U0454601

王荣华／译注

千家诗

双语版

A PRIMER OF ANCIENT POETRY

English-Chinese Edition

Translated, with Annotations by
WANG RONGHUA

中国人民大学出版社
·北京·

图书在版编目（CIP）数据

千家诗：双语版/王荣华译注 . -- 北京：中国人民大学出版社，2020.10
ISBN 978-7-300-27565-9

Ⅰ.①千… Ⅱ.①王… Ⅲ.①古典诗歌-诗集-中国-英、汉 Ⅳ.①I222.72

中国版本图书馆 CIP 数据核字（2019）第 232605 号

千家诗：双语版

王荣华　译注

Qianjiashi

出版发行		中国人民大学出版社			
社　　址		北京中关村大街 31 号		**邮政编码**	100080
电　　话		010 - 62511242（总编室）		010 - 62511770（质管部）	
		010 - 82501766（邮购部）		010 - 62514148（门市部）	
		010 - 62515195（发行公司）		010 - 62515275（盗版举报）	
网　　址		http://www.crup.com.cn			
经　　销		新华书店			
印　　刷		涿州市星河印刷有限公司			
规　　格		148 mm×210 mm　32 开本		**版　　次**	2020 年 10 月第 1 版
印　　张		10.875		**印　　次**	2020 年 10 月第 1 次印刷
字　　数		308 000		**定　　价**	58.00 元

P reface 前言

This book is entitled in Chinese phonetic alphabet—*Qianjiashi*, which means is poems written by one thousand poets. But there are only 226 poems by 122 poets in this book. Why? Because its source book—*Anthology of Poetry of Different Categories by One Thousand Bards* was composed of twenty-two volumes in fourteen sections, one hundred and thirty-three categories and four hundred and forty-two entries and totaled 1,281 quatrains and octaves by 368 poets. So, the words "one thousand" should not be treated as an exact figure, but an adjective to indicate a large number of poets. The compiler of this book was the then Minister of Engineering Mr. Liu Kezhuang (1187 – 1269), who was an important member of Folk Society School of literature. However, his collection was not for the purpose of enlightenment, but rather for the aim of appraisal and appreciation.

It was Xie Bingde (1226 – 1289) who rendered the book into a form of enlightenment for children. Xie was once a Chief Administrator of a prefecture, assistant ministers at several ministries. When the Yuan troops were invading, he rallied up over ten thousand militia with his own money and fought against the Yuan dynasty army. During the war, his wife, one daughter, two brothers and three nephews were killed by the aggressors. After the country was lost, he lived in seclusion, on teaching, selling his calligraphy and straw shoes he made at Jianyang, Fujian Province. He was finally identified and sent to the capital, where the Yuan rulers wanted him to work for the new regime. Xie refused and fasted for five days to death (he purposely ate a little food on the way up to the capital). It was during his secluded and teaching period he compiled the present form of this book. Neighbors of his asked him to teach their children, and it so happened that Liu Kezhuang was from this region and was very influential there. So he chose some poems from Liu's book and had it printed. Jianyang was one of the three printing centers of China at the time. It was profitable to print such a primer, which was so popular. Ever since this primer came into being, schools, both private and public, used this book to teach children poetry.

You may wish to know that *Three Hundred Tang Poems* came out much later. It was compiled by Heng Tang Tui Shi, whose original name was Sun Zhu (1711 - 1778). *Three Hundred Song Poems* was even later, it was compiled by Zhu Xiaozang (1857 - 1931), whose another name was a Villager from Shangjiang. These two books were not intended for children, but we must say they have been as popular as the primer.

The primer is divided into four parts: The first part is devoted to "seven-characters a line" quatrains, the second part to "seven-characters a line" octaves, the third part to "five-characters a line" quatrains and the fourth part to "five-characters a line" octaves.

The text of this writing is headed by translation of each poem, then the poem is presented in both the Chinese phonetic alphabet and Chinese characters, to be followed by some notes, which would provide some background knowledge about the poet and the poem and other things that the translator thought readers may need to know. An index of poets is attached at the end of the book.

Poetry is a way of expression. Poems in this book tell us how

Tang and Song poets responded to their living conditions, how they said farewell to their relatives and friends, how they missed their homes, how they appreciated their beautiful landscape and so on. When pupils learned these poems, in particular since the Song Dynasty, they were asked to use first of all their eyes, their mouths and their mind. In using their eyes, they should not miss any character in reading; in using their mouths they should read aloud, because they believed that after they had read aloud one thousand times, the meaning of what they read could come into their minds; in using their mind they should memorize what they were reading.

The purpose of this book is to draw a profile of ancient Chinese poetry to English readers. In spite of the unique forms of poetry, I hope readers can easily find out the emotions and impulses of the poets included in the book, to feel the "soul" of the ancient Chinese poets through their responses to their realities. Such an experience may help readers to have a grasp of what traditional Chinese culture is, and may further their understanding of contemporary Chinese and their culture.

The origin of the book was published by ZhongHua Book Co. in 2009, its text the publisher used was based on *Poetry by One thousand Bards with Illustrations and Annotations* printed by stone blocks by Shanghai Jinzhang Book Company.

这本书名叫《千家诗》，也就是说它收录了 1 000 名诗人的作品。然而，书中只有 122 位诗人的 226 首诗，这是怎么回事呢？因为其母体《分门纂类唐宋时贤千家诗选》共分 22 卷、14 门、133 类、442 目，收录了 368 位诗人的 1 281 首绝句和律诗。因此，所谓"千家"不是一个确切的数字，只是形容诗人之众。此诗选的编撰者刘克庄（1187—1269），号后村，曾任工部尚书，是江湖派最出色的诗人之一。然而，他辑诗的初衷不是为了启蒙后学，而是为了评判和欣赏。

将诗选缩减为儿童启蒙读物的是谢枋得（1226—1289）。他曾任江东提刑、江西招谕使、知信州，担任过六部侍郎。元军进犯后，他用自己的钱财，组织起万人民团反抗元军。在战争中，他的妻子、一个女儿、两个弟兄、三个侄子均遭杀害。战争失利后，他被迫隐姓埋名，逃亡福建，流寓建阳，以卖卜教书度日。后来他被人认出，被俘并送往元都北京。元军对他进行劝降，他予以严词拒绝，之后连续五日绝食（他在来北京的路上有意少食）而死。他在建阳隐居期间，编成了这本蒙学著作，由于他隐居处的街坊邻居请他教授他们的孩子，他就用这本书做教材。他编这本书的原因之一是，刘克庄就是建阳人，而且在当地影响巨大，对刘的诗选进行改编就成了很自然的事。更何况，建阳是当时中国的三大印刷中心之一。由于此书改编后，需求量大，因此印刷它是有利可图的。此书刊行之后，许多学堂、私塾都用它做教授儿童诗歌的教材。

读者或许知道《唐诗三百首》问世的时间要晚得多。其编者是蘅塘退士，此人原名孙洙（1711—1778）。《宋词三百首》就更晚了，其编者是朱孝臧（1857—1931），其别号上彊村民。这两部书不是专为儿童而编，但是我们必须说它们受欢迎的程度不亚于《千家诗》。

《千家诗》共分四卷：卷一是七绝，卷二是七律，卷三是五绝，卷四是五律。

本双语文本首先给出的是每首诗的英译，其次给出的是诗的中文文本并加注拼音，最后给出的是关于诗人和诗歌的背景材料以及译者认为读者需要了解的有关内容。

诗歌是表达的一种方式。本书所收诗篇告诉我们唐宋诗人是如何看待他们的生活条件、如何告别亲朋、如何思念家乡、如何欣赏秀美的景色的。孩童读诗的时候，特别是宋朝之后，要眼、嘴、脑并用。用眼阅读，不能丢掉一个字；用嘴高声朗读，人们坚信朗读千遍之后，诗歌中的含义就会入脑；用脑就是要记忆诗篇。

本书试图为英语读者提供一个关于中国古诗的梗概。除了解诗歌独特的形式外，我希望读者能感受到诗人们的感情和灵感，从诗人对他们所在现实的反应中触摸到中国古代诗人的"灵魂"。这种阅读经历会让读者对什么是中国传统文化有所领悟，进而促进他们对当代中国人及其文化的了解。

　　本译文所依据的中文文本是中华书局 2009 年出版的《千家诗》，其底本是上海锦章书局的石印本《绘图千家诗注释》。

目录

A Primer of
Ancient
Poetry 千家诗

Part I "Seven-Characters a Line" Quatrains
卷一 七绝

4

Part II   "Seven-Characters a Line" Octaves
卷二   七律

12

A **P**rimer of **A**ncient **P**oetry 千家诗

Part I "Seven-Characters a Line" Quatrains

卷一　七绝

The four-line poem in Chinese is "Jue Ju", and is written as "绝句". Fortunately it has an equivalent in English— "quatrain". The first Chinese character "绝" means to cut up a silk thread and the second character "句" means a sentence or a line of characters. So，the two characters mean to simplify the form. This form was finalized and formalized in the Tang Dynasty（618－709）. Since it evolved from archaic poetry forms，it has been referred to as a "modern poetic form". There have been two types of "Jue Ju" or Chinese quatrains：they are the "five-characters a line" ones and "seven-characters a line" ones. The first part of this primer devotes to the "seven-characters a line" ones. There are only fore lines in a quatrain. Normally the first，second and the fourth lines rhyme with a flat tone，and the third line ends with an oblique tone. This part collected ninety four poems. Now，let's look at each of them.

中文管四行诗叫"绝句"。幸运的是，英文里也有个对应的词叫"quatrain"。中文的"绝"字是剪断丝线的意思，"句"就是一句话或一行字的意思，两字连起来的意思是简化形式。绝句在唐朝（618—709）得以定型，是从古体诗演变而来的，因此，它也被称为"近体诗"。绝句分五言绝句和七言绝句。收入卷一的都是七言绝句。绝句只有四句，通常第一、第二和第四句以平声押韵。第三句的最后一个字往往是仄声。卷一收录诗九十四首。现在，让我们看看每一首的情况。

1. A Poem Prompted by a Spring Day

(Song) Cheng Hao

It was almost noon with scarce clouds and wind so gentle,
I've crossed the river and breezed along flowers and willow.
They don't pay heed to my outing thrill,
A kid snatching pleasure they thought I was trying to resemble.

In Chinese phonetic alphabet and Chinese characters:

chūn rì ǒu chéng
春 日 偶 成

（宋）程颢

yún	dàn	fēng	qīng	jìn	wǔ	tiān
云	淡	风	轻	近	午	天 ，

bàng	huā	suí	liǔ	guò	qián	chuān
傍	花	随	柳	过	前	川 。

shí	rén	bù	shí	yú	xīn	lè
时	人	不	识	余	心	乐 ，

jiāng	wèi	tōu	xián	xué	shào	nián
将	谓	偷	闲	学	少	年 。

Notes: The poet Cheng Hao （1032 - 1085） was a Neo-Confucianism philosopher in the Song Dynasty （960 - 1279）, with his younger brother Cheng Yi （1033 - 1107）, they established a new Confucian school, which has been very influential in China. The poem depicts how thrilled he was when taking an outing. Yet, ordinary people didn't understand why he was so excited by spring scenes and thought he was trying to imitate a youngster who is snatching a moment for pleasure. In the original poem, every lines rhymes but the third. In the translation I tried to rhyme to the end.

【说明】诗人程颢 （1032—1085） 是宋朝 （960—1279） 的一位理学家。他与其弟程颐 （1033—1107） 组成了重要的、很有影响力的理学学派。诗歌描写了诗人春游陶醉于大自然的美景，到了忘我的境地。当时的人不理解他内心的快乐，还以为他在学年轻人的模样，趁着大好时光忙里偷闲呢。原诗第三句不押韵，译文则一韵到底了。

2. A Spring Day
(Song) Zhu Xi

On a nice day I walked over green grass to the side of Sishui River,

The boundless scenery is on new attire.

Everywhere it is the east wind I encounter,

Spring is simply a riot of color.

In Chinese phonetic alphabet and Chinese characters:

chūn rì
春 日
（宋）朱熹

shèng rì xún fāng sì shuǐ bīn
胜 日 寻 芳 泗 水 滨 ，

wú biān guāng jǐng yì shí xīn
无 边 光 景 一 时 新 。

děng xián shí dé dōng fēng miàn
等 闲 识 得 东 风 面 ，

wàn zǐ qiān hóng zǒng shì chūn
万 紫 千 红 总 是 春 。

Notes: The poet Zhu Xi (1130 – 1200) is also a Neo-Confucian philosopher, who inherited the thoughts of the Cheng brothers we mentioned above by completing a new system—Objective Idealism. Some scholars say what this poem depicts is not spring scenery of the poem, but Zhu's adherence to Confucian thoughts. Because The Sishui River mentioned in the poem is in northern China, which was already occupied by the Jurchen people at the time he wrote the poem, and he was in the south. Sishui River area was where Confucius used to give his lectures, therefore the mention of the river alludes to his firm belief in Confucian thoughts. The original of the third line says literally that everywhere I could see the true face of the east wind. What my translation missed from the original is in the last line, which says literally "ten thousand purple colors and one thousand red make up a spring season". Or, when there is so much purple and red, it must be spring. Again, in the original, the third line does not rhyme, and this is a rule in the Chinese quatrains.

【说明】诗人朱熹（1130—1200）是一位理学家，他发展了一整套学说——客观唯心主义，从而继承了前面提到的二程的学说。有的学者认为此诗描绘的不是春景，而是他对孔子思想的坚持。因为泗水在北方，在宋南渡时早被金人侵占。朱熹未曾北上，当然不可能在泗水之滨游春吟赏。其实诗中的"泗水"是孔子弦歌讲学、教授弟子的地方。诗的第三句说：到处都可以看到春天的面目。最后一句的译文未能表现出"万紫千红总是春"。原诗的第三句不押韵，是绝句的一个规则。

3. Spring Night
(Song) Su Shi

An instant of spring night is worth one thousand gold pieces,
Flowers present pale scent, the moon casts shadows.
Song and pipe playing in the tower fade into distance,
The courtyard, where there is a swing, is in absolute silence.

In Chinese phonetic alphabet and Chinese characters:

chūn xiāo
春 宵
（宋）苏轼

chūn	xiāo	yí	kè	zhí	qiān	jīn
春	宵	一	刻	值	千	金 ，
huā	yǒu	qīng	xiāng	yuè	yǒu	yīn
花	有	清	香	月	有	阴 。
gē	guǎn	lóu	tái	shēng	xì	xì
歌	管	楼	台	声	细	细 ，
qiū	qiān	yuàn	luò	yè	chén	chén
秋	千	院	落	夜	沉	沉 。

Notes：Su Shi （1037 - 1101） was a man of letters，an artist and a calligrapher. The first line of this poem has become a catch phrase in China. We can detect the poet's subtle reproach in the poem of those who are leading a befuddled life and wasting their time in seeking pleasure and comfort.

【说明】苏轼（1037—1101）是位大文豪、艺术家、书法家。诗的第一句已经成为中国家喻户晓的妙句。我们从诗的最后两句可以读出作者对醉生梦死、贪图享乐、不惜光阴的人的深深谴责。

4. Early Spring in the Eastern Area of City
(Tang) Yang Juyuan

A refreshing and best scene in the eyes of bards is early spring，
The tender yellow of half of willow branches is only sojourning.
When the entire city is in full blossom，
Flower viewers would be packed in the streets，pushing and squeezing.

In Chinese phonetic alphabet and Chinese characters：

chéng dōng zǎo chūn
城 东 早 春

（唐）杨巨源

shī jiā qīng jǐng zài xīn chūn
诗 家 清 景 在 新 春，

lù liǔ cái huáng bàn wèi yún
绿 柳 才 黄 半 未 匀。

ruò dài shàng lín huā sì jǐn
若 待 上 林 花 似 锦，

chū mén jù shì kàn huā rén
出 门 俱 是 看 花 人。

Notes：Yang Juyuan （755–832） took a few posts in the government；his final job was a director of teaching affairs at the Imperial Academy. "The City" mentioned in the title is Chang'an, the capital of the Tang Dynasty. I must confess the translation of the second line does not fully express the meaning in the original，which says in early spring willion leaves and budding in tender yellow and only half of the willow branches have just turned yellow before they take on the green color. The original of the third line mentioned a place— "Shanglin"，which was an imperial garden in the Han Dynasty and was expanded in the Tang，and it used to imply the capital. The original of the last line says that everywhere outdoors there are flower viewers. In my translation the third line does not rhyme as in the original.

【说明】杨巨源（755—832）曾在政府机构任职，他最后一个职务是国子祭酒。题目中的"城"，指唐朝的都城长安。第二句的译文未能全部表现出原文的意思，其意是说：早春时，柳叶新萌，其色嫩黄，"半未匀"是说我们仿佛见到绿枝上刚刚露出的几个嫩黄的柳眼，绿色远未长开。第三句中的"上林"原是汉朝时的御花园，在唐朝得以扩建。此处代指首都。第四句说大街上到处都是看花的人。译文第三句也未押韵。

5. A Spring Night

(Song) Wang Anshi

Incense turned into ashes in the metal burner when water in the clepsydra is almost exhausted,

Wind is slight, yet cold.

Unable to sleep, spring is so annoying,

While the moon has cast flower shadows onto the balustrade.

In Chinese phonetic alphabet and Chinese characters:

chūn yè
春 夜

（宋）王安石

jīn	lú	xiāng	jìn	lòu	shēng	cán
金	炉	香	尽	漏	声	残 ，

jiǎn	jiǎn	qīng	fēng	zhèn	zhèn	hán
剪	剪	轻	风	阵	阵	寒 。

chūn	sè	nǎo	rén	mián	bù	dé
春	色	恼	人	眠	不	得 ，

yuè	yí	huā	yǐng	shàng	lán	gān
月	移	花	影	上	栏	杆 。

Notes: Wang Anshi (1021 – 1086) was a statesman, litterateur and a reformer of the Song Dynasty. He was conferred dukedom and was also named Duke Wang of Jing. He executed the second most important reform in the history of China. [The first one was in the State of Qin during the Warring States period (475 BC-221 BC) executed by Shang Yang.] After reading this poem, most readers would ask that if he was really annoyed by the spring scene? Why did he sit up all night? Most people guessed that he was seriously missing someone. But we don't know whom he was missing.

【说明】王安石（1021—1086）是宋朝一位政治家、文学家和

8

改革家。他被封为荆国公，世人称其为王荆公。他推行了中国历史上的第二次大的变法。[第一次大的变法是发生在战国时期（公元前475—公元前221年）的秦国，推行者是商鞅。] 大多数读者读完此诗后会问：春色真的让他烦恼吗？他为何整夜未眠？大多数人认为他是在思念一个人。然而，我们不知道这个人是谁。

6. Drizzle in Early Spring
(Tang) Han Yu

On the boulevard of the capital drizzle drops are moistening and fine,

It's all grass color over there, yet coming close it is nowhere to be seen.

In the whole year this is the best season,

Much better than the haziness and full willow green.

In Chinese phonetic alphabet and Chinese characters:

chū chūn xiǎo yǔ
初 春 小 雨

（唐）韩愈

tiān jiē xiǎo yǔ rùn rú sū
天 街 小 雨 润 如 酥 ，

cǎo sè yáo kàn jìn què wú
草 色 遥 看 近 却 无 。

zuì shì yì nián chūn hǎo chù
最 是 一 年 春 好 处 ，

jué shèng yān liǔ mǎn huáng dū
绝 胜 烟 柳 满 皇 都 。

Notes: Han Yu (768 – 824) was a famous litterateur and philosopher of the Tang Dynasty. The highest official position he held was a deputy minister in the Ministry of Personnel. He was ranked the first among the "Eight Great Writers of Tang and Song Dynasties". He was referred to as a "grand master of writing" and "a model of literary culture for a hundred generations". I wish to point out in the original the poet used "heavenly street" to refer to the capital, and he used "crispyor" and "shortening" to describe moistening of the rain. In the second line, the poet says it is grass color when looking from a distance. The poet used such words as "the best" when comparing the early spring to a full spring. You may wish to know that the poem also has a sub-title— "To Deputy Department Head of Ministry of Water Conservancy Mr. Zhang the Eighteenth in Early Spring".

【说明】韩愈（768—824）是唐朝的文学家和思想家。他最高的职务是吏部侍郎。在"唐宋八大家"中他排名首位，有"文章巨公"和"百代文宗"之名。我要指出的是原诗中作者用"天街"代指首都，用"润""酥"来描写细雨。第二句说从远处看是一片草色，走近后却看不到了。诗人用"最是一年春好处"说初春美过春天的其他时候。此诗还有一个副标题：《早春呈水部张十八员外》。

7. The New Year's Day
(Song) Wang Anshi

A year is gone with the sound of firecrackers,

When drinking herb wine, people felt the warmth of spring winds.

The rising sun shines on all the households,

Where new peach wood charms replaced the old on their doors.

In Chinese phonetic alphabet and Chinese characters:

yuán rì
元 日

（宋）王安石

bào	zhú	shēng	zhōng	yí	suì	chú
爆	竹	声	中	一	岁	除 ，

chūn	fēng	sòng	nuǎn	rù	tú	sū
春	风	送	暖	入	屠	苏 。

qiān	mén	wàn	hù	tóng	tóng	rì
千	门	万	户	曈	曈	日 ，

zǒng	bǎ	xīn	táo	huàn	jiù	fú
总	把	新	桃	换	旧	符 。

Notes: This poem is very popular in China. Chinese people celebrate Spring Festival, which is the Chinese New Year. In the original the poet gave the name of the herb—Tusu, which is a broad leaf grass and is the main content in the wine. According to historic records, the purpose of drinking such wine is to prevent plague. The poem also mentions a custom during the Spring Festival that is to replace old peach wood charm with new ones. In this custom Chinese household would place on each side of their gate a peach wood charm, usually a guardian name Shen Tu on the left side and another guardian named Yu Lei on the right side. Both are believed to have power to expel devils. It is obvious that such a custom carries simple wishes of Chinese families, which is to pursue good fortune and avoid disasters. The poem was composed in the year he began his reform plans, and we can see how delightful he was to be able to push forward his reform, and that he was confident that things new would replace things old.

【说明】此诗在中国非常有名。元日即中国春节，亦即中国新年。诗中提到的屠苏这种草药，是宽叶植物，用来泡酒。据史料记载，喝此酒可以驱邪避瘟疫。诗中还提到古代一种风俗，即农历正月初一时人们用新桃木做的木匾换下旧的，通常写有神荼名字的挂在门的左面、写有郁垒名字的挂在右面，用来压邪驱鬼。这些风俗表达了中国人朴素的愿望，那就是祈望好运、避免灾祸。此诗作于他开始改革之年。从诗中我们可以看到作者得以推行改革的兴奋之情，以及他对除旧布新的信念。

8. Attending the Imperial Banquet on the Night of the Lantern Festival
(Song) Su Shi

Pale moon and sparse stars are enveloping the Imperial Palace,
An aroma has been blowing down by the fairyland winds.
Officials stand at attention in the blazing lights,
As if awaiting the Jade Emperor, who would come by riding the environing red clouds.

In Chinese phonetic alphabet and Chinese characters:

shàng yuán shì yàn
上　元　侍　宴
（宋）苏轼

dàn	yuè	shū	xīng	rào	jiàn	zhāng
淡	月	疏	星	绕	建	章 ，
xiān	fēng	chuī	xià	yù	lú	xiāng
仙	风	吹	下	御	炉	香 。
shì	chén	hú	lì	tōng	míng	diàn
侍	臣	鹄	立	通	明	殿 ，
yì	duǒ	hóng	yún	pěng	yù	huáng
一	朵	红	云	捧	玉	皇 。

Notes: The Lantern Festival is on the fifteenth of lunar January, and the moon is full on that night and you don't see many stars. In the original that the aroma comes from the imperial incense burner. The way the officials stood, as the poet described was standing there stretching their necks like swans anticipating the emperor. The Jade Emperor is the highest God in Taoism.

【说明】元宵节在正月十五，此夜月圆星稀。诗中说的是香气被仙风从御香炉中吹来，官员们引颈肃立、恭候皇上。最后一句中的"玉皇"是中国道教中最大的神。

9. A Poem Prompted by the Spring Solstice
(Song) Zhang Shi

With remnant of ice and frost Spring Solstice came before the Spring Festival，

Grass and wood are the first to know spring was on its way.

Everywhere before me is vigor and vitality，

The green water ripples when the east wind blows in jollity.

In Chinese phonetic alphabet and Chinese characters：

lì chūn ǒu chéng
立 春 偶 成

（宋）张栻

lù huí suì wǎn bīng shuāng shǎo
律 回 岁 晚 冰 霜 少 ，

chūn dào rén jiān cǎo mù zhī
春 到 人 间 草 木 知 。

biàn jué yǎn qián shēng yì mǎn
便 觉 眼 前 生 意 满 ，

dōng fēng chuī shuǐ lù cēn cī
东 风 吹 水 绿 参 差 。

Notes：Zhang Shi（1130 - 1180）is a Neo-Confucian philosopher. The second line is well known. The poet believed grass and wood know the coming of spring much earlier than man. The rhyming of this poem is exceptional，it only rhymes in the second and fourth lines in the original.

【说明】张栻（1130—1180）是理学家。诗中第二句很有名，诗人认为对春天的到来，草木要比人敏感。此诗的押韵比较特殊，只在第二、四句押韵。

10. Return from Polo Playing
(Song) Chao Shuizhi

All the gates of the Imperial Palace are wide open,

Having played polo, the Emperor has returned but was drunken.

One is aged, the other is deceased, and they were the only ones out-spoken,

From now on no admonishment would be given.

In Chinese phonetic alphabet and Chinese characters:

dǎ qiú tú
打 球 图

（宋）晁说之

chāng	hé	qiān	mén	wàn	hù	kāi
阊	阖	千	门	万	户	开 ，
sān	láng	chén	zuì	dǎ	qiú	huí
三	郎	沉	醉	打	球	回 。
jiǔ	líng	yǐ	lǎo	hán	xiū	sǐ
九	龄	已	老	韩	休	死 ，
wú	fù	míng	zhāo	jiàn	shū	lái
无	复	明	朝	谏	疏	来 。

Notes: Chao Shuizhi (1059-1129) satirizes the imperial court of the Song by depicting the absurdity of Emperor Xuanzong of Tang, who indulged in polo playing and lived in luxury and dissipation. The poet called the Tang emperor "the third boy", because he was the third son of Emperor Ruizong of Tang. The poem mentioned two prime ministers Zhang Jiuling and Han Xiu, who were bold to criticize the wrong doings of the emperor. But when people like them left the political scene, the decline of the dynasty began. The names are omitted in translation, and instead "one" and "the other" are used, which may seem a bit rigid indeed.

【说明】晁说之（1059—1129）用嘲笑唐玄宗的方法来挖苦宋朝皇室。唐玄宗醉心于马球，生活奢靡放荡。诗中称他为"三郎"，因为他是唐睿宗第三子。诗中提到两位敢于批评皇上的宰相张九龄和韩休。然而，当这两位宰相退出政治舞台时，唐王朝就开始衰败了。译文中没有出现宰相的名字，只是用了"一位"和"另一位"，显得有些生硬。

11. A Palace Verse

(Tang) Wang Jian

The purple buildings opposite the Throne Hall are of multi-layer,

The cotton-rose on the palm of the bronze immortal is a jade-ware.

On the day the Emperor of Peace paid respect to his primogenitor,

He was on a five-color cloud cart and six dragons were his driver.

In Chinese phonetic alphabet and Chinese characters:

gōng cí
宫 词

（唐）王建

jīn diàn dāng tóu zǐ gé chóng
金 殿 当 头 紫 阁 重 ，

<pre>
xiān   rén   zhǎng shàng yù   fú   róng
仙   人   掌   上   玉   芙   蓉 。

tài   píng tiān   zǐ   cháo yuán rì
太   平   天   子   朝   元   日 ，

wǔ   sè   yún   chē   jià   liù lóng
五   色   云   车   驾   六   龙 。
</pre>

Notes："Palace Verse" is a category of poetry, which writes about trivial matters in the imperial court. Wang Jian (About 767 – 831) became a petty official at the age of 46. The highest position he held was a provincial governor. He was good at giving artistic generalizations to typical persons, events and environment. He was well known for his "One Hundred Palace Verses", and this is one of them. It has been said that when Li Hongzhang (1823 – 1901) visited Europe and Russia in 1896 in the capacity of the Special Envoy of the Qing Emperor, he used this poem as the verse of "the national anthem". As China's national anthem must be played at diplomatic functions, and at that time, there was no formal anthem, what Li did was that he picked from imperial court music a number to company this verse. The jade-ware is a plate made of jade, and was placed on the palm of the bronze figure and used to collect dew for the emperor, which was believed that drinking the dew can prolong life. This practice was started in the Han Dynasty. The so-called "five colors" used to be dark green, red, yellow, white and black. They were considered to be the proper colors in very ancient times. In ancient times "if a horse was over eight foot long, it was referred to as a dragon", according to records in the *Rites of the Zhou*.

【说明】"宫词"是诗歌的一个种类，大都描写皇宫里的琐事。王建（约767—831）46岁时才当了一个小官。其最高职务是刺史。他善于选择有典型意义的人、事和环境加以艺术概括，集中而形象地反映现实。他曾作"宫词一百首"，传诵一时。此诗是百首之一。

这首小诗相传还有一则故事：1896 年清政府派遣李鸿章（1823—1901）出使西欧与俄国，在欢迎仪式上要奏国歌，但当时清廷根本无国歌。于是，李鸿章临时找了唐朝诗人王建"宫词一百首"中的这首诗，加以改编，配以清代之宫廷音乐，作为"国歌"临时使用。玉芙蓉是指玉盘，放置在铜人的手掌上，为皇上接露水，据说饮这种露水可以长寿。这种做法始于汉朝。所谓"五色"是指青、赤、黄、白、黑，古代以此五者为正色。根据《周礼》所讲："马八尺以上为龙。"

12. Examination in the Throne Hall
(Song) Xia Song

The Sun-Moon pattern on the Emperor's robe is so splendid，

Moving like dragon and snake in my ink the banners so reflected.

With my fertile pen three thousand characters on classics were produced，

It was not yet noon when，standing alone on the red steps，all the Emperor's questions I have answered.

In Chinese phonetic alphabet and Chinese characters：

tíng shì
廷 试

（宋）夏竦

diàn	shàng	gǔn	yī	míng	rì	yuè
殿	上	衮	衣	明	日	月 ，

yàn	zhōng	qí	yǐng	dòng	lóng	shé
砚	中	旗	影	动	龙	蛇 。

zòng	héng	lǐ	yuè	sān	qiān	zì
纵	横	礼	乐	三	千	字 ，

dú	duì	dān	chí	rì	wèi	xiá
独	对	丹	墀	日	未	斜 。

Notes: Xia Song （985 - 1051） was a famous and capable official of the Song Dynasty. He was a paleographer and a poet. The highest position he held was Minister of Finance and Secretary General of the Privy Council. It was said that after the examination in the imperial hall, one senior official came to Xia Song and asked him to compose a poem on his experience of the exam he had just finished. And these four lines were what he wrote, almost immediately, for the senior official. The third line of the original clearly mentioned what the classics were *The Book of Rites* and *The Book of Music*, two of the six classics examination candidates were supposed to master. The poem eulogized the deeds and virtues of the imperial court in between lines.

【说明】夏竦（985—1051）是宋朝有名的能臣、古文字学家和诗人。曾任户部尚书、枢密使。据说他参加殿试后，一位高官让他写一首诗，表达他考试的感受。上面这四句诗就是他当场为那位高官所作。诗的第三句提到两部儒学经典：《礼记》和《乐记》，是科举应试者必读的六经中的两部。诗的字里行间歌颂了皇室的功德。

13. Paying Homage to the Palace of Huaqing
(Song) Du Chang

Having passed over ten postal relays in the south without stopping,

With morning wind and descending moon I entered into Huaqing.

On Chaoyuan pavilion the west wind is so strong,

In the yard where willows used to be the rain is slashing.

In Chinese phonetic alphabet and Chinese characters:

yǒng huá qīng gōng
咏 华 清 宫

（宋）杜常

xíng	jìn	jiāng	nán	shù	shí	chéng
行	尽	江	南	数	十	程 ，

xiǎo	fēng	cán	yuè	rù	huá	qīng
晓	风	残	月	入	华	清 。

cháo	yuán	gé	shàng	xī	fēng	jí
朝	元	阁	上	西	风	急 ，

dōu	rù	cháng	yáng	zuò	yǔ	shēng
都	入	长	杨	作	雨	声 。

Notes：Du Chang（no dates of birth and death available）was once the Minister of Engineering of the Song Dynasty. His grandmother was the first Queen of the Northern Song. Huaqing Palace was a suburb residence built in 723 for the Tang emperors. It has been famous for its resources in geothermal hot water, which was mainly used for bathing. Emperors in the Zhou，Qin，Han and Sui all had palaces built there. Emperor Xuanzong of Tang spent much time in here with his beauty concubine Yang Yuhuan. The Chaoyuan Pavilion was in the palace，according to some legends，Laozi，the founder of Taoism was once in this pavilion，and Emperor Xuanzong was a firm believer of Taoism. There have been quite a number of poems depicting the Huaqing Palace，and this one composed by Du Chang is regarded as one of the best.

【说明】杜常（无生卒年记载）曾任宋朝工部尚书。他祖母是宋朝第一位皇后。华清池是唐朝皇帝于723年修建的寝宫，它的地下热水资源广为人知，人们多用热水来沐浴。周、秦、汉、隋的皇帝都曾在此建有宫殿。唐玄宗经常在此处与杨贵妃寻欢作乐。朝元阁就在华清宫内。相传道教的创始人老子曾到过朝元阁，唐玄宗也笃信道教。写华清宫的诗很多。杜常这一首则被认为是最好的。

19

14. A Verse for "Clear and Even" Tune
(Tang) Li Bai

Rosy clouds want to be her dress and flowers to be her face,

Spring wind caresses on the balustrade and so thick is the dew on flowers.

Such a peerless beauty can be found either on the Mount where the Heavenly mother resides,

Or in the fairyland among the Nymphs.

In Chinese phonetic alphabet and Chinese characters:

qīng píng diào cí
清 平 调 词

（唐）李白

yún	xiǎng	yī	cháng	huā	xiǎng	róng
云	想	衣	裳	花	想	容 ，

chūn	fēng	fú	kǎn	lù	huá	nóng
春	风	拂	槛	露	华	浓 。

ruò	fēi	qún	yù	shān	tóu	xiàn
若	非	群	玉	山	头	见 ，

huì	xiàng	yáo	tái	yuè	xià	féng
会	向	瑶	台	月	下	逢 。

Notes: Li Bai (701 – 762) was the great romantic poet of the Tang Dynasty. He has been reputed as a "Poetry Immortal". He is the symbol of the climax of ancient poetry in China and he is a symbol of the Golden Age of Chinese poetry. His peer Du Fu described him thus: "when he set his pen on paper, wind and rain are startled; when he finished his poem, ghosts and deities begin to weep." "Clear and Even" tune was a tune with a set form, inherited from the Zhou Dynasty. This poem was one of the three poems composed by Li Bai on spot when Emperor Xuanzong of Tang was having a good time with his favorite concubine Yang Yuhuan in the imperial garden.

At that time Li Bai was a standing-by member of the Imperial College. Apparently this poem depicts the beauty of Yang Yuhuan. The word "want" in the first line has been normally interpreted as "connected with", that is to say when one sees the clouds, he would connect it with her dress; when one sees flowers, he would connect with her looks; or as "imagining", that is to imagine her dress as clouds and her looks as flowers.

【说明】李白（701—762）是唐朝伟大的浪漫主义诗人，被誉为"诗仙"。他是中国古代诗歌达到高峰的标志，是中国诗歌黄金时代的象征。与他同时代的诗人杜甫这样形容他："落笔惊风雨，诗成泣鬼神。""清平调"是一种歌的曲调，是从周朝传下来的，其用词有固定的格式。此诗是唐玄宗与杨贵妃在御花园赏花时，李白当场奉诏所作的三首诗之一。当时李白任翰林待诏。很显然，此诗写的是杨贵妃之美。诗中的"想"字，通常被解释为"联想到"，也就是说当人们看到云彩时，他们就会联想到贵妃的衣裙；当他们看到花朵时，就会联想到贵妃的面容。也有人将"想"字解释为"想象"，是说把她的衣裙想象成云彩，把她的面容想象成花朵。

15. Inscription on the Hotel Room Wall
(Song) Zheng Hui

Fearing spring cold, disturbing her nice dream is the aroma of bramble,

Gate after gate in the garden green swallows are staying idle.

The jade hairpin is already broken by her endless knocking, the light is out on the red candle,

She thought I would be on Mount Chang and calculating how much more I have to travel.

In Chinese phonetic alphabet and Chinese characters:

tí dǐ jiān bì
题 邸 间 壁

（宋）郑会

tú	mí	xiāng	mèng	qiè	chūn	hán
荼	蘼	香	梦	怯	春	寒 ，

cuì	yǎn	zhòng	mén	yàn	zǐ	xián
翠	掩	重	门	燕	子	闲 。

qiāo	duàn	yù	chāi	hóng	zhú	lěng
敲	断	玉	钗	红	烛	冷 ，

jì	chéng	yīng	shuō	dào	cháng	shān
计	程	应	说	到	常	山 。

Notes：Zheng Hui（no dates of birth and death available）
was once the assistant minister in the Ministry of Rites. It is a
disgusting habit of Chinese scholars in the old times，who always
wrote with their brush pen on walls as soon as they were inspired
and composed something. This guy wrote on the wall of a hotel
room. Don't think the hotel owner would ask him to white wash the
wall or to pay for smudging the wall，on the contrary，it was most
likely the owner would be very happy of have an inscription by a
famous scholar in his hotel. As we go on with this book you would
read more inscriptions. This poem described how much the poet
was missing his wife and home by way of imagining how his wife
was missing him. She was knocking her hairpin on the table
aimlessly，and when it broke and the taper light was gone，she
still stayed awake. Mount Chang is just a place her husband must
pass by on his way home.

【说明】郑会（无生卒日期记载）曾任礼部侍郎。在中国古代，
读书人有一个习惯，那就是一时兴起，用毛笔在墙上题字。郑会就
是在客栈的房间里题的字。不要以为，客栈主人会让他把字刷掉，
或做出赔偿。相反，要是有知名的学者题字，客栈老板会非常高

兴。本诗集还会提到很多题词。此诗写了诗人如何思念他的妻子和家乡，诗中想象他的妻子在夜里思念他的样子，她漫不经心地用发簪敲打着桌子，结果发簪断了，蜡烛也灭了，她仍无法入睡。常山是她丈夫回家必须经过的地方。

16. A Quatrain

(Tang) Du Fu

On green willow branches two orioles chirp，

Up in the air the wings of a row of egrets flap.

Outside the window is the one thousand year old snow on the West Hill strip，

Outside the gate are vessels，from the Wu State ten thousand miles away，berthed deep.

In Chinese phonetic alphabet and Chinese characters：

jué jù
绝 句

（唐）杜甫

liǎng gè huáng lí míng cuì liǔ
两　个　黄　鹂　鸣　翠　柳　，

yì háng bái lù shàng qīng tiān
一　行　白　鹭　上　青　天　。

chuāng hán xī lǐng qiān qiū xuě
窗　含　西　岭　千　秋　雪　，

mén bó dōng wú wàn lǐ chuán
门　泊　东　吴　万　里　船　。

Notes：Du Fu（712 - 770）is a great realistic poet of China and has been reputed as a "Poetry Saint". He composed over three thousand poems in his lifetime. This poem was written when he returned to his thatched cottage which still exists and is now a hot tourist spot outside the city of Chengdu and when An-Shi Rebellion was quelled. The poem constitutes a picture of spring, in which you hear the chirping of orioles, you see green and white colors; you see movements of the bird and the stillness of snow and mountain. What the poet presents to his readers is his joy and delight.

【说明】杜甫（712—770）是中国伟大的现实主义诗人，被誉为"诗圣"。他一生作诗 3 000 余首。这首诗是在安史之乱平息后他回到成都郊外的草堂后所写。此草堂现在仍然存在，成为了旅游热点。此诗勾画了一幅春色图，从中可以听到莺啼，可以看到绿白等颜色；有鸟飞的动态，也有雪和山脉的静态。诗里流露出诗人愉悦的心情。

17. The Cherry-Apple Flower
(Song) Su Shi

The east wind drags clouds gently away and the spring moon is spreading out,

Flower scent gets into fog, the moon moved to the corridor on her route.

Fearing flowers may fall into sleep in the dark night,

I tried to keep the taper light high over the red flower by the candle I lit.

In Chinese phonetic alphabet and Chinese characters:

　　　　　　　hǎi táng
　　　　　　　海　棠

　　　　　　　（宋）苏轼

dōng　fēng　niǎo　niǎo　fàn　chóng　guāng
东　　风　　袅　　袅　　泛　　崇　　光　，

24

xiāng	wù	kōng	méng	yuè	zhuǎn	láng
香	雾	空	蒙	月	转	廊 。

zhǐ	kǒng	yè	shēn	huā	shuì	qù
只	恐	夜	深	花	睡	去 ，

gù	shāo	gāo	zhú	zhào	hóng	zhuāng
故	烧	高	烛	照	红	妆 。

Notes：I am not sure if I got the title right in English. The title is a kind of plant called "Haitang", in the Chinese-English dictionary it is "Chinese flowering apple", which does not make much sense to me. Some dictionary explains it as a crab-apple, which seems like a hawthorn；some dictionary names it as "cherry-apple", which to me makes sense, because its fruit looks like cherry. I finally found a Latin term, which is very close to what the poet wanted to describe— "malus spectabilis", and this is what the poet was talking about. The second line says the moon had moved to the corridor, it means that the moon had left the flowers, and it must be very late at night.

【说明】我不敢肯定我是否将诗的题目翻译对了。诗的题目叫《海棠》，查中英字典，其英文表达是"Chinese flowering apple"。从这三个词我读不出什么内容；有的字典将它说成是"crab-apple"，听起来好像是山楂；有的字典给出的是"cherry-apple"。这个说明我倒是能够接受，因为海棠果看上去很像一种莓。我后来找到一个拉丁词，与诗人所要表达的内容很接近——"malus spectabilis"，此词的含义就是诗人要说的话。诗里说月亮已经转到廊子那边，已从花朵那里移开了，夜已很深了。

18. The Pure Brightness Day

(Tang) Du Mu

Drizzle drags on in the Pure Brightness season，
All travelers are feeling heart-broken.

When asking where can find a tavern,

A cowboy points at the Apricot Village in the far direction.

In Chinese phonetic alphabet and Chinese characters:

qīng míng
清　明

（唐）杜牧

qīng	míng	shí	jié	yǔ	fēn	fēn
清	明	时	节	雨	纷	纷 ，
lù	shàng	xíng	rén	yù	duàn	hún
路	上	行	人	欲	断	魂 。
jiè	wèn	jiǔ	jiā	hé	chù	yǒu
借	问	酒	家	何	处	有 ，
mù	tóng	yáo	zhǐ	xìng	huā	cūn
牧	童	遥	指	杏	花	村 。

Notes：Du Mu （803－852） is a great poet of the Tang Dynasty，has been reputed as the "junior Du Fu". He held quite a number of official positions and the highest one was a deputy department head in several ministries，he also served as a local governor at two places. This poem is very popular and has been often quoted，especially in the "Pure Brightness" season. There have been at least twenty different versions in English of this poem，which were formally published in China. The Pure Brightness Day is a very important occasion for Chinese. On this day people go to sweep the tombs of their deceased relatives. In English，this day is also named as "Tomb Sweeping Day"，"Mourning Day"，"Clear-and-Bright Feast"，"All Souls' Day"，and so on. I stick to the "Pure and Brightness Day"，because it is very close to the original in Chinese.

【说明】杜牧（803—852）是唐朝一位伟大的诗人，被誉为"小杜"。他在朝廷里担任过很多职务，最高做到监察御史，也曾在两个州任刺史。此诗很有名，经常被引用，尤其过"清明"

的时候。此诗的英译版本至少有 20 种，而且都在中国正式出版过。对中国人来说，清明节很重要，家人都要为已故的亲朋去扫墓。英语又称此节为"扫墓日""致哀日""清亮节""魂灵日"等。我用的是"Pure and Brightness Day"，因为此说法接近中文原意。

19．The Pure Brightness Day

(Song) Wang Yucheng

I spent the Pure Brightness Day without flowers and wine，
Such ascetic life is like that of a monk in the fane.

Yesterday I got newly enflamed kindling from the neighbor's kitchen，

At dawn I lit the lamp by the window and read in concentration.

In Chinese phonetic alphabet and Chinese characters：

qīng míng
清　明

（宋）王禹偁

wú	huā	wú	jiǔ	guò	qīng	míng
无	花	无	酒	过	清	明 ，
xìng	wèi	xiāo	rán	sì	yě	sēng
兴	味	萧	然	似	野	僧 。
zuó	rì	lín	jiā	qǐ	xīn	huǒ
昨	日	邻	家	乞	新	火 ，
xiǎo	chuāng	fēn	yú	dú	shū	dēng
晓	窗	分	与	读	书	灯 。

Notes：Wang Yucheng（954 - 1001）was a prose writer of the Song Dynasty，he was regarded as a forerunner of poetry and literary revolution in the Northern Song period. It was a custom，in the Tang and Song dynasties to put out fire on the Cold Food

Day, which are two days before the Pure and Brightness Day. That's why people had to enflamed new fires the next day. Apparently the poet wrote this verse on the second day of the Pure and Brightness Day.

【说明】王禹偁（954—1001），宋朝散文家，被称为北宋诗文革新运动的先驱。在唐宋两朝，寒食节在清明节的前两天，寒食节不点火是一种习俗。所以，寒食节过后家家要点火。很显然，此诗写于清明节次日。

20. The Day to Offer Sacrifice to the Land Deity
(Tang) Wang Jia

At the foot of Ehu Mount it is a good year for sorghum and paddy,

The gate is ajar, but pigsty and chicken coop are in safety.

When tree shadows become longer, people end their spring sacrificial party,

Every household is helping its drunks returning home happily.

In Chinese phonetic alphabet and Chinese characters：

shè rì
社 日
（唐）王驾

é	hú	shān	xià	dào	liáng	féi
鹅	湖	山	下	稻	粱	肥 ，

tún	zhà	jī	qī	duì	yǎn	fēi
豚	栅	鸡	栖	对	掩	扉 。

sāng	zhè	yǐng	xiá	chūn	shè	sàn
桑	柘	影	斜	春	社	散 ，

jiā	jiā	fú	dé	zuì	rén	guī
家	家	扶	得	醉	人	归 。

Notes: Wang Jia (851 -?) was once an assistant minister at the Ministry of Rites. He then resigned from his official post and led his life in solitude. Literally the title means "gathering on the community day" and there were two such days in one year, one in spring and one in autumn. The one in spring offers sacrifices to the Land Deity, after the ceremony, community members would stage performances, competition of skills followed by a feast. The third line in the original mentions two particular trees, which are mulberry and another one in the same family, whose Latin name is "cudrania tricuspidata" and they were common at places around Jiangxi Province.

【说明】王驾 （851—?） 曾任礼部侍郎。他辞职后过起了隐居生活。诗的题目的意思是 "人们在一起聚会"。一年中有两个社日，一个在春季，另一个在秋季。春季的社日先祭土地神，祭后民众集会竞技，进行各种类型的表演，集体欢宴，非常热闹。诗的第三句提到两种树，即桑树和柘树，柘树也属于桑科，其拉丁文的名称是 "cudrania tricuspidata"。这两种树在江西地区很常见。

21. The Cold Food Day

(Tang) Han Hong

In the spring everywhere in the capital catkins are flying around,

On the Cold Food Day branches of willow in the imperial court are being blown up by the east wind.

At dusk in the court people were busy to have candles delivered,

Light kitchen smoke effused from houses of the newly knighted.

In Chinese phonetic alphabet and Chinese characters:

hán shí
寒 食
（唐）韩翃

chūn	chéng	wú	chù	bù	fēi	huā
春	城	无	处	不	飞	花 ，

hán	shí	dōng	fēng	yù	liǔ	xiá
寒	食	东	风	御	柳	斜 。

rì	mù	hàn	gōng	chuán	là	zhú
日	暮	汉	宫	传	蜡	烛 ，

qīng	yān	sàn	rù	wǔ	hóu	jiā
轻	烟	散	入	五	侯	家 。

Notes: Han Hong (no dates of birth and death available) was one of "the ten geniuses in the Dali period (766 – 779)". He came to the capital with a military governor, for whom he had worked. Emperor Dezong of Tang appointed him a drafter of imperial edicts because of this poem, which was very popular, especially the first line. Cold food days are the two days before the Pure and Brightness Day. People mark this day to remember a gentleman and scholar, Mr. Jie Zhitui, who was on exile with Prince Chong'er of the State of Jin for nineteen years. When Chong'er became the monarch, Jie didn't want to be rewarded; he went up to a mountain and lived there with his mother. The monarch insisted in using Jie in his government, so he came to the mountain to see Jie. Jie refused to come down from the mountain, and then the monarch accepted a suggestion to set fire on three sides of the mountain, thinking Jie would come down from the side where there was no fire. Yet, when the fire was put out, people found Jie and his mother were burnt to death, still holding a tree tightly. In memory of Jie, the monarch issued an edict to name the two burning days "Cold Food Days", that is to say during these two days no fire should be used to heat food. Why the third line says palace maids were busy delivering candles? Because, the imperial court made itself an exception in using candles. The poet said the Han court was using candles on the two days. We don't know if this was true. We know that the poet was insinuating that the Tang court was making itself an exception. The last line in the original mentions five marquises, who were brothers of a Queen and were given such a title on the same day. The poet was saying not only the imperial court itself, but also families of nobles could use candles on the occasion.

【说明】韩翃（无生卒日期记载）是"大历十才子"之一。他曾为一位节度使工作，后跟随其至京城。唐德宗看了他写的这首诗后，让他做了中书舍人，可见这首诗名声之大，尤其是第一行。寒食节在清明节前两天，人们纪念的是介之推这位君子。介之推与晋国公子重耳在外逃亡 19 年，重耳登上王位后，介之推并不想得到奖赏，就与他的母亲跑到山上去居住。重耳想重用介之推，就来山上见他。然而，介之推仍不愿意下山。此时，重耳接受了一项建议，那就是从三面烧山，留下一面让介之推下山。可是，当大火被扑灭后，人们发现介之推和他的母亲紧紧地抱着一棵大树被烧死了。为了纪念介之推，晋文公颁布法令，将大火燃烧的两天作为"寒食节"，这两天里不准用火做饭、热饭。但是，第三句为什么说宫女在忙着传递蜡烛呢？因为皇室将自己作为例外了。诗人说汉室用蜡烛，我们不知这个说法是否准确。但是，诗人暗示唐室破例了。诗的最后一句提到的五侯是皇后的兄弟，此五人在同一天被封侯。诗人要说的是，除了皇室，还有贵族家庭在这两天也使用了蜡烛。

22. Spring South of Changjiang River

(Tang) Du Mu

For a thousand miles orioles sing amidst green that contrasts with red,

Wine shop banners flutter in the towns at mountain foot and by the riverside.

The four hundred and eighty monasteries built in the Southern Dynasties,

Are now under mist and rain as we so behold.

In Chinese phonetic alphabet and Chinese characters:

jiāng nán chūn

江 南 春

（唐）杜牧

qiān	lǐ	yīng	tí	lù	yìng	hóng
千	里	莺	啼	绿	映	红 ，

shuǐ	cūn	shān	guō	jiǔ	qí	fēng
水	村	山	郭	酒	旗	风 。

nán	cháo	sì	bǎi	bā	shí	sì
南	朝	四	百	八	十	寺 ，

duō	shǎo	lóu	tái	yān	yǔ	zhōng
多	少	楼	台	烟	雨	中 。

Notes： The land south of Changjiang River is vast. It is beautiful in the spring. It was quite developed since there were so many wine shops at mountain foot or by the riverside. The Southern Dynasties existed from AD 420 – 589 through four consecutive regimes, which all believed in Buddhism, that's why they had so many Buddhist monasteries built. The poet used "mist and rain" to strike a difference with the scene outside the monasteries.

【说明】长江之南地域广阔，春色优美，经济发达，河边山下有许多酒家。南朝是公元 420—589 年，前后共有四个政权。这些当政的，都信奉佛教，所以，才有这么多寺庙。诗人用"烟雨"二字强调了寺外不同的景致。

23. To Assistant Minister Gao

(Tang) Gao Chan

The fairyland peach is watered by dew,

By side of cloud the red apricot near the sun grow.

Only lotus in the cold rivers in autumn,

Never resent the east wind for not warming her and not letting her glow.

In Chinese phonetic alphabet and Chinese characters:

shàng gāo shì láng
上　高　侍　郎

（唐）高蟾

tiān	shàng	bì	táo	hé	lù	zhòng
天	上	碧	桃	和	露	种 ，
rì	**biān**	**hóng**	**xìng**	**yǐ**	**yún**	**zāi**
日	边	红	杏	倚	云	栽 。
fú	**róng**	**shēng**	**zài**	**qiū**	**jiāng**	**shàng**
芙	蓉	生	在	秋	江	上 ，
bù	**xiàng**	**dōng**	**fēng**	**yuàn**	**wèi**	**kāi**
不	向	东	风	怨	未	开 。

Notes: Gao Chan (no dates of birth and death available) was once a deputy Inspector General of the Tang Imperial Court. In the poem he described those who passed the national examination as jade peach in the heaven and red apricot near the sun and he compared himself to a lotus in cold autumn river. Those who have passed the examination would enjoy special kindness from the society and the imperial court. It was entirely a different story for those who failed such an examination, like the poet himself who had failed many times. The "east wind" in the last line represents the imperial court, to which the poet didn't resent for the unequal treatment. Actually the next year from the time he wrote this poem, he passed the examination and became qualified as a candidate to be given an official post.

【说明】高蟾（无生卒日期记载）曾在唐朝任御史中丞。诗中将通过科举考试者喻为天上的碧桃和日边的红杏，将自己比喻为寒冷秋日河里的芙蓉。高中皇榜的待遇极其优渥。然而，落榜者的情况，如诗人自己，多次未中，境遇就不可同日而语了。皇室被喻为"东风"。诗人倒是没有发"东风"的牢骚。事实上，此诗作后一年，高蟾中了进士，很快被朝廷启用。

24. A Quatrain
(Song) Monk Zhi Nan

I tied my small boat in the bower of an old tree,

With a goosefoot crane in hand I crossed to the east of bridge gladly.

Rain in the apricot season almost bedraggled my cloth,

Facing the wind that blows up willow branches I don't feel chilly.

In Chinese phonetic alphabet and Chinese characters:

jué jù
绝 句
（宋）僧志南

gǔ	mù	yīn	zhōng	jì	duǎn	péng
古	木	阴	中	系	短	篷 ，
zhàng	lí	fú	wǒ	guò	qiáo	dōng
杖	藜	扶	我	过	桥	东 。
zhān	yī	yù	shī	xìng	huā	yǔ
沾	衣	欲	湿	杏	花	雨 ，
chuī	miàn	bù	hán	yáng	liǔ	fēng
吹	面	不	寒	杨	柳	风 。

Notes: We don't know much about Zhi Nan. The name is

only a Buddhist title，not the person's name． This poem is a subtle and realistic description of how the monk felt about things in February—the early spring． I am not sure if "goosefoot" makes much sense，but it is a kind of old plant that can be used as a crane for elders．

【说明】我们对僧志南所知甚少，所有的和尚都可称为僧，志南是法号，并不是人的名字。此诗以细腻和现实的手法描写了诗人对早春二月景物的感受。蔾是一种树木，可用来做老人的手杖，但不知"goosefoot"一词是否是正确的译名。

25．Fail to Get into the Garden
(Song) Ye Shaoweng

Fearing I may leave clog teeth imprints on the dark green mosses，

Knocking on the gate for so long I wasn't given an excess．

Nobody can shut the garden's voluptuous spring scenes，

Out of its wall a red apricot flower sticks．

In Chinese phonetic alphabet and Chinese characters：

yóu yuán bù zhí
游　园　不　值
（宋）叶绍翁

yīng	lián	jī	chǐ	yìn	cāng	tái
应	怜	屐	齿	印	苍	苔 ，

xiǎo	kòu	chái	fēi	jiǔ	bù	kāi
小	扣	柴	扉	久	不	开 。

chūn	sè	mǎn	yuán	guān	bú	zhù
春	色	满	园	关	不	住 ，

yī	zhī	hóng	xìng	chū	qiáng	lái
一	枝	红	杏	出	墙	来 。

Notes：Li was the original name of Ye Shaoweng（no dates of his birth and death available）. He was adopted by the Ye family. No records showed he ever worked in the government. He lived in solitude for a long time in Hangzhou. The last two lines of this poem are very well known.

【说明】叶绍翁（他的生卒日期没有文字记载），原姓李。他之所以改姓叶是因为叶家收养了他。无任何资料说明他曾在朝廷当值过。他长期隐居杭州。诗的最后两句非常有名。

26. On My Visit
(Tang) Li Bai

The beautiful wine of Lanling smells tulip,
It shimmers amber in the jade cup.
If only the host can act like me and have too much of a drop,
I would not care if this is an alien place with no kinship.

In Chinese phonetic alphabet and Chinese characters：

kè zhōng xíng
客 中 行

（唐）李白

lán	líng	měi	jiǔ	yù	jīn	xiāng
兰	陵	美	酒	郁	金	香 ，
yù	wǎn	chéng	lái	hǔ	pò	guāng
玉	碗	盛	来	琥	珀	光 。
dàn	shǐ	zhǔ	rén	néng	zuì	kè
但	使	主	人	能	醉	客 ，
bù	zhī	hé	chù	shì	tā	xiāng
不	知	何	处	是	他	乡 。

Notes：Lanling, a town in today's Shandong Province. The word "xing" in the original title is one of the forms of poetry. The title actually means "a poem about my visit". Lanling wine was made from soaking tulip. Missing home was often the theme in old poems. Li Bai was missing home，he was aware that he was staying at an alien place. Yet the wine diluted his homesickness，and he was delightful and excited.

【说明】兰陵在今天的山东省。"行"是诗歌的一种。中文题目的意思是：我作客兰陵的诗。兰陵酒是泡郁金香草制成的。他乡作客之愁，是古代诗歌创作中一个很普遍的主题。李白作客他乡，乡愁正浓。但是，兰陵美酒稀释了他的愁思，让他愉悦兴奋起来。

27. Inscriptions on a Screen
(Song) Liu Jisun

Swallows twitter on the roof girder，
What they are talking has awoken the idler and dreamer.
Since nobody would know how I have been enraptured，
To go and see the Zhi Mount with my crane and wine is better.

In Chinese phonetic alphabet and Chinese characters：

tí píng
题 屏
（宋）刘季孙

ní	nán	yàn	zi	yǔ	liáng	jiān
呢	喃	燕	子	语	梁	间 ，
dǐ	shì	lái	jīng	mèng	lǐ	xián
底	事	来	惊	梦	里	闲 。
shuō	yú	páng	rén	hún	bù	jiě
说	与	旁	人	浑	不	解 ，
zhàng	lí	xié	jiǔ	kàn	zhī	shān
杖	藜	携	酒	看	芝	山 。

Notes：Liu Jisun （1033 - 1092） was a poet of the Northern

Song，often referred to as a "generous prodigy" by Su Shi. It was said that when Wang Anshi was in charge of legal affairs in the area south of the Changjiang River，he came to where Liu Jisun was the chief of Wine Regie. Wang was not satisfied with Liu's job，and he wanted to punish Liu. Just before he gave his order of punishment he saw this poem on the screen. He was then prodigal of praises and left without giving the punishment. The Zhi Mount is in Jiangxi Province，where the poet was working.

【说明】刘季孙（1033—1092），北宋诗人，苏轼称其为"慷慨奇士"。当年王安石做江东提刑时，巡查酒务到饶州，对在那里任酒业专卖官员的刘季孙的工作并不满意，要对其进行惩罚。就在王安石下达处罚命令之前，他看到了屏幕上的这首诗，对这首诗赞不绝口，就把处罚的事忘在脑后了。芝山在江西省鄱阳县北，作者当时在那里做官。

28. My Casual Versification
(Tang) Du Fu

It is sad to see beautiful spring scenes are coming to an end，
I strolled with stick in hand to the still flourishing land bar and behold.
Craze catkins are dancing with the wind，
Frivolous peach flowers are being carried away by the tide.

In Chinese phonetic alphabet and Chinese characters：

màn xìng
漫 兴

（唐）杜甫

duàn cháng chūn jiāng yù jìn tóu
断 肠 春 江 欲 尽 头，

zhàng	lí	xú	bù	lì	fāng	zhōu
杖	藜	徐	步	立	芳	洲	。

diān	kuáng	liǔ	xù	suí	fēng	wǔ
颠	狂	柳	絮	随	风	舞	，

qīng	bó	táo	huā	zhú	shuǐ	liú
轻	薄	桃	花	逐	水	流	。

Notes：This is the number five of "The Nine Casually Written Poems" of Du Fu. The poet bewailed the ending of spring. This is something catkins and peach flowers didn't really care. Catkins are craze and insane，peach flowers are frivolous，they are just like snobs in the society.

【说明】这是杜甫《绝句漫兴九首》中的第五首。春色将尽，诗人觉得心如刀割。然而，飘飞的柳絮和落地的桃花对即将逝去的春色毫不在乎。柳絮癫狂，桃花轻薄，它们与社会上的小人毫无二致。

29. Peach Flower at Qingquan Cottage
(Song) Xie Bingde

To hide from Qin troops I found this garden of peach flower，
The peach red tells me this is spring of another year.
I wish fallen flowers would not flow away in the river，
Some acquisitive fishermen may track them back here.

In Chinese phonetic alphabet and Chinese characters：

qìng quán ān táo huā
庆 全 庵 桃 花
（宋）谢枋得

xún	dé	táo	huā	hǎo	bì	qín
寻	得	桃	花	好	避	秦	，

táo	hóng	yòu	shì	yì	nián	chūn
桃	红	又	是	一	年	春	。

huā	fēi	mò	qiǎn	suí	liú	shuǐ
花	飞	莫	遣	随	流	水 ，

pà	yòu	yú	láng	lái	wèn	jīn
怕	有	渔	郎	来	问	津 。

Notes: Xie Bingde (1226 – 1289) was once a Chief Administrator of a prefecture, assistant ministers at several ministries. When the Yuan troops were invading, he rallied up over ten thousand militia with his own money and fought against the invaders. During the war, his wife, one daughter, two brothers and three nephews were killed by the aggressors. After the country was lost, he lived in seclusion, on teaching and selling his calligraphy and straw shoes he made at Jianyang, Fujian Province. He was finally identified and sent to the capital, where the Yuan rulers wanted him to work for the new regime. Xie refused and fasted for five days to death (he purposely ate very little on the way up to the capital). It was during his secluded and teaching period he compiled the primer form of this book, which was based on *Anthology of Poetry of Different Categories by One Thousand Bards* assembled by his peer Liu Kezhuang (1187 – 1269). In Xie's edition, there are 226 poems from 122 poets. As the English titles—*A Primer of Ancient Poetry* suggests the poems in this book are widely read by the Chinese people ever since this book came into being.

The Chinese character "an" can mean two things—one is a house or a hut, and two is a nunnery or a temple. The name in the title is close to the first definition of the character, and it was where the poet had been living. Since the poet had been staying away from public notice, he naturally thought of a similar case to himself, something Tao Yuanming, a great poet of the Jin Dynasty, wrote in the famous essay "Notes on the Peach Flower Fountain", which said that a fisherman found among peach flowers a place, where the descendants of Qin had been living in peace and enjoyed themselves and where their ancestors were hiding from the tyranny of the Qin emperor. When the fisherman came again with some officials, this place could no longer be found. That's why in the first line, the poet was saying the purpose of him finding this garden of peach flowers was to stay away from Qin, or in his case, from the tyranny of the Yuan troops. The last two lines expressed the poet's fear that he might be identified by some one like the fisherman in Tao Yuanming's story.

【说明】谢枋得（1226—1289）曾任江东提刑，江西招谕使，知信州，担任过六部侍郎。元军进犯后，他用自己的钱财，组织起万人民团反抗元军。在战争中，他的妻子、一个女儿、两个弟兄、三个侄子均遭杀害。战争失利后，他被迫隐姓埋名，逃亡福建，流寓建阳，以卖卜教书度日。后来他被人认出，被俘并送往元大都。元军对他进行劝降，他严词拒绝。之后连续五日绝食（他在来元大都的路上有意少食）而死。他在建阳隐居期间，编成了这本蒙学著作《千家诗》。这本书是以与他同辈的刘克庄（1187—1269）所编纂的《分门纂类唐宋时贤千家诗选》为蓝本的。谢的版本收录了122位诗人的226首诗。正如本书的英文书名 *A Primer of Ancient Poetry* 所示，此书问世后，读者的数目可谓庞大。

"庵"字在中文里有两重意思：其一，圆形草屋；其二，小庙。诗名与第一项定义接近，说的是诗人居住的地方。由于诗人有段时间远离了公众的注意力，他很自然地想到他的境遇与晋朝的大诗人陶渊明所著《桃花源记》里的情况有些类似。《桃花源记》说的是一个打鱼的人在桃花源里发现了一个地方，这个地方住着先秦的子民，他们无忧无虑地生活着。这些人的前辈为了躲避秦朝的暴政隐藏在桃花源。然而，当打鱼人带着官府的人回来时，却怎么也找不到这个地方了。这就是为什么在第一句，诗人说他之所以找到桃花源，是为了"避秦"，或者按他的情况说是为了"避元"。诗的最后两句表示出来诗人的担心，他害怕出现陶渊明故事中的打鱼人，那样就会找到他，认出他来。

30. Watching Peach Blossom at Xuandu Taoist Temple
(Tang) Liu Yuxi

Dust rises on the roads in the downtown capital，

Everyone says he just returned from flower watching at the temple.

Yet，the thousand and odd peach trees there，

Were planted after Liu was deposed and sent to exile.

In Chinese phonetic alphabet and Chinese characters：

xuán dū guàn táo huā
玄 都 观 桃 花

（唐）刘禹锡

zǐ	mò	hóng	chén	fú	miàn	lái
紫	陌	红	尘	拂	面	来 ，
wú	rén	bú	dào	kàn	huā	huí
无	人	不	道	看	花	回 。
xuán	dū	guàn	lǐ	táo	qiān	shù
玄	都	观	里	桃	千	树 ，
jìn	shì	liú	láng	qù	hòu	zāi
尽	是	刘	郎	去	后	栽 。

Notes：Liu Yuxi（772－842）served as chief administrator at several prefectures and the highest position he held was Acting Minister of Ministry of Rites. On surface the poem depicts the passion of people for going to watch peach blossom at the Xuandu Taoist Temple，yet in between lines the poem is a satire on the bigwigs of the time. The first two lines show how spectacular it was on the streets，packed with people and carts，all returning from flowers watching. However，ten years ago when the poet was in the capital，there were no peach blossom at all in that temple. Actually the poet was comparing the peach blossom to complacent upstarts，and flowers viewers to snobs who curried favor with those in power. The last line pointed out those seemingly important upstarts only emerged after the poet was squeezed out of the capital. Powerful as the mocking and satire of this poem，the poet was deposed and sent to exile again because of this poem.

【说明】刘禹锡（772—842）曾任几个州的刺史，最高做过礼部郎中。表面上看去，此诗写的是人们到玄都观看花的热情，字里行间讽刺了当时掌管朝廷大权的新官僚。第一二句写人们去玄都观看花的情景，展示出大道上人欢马叫、川流不息的热闹场面。自己10年前在长安的时候玄都观里根本没有桃花。诗人用10年里新生的桃树比喻得意忘形的新贵，用观花人比喻献媚新贵的小人。最后一句指出那些看上去地位显赫的新贵是在他被排挤出都城后才冒出头来的。由于此篇诗语讥怨，触怒当权者，诗人因此又遭贬逐。

31. Revisit the Xuandu Taoist Temple
(Tang) Liu Yuxi

Half of the hundred-acre yard is covered with mosses，
Peach blossom are all gone，rape flowers have taken their place.
Where are those peach planting Taoists?
Today again，Liu who visited before comes.

In Chinese phonetic alphabet and Chinese characters：

zài yóu xuán dū guàn
再 游 玄 都 观

（唐）刘禹锡

bǎi	mǔ	tíng	zhōng	bàn	shì	tái
百	亩	庭	中	半	是	苔 ，

táo	huā	jìng	jìn	cài	huā	kāi
桃	花	净	尽	菜	花	开 。

zhòng	táo	dào	shì	guī	hé	chù
种	桃	道	士	归	何	处 ，

qián	dù	liú	láng	jīn	yòu	lái
前	度	刘	郎	今	又	来 。

Notes：There is a preface in the poem，which said it had been fourteen years since he was sent to exile. When he came back again to see that half of the hundred-acre yard was covered with mosses，a big contrast with the previous poem，mosses would grow if there weren't many visitors. Now，peach blossom was gone，what you saw were only rape flowers. The poet asked where those Taoists who planted peaches are，or in other words where those upstarts are. The poet exclaimed：who would have predicted Liu，who was deposed，is back again.

【说明】原诗有一序言，说诗人遭贬后，已经过去了十四年，他又回到玄都观，观里百亩庭中半是苔，景象大为不同。观里没有人迹，自是要长出苔藓来。现在桃花已无踪影，满眼都是菜花。诗人便问，过去那些种桃花的道士哪里去了？或者说，过去的那些新贵哪里去了？诗人感叹道：谁能预料，我这被贬的刘郎今天又回来了！

32. The West Gully at Chuzhou

(Tang) Wei Yingwu

My only favorite is wild grass growing along a gully，

Deep in the trees orioles sing pleasantly.
When it rained at dusk spring tide comes in a hurry,
A boat is being blown sideways at the deserted ferry.

In Chinese phonetic alphabet and Chinese characters:

chú zhōu xī jiàn
滁 州 西 涧
（唐）韦应物

dú lián yōu cǎo jiàn biān shēng
独 怜 幽 草 涧 边 生 ，

shàng yǒu huáng lí shēn shù míng
上 有 黄 鹂 深 树 鸣 。

chūn cháo dài yǔ wǎn lái jí
春 潮 带 雨 晚 来 急 ，

yě dù wú rén zhōu zì héng
野 渡 无 人 舟 自 横 。

Notes：Wei Yingwu（737 - 792 or 793）was one of the pastoral poets of the Tang Dynasty. He squandered much time in his youth playing and he only started his studies seriously when he was twenty-two years old, he also began composing poems since that age. He served as chief administrator at several localities. Chuzhou is today's Chu County. Wei wrote this poem when he was the chief administrator there. He changed his disposition ever since he began writing poetry. He didn't desire much in life, he loved equanimity, and he swept his courtyard and burnt incense as soon as he got up. He used to walk by himself outside for a long time everyday. It may seem strange for him to favor wild grass by the riverside; he didn't like things big and conspicuous. This poem is a natural flow of his attitude toward life.

【说明】 韦应物（737—792 或 793）是唐朝的田园诗人之一。他年轻时荒废了很多时日，到 22 岁时才认真读书并开始诗歌创作。滁州即今日之滁县。他在滁州任刺史时写下了此诗。韦应物开始写诗后，性情大变。他对生活没有多少要求，喜爱恬静的日子，起床后，自己打扫院落，烧香，常常独自一人长时间地散步。他偏爱河边的幽草，不喜欢大的、显眼的事。这首诗自然地流露出他对待生活的态度。

33. Flower Shadows

(Song) Xie Bingde

Up on the jade terrace flower shadows are overlapping，
Several times I asked servant to sweep them away，but they persisted their being.
The sun has just rolled them up，
Yet，they are back again，and the moon was delivering.

In Chinese phonetic alphabet and Chinese characters：

huā yǐng
花　影
（宋）谢枋得

chóng	chóng	dié	dié	shàng	yáo	tái
重	重	叠	叠	上	瑶	台 ，
jǐ	dù	hū	tóng	sǎo	bù	kāi
几	度	呼	童	扫	不	开 。
gāng	bèi	tài	yáng	shōu	shí	qù
刚	被	太	阳	收	拾	去 ，
què	jiào	míng	yuè	sòng	jiāng	lái
却	教	明	月	送	将	来 。

Notes： This poem describes the interacting between flower shadow and light. Some people say the poet compared snobs to flower shadows，who are always around you and you just can not get away from them. It is disputable if the one who wrote this poem was Xie. Some critics held that it was Su Shi who wrote it，yet when checking all Su's works, there is no such a poem.

【说明】此诗写的是花影与光之间的相互作用。有人说诗人将花影比作小人，小人总是围着你转，想甩也甩不掉。这首诗的作者是不是谢枋得，是有争议的。有人说此诗系苏轼所作，然而，查遍苏轼所有的著作，也找不到此诗。

34. The North Mountain
(Song) Wang Anshi

The pond is full to the brim with green spring water from the North Mountain,

Waters in pools in various shapes glisten.

Sitting for a long time counting how many flowers have fallen,

Returned home late because of my slow searching of things still green.

In Chinese phonetic alphabet and Chinese characters:

běi shān
北 山
（宋）王安石

běi	shān	shū	lù	zhǎng	héng	bēi
北	山	输	绿	涨	横	陂 ，
zhí	qiàn	huí	táng	yàn	yàn	shí
直	堑	回	塘	滟	滟	时 。
xì	shǔ	luò	huā	yīn	zuò	jiǔ
细	数	落	花	因	坐	久 ，
huǎn	xún	fāng	cǎo	dé	guī	chí
缓	寻	芳	草	得	归	迟 。

Notes: Wang Anshi lived in the Zhongshan Mountains in Jinling (Nanjing) in his late years. No longer burdened with public duties, Wang was able to devote all his time to writing. The North

Mountain must be part of the Zhongshan Mountains. This poem conveys Wang's leisurely and easygoing mood; it was written after his meeting in 1084 with Su Shi, who was passing through Jinling. Wang was deeply moved by Su's visit. The two toured the mountains, enjoyed wine and poetry. Wang also went to the hotel where Su was staying in Jinling and returned the visit. Su furthered his understanding of Wang and he often remarked after their meeting that a person like Wang only appeared once in a few hundred years.

【说明】王安石晚年生活在金陵（今南京）的钟山。一旦除却公事的烦扰，王就将所有的时间都用来作诗。北山应该是钟山的一部分。此诗表现了他安然自得的情绪，写于 1084 年他与苏轼见面之后，苏当时路过金陵。苏轼来访，深深打动了王安石，两人一起游山，饮酒赋诗。王也到苏轼所住客栈回访。苏轼通过这些活动加深了对王的了解。此次会面后，他经常说："不知几百年，方有如此人物。"

35. On the Lake
(Song) Xu Yuanjie

Among blossoming red flowers orioles on trees keep chirping,

In fully grown grass along the banks and on the even surface of the West Lake egrets are whirring and fluttering.

On such a nice day when wind is so gentle, people are in a happy mood,

When the sun is setting, amidst the playing of flute and drum boats are returning.

In Chinese phonetic alphabet and Chinese characters:

hú shàng
湖 上

（宋）徐元杰

huā 花	kāi 开	hóng 红	shù 树	luàn 乱	yīng 莺	tí 啼 ，
cǎo 草	zhǎng 长	píng 平	hú 湖	bái 白	lù 鹭	fēi 飞 。
fēng 风	rì 日	qíng 晴	hé 和	rén 人	yì 意	hǎo 好 ，
xī 夕	yáng 阳	xiāo 箫	gǔ 鼓	jǐ 几	chuán 船	guī 归 。

Notes：Xu Yuanjie （1196－1246）was rector of the Imperial College and a drafter of imperial edicts. He was poisoned to death on his post of Assistant Minister of Engineering. This poem has been regarded as one of the best describing the West Lake，it portrayed the natural scenery of the lake，and the delightfulness of visitors as well.

【说明】徐元杰（1196—1246）曾任国子祭酒、中书舍人。他任工部侍郎时被人毒死。此诗被视为描写西湖的杰作，不但写出了湖光之美，而且写出了游湖人愉悦的心情。

36. My Casual Versification （7）
(Tang) Du Fu

The shattering poplar filaments look like a white blanket rolled out on the road，

The tender lotus leaves on the brook look like qreen coins overlapped.

Baby pheasants at the root of bamboo shoot nobody has noticed，

The newly hatched ducks are sleeping by their mother's side on the sand.

In Chinese phonetic alphabet and Chinese characters:

màn xìng qī
漫 兴 （七）
（唐）杜甫

sǎn	jìng	yáng	huā	pū	bái	zhān
糁	径	杨	花	铺	白	毡 ，

diǎn	xī	hé	yè	dié	qīng	qián
点	溪	荷	叶	叠	青	钱 。

sǔn	gēn	zhì	zǐ	wú	rén	jiàn
笋	根	雉	子	无	人	见 ，

shā	shàng	fú	chú	bàng	mǔ	mián
沙	上	凫	雏	傍	母	眠 。

Notes: In this poem each line presents an independent scene. On the whole, scenery in the suburb in early summer is being portrayed. The observation of the poet was so delicate that it revealed how much the poet had enjoyed the things he found in early summer.

【说明】这四句诗，一句一景。总体上展现了一幅美丽的初夏风景图。细致的观察描绘，透露出作者对初夏美妙自然景物的流连欣赏之情。

37. A Clear Day after Rain
(Tang) Wang Jia

Flowers displayed their fresh stamens and pistils before the rain,

After the rain, flowers under the leaves are nowhere to be seen.

To the other side of the wall bees and butterflies have flown,

The spring scene might have moved to the neighbor's garden.

In Chinese phonetic alphabet and Chinese characters:

yǔ qíng
雨 晴

（唐）王驾

yǔ	qián	chū	jiàn	huā	jiān	ruǐ
雨	前	初	见	花	间	蕊 ，

yǔ	hòu	quán	wú	yè	dǐ	huā
雨	后	全	无	叶	底	花 。

fēng	dié	fēn	fēn	guò	qiáng	qù
蜂	蝶	纷	纷	过	墙	去 ，

què	yí	chūn	sè	zài	lín	jiā
却	疑	春	色	在	邻	家 。

Notes：The difference before and after the rain shows how much the poet was attached to spring. Before the rain flower buds had just come out，but the rain came and deprived the poet of lively spring scenery. The poet was not the only one disappointed，bees and butterflies were also discontented and flew to the next door over the wall. Was it spring there? The last line fully expressed in a refreshing and vivid way how the poet felt about what he saw.

【说明】此诗以雨前所见和雨后情景相对比、映衬，展现出诗人一片惜春之情。雨前，花才吐出骨朵儿；雨一来，诗人眼中生机勃勃的春景就被赶跑了。失望的并非诗人一人，蜜蜂和蝴蝶也不满意，它们飞过墙，跑到邻居家去了。隔壁有春色吗？最后一句以令人耳目一新的方式，活灵活现地说出了诗人的感受。

38. Late Spring
(Song) Cao Bin

Out on the street nobody seems to care about fallen flower，

Dark green is slowly extending to every corner.

In forests there is no longer the sound of oriole twitter,

By the pond amidst green grass the croaking of frogs is the only thing you can hear.

In Chinese phonetic alphabet and Chinese characters:

chūn mù
春 暮
（宋）曹豳

mén	wài	wú	rén	wèn	luò	huā
门	外	无	人	问	落	花 ，

lù	yīn	rǎn	rǎn	biàn	tiān	yá
绿	阴	冉	冉	遍	天	涯 。

lín	yīng	tí	dào	wú	shēng	chù
林	莺	啼	到	无	声	处 ，

qīng	cǎo	chí	táng	dú	tīng	wā
青	草	池	塘	独	听	蛙 。

Notes：Cao Bin （1170－1250） served as one providing admonishment to the emperor, then the chief administrator in Fuzhou and finally an assistant minister in the Ministry of Rites. He was known for his straightforward manner. There had been a sad tone when poets were writing about late spring. But, this one by Cao Bin is different. He cherished no sentiment over the passing of spring; instead, he was full of joy and longing for the early summer. He juxtaposed blossoming flowers with green bower, singing of oriole with croaking of frogs, yet he emphasized more the latter. He was apparently an extoller of green bower and croaking of frogs. He gave a remarkakle and different touch to the scene of late spring.

【说明】曹豳（1170—1250）曾任左司谏、福州知府和礼部侍郎等职，以性情耿直著称。写暮春的诗往往笔调忧伤，但是曹豳的这首与众不同。他并不伤春，相反，他对夏天的到来充满渴望和喜悦。他将繁花与绿荫、莺啼与蛙叫并列，更看重绿荫和蛙叫。他笔下的暮春不同凡响。

39. Fallen Flowers

(Song) Zhu Shuzhen

Flowers on intertwined branches are in full blossom，

Wind and rain are trying to fasten withering of flowers，out of envy of flowers charm.

May the power of the Spring God always overwhelm，

So that lovely flowers will not fall on green mosses and keep their tender form.

In Chinese phonetic alphabet and Chinese characters：

luò huā
落 花
（宋）朱淑真

lián	lǐ	zhī	tóu	huā	zhèng	kāi
连	理	枝	头	花	正	开 ，

dù	huā	fēng	yǔ	biàn	xiāng	cuī
妒	花	风	雨	便	相	催 。

yuàn	jiào	qīng	dì	cháng	wéi	zhǔ
愿	教	青	帝	常	为	主 ，

mò	qiǎn	fēn	fēn	diǎn	cuì	tái
莫	遣	纷	纷	点	翠	苔 。

Notes：Zhu Shuzhen （1135 – 1180）was one of the most proliferous lady writers of both the Tang and Song dynasties. She died earlier of despondency resulted from her unhappy marriage. Some believed that she was a niece of Zhu Xi，a poet we mentioned in the foregoing. "Intertwined branches" are often used as a metaphor of a husband and his wife. This poem was composed when the poet was a young girl. She adored beautiful flowers and wanted very much to protect them. She had also suggested，by writing this poem，"true love" should be protected.

【说明】朱淑真（1135—1180）是唐宋最多产的女作家之一。她由于婚姻不幸，抑郁早逝。有人说她是朱熹的侄女，我们前面提到过朱熹这位诗人。"连理枝"常用来形容恩爱的夫妻关系。写此诗时，作家尚是一位年轻女子。她喜爱美丽的花朵，极力地要保护它们。在此诗中她提出要保护"真正的爱情"。

40. Visiting a Small Garden in Late Spring
(Song) Wang Qi

The fall of plum blossom is just like the removal of makeup from a girl，

The flourishing of cherry-apple is just like newly added red on the gill.

The flowering term ends with the blossom of bramble，

Over the wall covered with mosses only asparagus grows still.

In Chinese phonetic alphabet and Chinese characters：

chūn mù yóu xiǎo yuán
春　暮　游　小　园

（宋）王淇

yì	cóng	méi	fěn	tuì	cán	zhuāng
一	从	梅	粉	褪	残	妆 ，

tú	mǒ	xīn	hóng	shàng	hǎi	táng
涂	抹	新	红	上	海	棠 。

kāi	dào	tú	mí	huā	shì	liǎo
开	到	荼	蘼	花	事	了 ，

sī	sī	tiān	jí	chū	méi	qiáng
丝	丝	天	棘	出	莓	墙 。

Notes：We don't know much about this poet，except that he was on very good terms with Xie Bingde，the compiler of this anthology. Each line mentions one particular kind of plant. I am not sure if "plum blossom" is what the poet meant. It might be some kind of a bayberry. I wish I have got the rest right in the remaining three lines.

【说明】对这位诗人我们所知甚少，只知道他与谢枋得，亦即本诗集的编者过从甚密。每行诗都提到一种植物。我不敢肯定"梅粉"是指开败了的梅花，或许他指的是月桂。希望余下的三行我都说对了。

41．The Oriole Shuttle
(Song) Liu Kezhuang

Orioles are so fond of the forest；they jump from arbor to willow，

Their singing sometimes sounds like a loom working nice and slow.

March in Luoyang is beautiful as a brocade，

How much time is needed to have it woven by the oriole?

In Chinese phonetic alphabet and Chinese characters：

yīng suō
莺　梭
（宋）刘克庄

zhì	liǔ	qiān	qiáo	tài	yǒu	qíng
掷	柳	迁	乔	太	有	情 ，

jiāo	jiāo	shí	zuò	nòng	jī	shēng
交	交	时	作	弄	机	声 。

luò	yáng	sān	yuè	huā	rú	jǐn
洛	阳	三	月	花	如	锦 ，

duō	shǎo	gōng	fū	zhī	dé	chéng
多	少	工	夫	织	得	成 。

Notes: Liu Kezhuang (1187 – 1269) was once the Minister of Engineering in the Song Dynasty. He was well known for his open and aboveboard qualities. *The Complete Works of Liu Kezhuang* included over 5,000 poems, over 200 "Ci" poetry, 4 books of his writings on poetry and many prose. We talked about him in the foregoing; he was the one who compiled *The Anthology of Poetry of Different Categories by One Thousand Bards*. The word "spring" does not appear in this poem about spring. He likened the up and down flying of the oriole to a shuttle, the chirping of birds to working sound of a loom, and the flourishing flowers in the capital to a brocade. These metaphorical images are vivid and expressive.

【说明】刘克庄（1187—1269）曾任宋朝的工部尚书。他生性开朗、光明磊落。他的《后村先生大全集》收有他 5 000 多首诗、200 多首词和 4 本诗论。我们前面说到过他。他就是《分门纂类唐宋时贤千家诗选》的编者。这首描写春天的诗中未见一个"春"字，将黄莺的上下翻飞比喻为莺梭，将鸟的鸣叫比作织布机的声音，将都城盛开的鲜花比喻为织锦。这些比喻既形象又生动。

42. A Poem Prompted by Late Spring
(Song) Ye Cai

The shadows of two sparrows are moving on my desk,
Catkins are waftures setting down in my container of ink.
Sitting leisurely by the small window reading "The Book of Change",
Not knowing how much spring has gone in the time range.

In Chinese phonetic alphabet and Chinese characters:

mù chūn jí shì
暮 春 即 事

（宋）叶采

shuāng	shuāng	wǎ	què	xíng	shū	àn
双	双	瓦	雀	行	书	案 ，

diǎn	diǎn	yáng	huā	rù	yàn	chí
点	点	杨	花	入	砚	池 。

xián	zuò	xiǎo	chuāng	dú	zhōu	yì
闲	坐	小	窗	读	周	易 ，

bù	zhī	chūn	qù	jǐ	duō	shí
不	知	春	去	几	多	时 。

Notes：Ye Cai（no dates of birth and death available）was a student of Zhu Xi's disciple. He was a lecturer and member of the Imperial Academy. This poem describes how concentrated the poet was in reading. Ancient Chinese wrote with brush pens，which have a pointed end. One has to put the head of the pen into ink. Ink is usually produced by grounding a bar of ink in water. A container of ink is normally made of stone. *The Book of Change* is China's first canon，all scholars were supposed to learn it.

【说明】叶采（无生卒年记载）是朱熹弟子的学生，官至翰林学士兼侍讲。这首诗描写作者专心致志读书的样子。在古代，中国人用毛笔写字，毛笔的头是尖的，写字时要用笔尖蘸墨。墨汁是用墨在砚台里加水磨出来的。砚台通常是石头做的。《周易》是中国的第一部典籍，是每个书生必读之书。

43. Mountain Climbing

(Tang) Li She

I have been in a state of drowsy all day long,

Bracing myself up I climbed the mountain and suddenly learned the Spring will be gone.

Passing by a temple I ran into a monk and talked to him,
In my floating life I spent in leisure another half day's time.

In Chinese phonetic alphabet and Chinese characters:

dēng shān
登 山
（唐）李涉

zhōng	rì	hūn	hūn	zuì	mèng	jiān
终	日	昏	昏	醉	梦	间 ，
hū	wén	chūn	jìn	qiǎng	dēng	shān
忽	闻	春	尽	强	登	山 。
yīn	guò	zhú	yuàn	féng	sēng	huà
因	过	竹	院	逢	僧	话 ，
yòu	dé	fú	shēng	bàn	rì	xián
又	得	浮	生	半	日	闲 。

Notes：Li She （not dates of birth and death available） was once responsible of briefing the Crown Prince of imperial edicts and orders, but he was soon downgraded to a warehouse keeper, and finally during his late years became one senior instructor at the imperial college. Li She was well known during his time. He was once on a passenger boat, which was stopped by a group of bandits, who didn't rob the boat because they learned that Li She was on it. They, out of their respect of the poet, even gave him some thing valuable after he agreed to compose a poem for them. This poem was written after he was downgraded, he was very depressed and somnolent all day long. When he realized that the spring was to end soon, he braced himself up and climbed the mountain. The second line was also interpreted that he had a life before him and he could not afford to be so demoralized. His talk with the monk helped him to leave all his worried behind, and he felt in half a day's time he was able to perceive the meaning of life.

【说明】李涉 （无生卒年记载） 曾任太子通事舍人，但很快被

58

贬为司仓参军。晚年任国子博士。李涉活着的时候就享有盛名，他有一次乘船，遇到一帮强盗，当这些强盗知道李涉在船上时，非但没有抢劫，而且在李涉同意给他们写首诗后，他们出于对李涉的尊敬，还给了他一些值钱的东西。这首诗是作者被贬之后所写，他那时心情郁闷，昏昏沉沉。然而，当他意识到春天就要结束时，就打起精神，去登山。有人将诗中第二句解释为：还有新的生活等着他，他不能消沉下去。他与僧人的谈话，让他丢掉了各种烦恼。他觉得在半天的时间里他终于弄明白了人生的意义。

44. Chant of Lady Silkworm Raiser
(Song) Xie Bingde

In small hours cuckoo crows so loudly,

She is up to see if mulberry leaves are enough for worms, which are so many.

It is unbelievable when the moon is high over trees and the building,

Girl performers, have not returned, are still singing and dancing.

In Chinese phonetic alphabet and Chinese characters：

cán fù yín
蚕 妇 吟
（宋）谢枋得

zǐ	guī	tí	chè	sì	gēng	shí
子	规	啼	彻	四	更	时 ，
qǐ	shì	cán	chóu	pà	yè	xī
起	视	蚕	稠	怕	叶	稀 。
bù	xìn	lóu	tóu	yáng	liǔ	yuè
不	信	楼	头	杨	柳	月 ，
yù	rén	gē	wǔ	wèi	céng	guī
玉	人	歌	舞	未	曾	归 。

Notes: The poem compares the life of two different kinds of ladies. One is silkworm raisers, who had to get up at one or three o'clock to check if the mulberry leaves were enough for the worms; the other is lady performers, who were still singing and dancing in the small hours when the moon was going down. When silkworm raisers heard the singing, they could not comprehend why the girls were still not home yet. The question is whose life is harder. The silkworm raisers or the performers? The performers were providing entertainment to rich people, for their own living as well. The original of the first line mentions "the fourth hour", which is from one to three o'clock according to ancient Chinese way of time division.

【说明】本诗比较了两种女人的生活：一种是养蚕妇，她们凌晨就要起床检查蚕叶是否够吃；另一种女人是歌女，她们在月亮要落下去时，在凌晨还在歌唱跳舞。当养蚕妇听到歌女的歌声时，她们不明白这些歌女为何还没回家。问题是谁的生活更艰辛？是养蚕妇，还是歌女？歌女卖唱给富人，也是为了生计。原诗第一句提到的"四更"是中国古人的计时方法，指凌晨1点到3点之间。

45. Late Spring

(Tang) Han Yu

Plants and trees realized spring would leave sooner or later,
They tried hard to contend in beauty and ambrosial aroma.
Catkins and elm seeds lack talent and are mediocre,
The only thing they know is to fly without grace in the air.

In Chinese phonetic alphabet and Chinese characters:

wǎn chūn
晚 春
（唐）韩愈

cǎo	mù	zhī	chūn	bù	jiǔ	guī	
草	木	知	春	不	久	归	，

bǎi	bān	hóng	zǐ	dòu	fāng	fēi	
百	般	红	紫	斗	芳	菲	。

yáng	huā	yú	jiá	wú	cái	sī	
杨	花	榆	荚	无	才	思	，

wéi	jiě	màn	tiān	zuò	xuě	fēi	
惟	解	漫	天	作	雪	飞	。

Notes：Is this poem about late spring? The poet didn't tell us flowers are falling down and plants are withering. Instead，he told us plants and trees were contending in beauty and ambrosial aroma. Plants and trees had sense，they realized spring would soon be gone，they were grasping time to present to us a flourishing scene. Even catkins and elm seeds，which had no talents or capabilities，were also trying to add color to late spring. This is really a positive and refreshing poem. What helped the poet to reach this effect was his way of personification，he gave sense and feelings to plants，to trees of willow and elm.

【说明】此诗是写暮春的吗？诗人不写百花稀落、暮春凋零，却写草木因留春而争奇斗艳的动人情景。草木亦有知，它们知道春将不久矣，便抓紧时间呈现出万紫千红的样子。就连那没有什么姿色的杨花和榆钱也要为暮春添色。这是一首积极，且令人耳目一新的诗。拟人化的写作手法，让草木、杨柳和榆树也动情，帮诗人达到了好的效果。

46. Sorrow over the Elapse of Spring
（Song）Yang Wanli

I thought this spring would be full of happy events，

The east wind was let down again against my intents.
In previous years I didn't have the heart to watch flowers,
I was ridden by either worries or illness.

In Chinese phonetic alphabet and Chinese characters:

shāng chūn
伤 春

（宋）杨万里

zhǔn	nǐ	jīn	chūn	lè	shì	nóng
准	拟	今	春	乐	事	浓 ，

yī	rán	wǎng	què	yī	dōng	fēng
依	然	枉	却	一	东	风 。

nián	nián	bú	dài	kàn	huā	yǎn
年	年	不	带	看	花	眼 ，

bú	shì	chóu	zhōng	jí	bìng	zhòng
不	是	愁	中	即	病	中 。

Notes: Yang Wanli (1127-1206) had many official titles, among them senior instructor at the imperial college, chief administrator in big cities, department head at the Ministry of Personnel, senior secretary at the Imperial Court were the most important ones. It was said that he composed over twenty thousand poems during his lifetime, but only 4,200 of them are still available. His complete works are consisted of 133 volumes. Most themes of his poetry were things in the nature as he remarked once, "I do not listen to cliches, I only listen to the nature." Things big as high mountains and long rivers, and things small as bees and butterfly can all enter into his poetry. He said, "There would be no poetry if there were no mountains." "Where would novel lines come from if there were no marvelous scenery?" His poems on natural objects can best embody the artistic characters of his poetry.

【说明】杨万里（1127—1206）从政经历丰富，他当过宝谟阁

62

文士、几个地方官、吏部官员以及枢密院检详官等。据说，他一生作诗两万多首，留存下来的只有 4 200 首。他的作品共 133 卷。他的很多诗写的是大自然，正如他自己说的那样："不听陈言只听天。"自然界的一切，大到高山流水，小到游蜂戏蝶，无不收录入诗。他说："无山安得诗。""不是风烟好，何缘句子新?"他描写自然景物的诗歌最能体现他的诗歌艺术特色。

47. Seeing off Spring

(Song) Wang Ling

Despite withering some flowers in March still bloom，
Every day to my eaves sparrows come.
Cuckoos cry to bleeding at mid-night，
Believing they could call the spring back as they so expect.

In Chinese phonetic alphabet and Chinese characters：

sòng chūn
送 春
（宋）王令

sān	yuè	cán	huā	luò	gèng	kāi
三	月	残	花	落	更	开 ，
xiǎo	yán	rì	rì	yàn	fēi	lái
小	檐	日	日	燕	飞	来 。
zǐ	guī	yè	bàn	yóu	tí	xuè
子	规	夜	半	犹	啼	血 ，
bú	xìn	dōng	fēng	huàn	bù	huí
不	信	东	风	唤	不	回 。

Notes：Wang Ling (1032 – 1059) never worked in the government system. He made a living by teaching. Wang Anshi thought highly of his poetry. In the poem he said that in March flowers may bloom despite their withering; some sparrows may still come for a visit. The last two lines have been on the lips of Chinese readers. The lines expressed confidence and positive attitude, cuckoos kept on crying, even though they were bleeding from crying, for they firmly believe spring would come back when hearing their cry.

【说明】王令（1032—1059）从未在朝廷供职，靠教书度日。王安石对他的诗评价很高。诗中说暮春三月，花谢了又开，小小的屋檐下天天有小燕子飞来。后两句表现出充满信心和积极的态度，为中国读者所熟知。子规尽管啼血，仍叫个不停，因为它们坚信叫声能唤回春天。

48. Seeing off Spring on the Last Day of March
(Tang) Jia Dao

This is the thirtieth day of the third month,
Departing from my body are the spring scenes, which I painstakingly intonate with.
Tonight your gentleman may sit up with me,
Before the morning bell strikes spring is still with us anyway.

In Chinese phonetic alphabet and Chinese characters：

sān yuè huì rì sòng chūn
三 月 晦 日 送 春

（唐）贾岛

sān	yuè	zhèng	dāng	sān	shí	rì
三	月	正	当	三	十	日 ，
fēng	guāng	bié	wǒ	kǔ	yín	shēn
风	光	别	我	苦	吟	身 。
gòng	jūn	jīn	yè	bù	xū	shuì
共	君	今	夜	不	须	睡 ，
wèi	dào	xiǎo	zhōng	yóu	shì	chūn
未	到	晓	钟	犹	是	春 。

Notes：Jia Dao（779 - 843）became a monk when he was young. He started to compose poetry after he resumed secular life and was noted for his painstaking efforts in repeated diction. In the late Tang period，Jia Dao and a few others formed a school known for their deliberate diction. His works were collected in the ten-volume *Changjiang Anthology*. This poem described how he sat up all night with his friends crooning their poems and drinking，and enjoyed the last night of spring.

【说明】贾岛（779—843）早年出家为僧，还俗后开始写诗。他写诗时字斟句酌，醉心于词句的琢磨。他与其他几个诗人在晚唐组成了"苦吟派"。他的作品大都收入十卷本的《长江集》中。此诗写诗人与友人长坐不睡，与那即将逝去的春天共守最后一个春夜。

49. Early Summer amidst My Journey

(Song) Sima Guang

Rain has just stopped and it is a clear and warm day of April，
Opposite the gate things are so distinctive on the South Hill.
There are no longer catkins flying with wind in the air，
There are only those always bloom to the sun，the sunflower.

In Chinese phonetic alphabet and Chinese characters：

kè zhōng chū xià
客 中 初 夏
（宋）司马光

sì yuè qīng hé yǔ zhà qíng
四 月 清 和 雨 乍 晴 ，

nán shān dāng hù zhuǎn fēn míng
南 山 当 户 转 分 明 。

gèng wú liǔ xù yīn fēng qǐ
更 无 柳 絮 因 风 起 ，

wéi yǒu kuí huā xiàng rì qīng
惟 有 葵 花 向 日 倾 。

Notes：Sima Guang （1019－1086） was a historian and man of letters. He served four emperors of the Song Dynasty. He was the chief compiler of China's first chronicle history—*Comprehensive Mirror in Aid of Governance*. He was conferred "The Grand Tutor" as the posthumous title. This is a poem about early summer. It was nice and warm after rain. The poet didn't like the fine drops of rain at the Southern Hill，he was pleased there were no longer any catkins，fortunately there was things he liked most— the sunflowers. This may imply that the poet didn't want to be catkins，which fly with the wind like those who always bowed unctuously and never boldly voiced their own views，and that he wished to be a sunflower，which is sunny，treasures sunlight and smiles all the time.

【说明】司马光（1019—1086）是历史学家和文学家，曾在四位皇帝手下为臣，是《资治通鉴》的编撰者。去世后获"太师"谥号。此诗写的是初夏，雨后，天气温暖舒适。诗人不喜欢雨丝蒙蒙的南山，柳絮不再翻飞让他高兴。可喜的是还有他最喜欢的向日葵。这几句话是说诗人不想做随风飞舞的柳絮，不想成为一个假惺惺点头哈腰、不敢亮出自己观点的人。他想做一棵向日葵，阳光、珍惜光明，微笑始终。

50. An Appointment

(Song) Zhao Shixiu

When plum turned yellow rain began to hang on over every household,

In the pond encircled by thick grass frogs croaked.

The guest on appointment didn't turn up and midnight has passed,

Snuff fell from my knocking of a chess piece, I was so bored.

In Chinese phonetic alphabet and Chinese characters:

yǒu yuē
有 约

（宋）赵师秀

| huáng | méi | shí | jié | jiā | jiā | yǔ |
| 黄 | 梅 | 时 | 节 | 家 | 家 | 雨 ， |

| qīng | cǎo | chí | táng | chù | chù | wā |
| 青 | 草 | 池 | 塘 | 处 | 处 | 蛙 。 |

| yǒu | yuē | bù | lái | guò | yè | bàn |
| 有 | 约 | 不 | 来 | 过 | 夜 | 半 ， |

| xián | qiāo | qí | zǐ | luò | dēng | huā |
| 闲 | 敲 | 棋 | 子 | 落 | 灯 | 花 。 |

Notes：Zhao Shixiu (1170 – 1220) was a direct descendant in the eighth generation of the first emperor of the Song. He was reputed as a "wizard" and one of the "Four Souls of the Yongjia Period". He opened up a special poetry school—the Folk Society School in the Southern Song period. He died in Hangzhou and was buried at the West Lake. When plum turns yellow, a rainy season is started for about a month. The pond is full of water, and frogs are croaking everywhere. The visitor didn't turn up, perhaps it was the rain, which has stopped him from coming. The poet was fidgeting, he was knocking a chess piece on the table, he was repeating such dull and mechanical movement and as a result, snuffs fell from the candle stick, the frustration of the poet was thus portrayed with minute care.

【说明】赵师秀（1170—1220）是宋太祖八世孙，"永嘉四灵"之一，人称"鬼才"，开创了南宋江湖派。他死在杭州，葬在西湖。梅子由青转黄之时，长达一个月左右的黄梅天就开始了。池塘水满，处处都是蛙声。约好的人没有露面，可能雨水阻住了他的路。诗人坐立不安，用围棋子敲打着桌子，他重复着这个单调机械的动作，结果灯花被敲了下来。诗人无奈的心情被惟妙惟肖地写了下来。

51. Up from a Nap in Early Summer
(Song) Yang Wanli

After eating plum, the sour tastes still remain,
On the window gauze there is some green of plantain.
Up from a nap in a long day I am so boring,
I just watch how children are trying to catch the catkin.

In Chinese phonetic alphabet and Chinese characters:

xián jū chū xià wǔ shuì qǐ
闲 居 初 夏 午 睡 起

（宋）杨万里

méi zǐ liú suān ruǎn chǐ yá
梅 子 留 酸 软 齿 牙 ，

bā jiāo fēn lù yú chuāng shā
芭 蕉 分 绿 与 窗 纱 。

rì cháng shuì qǐ wú qíng sī
日 长 睡 起 无 情 思 ，

xián kàn ér tóng zhuō liǔ huā
闲 看 儿 童 捉 柳 花 。

Notes: In the original, the poet said that the sour taste has softened his teeth. He said in the second line the plantain has divided its green with the window gauze. The translation omitted "since I had nothing to do" before watching children play in the last line.

【说明】原文第一句说梅子留酸软齿牙，第二句说芭蕉把它的绿色也分到了窗纱上，最后一句观看孩童捉柳花前面的"闲"字在英文里被省略掉了。

52. On the Way to Sanqu Prefecture

(Song) Zeng Ji

When plum turned yellow, it has been sunny,

My boat reached the end of the rivulet and I took the mountain

way.

Green is no less than that on road coming over,

More pleasant here is that orioles are chirping with jollity.

In Chinese phonetic alphabet and Chinese characters：

sān qú dào zhōng
三 衢 道 中

（宋）曾几

méi	zǐ	huáng	shí	rì	rì	qíng
梅	子	黄	时	日	日	晴 ,

xiǎo	xī	fàn	jìn	què	shān	xíng
小	溪	泛	尽	却	山	行 。

lù	yīn	bù	jiǎn	lái	shí	lù
绿	阴	不	减	来	时	路 ,

tiān	dé	huáng	lí	sì	wǔ	shēng
添	得	黄	鹂	四	五	声 。

Notes： Zeng Ji （1084－1166） served in the government as
Chief of Justice at a few prefectures and a Deputy Minister of Rites.
He was a passionate traveler all his life. When plum turns yellow,
it should be a rainy season, yet for the poet it turned out to be
sunny for a few consecutive days. When the poet reached the end of
the rivulet, he still wanted to see more, so he began to climb up
the mountain. The green and bower was as much as the on the way
over, a pleasant difference is the chirping of orioles in the
mountain. The poet imbued his own feeling subtly in his description
of fine early summer scenery of the mountain areas in the western
part of Zhejiang Province.

【说明】曾几（1084—1166）曾任江西、浙西提刑，秘书少监，礼部侍郎。一生酷爱游玩。当青梅变黄，雨季就来了。然而，诗人却遇上连续多日的艳阳天。诗人乘轻舟泛溪而行，溪尽而兴不尽，于是舍舟登岸，沿山路步行。山路上苍翠的树，与来的时候一样浓密；深林中传来几声黄鹂的欢鸣声，比来时更添了些幽趣。诗人在对浙江西部山区初夏的优雅景致描写时悄悄地注入了自己的情感。

53. Inspired by What I See

(Song) Zhu Shuzhen

The swaying bamboo casts its clear shadow on the window,

To the setting sun pairs of birds clamorously crow.

Up in the air no more catkins are flying and neither is there any cherry apple,

Days are longer and the weather makes people sleepy and dull.

In Chinese phonetic alphabet and Chinese characters:

jí jǐng
即 景

（宋）朱淑真

zhú	yáo	qīng	yǐng	zhào	yōu	chuāng
竹	摇	清	影	罩	幽	窗，
liǎng	**liǎng**	**shí**	**qín**	**zào**	**xī**	**yáng**
两	两	时	禽	噪	夕	阳。
xiè	**què**	**hǎi**	**táng**	**fēi**	**jìn**	**xù**
谢	却	海	棠	飞	尽	絮，
kùn	**rén**	**tiān**	**qì**	**rì**	**chū**	**cháng**
困	人	天	气	日	初	长。

Notes: In the poem, clear shadow and window are in a static state; the shaking bamboo and singing birds are in a motional state. When cherry apple are gone, when there is no more catkins

70

in early summer，days become longer. The person in the poem is a lonely young wife. She must have been bored on such a day.

【说明】诗中清雅的影子和幽静的窗子写的是静物；抖动的竹子和鸣叫的鸟儿写的是动态。初夏海棠凋谢、柳絮飞尽后，日子就变长了。诗中所写人物是一位孤独的少妇，在这样的日子里她肯定觉得很无聊。

54. A Feast at the Zhang Garden
(Song) Dai Fugu

Newly born ducklings frolic in shallow and deep parts of the pond，

It's half cloudy at this time when plums have ripened.

Drink in the east garden，we are drunk when get to the west park，

Picking all the loquat off the tree is just like a strip of all its color of gold.

In Chinese phonetic alphabet and Chinese characters：

chū xià yóu zhāng yuán
初 夏 游 张 园

（宋）戴复古

rǔ　yā　chí　táng　shuǐ　qiǎn　shēn
乳 鸭 池 塘 水 浅 深 ，

shú　méi　tiān　qì　bàn　qíng　yīn
熟 梅 天 气 半 晴 阴 。

dōng　yuán　zài　jiǔ　xī　yuán　zuì
东 园 载 酒 西 园 醉 ，

zhāi　jìn　pí　pá　yí　shù　jīn
摘 尽 枇 杷 一 树 金 。

Notes：Dai Fugu （1167 - 1252?） never worked in the government.

He was regarded as one of the Folk Society School. He died when he was over eighty. A dictionary explains what "loquat" is: evergreen tree of warm regions having fuzzy yellow olive-sized fruit with a large free stone; native to China and Japan. The poet used "color of gold" instead of "fuzzy yellow" for its fruit. When the fruits are ripening, they do look like golden pieces hanging on the tree.

【说明】戴复古（1167—1252?）一生不仕，江湖派诗人，卒年八十余。字典解释"枇杷"为热带常青树，其果大如橄榄，呈泛黄色，内有较大硬核，生长在中国和日本。诗人写其果实用的是"金"黄，而不是"泛黄"。果实成熟后，就像金子挂在树上一样。

55. An Account of My Visit to the Southern Tower at E Zhou

(Song) Huang Tingjian

Looking around the mountain, the sky blends with water in the distance,

Leaning on the balustrade I noticed for ten miles it's filled with lotus flavors.

Refreshing breeze and bright moon are footloose,

They come together from the south to render the southern tower into coolness.

In Chinese phonetic alphabet and Chinese characters:

è zhōu nán lóu shū shì

鄂 州 南 楼 书 事

（宋）黄庭坚

sì gù shān guāng jiē shuǐ guāng

四 顾 山 光 接 水 光，

píng	lán	shí	lǐ	jì	hé	xiāng
凭	栏	十	里	芰	荷	香 。

qīng	fēng	míng	yuè	wú	rén	guǎn
清	风	明	月	无	人	管 ，

bìng	zuò	nán	lái	yí	wèi	liáng
并	作	南	来	一	味	凉 。

Notes: Huang Tingjian （1045 – 1105） was the founder of the Jiangxi School of poetry, a famous calligrapher. His life was full of ups and downs, was continuously framed. For instance, he was downgraded to the middle of Sichuan for six years, and after he was back to the capital for only a few months, he was again deposed and sent to Wuhan, where he had this poem composed when he was comparing himself to the moon and the breeze, which in his eyes were so unconstraint. We can detest his melancholy and resentful mood from this poem.

【说明】黄庭坚（1045—1105）开创了江西诗派，是一位大书法家。他仕途坎坷，多次被陷害。譬如，他被贬到四川中部 6 年，回京后仅仅几个月，就又被贬到武汉。这首诗就是在武汉写的，他把无拘无束的自己比作清风明月。字里行间我们可以感觉到诗人悲凉和郁闷的心情。

56. In the Mountain Kiosk in Summer
（Tang）Gao Pian

On long summer days the thick forest is so verdant,

Reverted images onto the pond buildings project.

Glittering curtains rise with wind,

Flower stands are full of rose, its smell is filling up the yard and it's so fragrant.

In Chinese phonetic alphabet and Chinese characters:

shān tíng xià rì
山 亭 夏 日

（唐）高骈

lù shù yīn nóng xià rì cháng
绿 树 阴 浓 夏 日 长 ，

lóu tái dào yǐng rù chí táng
楼 台 倒 影 入 池 塘 。

shuǐ jīng lián dòng wēi fēng qǐ
水 晶 帘 动 微 风 起 ，

mǎn jià qiáng wēi yí yuàn xiāng
满 架 蔷 薇 一 院 香 。

Notes：Gao Pian（821－887）was a famous general in the late Tang period. He served as a Military Governor at five places. He dealt a heavy blow on the Huang Chao insurrectionary army，but was finally taken in by the rebels' maneuver and lost one of his commanders. All his reputation was ruined by this defeat. He was buried alive by one of his subordinates. The poet depicted summer scene with painting technique：the green trees，shades，reverted images of buildings，ripples in the pond，full stands of roses. Such a colorful and peaceful scene was portrayed by the poet standing on the mountain kiosk. Even though the poet and the kiosk didn't appear in the poem，we do see a leisurely poet and the kiosk from which he was viewing the scenery.

【说明】高骈（821—887），晚唐诗人、名将，曾任五镇节度使。多次重创黄巢起义军。然而，他之后在一次战斗中失利，并损失了一员大将，这次失败使他身败名裂，后来被其部下活埋。这首诗的创作使用了绘画手法：绿树阴浓、楼台倒影、池塘水波、满架蔷薇构成了一幅色彩艳丽、笔调清和的图画。这一切都是诗人站在高山上的亭子中描绘下来的。诗中虽然没有出现诗人和亭子，但是，我们读诗时仿佛看到了诗人和一座山亭。

57. Farmers' Life

(Song) Fan Chengda

Farmers till land in daytime and at night spin ramie thread,

Sons and daughters of villagers have to shoulder family load.

Tilling and spinning naive children haven't learned,

Yet, under the mulberry tree they are watching how to have melons planted.

In Chinese phonetic alphabet and Chinese characters:

tián jiā
田 家

（宋）范成大

zhòu	chū	yún	tián	yè	jì	má
昼	出	耘	田	夜	绩	麻 ，

cūn	zhuāng	ér	nǚ	gè	dāng	jiā
村	庄	儿	女	各	当	家 。

tóng	sūn	wèi	jiě	gōng	gēng	zhī
童	孙	未	解	供	耕	织 ，

yě	bàng	sāng	yīn	xué	zhòng	guā
也	傍	桑	阴	学	种	瓜 。

Notes: Fan Chengda (1126 – 1193) was one of the Four Great Poets in the middle recovery period of the Southern Song Dynasty (the other three are Yang Wanli, Lu You and You Mao). He was regarded as the agglomeration of the eclogues of the time, and his most representative work is *A Consort of Verve in Composing Eclogues of Four Seasons*, which collected sixty poems, and this is one of them. The first two lines tell us that sons and daughters of villagers had ruled the roast at their early ages and worked hard day and night. The last two lines present vividly and joyfully the naivete of children in the countryside who are eager to labor.

58. Life in the Village

(Song) Weng Juan

Green is all over the hill and fields and the rice paddy looks white under the sky,

It is so misty with rain amidst cuckoo cry.

No one stays idle in the April countryside,

Having finished silkworm breeding rice seedlings have to be transplanted.

In Chinese phonetic alphabet and Chinese characters：

cūn jū jí shì
村 居 即 事

（宋）翁卷

lǜ biàn shān yuán bái mǎn chuān
绿 遍 山 原 白 满 川 ，

zǐ guī shēng lǐ yǔ rú yān
子 规 声 里 雨 如 烟 。

xiāng cūn sì yuè xián rén shǎo
乡 村 四 月 闲 人 少 ，

cái liǎo cán sāng yòu chā tián
才 了 蚕 桑 有 插 田 。

Notes：Weng Juan（no dates of birth and death available）was a common folk all his life. He had been reputed as a countryside poet. He travelled a lot for purpose of composing poems，his foot prints can be tracked in many southern provinces. His hair turned grey earlier because of composing poems，his life had been poor and had nothing to live on except writing. The previous poem by Fan Chengda was written with briskness，yet this one by Weng is full of charm. The background of Weng's poem is much bigger with green and white as its base color，on which the misty and rainy weather of April was portrayed with melodious call of cuckoos. If we close our eyes and ponder，we may see on the vast fields many moving spots，which are farmers with their bamboo hats and straw rain coats busy transplanting rice seedlings.

【说明】翁卷（无生卒年记载）一生为平民，被誉为乡村诗人。为了作诗，他到过很多地方，很多南方的省份都留下了他的足迹。由于作诗，他的头发很早就变白了，他一生贫困，除了作诗，无以为生。前面提到的范成大的诗声调清脆，翁卷此诗则充满魅力。翁诗背景阔大，绿和白成为诗中画面的底色，细雨如烟典型刻画了江南乡村四月的烟雨天气，杜鹃声声更显得悠扬动人。我们如闭目凝想，就仿佛看到江南辽阔田间一个个活动着的圆点，那是农夫头戴斗笠、身穿蓑衣，在田间插秧呢！

59. For Pomegranate Flower

(Tang) Han Yu

Pomegranate flowers are so brilliantly red in May,
Behind thick branches the little ones are so many.
Where they grow is not open to vehicle and horses，
The flowers can only fall on mosses to cover the wild country.

In Chinese phonetic alphabet and Chinese characters：

tí liú huā
题 榴 花

（唐）韩愈

wǔ yuè liú huā zhào yǎn míng
五 月 榴 花 照 眼 明，

zhī jiān shí jiàn zǐ chū chéng
枝 间 时 见 子 初 成。

kě lián cǐ dì wú chē mǎ
可 怜 此 地 无 车 马，

diān dǎo cāng tái luò jiàng yīng
颠 倒 苍 苔 落 绛 英。

Notes：My translation fails to render that the pomegranate flowers brightened the eyes of viewers, so said in the original of the first line. The poet showed his sympathy to fallen flowers, which were on the mosses in the wild country, which had fewer people to appreciate. Some critics say that the last two lines also expressed his sympathy towards those friends who were most talented, yet were placed in remote areas, where they were not able to exhibit their capability.

【说明】原诗第一句"榴花照眼明"在我的译文中未能译出。诗人对落地的石榴花花瓣深表同情，它们落在了荒郊野外的苔藓上，这些地方鲜有路人去观赏。有评论认为，诗的最后两句说的是他那些有才干却被发配到边远地区的朋友，对他们无从展示他们的才能表示了同情。

60. An Evening in the Country
(Song) Lei Zhen

The pond brims with water and is encircled by grass,
The setting sun is being hung halfway on the mountain, and such is reflected in the cold ripples.

A cowboy is going back home and sitting sideways on the cow's back,
He is blowing a short flute and plays numbers he likes most.

In Chinese phonetic alphabet and Chinese characters:

cūn wǎn
村 晚
（宋）雷震

cǎo	mǎn	chí	táng	shuǐ	mǎn	bēi	
草	满	池	塘	水	满	陂	，
shān	xián	luò	rì	jìn	hán	yī	
山	衔	落	日	浸	寒	漪	。
mù	tóng	guī	qù	héng	niú	bèi	
牧	童	归	去	横	牛	背	，
duǎn	dí	wú	qiāng	xìn	kǒu	chuī	
短	笛	无	腔	信	口	吹	。

Notes: We don't know much about this poet. The poet was viewing the evening of the country with an appreciative eye, the pond, the setting sun half way on the mountain, the ripples, the cowboy sitting on the cow sideways and plays whatever the number that came to his mind on his flute. It must be a big contrast with the poet's life in the downtown.

【说明】我们对此诗人雷震了解甚少。诗人是带着一种欣赏的目光去看村晚的，池塘、山中的落日、波纹、横坐牛背上的牧童、牧童信口所吹的曲子都是诗人爱看爱听的，这些与诗人喧嚣的闹市生活有很大的反差。

61. Wall Inscription on Mr. Huyin's Cottage
(Song) Wang Anshi

The beam is so clean and without mosses in the thatched cottage,

The owner has planted flowers and trees on orderly beds divided by the ridge.

Outside a river circles and protects the fields,

When push the gate open dark green from the two mountains meets our eyes.

In Chinese phonetic alphabet and Chinese characters:

shū hú yīn xiān shēng bì
书 湖 阴 先 生 壁
（宋）王安石

máo yán cháng sǎo jìng wú tái
茅 檐 常 扫 净 无 苔，

huā mù chéng xī shǒu zì zāi
花 木 成 蹊 手 自 栽。

yì shuǐ hù tián jiāng lù rào
一 水 护 田 将 绿 绕，

liǎng shān pái tà sòng qīng lái
两 山 排 闼 送 青 来。

Notes: Huyin was a neighbor of the poet when he was living in Jinling. It was not easy to keep mosses away in a wet environment, but Huyin did it. So the cottage was very clean. The fields were so orderly tended. The way the river is protecting the fields is very much like a mother protecting her child. And when you push the gate open, the dark green color of two mountains was coming down on you. Such a way of depicting scenery is peculiar yet natural, the refined diction left no sign that the words had been chosen with much weighing and deliberation.

【说明】诗人住在金陵时，湖阴是他的邻居。在潮湿的环境里不长苔藓太难了，可是湖阴先生做到了，他的庭院非常清洁。田地里的庄稼也很规整。小河就像母亲保护孩子那样看护着田野。推开庭院的大门，两山的翠绿立即进入眼帘。这种写法很新奇，也很自然。诗中字词用得精妙，毫无人为斧凿的迹象。

62. The Dark Attire Lane

(Tang) Liu Yuxi

By the side of Rose Finch Bridge there are wild plants and flower,

The setting sun is low at the entrance of the Lane of Dark Attire.

Those swallow that used to play before the halls of very rich families,

Are now flying into homes of common folks.

In Chinese phonetic alphabet and Chinese characters:

wū yī xiàng
乌 衣 巷

（唐）刘禹锡

zhū	què	qiáo	biān	yě	cǎo	huā
朱	雀	桥	边	野	草	花 ，

wū	yī	xiàng	kǒu	xī	yáng	xiá
乌	衣	巷	口	夕	阳	斜 。

jiù	shí	wáng	xiè	táng	qián	yàn
旧	时	王	谢	堂	前	燕 ，

fēi	rù	xún	cháng	bǎi	xìng	jiā
飞	入	寻	常	百	姓	家 。

Notes: This is one of the "Five Themes on Jinling" —poems by Liu, and a most famous one expressing his reflections on things he saw. When Liu wrote this poem, he had not yet been to this former capital of the Six Dynasties. A friend of his composed five poems on historic sites of Jinling and sent to him, so his five poems were all replies to his friend. The Dark Attire Lane used to be the busiest and prosperous area, where nobilities lived in the Six Dynasties periods, but by the time of writing their poems in the Tang Dynasty wild grass was overgrown by the famous Rose Finch

Bridge and there were no traffic at all at the entrance of the lane. The original of the third line mentions two specific families—Wang and Xie. Wang refers to the family of Wang Dao（276 - 339），a founder of the Eastern Jin Dynasty. Xie refers to Xie An（320 - 385），who was once a Prime Minister of the Eastern Jin Dynasty. The two families not only enjoyed political power but also much wealth.

【说明】此诗是刘禹锡《金陵五题》中的一首，是表达他对所观察事物的看法的最有名的一篇。刘写此诗时，尚未去过六朝的这座古都。他的一位朋友就金陵的五处历史遗迹写了五首诗送给他，他便和了五首。乌衣巷曾是金陵最繁华忙碌的地方，也是六朝贵族生活的地方。但是，到了唐朝他们写诗的时候，乌衣巷口、朱雀桥边却长满了野草。诗的第三句提到两个家族，即王、谢两家。王指建立了东晋的王导（276—339），谢指谢安（320—385），这两个家族曾握有大权，且富可敌国。

63. Seeing off Yuan Er before His Mission at An Xi
(Tang) Wang Wei

The morning drizzle at Weicheng has moistened the dusty road，

In the light grey guest house willow branches are so tender and mild.

May I ask you to drink one more cup of wine?

For outside the Yangguan Pass in the west you will not find dear ones again.

In Chinese phonetic alphabet and Chinese characters：

sòng yuán èr shǐ ān xī
送 元 二 使 安 西

（唐）王维

wèi chéng zhāo yǔ yì qīng chén
渭 城 朝 雨 浥 轻 尘 ，

kè shè qīng qīng liǔ sè xīn
客 舍 青 青 柳 色 新 。

quàn jūn gèng jìn yì bēi jiǔ
劝 君 更 尽 一 杯 酒 ，

xī chū yáng guān wú gù rén
西 出 阳 关 无 故 人 。

Notes：Wang Wei （700－761） was born in the family of a Buddhist. He was the representative of the Tang eclogue poetry, and was reputed as a "poetic Buddha". The highest official position he had was a Prime Minister. He was good at music and painting. He played Pipa—a four-string plucking instrument. His paintings were as famous as his poetry. He passed away as soon as he finished his farewell letters to his brother and friends. Wang's friend was going to the northwest frontier to work; this poem was composed to say farewell to his friend—Yuan Er. Its words were set to music later. Weicheng is today's Xianyang, where the poet saw off his friend. An Xi was the headquarters of the frontier army. The Yangguan Pass was at the end of the Hexi Corridor. Further west would be the so-called Western Regions, where it was less developed, yet the Tang Dynasty had many contacts with these regions. Going to the Western Regions was considered a feat of daring. When the poet was proposing one more toast, he was doing it with profound feelings, and it contained his best wishes, for ahead of his friend it was a long and difficult journey.

【说明】王维（700—761）出生于一个信奉佛教的家庭。他是唐朝田园诗派的代表，以"诗佛"著称。官至尚书右丞。他工音律、善作画。他的琵琶弹得很好，琵琶是一种四弦弹拨乐器。他的画作像他的诗作一样有名。他临终前，写信给兄弟亲友，写完后舍笔而绝。王维的朋友元二要出使西北边境，这首诗就是为送别元二而写。此诗后来被谱成曲子。渭城即今日之咸阳，王就是在咸阳送别元二的。安西是安西都护府的简称，元二要去的就是这个地方。阳关在河西走廊的尽头。再往西走就是西域了。西域是比较荒凉的地方，但是唐朝与西域接触很多。到西域去那时是一种勇敢的行为。诗人劝元二再饮一杯酒时，他的感情是真挚的，酒中有他最好的祝愿，因为元二要走的路既漫长又艰苦。

64. Inscription on the Stele at the North Pavilion
(Tang) Li Bai

I am demoted like Jia who was sent to exile to Changsha,
Looking west to Chang An，there isn't home any longer.
Someone is playing a jade flute on this Yellow Crane Tower，
What are falling in this Riverside City in May seem to be plum flowers.

In Chinese phonetic alphabet and Chinese characters：

tí bèi xiè bēi
题 北 榭 碑
（唐）李白

yì wéi qiān kè qù cháng shā
一 为 迁 客 去 长 沙 ，
xī wàng cháng ān bú jiàn jiā
西 望 长 安 不 见 家 。
huáng hè lóu zhōng chuī yù dí
黄 鹤 楼 中 吹 玉 笛 ，
jiāng chéng wǔ yuè luò méi huā
江 城 五 月 落 梅 花 。

Notes：The original of the first line does not specify who was demoted and sent to exile to Changsha, yet those who are familiar with China's history would instantly know the poet was comparing himself to Jia Yi (200 BC-168 BC). Jia was a statesman and a great thinker. When the emperor was going to confer to Jia a dukedom, many officials with invested interest rose to slander him, and then he was demoted and sent to exile to Changsha. Jia died of melancholy at the age of thirty-three. Why did Li Bai compare to Jia? Because he was passing through Wuchang on his way to Yelang, a remote southern county, where he was sent to exile to, and his experience was very much the same like that of Jia Yi. Such comparison revealed that he was full of resentment and that he was saying he was as innocent as Jia Yi. The Yellow Crane Tower is on the southern bank of Changjiang River and on the peak of the Snake Mountain in Wuchang. It was first built in 223 AD. The poet was looking in the direction of his way over, many miles away from the capital, where his home was. While he was deeply depressed, he heard someone was playing a flute, and the music of "The Falling Plum Flower". It was in May, but the poet felt that plum flowers were falling down as in winter, because he was cold, sad, alone and desolate.

【说明】原诗第一句没有明确指出谁被贬到长沙，熟悉中国历史的人会立即想到被贬的人是贾谊（公元前 200—公元前 168）。贾是一位政治家和思想家。当皇帝即将封他为公爵时，很多既得利益者站出来对他进行诽谤，结果他就被贬到长沙去了。贾谊 33 岁时郁郁不得志而死。李白为何将自己比作贾谊呢？因为，他去夜郎路过武昌，夜郎是他被放逐的地方，在遥远的南方，而这个经历与贾谊非常相似。这一比，说明李白当时牢骚满腹，他认为自己与贾谊一样无辜。黄鹤楼在长江南岸，在武昌蛇山山顶，始建于公元 223 年。诗人当时在楼上观看他来时所走过的路，已经离开京城很远了。而他的家曾安在京城。在他情绪低落时，听到有人吹笛子，吹的是《梅花落》。当时虽是 5 月，可是诗人觉得好像在冬天，梅花似乎落了，他感到寒冷、悲伤、寂寞、凄凉。

65. Inscription at Huainan Temple

(Song) Cheng Hao

I rest when I want to for I have been shuttling between south and north,

White duckweed has been blown away in the river and autumn has come forth.

I am not one of those who sigh for the arrival of autumn,

Let the mountain on this bank at dusk face its opposite and sorrowful peer in gloom.

In Chinese phonetic alphabet and Chinese characters:

tí huái nán sì
题 淮 南 寺
（宋）程颢

nán qù běi lái xiū biàn xiū
南 去 北 来 休 便 休，

bái pín chuī jìn chǔ jiāng qiū
白 蘋 吹 尽 楚 江 秋。

dào rén bù shì bēi qiū kè
道 人 不 是 悲 秋 客，

yī rèn wǎn shān xiāng duì chóu
一 任 晚 山 相 对 愁。

Notes: This poem smells a bit Zen Buddhism. When everyone was sad about the coming of autumn, he said he wasn't. Was he really so graceful, so elegant and unconventional? Not really. He wanted to rest, because he was tired; he saw white duckweed was being blown away, because he was sensitive to the change in nature, he let the mountains on each side of the river face each other in gloom, because he was gloomy.

【说明】此诗有些禅的味道。秋天来了，大家都不高兴，他却不以为然。他真的那么旷达，那么超凡脱俗吗？其实未必。他想休息，因为他累了；他看到白蘋已被吹得无影无踪了，说明他对大自然的变化还是敏感的。他让两山相对愁，因为他在愁呀。

66. The Autumn Moon
(Song) Zhu Xi

The limpid rivulet water flows past the emerald mountain top,

The vitreous moon light and clear flowing water form a sheer autumn scope.

The mortal world is now far away,

White clouds and yellow leaves can freely display their beauty.

In Chinese phonetic alphabet and Chinese characters:

qiū yuè
秋 月

（宋）朱熹

qīng xī liú guò bì shān tóu
清 溪 流 过 碧 山 头 ，

kōng shuǐ chéng xiān yī sè qiū
空 水 澄 鲜 一 色 秋 。

gé duàn hóng chén sān shí lǐ
隔 断 红 尘 三 十 里 ，

bái yún huáng yè gòng yōu yōu
白 云 黄 叶 共 悠 悠 。

Notes: How could water flows past a mountain top? It was the reflection of the mountain top in the rivulet, and the water flowed past the converted image of the mountain top in the rivulet. The second line says the moon and the water merged into one color. The original of the third line gives a specific distance—thirty miles, the noise of the mortal world was thirty miles away; the white clouds and the red leaves on the mountain were peaceful and carefree. Apparently, the poet was cheerful and light-hearted at the time of composing the poem. We should note the title is "The Autumn Moon", yet what the poet wrote in the poem were the rivulet, the mountain top, the blue sky, the floating clouds and the carefree tree leaves, and they all reflect the beauty of the moon.

【说明】溪水如何流过碧山头呢？原来是溪水里映射的山头的样子。第二句说夜空与溪水合成了一个颜色，第三句给出了三十里这样的具体数字，说人世间的喧闹在三十里之外。那里白云和红叶悠然自得。很显然，写诗时作者心态轻松怡然。我们应该注意，此诗的名称是《秋月》，可是诗人写的是溪水、山顶、蓝天、流动的云、悠闲的树叶，却都写出了月色之美。

67. At Night on the Double Seventh Day
(Song) Yang Pu

What would people do if the weaving girl does not meet her cowboy friend?

I would invite her to weave, with a golden shuttle in the sky, a brocade.

Every year people plea to the weaving girl for more deftness and craft,

Yet, in this world skills and art are already adequate.

In Chinese phonetic alphabet and Chinese characters：

qī xī
七　夕

（宋）杨朴

wèi　huì　qiān　niú　yì　ruò　hé
未　会　牵　牛　意　若　何，

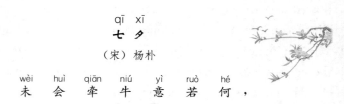

<pre>
xū   yāo   zhī   nǚ   nòng jīn   suō
须   邀   织   女   弄   金   梭 。
nián nián qǐ   yǔ   rén   jiān qiǎo
年   年   乞   与   人   间   巧 ，
bú   dào   rén   jiān qiǎo jǐ   duō
不   道   人   间   巧   几   多 。
</pre>

Notes：Yang Pu （921－1003） was a recluse all his life. He refused to be an official, even when the emperor personally gave him an offer. He often lay down in thick grass to ponder on his lines, and he would note down right away the good words that came to his mind. On the night of the seventh day in July lunar calendar is a festival occasion, people refer to it as either "the Festival to Plead for Skills" or "the Daughters' Day". On that night every year, the Altair on one side of the Milky Way and the Vega on the other side were looking at each other. According to a Chinese legend, the incarnation of the Altair was a cowboy who fell in love with a girl weaver, who is the incarnation of Vega. They could only meet once in a year on a bridge, constructed temporarily by magpies, and the meeting is the night on the seventh of each July lunar calendar. It has been a custom to plead, on the very night, to the Girl Weaver for some skills of needlework.

【说明】杨朴（921—1003）一生隐居。他终生不仕，皇帝赐给他官做，他都予以谢绝。他常常躺在草地上思考他的诗句，灵感来时，他立即把得到的字词记下来。阴历七月初七的夜晚是个节日，人们管它叫"乞巧节"或"女儿节"。每年这一晚，牵牛星在银河的一端，织女星在银河的另一端，相互张望。根据中国的一个传说，牵牛星的前身是一个牛郎，他爱上了织女，这个织女化成了织女星。他们每年阴历七月七日的夜晚可以在夜空的鹊桥上见一次面。每年的这个夜晚女孩们向织女学习一些针线活的技巧已经成为一种风俗。

68. The First Day of Autumn

(Song) Liu Han

When raucous call of baby crows fades away the screen stands there in its lonely jade color,

I sensed some new cool on the pillow as if a fan is sending a current of air.

I got up to see, the autumn is not yet here,

Only in the moonlight and on the steps fallen leaves of phoenix trees scatter.

In Chinese phonetic alphabet and Chinese characters:

lì qiū
立 秋

（宋）刘翰

rǔ	yā	tí	sàn	yù	píng	kōng
乳	鸭	啼	散	玉	屏	空 ，
yī	zhěn	xīn	liáng	yī	shàn	fēng
一	枕	新	凉	一	扇	风 。
shuì	qǐ	qiū	shēng	wú	mì	chù
睡	起	秋	声	无	觅	处 ，
mǎn	jiē	wú	yè	yuè	míng	zhōng
满	阶	梧	叶	月	明	中 。

Notes: Liu Han (no dates of birth and death available) was a famous doctor of Chinese Medicine. He worked in the government as a chief of the protocol department, a tribute supervisor in the Pharmacy Bureau, and then an assistant Minister of Engineering. On the third line the original says poet was up to look for autumn sounds, such as the rustle in the air. The translation is different, but the effect is the same, A phoenix tree is also referred to as a Chinese parasol.

【说明】刘翰（无生卒年记载）是著名的中医，曾任朝散大夫、尚药奉御、检校工部员外郎、翰林医官使等职。第三句原文说诗人醒来后寻找秋天的声音，如树木萧瑟的声音。译文换了说法，效果相同。梧桐树也可叫作"Chinese parasol"。

69. An Autumn Night
(Tang) Du Mu

Under the taper light of the silver candle the painted screen looks a bit icy,

A maid is patting on fire-worms with a small silk fan，vainly.

Under the lunar light the stone steps seem so chill，

Staring at the Altair and Vega she sits still.

In Chinese phonetic alphabet and Chinese characters：

qiū xī
秋 夕

（唐）杜牧

yín	zhú	qiū	guāng	lěng	huà	píng
银	烛	秋	光	冷	画	屏 ，
qīng	luó	xiǎo	shàn	pū	liú	yíng
轻	罗	小	扇	扑	流	萤 。
tiān	jiē	yuè	sè	liáng	rú	shuǐ
天	阶	月	色	凉	如	水 ，
wò	kàn	qiān	niú	zhī	nǚ	xīng
卧	看	牵	牛	织	女	星 。

Notes：This is a poem about a palace maid，who had been neglected or forgotten. Why do we say so? Because of the fire-worms. Firstly，which only grow and live at places where weeds are overgrown. Secondly，she was trying to catch a fire-worm. Such an action tells us that she had nothing else to do，and she was boring. Thirdly，the small fan also speaks. It was autumn，she was still using a fan, and in many previous poems it was mainly deserted wives who use a fan this way. The night was already late, and the steps in the palace seemed so chilly, she should have gone to bed. But she was sitting still on the steps and looking up at the Altair and Vega, being touched by the story of the cowboy and the weaver girl. She was lost in her thought and desire for love.

【说明】此诗写的是一位被忽视、被遗忘的宫女。我们为什么这么说呢？根据就是流萤。第一，萤总是生在冢间草丛那些荒凉的地方。第二，宫女在扑打流萤，说明她无所事事，很无聊。第三，那把小扇自己说话了——已经是秋天了，她还在用扇子。在很多诗里，秋天用扇子的都是被遗弃的女人。夜已经很深，皇宫里的台阶是冰凉的，她本该入睡了，却坐在冰冷的台阶上，望着天上的牵牛星和织女星，被牛郎织女的故事深深打动着。她陷入了深思，渴望爱情。

70. The Mid-Autumn Moon

(Song) Su Shi

When evening clouds have been stored away chilliness spills over,

The bright moon is high and the rays of the Milky Way soundlessly pour.

During my lifetime this beautiful night cannot stay longer,

I don't know where I would see such glowing moon next year.

In Chinese phonetic alphabet and Chinese characters:

zhōng qiū yuè
中　秋　月

（宋）苏轼

mù　yún　shōu　jìn　yì　qīng　hán
暮　云　收　尽　溢　清　寒，

<table>
<tr><td>yín
银</td><td>hàn
汉</td><td>wú
无</td><td>shēng
声</td><td>zhuàn
转</td><td>yù
玉</td><td>pán
盘 。</td></tr>
<tr><td>cǐ
此</td><td>shēng
生</td><td>cǐ
此</td><td>yè
夜</td><td>bù
不</td><td>cháng
长</td><td>hǎo
好 ，</td></tr>
<tr><td>míng
明</td><td>yuè
月</td><td>míng
明</td><td>nián
年</td><td>hé
何</td><td>chù
处</td><td>kàn
看 。</td></tr>
</table>

Notes：This poem is about the poet's re-union with his kid brother，after they had departed for a long time，and how they appreciated the moon together. The poet said that the moon came out and rolled up the clouds and stored them away，as a result，the sky was filled with chilliness. The poem is about the mid-autumn moon，but in the whole poem there is no mention of the word moon in the Chinese original. The original of the second line describes the moon as a "jade plate". The poet was sighing that such a night in his life was too short and he was not sure where he would be the same night next year. Mid-autumn has been a time of family re-union to celebrate harvest. Mid-autumn moon has been a favorite topic for ancient poets.

【说明】这首诗写的是诗人与胞弟久别重逢、共同赏月的情景。诗人说月亮出来了，把云彩卷起来收走了，结果天空充满了寒气。诗写的是中秋，但诗中未见"中秋"二字。诗的第二句将月亮称为"玉盘"；诗人叹道他生命中的这个夜晚太短暂了，他不知道明年此时会在何处。中秋是家人团聚、庆祝丰收的时刻。很多古代的诗人都写中秋。

71. Thoughts on the Riverside Tower
(Tang) Zhao Gu

On the riverside tower alone I am downcast，
Water is shimmering in the moonlight.
Where are those who were with me appreciating the moon?
It seems somewhat the same as last year's scene.

In Chinese phonetic alphabet and Chinese characters:

jiāng lóu yǒu gǎn
江 楼 有 感
（唐）赵嘏

dú	shàng	jiāng	lóu	sī	qiǎo	rán
独	上	江	楼	思	悄	然 ，

yuè	guāng	rú	shuǐ	shuǐ	rú	tiān
月	光	如	水	水	如	天 。

tóng	lái	wán	yuè	rén	hé	zài
同	来	玩	月	人	何	在 ，

fēng	jǐng	yī	xī	sì	qù	nián
风	景	依	稀	似	去	年 。

Notes: Zhao Gu（806 -?）achieved recognition for his poetry very early in his life. The emperor heard about his name and wanted to appoint him an official, yet the emperor was annoyed and dropped his idea when reading one of his poems, in which Zhao scoffed at the First Emperor of Qin. So, all his life Zhao was not a big official. Zhao's wife was a beauty, one day when she was visiting a temple fair; she was singled out and taken away by force by the military governor of the province. When Zhao heard about it, he wrote a poem to express his bitterness. The poem was quickly on the lips of common folks. The military governor also heard about this poem, he realized he had gone too far on this matter, and returned the lady to Zhao with a letter of apology. When the couple finally met, they cried in each other's arms. The wife cried all night and such a dramatic change took her life away, she died the next morning. Zhao was extremely grieved. He buried her at a higher place where she could have much more sunshine.

【说明】赵嘏（806—?）年轻时就享有诗名。皇帝听说他的大名，起初想重用他，后来读过赵的一首诗后又改变了主意。这是一首嘲笑秦始皇的诗。赵的一生没当过大官。他的夫人是个美人，一日，她逛庙会时被浙江的督军看上，被强行掳走。赵蝦听到这个消息后写了一首诗，一诉心中的凄凉。此诗很快传播开来。当浙江的督军听说这首诗后，觉得自己做得太过分了，便写了一封道歉信，把赵妻送了回去。夫妻俩见面后，相拥而泣。赵妻哭泣了一夜，生活中的剧烈变化要了她的性命，第二天一早她就撒手人寰了。赵悲痛欲绝，将妻子埋在了容易被太阳照射到的高岗之上。

72. Inscription on the Hotel Wall in Linan
(Song) Lin Sheng

Hills in the distance and buildings before our eyes overlap,
When will the song and dance on the West Lake stop?
Intoxicated by the sultry atmosphere are men of grand title,
Who take Hangzhou as their former capital.

In Chinese phonetic alphabet and Chinese characters:

tí lín ān dǐ
题 临 安 邸
（宋）林升

shān wài qīng shān lóu wài lóu
山 外 青 山 楼 外 楼 ，

xī hú gē wǔ jǐ shí xiū
西 湖 歌 舞 几 时 休 。

nuǎn fēng xūn dé yóu rén zuì
暖 风 熏 得 游 人 醉 ，

zhí bǎ háng zhōu zuò biàn zhōu
直 把 杭 州 作 汴 州 。

Notes: Lin Sheng（1106 - 1171）only served one term as chief administrator of a county. This poem pin-pointed directly at the ruling regime, which had lost the northern part of the country and became content to exercise sovereignty only over the south.

The poem expressed the pent-up grief and indignation of common folks. The ruling court took Hangzhou as their capital，which was in Bianzhou before，the last line mentioned in the original specifically Bianzhou. Why did the imperial court lose the northern part? Because they had no will to fight against invaders，and were indulged in extravagant life. After they moved to the south，they remained the same，had no desire at all to recover the lost land.

【说明】林升（1106—1171）当过一任县令。此诗直指丢掉了北方国土而在南方偏安一隅的南宋王朝。此诗一抒老百姓心中的愤懑。宋朝都城本在汴州，现在却将杭州当成都城。北方的国土是怎样丢失的呢？因为朝廷没有抗击侵略者的决心，一味苟且偷安，寻欢作乐。来到南方后，他们的本性未改，没有一丝收复国土的愿望。

73．Seeing off Lin Zifang outside the Jing Ci Temple at Sunrise
(Song) Yang Wanli

After all this is the West Lake in June，

Compare with other seasons its present beauty is unique and alone.

Large lotus leaves merge with the sky in boundless green，

The red water lilies under the sun are refreshing and sheen.

In Chinese phonetic alphabet and Chinese characters：

xiǎo chū jìng cí sì sòng lín zǐ fāng
晓　出　净　慈　寺　送　林　子　方

（宋）杨万里

bì　jìng　xī　hú　liù　yuè　zhōng
毕　竟　西　湖　六　月　中，

fēng	guāng	bù	yǔ	sì	shí	tóng
风	光	不	与	四	时	同 。

jiē	tiān	lián	yè	wú	qióng	bì
接	天	莲	叶	无	穷	碧 ，

yìng	rì	hé	huā	bié	yàng	hóng
映	日	荷	花	别	样	红 。

Notes：It seems a bit abrupt to begin the poem with "after all". The scenery of the West Lake in June is different from all other seasons. Why? Because of its "boundless green" and "unique red", this cannot be seen in spring, autumn or winter, and not even in other months of summer. The first and second lines are somewhat general and intangible; the third and forth lines are specific and actual. Lotus leaves and flowers belong to the feminine category, yet they are described with such masculine words like the "sky" and "sun". The feminine and the masculine are well blended in the poem. The poet and Lin Zifang were bosom friends, while Lin served as the secretary of the emperor, the poet was the tutor of the prince. As the title of this poem suggests Lin was going to Fuzhou to be the Chief Administrator there. In the poem the poet was inferring that the West Lake is the capital, "in June" is alluded to the imperial court; the second line was saying working in the capital has a lot advantages than working at localities; lotus leaves and red water lily were alluded to Lin. In one word, the poet was hinting to Lin he should not go to Fuzhou. But Lin was not smart enough to see the real meaning of the poem. He said goodbye and thanked the poet for the poem and went to Fuzhou, and since then we never heard about him again.

【说明】用"毕竟"二字来开始一首诗似乎有些突兀。六月的西湖不同于其他时节。为何？因为其"无穷碧"和"别样红"，此二者春秋冬都看不到，在夏天的其他月份里也看不到。头两句很概括、空泛，后两句则很具体、实在。荷叶、荷花属阴性物品，但却用"天""日"这样阳性的字来描绘。所以，诗中阴阳是平衡的。诗人与林子方是知音，林担任直阁秘书时，诗人是秘书少监、太子侍读。正如诗的题目所示，林要到福州任知府。诗中将都城暗指为西湖，"六月"暗指皇室；诗的第二句说在都城工作比在地方工作有很多好处。诗人将林比作莲叶与荷花，暗示林不要去福州。但是，林未能看出此诗的真意。他向诗人为他作诗表示了谢意，道了声再见，就去了福州。他这一去，就再也没有消息了。

74. Drinking on the Lake while the Rain Resumed after It Had Stopped

(Song) Su Shi

It has just turned nice and clear and the water is twinkling,

It rained again, hills are obscure behind the haze and all is so intriguing.

If we take the West Lake to Xi Shi, the Beauty in comparing,

Both light and heavy make-ups would be becoming.

In Chinese phonetic alphabet and Chinese characters:

yǐn hú shàng chū qíng hòu yǔ
饮 湖 上 初 晴 后 雨

（宋）苏轼

shuǐ guāng liàn yàn qíng fāng hǎo
水 光 潋 滟 晴 方 好，

shān sè kōng méng yǔ yì qí
山 色 空 蒙 雨 亦 奇。

yù bǎ xī hú bǐ xī zǐ
欲 把 西 湖 比 西 子，

dàn zhuāng nóng mǒ zǒng xiāng yí
淡 妆 浓 抹 总 相 宜。

Notes: Xi Shi was a well-known beauty of the State of Yue in the Spring and Autumn Period and was one of the four most graceful beauties of China. The first two lines describe the lake and hills in both sunny days and rainy climate. Some critics say these two lines are a high artistic generalization of the character of the West Lake，and all other poems about the lake can be replaced by these two lines. The West Lake is always beautiful，no matter it is a fine day or a rainy day. It is just like Xi Shi，who was always beautiful，no matter she had a light or heavy make-up.

【说明】西施是春秋时越国有名的美人，是中国四大美人之一。诗的上半首既写了西湖的水光山色，也写了西湖的晴姿雨态。有评论家说这两句是对西湖特点所做出的高度的艺术概括。所以其他写西湖的诗句完全可以被这两句代替。西湖总是美的，不管是晴天还是雨天，就如同西施一样，不管是浓妆还是淡妆，都很美丽。

75. On Duty

(Song) Zhou Bida

At dusk crows were returning to their nest on the pagoda trees along both sides of the road，

The court official called me in，the Emperor gave an audience and tea was bestowed.

Back to the academy office I was sober and astir，

Until the crescent moved up to the crape myrtle flower.

In Chinese phonetic alphabet and Chinese characters：

rù zhí
入　直

（宋）周必大

lǜ　huái　jiá　dào　jí　hūn　yā
绿　槐　夹　道　集　昏　鸦，

chì	shǐ	chuán	xuān	zuò	cì	chá
敕	使	传	宣	坐	赐	茶 。

guī	dào	yù	táng	qīng	bú	mèi
归	到	玉	堂	清	不	寐 ，

yuè	gōu	chū	shàng	zǐ	wēi	huā
月	钩	初	上	紫	薇	花 。

Notes：Zhou Bida（1126 - 1204）was an outstanding statesman and man of letters，has been regarded as leader of the literary world. He held many official positions，the highest were deputy Prime Minister，Tutor of Prince and so on. He wrote over 80 titles of book in 200 volumes.

【说明】周必大（1126—1204）是卓越的政治家和文学家，被视为文学界的领袖。他一生有过很多头衔，如右丞相、敷文阁待制、侍讲等。著书 80 余种，有作品 200 卷。

76. Mounting the Canopy Kiosk on a Summer Day
(Song) Cai Que

Behind the cocoon paper screen，with a stone pillow I lay down on a square bamboo bed，

I had a long dream in my nap，the book dropped from my tiring hand.

When woke up I chucked for things went through in my dream，

Suddenly from the river some clear notes of a fisherman's flute came.

In Chinese phonetic alphabet and Chinese characters：

xià rì dēng chē gài tíng
夏 日 登 车 盖 亭

（宋）蔡确

zhǐ	píng	shí	zhěn	zhú	fāng	chuáng
纸	屏	石	枕	竹	方	床 ，

shǒu	juàn	pāo	shū	wǔ	mèng	cháng
手	倦	抛	书	午	梦	长 。

shuì	qǐ	wǎn	rán	chéng	dú	xiào
睡	起	莞	然	成	独	笑 ，

shù	shēng	yú	dí	zài	cāng	làng
数	声	渔	笛	在	沧	浪 。

Notes: Cai Que (1037 – 1093) served as the Right and Left Prime Minister for many years before he was deposed to prefectures, where he worked in the capacity of their chief administrator. This poem described the idle life of the poet after he was deposed from the capital and his desire for a solitary life. The original of the first line says that the screen was made of paper; actually it was made of rattan peel and cocoons. Some critics tried to figure out what the poet dreamt in his nap. His family was poor and he had no decent clothing when he was twenty years old. After he was enrolled at the national examination, he had been working for the government for over twenty years, the highest position he held was that of a prime minister. Then he was deposed to the place where he wrote this poem. His entire life seemed like a big dream, from which he wanted to lead a solitary life. The sound of flute drifted over from a river and woke him up.

【说明】蔡确（1037—1093）在被贬州府前，曾任左右丞相多年。这首诗刻画了作者被贬后的闲散心态和对隐居生活的向往。诗的第一句说屏风是用纸做的，实际上，它是用藤子皮和蚕茧做的。有些评论人士试图猜出诗人午睡时做的什么梦。他 20 岁时，家里贫穷，没有像样的衣服穿。自中举后，他为朝廷工作了 20 多年，最高的职务是丞相。之后，就被贬到作这首诗的地方。他整个人生就像一场梦，他梦想过上隐居的生活。河上飘来的笛声吵醒了他。

77. On Duty at the Imperial Academy

(Song) Hong Zikui

In the still night deeply behind the locked palace gates,

I wrote with ease on jute paper in thick ink the appointment of
two prime ministers on the imperial edicts.

When palace guards were telling time in their regular chant just
before dawn,

The crape myrtle flowers were soaked in the moonlight of the morn.

In Chinese phonetic alphabet and Chinese characters:

zhí yù táng zuò
直 玉 堂 作

（宋）洪咨夔

jìn	mén	shēn	suǒ	jì	wú	huá
禁	门	深	锁	寂	无	哗 ，

nóng	mò	lín	lí	liǎng	xiàng	má
浓	墨	淋	漓	两	相	麻 。

chàng	chè	wǔ	gēng	tiān	wèi	xiǎo
唱	彻	五	更	天	未	晓 ，

yí	chí	yuè	jìn	zǐ	wēi	huā
一	墀	月	浸	紫	薇	花 。

Notes: Hong Zikui (1176－1236) served as Chief Supervisor,
Edict-Drafter and Minister of Justice in the royal court of the Song. He
wrote over 900 poems. This poem recorded how he was on night duty in
the imperial court. The poem begins with palace gates, which separates
the mortal world and the court of the so-called Son of the Heaven—the
emperor. From the first two lines we can sense the pride of the poet,
who was the one to write for the emperor's appointment of two prime
ministers. Jute paper was made of hemp, cloth and other materials. In
ancient times, palace guards would chant to mark specific hours; the
third line in the original gives the specific time—the fifth hour,

which is equal to 3am to 5am nowadays. In between the lines we could see the graceful and decorous mien, capability and enchanted state of mind of the poet.

【说明】洪咨夔（1176—1236）曾任监察御史、中书舍人、刑部尚书等职。他写过 900 首诗。这首诗记载了他在皇室值班的情况。诗里首先提到的是门，一扇将皇室与俗世隔开的大门。诗的前两句流露出诗人的自豪，因为他亲笔起草了皇帝对两位丞相的任命书。麻纸是用麻、布和其他材料做成的纸。古时候，宫中卫士都要高声报时。此刻，诗的第三句指出卫士们报的是五更，亦即清晨 3 点到 5 点。字里行间我们可以看出诗人优雅端庄的风度、高超的能力及其欢喜的心态。

78. Bamboo Buildings

(Tang) Li Jiayou

A lofty petty official, whose job is easy, does not regard the life of a marquis as desirable,

High buildings made of bamboo, grew in the area west to the river, are so ideal.

The cattail leaf fan is of no use since the south wind is gentle,

Taking off the gauze cap I often doze off opposite the playing water fowl.

In Chinese phonetic alphabet and Chinese characters:

zhú lóu
竹 楼
（唐）李嘉佑

ào　lì　shēn　xián　xiào　wǔ　hóu
傲　吏　身　闲　笑　五　侯 ，

xī　jiāng　qǔ　zhú　qǐ　gāo　lóu
西　江　取　竹　起　高　楼 。

nán	fēng	bú	yòng	pú	kuí	shàn
南	风	不	用	蒲	葵	扇 ，

shā	mào	xián	mián	duì	shuǐ	ōu
纱	帽	闲	眠	对	水	鸥 。

Notes：Li Jiayou （719? – 781?） began his official career as a proof-reader，he took a few offices in the capital before he became a chief administrator in two prefectures. This poem was written when he was working in Jiangxi Province，where bamboo buildings were common in the Tang Dynasty.

【说明】李嘉佑 （719? —781?） 的仕途从担任秘书省正字开始，他在京城担任几个职务后到地方做了两任刺史。此诗是他在江西当官时所作，唐朝时江西有很多竹子做的建筑。

79. On Duty at the Edict Drafting Office

(Tang) Bai Juyi

There is nothing to write and it's deadly still in the Edict Drafting Office，

In the drum and bell towers the water clock seems working at a slow pace.

In the twilight I sit alone without company，

The only one to be paired with the crape myrtle flower is me, the deputy.

In Chinese phonetic alphabet and Chinese characters：

zhí zhōng shū lìng
直 中 书 令

（唐）白居易

sī	lún	gé	xià	wén	zhāng	jìng
丝	纶	阁	下	文	章	静 ，

zhōng	gǔ	lóu	zhōng	kè	lòu	cháng
钟	鼓	楼	中	刻	漏	长 。

dú	zuò	huáng	hūn	shuí	shì	bàn
独	坐	黄	昏	谁	是	伴 ，

zǐ	wēi	huā	duì	zǐ	wēi	láng
紫	薇	花	对	紫	薇	郎 。

Notes：Bai Juyi （772 - 846） is a great realistic poet of China. He has been reputed as a "Poetry Demon" and a "Poetry King". He was a member of the Royal Academy of the Tang Dynasty, instructor of the Crown Prince, an admonisher and chief administrator at several localities. Most influential poems are Song of Eternal Hatred, The Old Charcoal Seller and Song of Pipa.

【说明】白居易 （772—846） 是中国一位伟大的现实主义诗人。他有"诗魔"之称，又被誉为"诗王"。官至翰林学士、太子左赞善大夫、左拾遗，并在地方上做过刺史。他最有名的诗作是《长恨歌》《卖炭翁》《琵琶行》。

80. Reflections on Reading
(Song) Zhu Xi

The half-acre square pond is like an opened mirror,
In the pond sky light and shadows of clouds are moving together.
Why is the water so limpid and clear?
Because water in its head stream is clean and fresh for ever.

In Chinese phonetic alphabet and Chinese characters：

guān shū yǒu gǎn
观 书 有 感

（宋）朱熹

bàn	mǔ	fāng	táng	yì	jiàn	kāi
半	亩	方	塘	一	鉴	开 ，

tiān	guāng	yún	yǐng	gòng	pái	huái
天	光	云	影	共	徘	徊 。

wèn	qú	nǎ	dé	qīng	rú	xǔ
问	渠	那	得	清	如	许 ，

wéi	yǒu	yuán	tōu	huó	shuǐ	lái
为	有	源	头	活	水	来 。

Notes：The title is Reflections on Reading. By saying that the head stream makes the water in the pond limpid and clear，the poet is telling us：reading is like the head stream，through reading new knowledge can be continuously obtained，things new can be accepted. The poem successfully turns what we sense in our minds into specific images that we can see and feel.

【说明】诗的题目是《观书有感》。诗中说池塘里的水之所以清澈明净，因为是有源头的活水。诗人是想说阅读就像源头之水，通过阅读可以不断地获取新知识，可以接受新生事物。此诗成功地将我们心中的感悟转化成我们可以看到、可以感觉到的具体形象。

81. Float the Boats
(Song) Zhu Xi

Last night water in the spring season rose in the river，
The great ships were lifted as light as a feather.
The ships didn't move an inch and always denied a myriad of pushing power，
Now they can flow freely in the river's center.

In Chinese phonetic alphabet and Chinese characters：

fàn zhōu
泛 舟
（宋）朱熹

zuó yè jiāng biān chūn shuǐ shēng
昨 夜 江 边 春 水 生，
méng chōng jù jiàn yí máo qīng
艨 艟 巨 舰 一 毛 轻。
xiàng lái wǎng fèi tuī yí lì
向 来 枉 费 推 移 力，
cǐ rì zhōng liú zì zài xíng
此 日 中 流 自 在 行。

Notes：The poet used the rising level of water to indicate the importance of the burst of art inspiration. Some critics said that the poet might be pondering how to write very big Chinese characters with his brush pen. He felt that as soon as an inspiration caught on him，he was free in his calligraphy. Other critics said that the poem is suggesting one has to accumulate and refine his skills to a certain point，like the water level that can float a boat；he would then be at home with his artistic creation.

【说明】诗人用水的深浅来说明获取艺术灵感的重要性。有评论者认为，诗人是在考虑如何用毛笔题字，他感觉灵感一来，挥洒起毛笔就非常自由。也有评论者说，要达到挥洒自如的程度，就需要积累，就需要将技巧练习纯熟，如同水涨到一定程度，就可以将船浮起来一样，这样就可以随心所欲地进行艺术创作了。

82. The Cold Spring Pavilion
(Song) Lin Zhen

The clearness of the deep spring inspires poetic mood，
The spring itself knows if the water has been cold in the years passed.

When its water flows to the West Lake it carries song and dance boats around,

To look back at the mountain, the water realizes its clearness has changed.

In Chinese phonetic alphabet and Chinese characters:

lěng quán tíng
冷 泉 亭
（宋）林稹

yí	hóng	qīng	kě	qìn	shī	pí
一	泓	清	可	沁	诗	脾 ，

lěng	nuǎn	nián	lái	zhǐ	zì	zhī
冷	暖	年	来	只	自	知 。

liú	chū	xī	hú	zǎi	gē	wǔ
流	出	西	湖	载	歌	舞 ，

huí	tóu	bù	sì	zài	shān	shí
回	头	不	似	在	山	时 。

Notes: Lin Zhen (no dates of birth and death available) was a genius of the Song Dynasty. He composed a hundred palace verses. In the poem Lin resented the reckless squandering by the rich families. By comparing the spring water up on the mountain and down into the lake, he was saying the water is clear up in the mountain and is marred in the lake. Once the water became foul, it would be difficult to resume its original nature. The poet may wish to suggest in this poem that man should consciously keep himself clean.

【说明】林稹（无生卒年记载）是宋朝的才子。他写过100首宫词。林在诗中对富户官僚的穷奢极侈表示了不满。通过比较山上的泉水和湖里的泉水，林说山上的泉水是清洁的，湖里的水已然脏了。水一旦变得污浊，要它恢复本性就困难了。诗人或许想说人要有意识地保持自己的清洁。

83. A Winter Scene

(Song) Su Shi

When lotus withers its broad leaves that used to ward off rain are gone,

Defying cold and frost only the branches of languishing chrysanthemum are fighting on.

You must remember the best season in the year,

Which is when orange is yellow and tangerine is greener.

In Chinese phonetic alphabet and Chinese characters:

dōng jǐng
冬 景

（宋）苏轼

hé	jìn	yǐ	wú	qíng	yǔ	gài
荷	尽	已	无	擎	雨	盖

jú	cán	yóu	yǒu	ào	shuāng	zhī
菊	残	犹	有	傲	霜	枝

yì	nián	hǎo	jǐng	jūn	xū	jì
一	年	好	景	君	须	记

zuì	shì	chéng	huáng	jú	lǜ	shí
最	是	橙	黄	橘	绿	时

Notes: The poem has a subtitle—To Liu Jingwen, who was the Military Commander of Zhejiang Province, stationed in Hangzhou. The poet was the Chief Administrator of Hangzhou. The two were good friends. The first two lines describe a bleak scene of early winter. The last two lines tell us the desolate period also sees rich harvest of fruits, therefore such a season is the best of the year. Since Liu was fifty-eight years old and the poet was fifty-five, the hidden meaning of the poem is saying they are experiencing a golden phase of life, they should be optimistic and forge ahead. The poet praised Liu's integrity subtly by way of portraying an early winter scene. The poet didn't know when composing this poem that he would soon be sent to exile to Hainan, the life there would be much harder. Yet, the broad-minded poet adapted to the changes of conditions and was not dejected at all. So, in that sense, this poem was also written for himself.

【说明】原诗有个副标题——《赠刘景文》。刘是浙江的督军，驻守杭州。诗人当时是杭州刺史，与刘是好友。头两句写的是初冬荒凉的景象。后两句告诉我们，果实是在凄凉的日子里获取的，因此，是一年中最好的季节。当年，刘已经五十有八，诗人也已五十五了。这个年纪正值壮年，他们应该在生活中乐观向前。诗人用写初冬的景色，巧妙地称赞了刘的人品。诗人写此诗时不知他很快会被派往海南，海南的生活要艰苦多了。后来心胸宽广的诗人很快适应了条件的变化，并未灰心丧气。从这一点来说，这首诗是写给诗人自己的。

84. Berthed at Night beside the Maple Bridge
(Tang) Zhang Ji

Algidity prevails when the moon is down and ravens crow,
Maple trees and lights on other fishing boats are facing the Choumian Hill.
The Chill Mount Temple is outside the Gusu city wall,
At the midnight bell my visiting boat is about to call.

In Chinese phonetic alphabet and Chinese characters:

fēng qiáo yè bó
枫　桥　夜　泊

（唐）张继

yuè　luò　wū　tí　shuāng　mǎn　tiān
月　落　乌　啼　霜　满　天，

江 枫 渔 火 对 愁 眠 。
jiāng fēng yú huǒ duì chóu mián

姑 苏 城 外 寒 山 寺 ，
gū sū chéng wài hán shān sì

夜 半 钟 声 到 客 船 。
yè bàn zhōng shēng dào kè chuán

Notes: Zhang Ji (no dates of birth and death available) served as a censor and a judge at the Salt and Iron Department of a prefecture. There are less than fifty of his poems in existence, of which this poem is most famous. The first line depicts what the poet heard, saw and sensed (respectively the ravens crow, the setting moon and algidity). The second line depicts the scenery around the maple bridge; the poet drew a night scene of a southern water town, full of sentiment and meaning, with a bridge, maple trees, water, a temple and a bell. The Chill Mount Temple was built in the Southern Dynasties and named after a monk of the same name. It was rebuilt many times. The present temple was rebuilt after the decline of the Taiping Heavenly Kingdom. The bell of the temple was taken away by Japanese during the Second World War.

【说明】张继（无生卒年记载）曾任一个州的盐铁判官。他有差不多 50 首诗存世，其中最有名的就是这首《枫桥夜泊》。第一句写诗人所听到、看到和感觉到的事物（乌鸦的啼叫、下落的月亮和满天的寒气）。第二句写枫桥的景致。诗人画了一幅南方水城的夜景，景色里有桥、枫树、水、庙，还有钟，富有情感，也有意义。寒山寺修建于南朝，名字取自一位和尚，被重修过多次。现在的寺庙是太平天国失败后重修的。但是，寺里的钟在二战期间被日本人抢走了。

85. A Winter Night
(Song) Du Lei

A guest has come in the cold night, I invited him to have tea instead of wine,

Water is boiling on the bamboo stove and the burning wood let out a groan.

Even though moon outside the window is the same as usual,

The blossoming winter-sweet flowers have made the night so special.

In Chinese phonetic alphabet and Chinese characters:

hán yè
寒 夜
（宋）杜耒

hán yè kè lái chá dāng jiǔ
寒 夜 客 来 茶 当 酒 ，

zhú lú tāng fèi huǒ chū hóng
竹 炉 汤 沸 火 初 红 。

xún cháng yí yàng chuāng qián yuè
寻 常 一 样 窗 前 月 ，

cái yǒu méi huā biàn bù tóng
才 有 梅 花 便 不 同 。

Notes: Du Lei (? – 1225) served as chief of clerical staff in a local government. He died during one armed rebellion. The first line has been a pet phrase. But, it meant more than it seems. First of all the guest must be a frequent visitor, and that's why the host didn't prepare wine and the visitor didn't mind drinking tea. Secondly, the visitor must have much to share with the host, since he came in a very cold night, and the two must be very good friends. The "bamboo stove" in the original of the second line refers to a bamboo casing of the stove. The second line also says that the water is boiling and the fire had just become red. The translation went a bit too far, yet it is more vivid to say the burning wood let out a groan, to rhyme with the first line. When the poet said that the blossoming winter-sweet flowers had made the night different, the understatement is that it was the guest who made the night special.

【说明】杜耒（? —1225）曾在地方政府做过主簿，死于军乱。此诗第一句已经变成一种口头禅。但是，它的含义并非表面上这么简单。第一，客人肯定是一位常客，所以，主人没有准备酒，客人饮茶也并不在意。第二，他一定不是俗人，与主人定有共同的语言；在寒冷的夜晚有兴出访，肯定与主人是好友。第二句中的"竹炉"不是说炉子是用竹子做的，是指炉子外面包了一层竹子。第二句还说，炉火已经烧红，茶汤已经煮沸。第二句的译文有些过头，说燃烧着的木材发出了呻吟声，以便与第一句押韵。诗人说梅花使得夜晚大不同前，实际上是在赞美来客，由于他的到来，此夜才更有意义。

86. Moon in the Frosty Night
(Tang) Li Shangyin

When wild geese started their southward flight their honking has replaced cicada chirping,

I see water blinds into the sky on top of the hundred feet high building.

Both Goddesses Frost and Moon can withstand cold,

Even in such moonlight and frost, each wanted to be the beauty of the world.

In Chinese phonetic alphabet and Chinese characters:

shuāng yè
霜 夜

（唐）李商隐

chū wén zhēng yàn yǐ wú chán
初　闻　征　雁　已　无　蝉，

bǎi chǐ lóu tái shuǐ jiē tiān
百　尺　楼　台　水　接　天。

qīng nǚ sù é jù nài lěng
青　女　素　娥　俱　耐　冷，

yuè zhōng shuāng lǐ dòu chán juān
月　中　霜　里　斗　婵　娟。

Notes：Li Shangyin（approx. 813 - approx. 858）didn't do well in the government because of his disposition. His no-title love poems have been most popular. He and Du Mu have been reputed as "junior Li and Du" in contrast to "senior Li and Du"—Li Bai and Du Fu. The poet used two legendary figures to depict the moon in the frosty night. In the Han nationality legends there have been a Goddess of Frost and a Goddess of the Moon. It has been said that the latter took some elixir by mistake and flew up to the moon and has been staying there since. Literally the last line says that the Goddess of Frost and the Goddess of Moon are contending with each other for who is more beautiful and graceful. The last two characters are a synonym of moon or a beauty. The poet presented to us the ambience of a clear autumn and the spirit of the moon at a frosty night. Such a spirit is also a natural flow of the lofty, unworldly，honest and frank disposition of the poet.

【说明】李商隐（约 813—约 858），由于他的性情，在仕途上没有大的作为。其无题爱情诗被广为传诵。他与杜牧被称为"小李杜"，此称谓是与李白与杜甫比较而来。诗人用了两个传说中的人物来写霜夜。在汉民族的传说里青女是主管霜雪的女神，素娥即嫦娥。嫦娥是因为误吃了一种药，才飞到月亮上去，而且一直待在那里。诗的最后一句说青女与素娥争奇斗艳。最后两个字代指月亮或美女。诗人烘托出秋高气爽的氛围，描绘了秋夜霜月的精神。这种精神是他性格中高标绝俗、耿介不随的一面的自然流露。

87. Plum Blossom

(Song) Wang Qi

Not being tainted by dust in the least,

Out of its won will it usually stays beside bamboo fences and thatched hut.

Ever since taking a plum lover as a friend by mistake,

Up to now plum blossom has been the main content for poets in their mockery and talk.

In Chinese phonetic alphabet and Chinese characters：

méi
梅

（宋）王淇

bú　shòu　chén　āi　bàn　diǎn　qīn
不　受　尘　埃　半　点　侵　，

zhú　lí　máo　shè　zì　gān　xīn
竹　篱　茅　舍　自　甘　心　。

zhǐ　yīn　wù　shí　lín　hé　jìng
只　因　误　识　林　和　靖　，

rě　dé　shī　rén　shuō　dào　jīn
惹　得　诗　人　说　到　今　。

Notes：Wang Qi（no dates of birth and death available）served as chief of clerical staff at a prefecture government office, then became a proof-reader at the imperial college and later became an edict-drafter. He ended his official career with the position of an assistant minister at the Ministry of Rites. The original of the third line mentions the name of the plum lover—Lin Hejing（967 – 1028）， who led a life of recluse with plum blossom and cranes as his life-long company. The poet was saying that because of the influence of Lin poets always wrote about plum. The first two lines outline a lofty image of the plum for us.

【说明】王淇（无生卒年记载）曾任地方主簿、馆阁校勘、集贤校理，知制诰，官至礼部侍郎。诗的第三句提到一位爱梅人——林和靖（967—1028）。林终生以梅和仙鹤为伴，过着隐居的生活。最后两句说，由于林和靖的影响，诗人经常写竹子。诗的头两句描绘了梅之高洁。

88. Early Spring

(Song) Bai Yuchan

There are two or three blossoms on the south facing plum branches，

In the snow I savor the pinky white and the delicate fragrance.

Sparse smell stains on the fog and thick aroma has melted into moonlight，

The smell is strong over the deep pool and on the sand it is faint.

In Chinese phonetic alphabet and Chinese characters：

zǎo chūn
早 春

（宋）白玉蟾

nán	zhī	cái	fàng	liǎng	sān	huā
南	枝	才	放	两	三	花 ，
xuě	lǐ	yín	xiāng	nòng	fěn	xiē
雪	里	吟	香	弄	粉	些 。
dàn	dàn	zhuó	yān	nóng	zhuó	yuè
淡	淡	著	烟	浓	著	月 ，

shēn　shēn　lǒng　shuǐ　qiǎn　lǒng　shā
深　　深　　笼　　水　　浅　　笼　　沙　。

Notes：Bai Yuchan （1194 -?） was a Taoist leader with the title of Purple Clarity Distinct Taoist True Master，has been regarded as one of the five southern forerunners of Complete Truth of Taoism. His original family name was Ge and was adopted by the Bai family. The poet was saying there were only two or three plum blossoms in early spring when he walked on snow to appreciate the plum under moonlight. The poet observed and felt so keenly that the plum smell is sparse in the fog and thick in the moonlight，stronger in the pool and faint on the sand. Some critics noticed the neat parallel antithesis in the poem.

【说明】白玉蟾（1194—?），著名道教领袖，号琼绾紫清真人，全真教南方五祖之一。原姓葛，后被白家收养。诗人说早春的梅花刚开过两三次，他在雪中散步，在月光下赏月。诗人敏锐地观察到：梅花香味在雾里是淡的，在月光下却是浓的；在池塘里是浓的，在沙滩上却是淡的。不少评论者认为此诗对仗工整。

89. Snow and Plum （1）
（Song）Lu Meipo

Each of plum and snow regards itself as symbol of early spring，and none gives up to the other，

All bards have to stop composing，they don't know which is better.

Plum blossom is not as white as snowflakes，to be fair，

And snowflakes are not as fragrant as plum flower.

In Chinese phonetic alphabet and Chinese characters：

xuě méi　qí yī

雪 梅 （其一）

（宋）卢梅坡

méi	xuě	zhēng	chūn	wèi	kěn	xiáng
梅	雪	争	春	未	肯	降 ，

sāo	rén	gé	bǐ	fèi	píng	zhāng
骚	人	阁	笔	费	评	章 。

méi	xū	xùn	xuě	sān	fēn	bái
梅	须	逊	雪	三	分	白 ，

xuě	què	shū	méi	yí	duàn	xiāng
雪	却	输	梅	一	段	香 。

Notes：There isn't much record about poet. We figure his name we are using must be his pseudonym—a slope covered by plum. Before him poets treated both snow and plum as messengers of spring. Some of them said that with plum snow heralded the coming of spring，others said that because of snow plum seemed loftier. But this poet of the Song Dynasty let the two of them dispute on who is the orthodox envoy of spring. This is really a novel and unique way of describing both.

【说明】关于卢梅坡的记录很少。我们觉得诗人用的是假名——长着梅花的山坡。在他之前，诗人把雪和梅都视为春天的信使。有的诗人说梅雪预示春天就要来了，有的诗人说雪梅更高贵。但是宋代这位诗人却让梅雪自己争论谁是春天正统的使者。这种写雪梅的方法很新奇独特。

90. Snow and Plum (2)

(Song) Lu Meipo

It is listless if there is only plum without snow，

It is vulgar if there is only snow without poems to give a satisfaction glow.

At dusk when the poem was composed it is again snowing,
Together with plum blossom it is a full spring.

In Chinese phonetic alphabet and Chinese characters:

xuě méi　qí èr
雪 梅 （其二）
（宋）卢梅坡

yǒu	méi	wú	xuě	bù	jīng	shén
有	梅	无	雪	不	精	神 ，

yǒu	xuě	wú	shī	sú	liǎo	rén
有	雪	无	诗	俗	了	人 。

rì	mù	shī	chéng	tiān	yòu	xuě
日	暮	诗	成	天	又	雪 ，

yǔ	méi	bìng	zuò	shí	fēn	chūn
与	梅	并	作	十	分	春 。

Notes: In this second poem about snow and plum the poet added "poetry" into the disputing parties. The three—snow plum and poetry have to be together to make a full and most beautiful spring. The poet contended that if there was only plum without snow, there would be no vivacity in the spring; and if there were only snow and plum without poetry, there would be no grace, charm, no loveliness, no refinement and no elegance in the spring. We can see how crazy the poet was about plum and how obsessed he was with snow and poetry.

【说明】诗人在第二首关于"雪梅"的诗中加入了"诗"字，最美丽的春天必须雪、梅、诗三者俱备。诗人主张只有梅没有雪，春天则无生气；只有雪梅没有诗，春天则无优雅、无魅力、无活力、无纯洁、无高雅。我们可以看出诗人爱梅几近癫狂，爱雪爱诗已到痴迷的程度。

91. In Reply to Zhong Ruoweng

Mu Tong

The carpet of green grass stretches out for six or seven miles,

In the evening breeze you can hear three or four flute notes.

Having returned home he had a good meal at sun set,

Lying on the ground with the straw rain coat on while the moon is so bright.

In Chinese phonetic alphabet and Chinese characters:

dá zhōng ruò wēng
答　钟　弱　翁

牧童

cǎo	pū	héng	yě	liù	qī	lǐ
草	铺	横	野	六	七	里，
dí	nòng	wǎn	fēng	sān	sì	shēng
笛	弄	晚	风	三	四	声。
guī	lái	bǎo	fàn	huáng	hūn	hòu
归	来	饱	饭	黄	昏	后，
bù	tuō	suō	yī	wò	yuè	míng
不	脱	蓑	衣	卧	月	明。

Notes: Zhong Ruoweng had been repeatedly deposed in his official career. Once he was travelling with a Taoist. Pointing at the open country, the green grass, Zhong asked the Taoist if he could compose a poem on them. At this juncture, a cowboy (Mu Tong in English means a cowboy.) was coming into the courtyard, and the Taoist said, I don't have to make a verse, this child can. At the request, the cowboy uttered out this poem. Of course "cowboy" is a pseudonym and we don't know who he was. In this poem, the cowboy was persuading Zhong to forsake his official life and to live in leisure and comfort. We can taste in this poem the repose and easiness of the life style of "working when the sun is up

and resting when the sun is down. " In the poem the cowboy seems
to be an incarnation of a wise man giving Zhong some orientations.

【说明】钟弱翁在官场多次被贬。一次，他与一位道士一起游
历时，指着空旷的田野和绿油油的草地，让道士作一首诗。这时，
一个牧童（牧童英文里叫 cowboy）进了院子，道士便说，我不用
作诗了，这个小孩会作。于是乎，这个孩子顺口说出了这首诗。
"牧童"当然是个代称，我们不知道他是谁。在这首诗里，牧童劝
钟放弃仕途，过清闲舒适的日子。我们从诗里可以品味到"日出而
作、日落而归"般的安逸的生活。在诗里牧童是一位智者的化身，
为钟指明了方向。

92. To Berth at the Qinhuai River
(Tang) Du Mu

While mist hangs over the chilly river moonlight casts on the
white sand，

For easy access to a wine shop I berthed my boat at night by
the riverside.

Singing girls bear no grudge against loss of their country，

They，on the other side，are still singing "The Rear Yard
Flower" with joy.

In Chinese phonetic alphabet and Chinese characters：

bó qín huái
泊 秦 淮
（唐）杜牧

yān lǒng hán shuǐ yuè lǒng shā
烟   笼   寒   水   月   笼   沙 ，
yè   bó   qín   huái   jìn   jiǔ   jiā
夜   泊   秦   淮   近   酒   家 。

<table>
<tr><td>shāng</td><td>nǚ</td><td>bù</td><td>zhī</td><td>wáng</td><td>guó</td><td>hèn</td></tr>
<tr><td>商</td><td>女</td><td>不</td><td>知</td><td>亡</td><td>国</td><td>恨，</td></tr>
<tr><td>gé</td><td>jiāng</td><td>yóu</td><td>chàng</td><td>hòu</td><td>tíng</td><td>huā</td></tr>
<tr><td>隔</td><td>江</td><td>犹</td><td>唱</td><td>后</td><td>庭</td><td>花。</td></tr>
</table>

Notes：The Qinhuai River is a branch on the lower reaches of the Yangtze River. It flows through the entire city of Nanjing. A section of it, five kilometers long in the down town area, used to be the busiest spot in the Southern Dynasties period, which was crowded with famous entertainment facilities and restaurants. The first line delineates a chilly night scene with mist, water, moon and sand, which are pieced together with the words of "over...cast". At the mention of Qinhuai River in the second line, the poet set his thoughts on the past. The poet was blaming the singing girls for their lack of patriotism, because they were still singing "The Rear Yard Flower", which was composed by the ruler of the last regime in the Southern Dynasties period, it was said when the state was lost, the ruler was having a good time with his concubines. So, the song had been regarded as a symbol of the loss of homeland. By the time this poem was written, the Tang Dynasty was on its decline. The poet was, actually, castigating at those who asked the girls to sing such a song. The word "still" called forth his pain upon hearing the song and evoked his denunciation of the rulers of his time, who were no different in their indulgence in extravagance and who learned no lesson at all from emperors and kings before them. This poem has been regarded as the best of "seven-character a line" quatrains of the Tang Dynasty.

【说明】秦淮河是长江下游的一段，横穿整个南京城。此河在市中心 5 公里长的一段在南朝曾是最繁华的地方，那时到处是有名的娱乐场所和酒家。诗的第一句的烟、水、月和沙四个字用一个"笼"字串了起来，描写了寒夜。第二句提到秦淮河时，诗人便想起了过去。他责怪歌女没有爱国情怀，因为她们仍在唱着《后庭花》。此曲是南朝最后一个政权的统治者作的。据说当国家失陷时，他正与他的嫔妃作乐。这个曲子就是一种亡国之音。写此诗时，唐朝已经开始败落。因此，诗人是在谴责那些让歌女唱亡国之音的人。"犹"字道出了诗人听到这个曲子时的心痛，激起了诗人对当时统治者的谴责，这些统治者没有从前朝的帝王学到任何教训，仍过着糜烂的生活。此诗被视为唐朝七绝之冠。

93. The Returned Wild Goose

(Tang) Qian Qi

Why do you wild geese leave the rivers on a whim?

Since the water is so green，sand so clean and with mosses the banks are in such a trim.

Every night the River Goddess plucked the twenty-five string lute，

We could no longer put up with such a torture and that's the reason for our revisit.

In Chinese phonetic alphabet and Chinese characters：

guī yàn
归 雁

（唐）钱起

xiāo	xiāng	hé	shì	děng	xián	huí
潇	湘	何	事	等	闲	回 ，
shuǐ	bì	shā	míng	liǎng	àn	tái
水	碧	沙	明	两	岸	苔 。
èr	shí	wǔ	xián	tán	yè	yuè
二	十	五	弦	弹	夜	月 ，
bù	shèng	qīng	yuàn	què	fēi	lái
不	胜	清	怨	却	飞	来 。

Notes：Qian Qi，a famous poet of the Tang Dynasty. We don't have his dates of birth and death. We know he is the uncle of a famous monk calligrapher Huai Su. He reached recognition of his poetry when he was young and was regarded one of the Ten Talents of the Da Li period (766 – 779) during the reign of Emperor Daizong of Tang. Wild goose is a kind of migrant bird, every spring it would fly from the south to the north. Knowing this is a natural phenomenon, the poet insisted to ask wild goose: why do you leave the rivers in the south on a whim? It is said in a legend that the Goddess of River Xiang was good at plucking a lute with fifty strings. Because the sound was too plaintive, the Emperor Shun asked the Goddess to reduce half of the strings. She did, yet the notes were still sad, and they were too much for the wild geese to put up with, and they left the Xiao and Xiang rivers and returned to where they were in the north. On surface, the poet was writing about wild geese, actually he was describing how people felt in the spring night. What did they feel? The poet didn't say, his readers have to imagine by themselves.

【说明】钱起系唐朝著名诗人，无生卒年可考。他是大书法家怀素和尚的叔叔，年轻时就享有诗名，是唐代宗大历（766—779）年间十才子之一。大雁是一种候鸟，每年春天由南往北飞。诗人知道这是个自然现象，但是他依旧问道：为何如此随便就离开了这么好的地方？据说湘夫人擅于鼓瑟。由于瑟的声调太过悲戚，舜帝就让湘夫人将琴弦减去一半。她虽减去了一半弦，但是，其音符仍很凄惨，大雁实在听不下去了，便告别湘江和潇江，回到它们北方的住处。表面上看，此诗写的是大雁，实际上写的是人们对春夜的感受。他们的感受是什么？诗人并未讲，读者只好自己去想象了。

94. Wall Inscription
Anonymous

A skein of couch grass is so jumbled,

When it caught fire, its flame may roar to the sky yet it can be easily distinguished.

Unlike the old tree roots being burnt in the furnace,

Whose burning is slow and the warmth they give endures.

In Chinese phonetic alphabet and Chinese characters:

tí bì
题 壁

无名氏

yí tuán máo cǎo luàn péng péng
一 团 茅 草 乱 蓬 蓬,

mò dì shāo tiān mò dì kōng
蓦 地 烧 天 蓦 地 空。

zhēng sì mǎn lú wēi gǔ duò
争 似 满 炉 煨 榾 柮,

màn téng téng dē nuǎn hōng hōng
慢 腾 腾 地 暖 烘 烘。

Notes: This is a poem written in the Song Dynasty. The first two lines describe that a skein of couch grass can easily catch fire and the fire can quickly expand, yet it is ease to put out. It is a different story with an old and rotten tree root, and when people burn it, its flame is small and its burning speed is slow, but the warmth it provides is much longer. The poet didn't say which is better. The two kinds of fires were likened to two types of persons; one type can burst out their power very quickly while the power of the other type can endure much longer. Apparently, the poet refused short and exhaustive brilliance and stood for solid and persistent warmth.

【说明】 这是一首宋诗。前两句写一团茅草很容易被点燃, 火势会很快地蔓延开来。但是, 扑灭它也很容易。对老树根疙瘩来说，情况就不一样了。当人们点燃它的时候，火焰很小，燃烧的速度也很慢。但是，它所提供的热度却很长久。诗人并没有说哪种火更好。两种火可比喻成两种人。一种人的力量可以突然爆发，另一种人的力量却可持久。很显然，诗人不喜欢力量被消耗后取得的短暂的辉煌，更热爱牢固的、用之不竭的热量。

A Primer of Ancient Poetry 千家诗

Part II "Seven-Characters a Line" Octaves

卷二　七律

The eight-line poem in Chinese is called "lüshi". Fortunately it also has an equivalent in English— "octave". The first Chinese character "lü" means to regulate and the second character "shi" means poem. So, the two characters together mean a regulated poem. This form appeared in the Southern and Northern Dynasties period (420 – 589) and matured in the Tang Dynasty (618 – 709). Since it evolved from archaic poetry forms, it has also been referred to as a "modern poetic form". There have been two types of "lüshi" or Chinese octaves; they are the "five-characters a line" ones and "seven-characters a line" ones. The second part of this primer devotes to the "seven-characters a line" one. There are two rules "seven-characters a line" octaves have to follow. First, each line must have seven characters; so there are fifty-six characters in the whole poem, which doubles that of the "seven-characters a line" quatrains. Second, the third line and the fourth line should be antitheses, the fifth line and the sixth line should also be antitheses. That is to say, the meaning of words in the fourth line should be in the same category with that in the third, and the part of speech in the two lines should be the same and in the same order. The same applies to line five and line six. There are no strict requirements on the first and the last two lines in antitheses. That is to say Chinese octave rhymes at the end of every other line. This part collected forty-eight poems.

八行一首的诗在汉语里叫"律诗"。幸运的是，英文也有对应的词——"octave"。"律"字是调节、控制的意思，"律诗"就是有规矩的诗。律诗出现在南北朝时期（420—589），成熟于唐朝（618—709）。由于律诗从古体诗演变而来，它也被称为"近体诗"。律诗有两种：一种是五言律诗，一种是七言律诗。本蒙学教材的第二部分专讲七言律诗。七言律诗必须符合如下两条要求：第一，每行七个字，所以每首律诗共有五十六个字，这个字数是"七绝"的两倍。第二、第三句和第四句必须对仗，第五句和第六句也必须对仗。也就是说第四句字词的含义与第三句的字词必须属于同一类；它们的词性必须相同，在句中的位置必须相同。第五句和第六句的要求也是如此。对起始的两句和结尾的两句并无严格的对仗要求。也就是说律诗隔行押韵。卷二共收有律诗四十八首。

1. Early Morning Audience at the Daming Palace

(Tang) Jia Zhi

Silver candle light lit up the purple path,

Spring at day break in the Forbidden City seemed a bit hazy.

A thousand feeble willow branches were caressing the palace gates,

A hundred ways of oriole singing were convoluting the Hall of the Monarchy.

The walking rapiers and jade pendants clanged softly while officials moved up the royal steps,

Their attires and caps were tainted by the smell of the incense of the regality.

All of them in the Chancery benefited from the care of the emperor,

Day after day they devoted to the cause of His Majesty.

In Chinese phonetic alphabet and Chinese characters:

zǎo cháo dà míng gōng
早　朝　大　明　宫

（唐）贾至

yín 银	zhú 烛	cháo 朝	tiān 天	zǐ 紫	mò 陌	cháng 长，
jìn 禁	chéng 城	chūn 春	sè 色	xiǎo 晓	cāng 苍	cāng 苍。
qiān 千	tiáo 条	ruò 弱	liǔ 柳	chuí 垂	qīng 青	suǒ 琐，
bǎi 百	zhuàn 啭	liú 流	yīng 莺	rào 绕	jiàn 建	zhāng 章。
jiàn 剑	pèi 佩	shēng 声	suí 随	yù 玉	chí 墀	bù 步，
yī 衣	guān 冠	shēn 身	rě 惹	yù 御	lú 炉	xiāng 香。
gòng 共	mù 沐	ēn 恩	bō 波	fèng 凤	chí 池	shàng 上，

<table>
<tr><td>zhāo</td><td>zhāo</td><td>rǎn</td><td>hàn</td><td>shì</td><td>jūn</td><td>wáng</td></tr>
<tr><td>朝</td><td>朝</td><td>染</td><td>翰</td><td>侍</td><td>君</td><td>王 。</td></tr>
</table>

Notes：Jia Zhi（718 - 772）was an important poet of the Tang Dynasty. *The Complete Collection of Tang Poetry* devoted one volume to his poems. He served as Chief of Chancery and a Standing-by Admonisher. This poem depicts how a regular morning audience was conducted. Some critics said that every character in the poem was good，that the poem provided a decent ceremony and a pleasing tonality. For purpose of fluency，my translation missed the following points：the third line in the original stressed relief sculpture on the gates，the fourth line mentions the name of a particular palace—the Jian Zhang Hall，the seventh line mentions the place where the poet and others worked—a pond for phoenix，which was used as a synonym of the Chancery，finally the last line gives the specific way the officials work—to write with the brush pen and ink. I tried to produce antithesis as well in the translation. For instance，in the third and fourth lines，a thousand vs. a hundred，feeble willow branches vs. ways of oriole singing，caressing vs. convoluting，palace gates vs. hall of the monarchy. The antitheses can also be found in the fifth and sixth lines. I also tried to rhyme at the end of every other line，and hoping this can sound alright in English.

【说明】贾至（718—772）是唐朝一位重要的诗人。《全唐诗》中他的诗作专有一卷。他曾任中书舍人，后官至右散骑常侍。此诗写的是百官上朝的场面。有的评论家说：整体气象轩冕，无一字不佳。为使译文流畅起见，译文未译出如下内容：第三句所说门上的浮雕，第四句所提建章宫，第七句所提诗人及其他人工作的地方——凤池，即中书省所在地，最后一句所说官员如何工作——用笔墨工作。我在译文中也试图对仗。譬如，第三句和第四句中千对百、弱柳对黄莺、抚摸对缠绕、宫门对大殿等。第五句、第六句也试图对仗。我也试图隔行押韵，希望这样的英文能说得过去。

2. In the Tune of Jia's Morning Audience
(Tang) Du Fu

Water dropping from the clepsydra heralds the coming of dawn,

Spring in the imperial palace sees red peach flowers.

Banners embroidered with dragons and snakes are fluttering in the sunshine,

Amidst soft breeze sparrows and swallows are flying high over the palace eaves.

When the audience is over the sleeves of the poet are filled with the aroma of incense,

Back to the office he completed an exquisite verse.

Why does glory befalls on this family whose members have been edict drafters?

You would have an answer if look at the one now in charge of the Chancery office.

In Chinese phonetic alphabet and Chinese characters：

hè jiǎ shě rén zǎo cháo
和 贾 舍 人 早 朝
（唐）杜甫

wǔ	yè	lòu	shēng	cuī	xiǎo	jiàn
五	夜	漏	声	催	晓	箭 ，
jiǔ	chóng	chūn	sè	zuì	xiān	táo
九	重	春	色	醉	仙	桃 。
jīng	qí	rì	nuǎn	lóng	shé	dòng
旌	旗	日	暖	龙	蛇	动 ，
gōng	diàn	fēng	wēi	yàn	què	gāo
宫	殿	风	微	燕	雀	高 。

<table>
<tr><td>cháo</td><td>bà</td><td>xiāng</td><td>yān</td><td>xié</td><td>mǎn</td><td>xiù</td></tr>
<tr><td>朝</td><td>罢</td><td>香</td><td>烟</td><td>携</td><td>满</td><td>袖，</td></tr>
<tr><td>shī</td><td>chéng</td><td>zhū</td><td>yù</td><td>zài</td><td>huī</td><td>háo</td></tr>
<tr><td>诗</td><td>成</td><td>珠</td><td>玉</td><td>在</td><td>挥</td><td>毫。</td></tr>
<tr><td>yù</td><td>zhī</td><td>shì</td><td>zhǎng</td><td>sī</td><td>lún</td><td>měi</td></tr>
<tr><td>欲</td><td>知</td><td>世</td><td>掌</td><td>丝</td><td>纶</td><td>美，</td></tr>
<tr><td>chí</td><td>shàng</td><td>yú</td><td>jīn</td><td>yǒu</td><td>fèng</td><td>máo</td></tr>
<tr><td>池</td><td>上</td><td>于</td><td>今</td><td>有</td><td>凤</td><td>毛。</td></tr>
</table>

Notes：Du Fu and Jia Zhi were peers. The first half of the poem is devoted to the audience. The original of the first line contains such words as the clepsydra urges the drawn arrow，what it means is that when the water is of a certain level，one arrow would come up to the surface to mark time. The second line describes the imperial palace as one on the ninth layer of the sky，it also describes red peach flower as a drunken immortal peach. The poet thought when a person is drunk，his face is red，and he presumed the same would happen to peach flowers. The second half is full of praises of Jia Zhi. In the Chinese language，a good poem is compared to pearl and jade wares，that is why the original of the sixth line says that by maneuvering the brush pen a poem as good as pearl and jade ware is completed. Jia Zhi's father was，as his son，the Chief of the Imperial Chancery. This is why the poet said for glory befalls on this family whose members had been edict drafters，which is a glory and honor. In the literary circle，if a son inherits and develops his father's studies，such a son is regarded as a "phoenix feather". So，the last line of the poem says that the one now in charge of the Chancery office. I didn't try purposely to produce antitheses. The translation also rhymes at the end of the other line.

【说明】杜甫与贾至是同时代人。诗的前半部分写的是早朝的情况。第一句说漏声催晓箭，是讲漏壶里的水达到一定水平，一支箭会跳上来指明时间。第二句说皇宫有似九重天，并将红色的桃花比作醉仙桃。诗人想说一个人喝醉了，脸色就会发红，便以为桃花也是如此。诗的下半部分夸奖了贾至。汉语里有将好诗比作珍宝的说法，因此，诗的第六句才说：诗成珠玉在挥毫。贾至的父亲与贾至一样曾任中书舍人，因此杜甫才说世掌丝纶。丝纶即丝纶阁，是中书省的所在地。对贾至一家来说这是无与伦比的荣耀。在文学界，如果儿子继承了父亲的学业，这个儿子会被看作"凤毛"。因此，诗的最后一句说：池上于今有凤毛。我没有在译文中特意地去对仗。译文也是隔行押韵。

3. In the Tune of Jia's Morning Audience
(Tang) Wang Wei

Guards with red scarf are shouting that it is time of the dawn,

The leather robe with green clouds patterns has just been sent into the regal chamber.

Palace gates in the Forbidden City are being opened,

All officials and foreign envoys are bending to the emperor.

A sea of long-handled fans is moving ahead in the morning sun,

Slowly rising around the emperor is the light smoke from the incense burner.

After the audience Jia has to draft an edict on the five-color paper,

He is now back in the office with clanging of his jade pendants and walking rapier.

In Chinese phonetic alphabet and Chinese characters：

hè jiǎ shě rén zǎo cháo
和 贾 舍 人 早 朝

（唐）王维

jiàng zé jī rén bào xiǎo chóu
绛 帻 鸡 人 报 晓 筹，

<table>
<tr><td>shàng
尚</td><td>yì
衣</td><td>fāng
方</td><td>jìn
进</td><td>cuì
翠</td><td>yún
云</td><td>qiú
裘</td><td>。</td></tr>
<tr><td>jiǔ
九</td><td>tiān
天</td><td>chāng
阊</td><td>hé
阖</td><td>kāi
开</td><td>gōng
宫</td><td>diàn
殿</td><td>，</td></tr>
<tr><td>wàn
万</td><td>guó
国</td><td>yī
衣</td><td>guān
冠</td><td>bài
拜</td><td>miǎn
冕</td><td>liú
旒</td><td>。</td></tr>
<tr><td>rì
日</td><td>sè
色</td><td>cái
才</td><td>lín
临</td><td>xiān
仙</td><td>zhǎng
掌</td><td>dòng
动</td><td>，</td></tr>
<tr><td>xiāng
香</td><td>yān
烟</td><td>yù
欲</td><td>bàng
傍</td><td>gǔn
衮</td><td>lóng
龙</td><td>fú
浮</td><td>。</td></tr>
<tr><td>cháo
朝</td><td>bà
罢</td><td>xū
须</td><td>cái
裁</td><td>wǔ
五</td><td>sè
色</td><td>zhào
诏</td><td>，</td></tr>
<tr><td>pèi
珮</td><td>shēng
声</td><td>guī
归</td><td>dào
到</td><td>fèng
凤</td><td>chí
池</td><td>tóu
头</td><td>。</td></tr>
</table>

Notes：This poem successfully delineates the solemn and gorgeous atmosphere of the morning audience at the Da Ming Palace of the Tang Dynasty by using descriptions of minute details and rendering of palace scenes，scenes before the audience，during the audience and after the audience. The poem begins with two actions：to report dawn（please refer to poem No. 77 of the last part）and to deliver the emperor's leather robe. The original uses the palace gates in the Forbidden City in the legend as a synonym of the regal chamber. The fourth line uses such words as envoys from ten thousand countries coming to call on the Tang emperor. It is certainly an exaggeration，but it is true that there were many foreign envoys in that period. The Chinese character "bai" means to show respect to the emperor，in the translation I used the word "bending"，to be on the safe side，because I am not sure if officials and foreign envoys kowtowed to the emperor at that time. In this line，the poet uses crown and its tassels as a synonym of the emperor. The last two lines indicate to the readers that Jia was a much preferred official of the emperor.

【说明】这首诗将唐朝大明宫的早朝之庄严与华贵成功地表现了出来。其表现手法细腻，将早朝前、早朝时和早朝后宫殿的情况表达得很清楚。全诗以两个动作开始：一是报晓（参阅卷一第77首诗），一是送皇帝的裘衣。原诗用传说中的九天阊阖来比喻皇宫。第四句说万国的使节来拜见皇帝，这个词当然有些夸张，然而，那时确实有很多外国使节来大唐。汉语里的"拜"是表示尊重的举止，我的译文用了"躬身"，这样比较保险，因为外国使节和使臣不大会向唐朝皇帝磕头。第四句用冕旒代指皇上。诗的最后两句暗示贾至是皇帝喜爱的臣子。

4. In the Tune of Jia's Morning Audience

(Tang) Cen Shen

When roosters crow the light of dawn on the purple path is cold,

Spring is at its best in the imperial palace when orioles sing.

At the bell of dawn all gates are opened,

Officials are coming up the steps with guards of honor saluting.

Stars have just faded out; flowers greet rapiers and jade pendants,

Willow branches are brushing the banners and dews are drying.

Only the Chief of the Chancery is so unique,

His poems are too elegant to find echoing.

In Chinese phonetic alphabet and Chinese characters:

hè jiǎ shě rén zǎo cháo
和 贾 舍 人 早 朝

（唐）岑参

jī   míng   zǐ   mò   shǔ   guāng hán
鸡   鸣   紫   陌   曙   光   寒，

<table>
</table>

莺啭皇州春色阑。

金阙晓钟开万户，

玉阶仙仗拥千官。

花迎剑佩星初落，

柳拂旌旗露未干。

独有凤凰池上客，

阳春一曲和皆难。

Notes: Cen Shen (715 – 770) worked as an official designated to the crown prince and then a chief of administration of a prefecture. There are three hundred and sixty poems of his still available. His poems on frontier and army life and on the culture and customs of minority groups are more famous. The third line in the original mentions in particular a golden hall, which is actually the bell tower. The fourth line describes the steps with the word jade, and uses a numeral—a thousand before officials. The seventh line uses the words the phoenix pond as a synonym of the royal chancery. The last line uses what has been considered a most elegant song named "The Sunny Spring", most difficult to echo to, to compare with the poems of Jia.

After two most influential poets have responded in the same tune and theme of Jia's poem, Cen still ventured to echo. It was a difficult task. Critics said the way Cen rhymed was very risky; he used such words as "han, lan, gan and nan", which have been used in poems with sad tones, but Cen managed very well. Most critics agreed that the antitheses Cen produced in this poem is neat and proper. Even though Cen used some grand and splendid words, they do not seem to be over stately.

5. A Poem on the Lantern Festival at the Order of the Emperor

(Song) Cai Xiang

Lanterns lit and hung on the walls looked like mountain tops,

The emperor and his retinue have appeared at the main entrance.

His Majesty's presence was not to watch the lanterns,

Rather, he wanted to share the joy of all his subjects.

The clear and bright moon wished to eternalize this night,

All flesh who enjoy daily concord wished to prolong such moments.

Why did people all bless His Majesty?

Because in over forty years of his reign he gave the people so much love and favors.

In Chinese phonetic alphabet and Chinese characters:

shàng yuán yīng zhì
上 元 应 制

（宋）蔡襄

高 列 千 峰 宝 炬 森 ，
gāo liè qiān fēng bǎo jù sēn

端 门 方 喜 翠 华 临 。
duān mén fāng xǐ cuì huá lín

宸 游 不 为 三 元 夜 ，
chén yóu bú wèi sān yuán yè

乐 事 还 同 万 众 心 。
lè shì hái tóng wàn zhòng xīn

天 上 清 光 留 此 夕 ，
tiān shàng qīng guāng liú cǐ xī

人 间 和 气 阁 春 阴 。
rén jiān hé qì gé chūn yīn

要 知 尽 庆 华 封 祝 ，
yào zhī jìn qìng huá fēng zhù

四 十 余 年 惠 爱 深 。
sì shí yú nián huì ài shēn

Notes: Cai Xiang （1012－1067） was a calligrapher, statesman and an expert of tea of the Song Dynasty. He was a scholar at the imperial library, chief administrator of several important cities. He wrote *Manual of Lichee*, which identified thirty-two kinds of lichee, specified their place of produce, the functions of the fruit, ways of processing, storage and transportation. He also wrote *The Inventory of Tea*, which expounded on how to discriminate and savor tea, and what tea sets to use.

This poem was composed at the order of Emperor Renzong of Song. The original of the third line mentions three types of festival nights, one is the fifteenth of January, the second is the fifteenth of July and the third one the fifteenth of August. These are all lunar calendars. The second is the Devil's Day and the third is the Mid-Autumn Day. The original of the seventh line mentioned wishes at Huafeng, which was a classical allusion of three wishes people gave to Sovereign Yao at the beginning of China's history, namely longevity, wealth and many sons.

【说明】蔡襄（1012—1067）是宋朝的一位书法家、政治家和茶叶专家。官至明殿学士，曾任几个地方的知府。他所著《荔枝谱》根据产地、果品的性能、加工的方法、储存及运输等因素将荔枝分为 32 类。他所著《茶录》阐述了如何鉴别茶品、如何品茶、如何选择茶具。

此诗是应宋仁宗之命而作。第三句提到了三种节日的夜晚，一是阴历正月十五、二是七月十五、三是八月十五。第二个是鬼节、第三个是中秋节。诗的第七句提到的华封祝，是中国历史早期人们对尧帝的三个祝愿，即长寿、财富和多子多孙。

6. A Poem on the Lantern Festival at the Order of the Emperor
(Song) Wang Gui

Snow has thawed, moonlight is pouring onto the terrace,
Numerous big candles cast light on the huge fans behind the emperor.

It seems two fairy maids are helping the emperor to get off his carriage in the clouds,
Guards of honor look like the Six Turtles in the legend, who in the sea are a mountain mover.

People in the capital are drinking wine, the feast is as grand as that of the Zhou ruler,
Even though the Han emperor wrote poetic prose, there is still something to desire.

Everyone is happy and notations of peace are sounding everywhere,
His Majesty dries up one more cup and his mood is even heartier.

In Chinese phonetic alphabet and Chinese characters:

140

shàng yuán yīng zhì
上 元 应 制

（宋）王珪

雪 消 华 月 满 仙 台 ，
xuě xiāo huá yuè mǎn xiān tái

万 烛 当 楼 宝 扇 开 。
wàn zhú dāng lóu bǎo shàn kāi

双 凤 云 中 扶 辇 下 ，
shuāng fèng yún zhōng fú niǎn xià

六 鳌 海 上 驾 山 来 。
liù áo hǎi shàng jià shān lái

镐 京 春 酒 沾 周 宴 ，
gǎo jīng chūn jiǔ zhān zhōu yàn

汾 水 秋 风 陋 汉 才 。
fén shuǐ qiū fēng lòu hàn cái

一 曲 升 平 人 尽 乐 ，
yī qǔ shēng píng rén jìn lè

君 王 又 尽 紫 霞 杯 。
jūn wáng yòu jìn zǐ xiá bēi

Notes：Wang Gui （1019－1085） served three Song emperors. He was a high ranking official. There are sixty volumes of his writings and poems available. The metaphors he used seem a bit abrupt and obscure—the fairy maids and the six turtles. The legend of the six turtles says they could prop up the entire earth. "Gaojing" in the original of the fifth line was the capital of the Zhou Dynasty, he used it as a synonym of his own capital, by mentioning "banquet in the Zhou", he wanted to say that banquets in his dynasty were also as grand. He sited Emperor Wu of Han, who wrote a poetic prose on the "Autumn Wind on the Fenshui River," for purpose of saying the Song emperors were more talented. He said in the last line that the emperor's cup—the Purple Cloud cup—was filled up again. So, you can see the translation missed out "autumn wind on the Fenshui River" and the name of the cup.

【说明】王珪（1019—1085）是三朝元老，官至宰相。现仍有他的六十卷诗文存世。他所用比喻——双凤和六鳌有些突兀、晦涩。六鳌在传说里可以举起整个天地。原诗第五句所言"镐京"是周朝的首都，他用来指代自己的都城。他用"周宴"是想说他所在的王朝的宴会同样很豪华。他引用了汉武帝在汾水所作《汾水秋风辞》，是想说宋朝的皇帝更多才。他在最后一句说皇上的紫霞杯又被斟满了。应注意的是译文中没有出现"汾水秋风"和杯子的名称。

7. At His Majesty's Dinner

(Tang) Shen Quanqi

The daughter of the emperor is fond of immortals,

Her newly built villa is a skyscraper.

The rockwork in the garden looks like the Ridge of Phoenix Call,

The pond is even bigger than the Weishui River.

The golden ring handles on the doors of the dancing hall shine like the sun,

The draperies of her dressing room are in the emerald color.

Following the emperor officials come to congratulate the completion of the villa,

They toast the emperor longevity whilst the playing of a joyful number.

In Chinese phonetic alphabet and Chinese characters：

shì yàn

侍 宴

（唐）沈佺期

huáng jiā guì zhǔ hào shén xiān
皇　家　贵　主　好　神　仙，

別业初开云汉边。
山出尽如鸣凤岭，
池成不让饮龙川。
妆楼翠幌教春住，
舞阁金铺借日悬。
敬从乘舆来此地，
称觞献寿乐钧天。

Notes: Shen Quanqi (656?–714) served as Chief of Chancery of the royal court and as a teacher and butler at the residence of a princess. He was the one who was said to have finally cemented the forms of the regulated poems. The poet was invited to dinner at the newly completed villa of the princess, and there he was asked to compose this poem. There is no such word as "skyscraper" in the original, what was used is even more exaggerated: the villa was built by the side of the Milky Way. The Ridge of Phoenix Call was where the Zhou Dynasty, which lasted for over eight hundred years, emerged. Weishui River or the river, where dragons used to drink, was the place King Wen of Zhou began his career. For rhyming purpose, I changed the original sixth line into the fifth. The original fifth line says that the aim of using emerald was to give a spring atmosphere all year round. The last line does give the title of the number being played— "At the Center of Sky". This poem brought much trouble to the poet, the princess said its words were too flowery. As a matter of fact, he undesignedly revealed the extravagant conditions of the princess, and this was one of the reasons of his death. He was actually a victim of the political struggles within the royal court.

8. In Reply to Ding Yuanzhen

(Song) Ouyang Xiu

I wonder if spring wind would ever come to this frontier,

It's already February in this hilly city and there are no flowers anywhere.

Weighing down branches the lumps of undissolved snow looks like oranges that have weathered the winter,

Bamboo shoots that will pullulate, having been startled by the spring thunder.

I missed home when hearing at night the honking of returning wild geese,

In sickness and soreness of vicissitudes I spent the New Year.

Since there were so many flowers in Luoyang to relish as a pleasure,

I don't have to sigh for the late arrival of wild flowers here.

In Chinese phonetic alphabet and Chinese characters:

dá dīng yuán zhēn
答 丁 元 珍
（宋）欧阳修

chūn	fēng	yí	bú	dào	tiān	yá
春	风	疑	不	到	天	涯 ，

èr	yuè	shān	chéng	wèi	jiàn	huā
二	月	山	城	未	见	花 。

cán	xuě	yā	zhī	yóu	yǒu	jú
残	雪	压	枝	犹	有	橘 ，

dòng	léi	jīng	sǔn	yù	chōu	yá
冻	雷	惊	笋	欲	抽	芽 。

yè	wén	tí	yàn	shēng	xiāng	sī
夜	闻	啼	雁	生	乡	思 ，

bìng	rù	xīn	nián	gǎn	wù	huá
病	入	新	年	感	物	华 。

céng	shì	luò	yáng	huā	xià	kè
曾	是	洛	阳	花	下	客 ，

yě	fāng	suī	wǎn	bù	xū	jiē
野	芳	虽	晚	不	须	嗟 。

Notes: Ouyang Xiu （1007－1072） was reputed as one of the Eight Men of Letters in the Tang and Song dynasties, a leader in the literary circle. The highest positions he held were Deputy Head of the Privy Council, Deputy Prime Minister and Tutor of the Prince. He wrote over five hundred proses, among them "Note on the Feng Le Pavilion" and "Notes on the Pavilion of the Old Drunken Man" cause some sensation at his time. This poem was written when he was head of the Xiazhou County. Ding Yuanzhen, who was a military officer in the same county, wrote our poet one verse, and this one was composed to answer Ding. Xiazhou County is in today's Hubei Province, but at that time, it was at the frontier. Our poet was demoted to the lowest rank, because of his failure in defending a colleague, and Ding was trying to console him in his poem. The February in the poem was in lunar calendar, and in solar calendar it should be March. The poet said he was homesick, where was his home? He was born in Sichuan, he stayed in the then capital—Kaifeng for quite long. He mentioned about Luoyang, a city not far from Kaifeng and was famous for peony. The last two lines show that he was not discouraged by the demotion—he had the pleasure to have seen so many beautiful flowers in his life, and he didn't have to resent about the late blossom of flowers at Xiazhou.

【说明】欧阳修（1007—1072）是唐宋八大家之一，文学界领袖。官至枢密副使、参知政事、太子少师。他作散文 500 余篇，其中《丰乐亭记》和《醉翁亭记》在当时就引起轰动。此诗是他任峡州县令时所作。丁元珍当时在峡州当判官。峡州在如今的湖北，当时却是边塞。我们的诗人由于为一位同僚辩护未果，被贬到最低级别。丁元珍于是作诗对他进行安慰。诗中所说二月是阴历，阳历则是三月。诗人说他想家了。然而他家在哪里呢？他生在四川，在首都开封待过很长时间。他提到了洛阳，离开封不远，是牡丹之城。最后两句说遭贬并未使他气馁，他一生有幸目睹了这许多美丽的花朵，所以，在峡州花开得晚也没什么可抱怨的。

9. A Chant for Inserting Flowers
(Song) Shao Yong

Flowers and tiny stems in my hair are reflected on the wine cup,

Inside the cup there are images of flowers and branches.

Having lived through two generations of peace,

I have witnessed the golden periods in four reigns.

My muscles and bones are nonetheless in good shape,

Especially I enjoy today when flowers are in full blossoms.

Flower images float in the wine, where red light flushes,

I can not but return home only after I get drunk before the flowers.

In Chinese phonetic alphabet and Chinese characters：

chā huā yín
插 花 吟
（宋）邵雍

tóu	shàng	huā	zhī	zhào	jiǔ	zhī
头	上	花	枝	照	酒	卮 ，

jiǔ	zhī	zhōng	yǒu	hǎo	huā	zhī
酒	卮	中	有	好	花	枝 。

shēn	jīng	liǎng	shì	tài	píng	rì
身	经	两	世	太	平	日 ，

yǎn	jiàn	sì	cháo	quán	shèng	shí
眼	见	四	朝	全	盛	时 。

kuàng	fù	jīn	hái	cū	kāng	jiàn
况	复	筋	骸	粗	康	健 ，

nǎ	kān	shí	jié	zhèng	fāng	fēi
那	堪	时	节	正	芳	菲 。

jiǔ	hán	huā	yǐng	hóng	guāng	liū
酒	涵	花	影	红	光	溜 ，

zhēng	rěn	huā	qián	bú	zuì	guī
争	忍	花	前	不	醉	归 。

Notes：Shao Yong（1011 - 1077）was a Taoist. He refused several times offers for being an official. He was a recluse for most part of his life. Culture was very developed in the Northern Song Dynasty. The literati enjoyed a higher social position in this period. "The four reigns" means the rule of four emperors. During their reigns there was no trouble at all at the borders, and it was a peaceful period. What he did was reading, drinking and composing poems. This poem was written in his later years, and it shows how much he enjoyed himself in a time of peace.

【说明】邵雍（1011—1077）是一位道士，他多次拒绝做官，一生大部分时间过着隐居的生活。北宋时期文化发达，文人的社会地位较高。"四朝"指四位皇帝，这四朝期间，边境无事，是和平时期。他平日读书、饮酒、作诗。此诗作于其晚年，表现了和平时期他是如何享受生活的。

10. An Allegory

(Song) Yan Shu

Ever since she left in her cart, she is nowhere to be seen,

She disappeared like the clouds above the mountain.

We were together with peach flowers in the yard under the

moon,

Watching dancing catkins while a gale was gently blown.

A hangover persisted for a few days, I felt alone,

During the Cold Food Days, what I see is a bleak scene.

I wrote her a letter, I don't know to where to post it,

Everywhere the high mountains and long rivers are a confine.

In Chinese phonetic alphabet and Chinese characters:

yù yì

寓 意

（宋）晏殊

yóu	bì	xiāng	chē	bú	zài	féng
油	壁	香	车	不	再	逢 ，
xiá	yún	wú	jì	rèn	xī	dōng
峡	云	无	迹	任	西	东 。
lí	huā	yuàn	luò	róng	róng	yuè
梨	花	院	落	溶	溶	月 ，
liǔ	xù	chí	táng	dàn	dàn	fēng
柳	絮	池	塘	淡	淡	风 。
jǐ	rì	jì	liáo	shāng	jiǔ	hòu
几	日	寂	寥	伤	酒	后 ，
yì	fān	xiāo	sè	jìn	yān	zhōng
一	番	萧	瑟	禁	烟	中 。
yú	shū	yù	jì	hé	yóu	dá
鱼	书	欲	寄	何	由	达 ，
shuǐ	yuǎn	shān	cháng	chù	chù	tóng
水	远	山	长	处	处	同 。

Notes: Yan Shu（991 - 1055）took part in the national examination when he was only fourteen years old. He was reputed as a child prodigy. He passed the examination and qualified to be an official, and he was given a job of a proof reader at the Secretariat of the royal court. He held a number of high positions in the government, to list a few: Chief Admonisher, Chief of the Privy Council, Minister of Rites, Minister of Punishment, Minister of Defense, and in 1042 he became the Prime Minister. He set up a few schools of national influence. He had a queue of students, such as Fan Zhongyan, Kong Daofu and Wang Anshi. He recommended quite a number of calibers to the cabinet, among them Han Qi became the Prime Minister for three emperors. He was more famous with his "Ci" poems, and he wrote over ten thousand of them. But, only one hundred and thirty-six survived in the form of a book, one hundred and sixty of his poems have been included in the *Complete Anthology of Song Poetry* and 53 prose essays have been included in the *Complete Collection of Song Writings*. This is apparently a love poem. Yet, as the titles suggests, the poet might allude to something else, something he treasured and loved. The lady who left in her cart is only a synonym. The original of the first line gives a special type of the cart—its compartment was painted on the outside.

【说明】晏殊（991—1055）14 岁时就参加了殿试，被誉为神童。他考试通过后，被任命为秘书正字，然后，做过一系列高官，如参知政事、枢密使、礼部、刑部和兵部尚书，1042 年任宰相。他建立了几所有全国影响的学校，门徒可以排成一长串，如范仲淹、孔道辅和王安石等。他为内阁推荐过不少人才，如韩琦后来担任过三朝宰相。他所作词更有名，作词上万首，然而，只有 136 首词在书中存留下来。他有 160 首诗被收进《全宋诗》，53 篇散文被收进《全宋文》。此诗显然是一首爱情诗。正如诗的名称所暗示的，诗里别有寓意，有他所珍爱的东西。乘车而去的伊人只是一个代名词。诗的第一句说出了那女子所乘的是油壁香车。

11. A Note on the Cold Food Day

(Song) Zhao Ding

A few gates are open in the village that seems a bit dreary,

Willow branches are stuck on each gate to mark this year's All Souls' Day.

The customs of not cooking with fire on the Cold Food Day have not reached this area,

Sweeping tombs is practiced by each family.

No sacrifices are offered at the Mausoleums of the previous dynasties,

Peach flowers on the hills and by brooks are growing tenaciously.

Just let me get drunk and lie on the ground covered with mosses,

The sounding of bugle for shutting the city gate does not bother me.

In Chinese phonetic alphabet and Chinese characters:

hán shí shū shì
寒 食 书 事

（宋）赵鼎

jì	jì	chái	mén	cūn	luò	lǐ
寂	寂	柴	门	村	落	里 ，

yě	jiào	chā	liǔ	jì	nián	huá
也	教	插	柳	纪	年	华 。

jìn	yān	bú	dào	yuè	rén	guó
禁	烟	不	到	粤	人	国 ，

shàng	zhǒng	yì	xié	páng	lǎo	jiā
上	冢	亦	携	庞	老	家 。

hàn	qǐn	táng	líng	wú	mài	fàn
汉	寝	唐	陵	无	麦	饭 ，

shān	xī	yě	jìng	yǒu	lí	huā
山	溪	野	径	有	梨	花 。

<pre>
yī   zūn   jìng jí   qīng tái wò
一   樽   竟   藉   青   苔   卧 ，
mò   guǎn chéng tóu zòu   mù jiā
莫   管   城   头   奏   暮   笳 。
</pre>

Notes：Zhao Ding（1085 - 1147）was a statesman and one of the most famous Prime Ministers in China's history. As a matter of fact he took twice the office of the Prime Minister，but he was demoted repeatedly because of his firm stand on resisting aggressors. Knowing his political enemy would not give up persecuting him，he starved himself to death. This poem was written when he was demoted to Chaozhou in today's Guangdong Province，where the custom of not using fire to make or heat food during the two days before the Tomb-Sweeping Day had not been practiced during his time. But tomb sweeping on the Tomb-Sweeping Day had been carried over and very often whole families would go to the graveyard to remember their deceased members. The poet mentioned in particular the practice of hanging willow branches on the gates of villagers on the Tomb-Sweeping Day，which was also a custom to mark a Spring. The original of the fourth line mentions a Pang of the Eastern Han period，who declined several offers of being an official and was known for bringing his entire family to sweep tombs of his ancestors. The original of the fifth line named two previous dynasties—Han and Tang Dynasty. The seeming repose mood of the poem contains strong passion of the poet：his resentment against the Song rulers who lost the northern territory and his indignation against the Jin aggressors who took over the north. The description of the Cold Food Day also carries a deep and forlorn perception of the poet on history and life.

【说明】赵鼎（1085—1147）是一位政治家，中国历史上最有名的宰相之一。实际上，他当了两任宰相，但是由于他坚定地主张抗击侵略者，被不断地降级。他知道自己的政敌不会放弃对他的迫害，最后将自己活活饿死。他被贬到当今广东的潮州时写了这首诗。那时，清明节前两天不准用火的习俗尚未传到广东。但是，清明扫墓的做法已经开始了，而且清明这天往往都是全家人出动。诗人特别提到清明时村民们在门上挂柳条，这也是表明春天到来的做法。原诗第四句提到了东晋的庞德公，此公以谢绝出仕、带领全家为先祖扫墓著称。第五句提到了汉唐两代。此诗看上去安宁的情态饱含诗人强烈的情感：他对失去北方国土的宋朝当政者的怨恨以及他对金朝侵略者的愤怒。对寒食节的描写也流露出他对历史和生活深刻的观察和凄凉之情。

12. All Souls' Day

(Song) Huang Tingjian

On All Souls' Day peach and plum flowers are in blossom,
The fields with neglected tombs are in gloom.

The roaring thunder has waken up dragons and snakes from their dormancy,

With enough spring rain grass and plants have sprouted in tendering charm.

One begged food from sacrifice offerings and lied to his wife,

There was one scholar who preferred to be burnt to death to being in the officialdom.

A thousand years later who would be regarded virtuous or vicious?

To be buried in a tomb covered with wild grass is the same doom.

In Chinese phonetic alphabet and Chinese characters:

清　明

（宋）黄庭坚

| jiā | jié | qīng | míng | táo | lǐ | xiào |
| 佳 | 节 | 清 | 明 | 桃 | 李 | 笑 ， |

| yě | tián | huāng | zhǒng | zhǐ | shēng | chóu |
| 野 | 田 | 荒 | 冢 | 只 | 生 | 愁 。 |

| léi | jīng | tiān | dì | lóng | shé | zhé |
| 雷 | 惊 | 天 | 地 | 龙 | 蛇 | 蛰 ， |

| yǔ | zú | jiāo | yuán | cǎo | mù | róu |
| 雨 | 足 | 郊 | 原 | 草 | 木 | 柔 。 |

| rén | qǐ | jì | yú | jiāo | qiè | fù |
| 人 | 乞 | 祭 | 余 | 骄 | 妾 | 妇 ， |

| shì | gān | fén | sǐ | bù | gōng | hóu |
| 士 | 甘 | 焚 | 死 | 不 | 公 | 侯 。 |

| xián | yú | qiān | zǎi | zhī | shuí | shì |
| 贤 | 愚 | 千 | 载 | 知 | 谁 | 是 ， |

| mǎn | yǎn | péng | hāo | gòng | yī | qiū |
| 满 | 眼 | 蓬 | 蒿 | 共 | 一 | 丘 。 |

Notes： This poem was composed in 1103，when the poet was demoted again to Guangxi Province，a southern most and remotest place at the time. The poet passed away only ten months after this poem. The poet went out on the Tomb-Sweeping Day，while he saw things very lively，such as peach and plum flower blossoms. He also saw things sad and gloomy，for instance the neglected tombs in the fields. At this time of the year，so many things have come to life，the thunder startled everything in the nature，including grass and plants，which have sprouted. He then remembered a person in the State of Qi，who begged food from those offering sacrifices to their deceased ones at the graveyard，and when he came home he bragged that he was treated by someone rich and important. His wife was doubtful and on the next Tomb-Sweeping Day she followed him and found out what he actually did. The poet thought，very naturally，of Jie Zhitui who died from fire and refused to come down the mountain to be an official in the royal court of the State of Jin, and for whom the Cold Food Day was to commemorate. The poet exclaimed that one thousand years later, between the two he mentioned, who would be regarded virtuous and vicious. No matter how good or bad a person is, his fate and doom is the same—to be buried in a tomb and covered by earth and wild grass. Despite the liveliness he saw in the nature, his heart was filled with dreariness. Yet, we can still see what the poet stood for, since he despised ugliness in life.

【说明】此诗作于 1103 年，那年诗人被再次贬到广西，而当时那里是最南端、最遥远的地方。此诗写后 10 个月作者就去世了。清明那天，诗人出门，看到满眼生机，桃李绽包吐艳；也看到凄惨之景，野外田间的荒冢。每年此时雷声惊天动地，惊醒了冬眠的龙蛇百虫，春雨充沛，郊外原野上草木嫩绿。他还想到当年那齐国人乞食于坟墓之间，还向妻妾夸耀；他妻子不相信他，并在第二年尾随他来到坟地，发现了他的所作所为。诗人很自然地想到被火烧死、不贪图公侯的富贵的介之推，寒食节就是为了纪念他而设立的。诗人感叹道，像那位齐人与介之推，究竟谁贤谁愚，千百年后又有谁知道呢？不管谁贤谁愚，最后都要被掩埋在长满野草的荒坟中。尽管大自然处处生机，可诗人的心中却充满凄凉。我们可以感到诗人蔑视生活中的丑陋，也知道他坚持什么。

13. All Souls' Day
(Song) Gao Zhu

So many graveyards are on the top of south and north hills,
On the All Souls' Day many families are sweeping tombs.
After being burnt joss paper turned into white butterflies,
Like cuckoo cried to bleeding sweepers have shed many tears.
At night foxes would sleep on the tombs,
When returned home children would chat and laugh before

lamps.

While alive one should get drunk whenever there is wine，

Because not even one drop of wine has made its way to the Nine Springs.

In Chinese phonetic alphabet and Chinese characters：

qīng míng
清　明
（宋）高翥

nán	běi	shān	tōu	duō	mù	tián
南	北	山	头	多	墓	田 ，
qīng	míng	jì	sǎo	gè	fēn	rán
清	明	祭	扫	各	纷	然 。
zhǐ	huī	fēi	zuò	bái	hú	dié
纸	灰	飞	作	白	蝴	蝶 ，
lèi	xuè	rǎn	chéng	hóng	dù	juān
泪	血	染	成	红	杜	鹃 。
rì	luò	hú	lí	mián	zhǒng	shàng
日	落	狐	狸	眠	冢	上 ，
yè	guī	ér	nǚ	xiào	dēng	qián
夜	归	儿	女	笑	灯	前 。
rén	shēng	yǒu	jiǔ	xū	dāng	zuì
人	生	有	酒	须	当	醉 ，
yì	dī	hé	céng	dào	jiǔ	quán
一	滴	何	曾	到	九	泉 。

Notes：Gao Zhu（1170 – 1241）was never an official and lived on teaching. He travelled quite extensively and was an important member of the Folk Society School. His paintings were also famous. He lived in a hut by a lake in his late years. You may wish to know that Chinese used to burn joss paper before tombs of their deceased relatives for them to use in the nether world. Zhuangzi（369 BC-286 BC），a philosopher of the Warring States period wrote in one of his essays that he once dreamt of becoming a butter flying freely and when he woke up he realized he was dreaming lying on his bed, he was not sure if he was the butterfly in the dream or the Zhuangzi in the dream of the butterfly. Since this story, the butterfly has served as a media between the mortal world and the nether world. The "Nine Spring" are where the deceased would live; it is also called the "Yellow Spring".

【说明】高翥（1170—1241）终身布衣，以教书为生。他游荡江湖，是江湖派重要诗人。他的画也甚有名声，晚年就生活在湖边一个简陋的草屋里。你或许也知道，中国人会在墓前给死去的故人烧纸钱，让他们在阴间用。战国时期的哲学家庄子（公元前369—公元前286年）在一篇文章里写道，他曾在梦里变成了蝴蝶自由地飞翔，当他醒来后他意识到自己在做梦，他不清楚，他到底是梦里的蝴蝶，还是蝴蝶梦里的庄子。自有了这个故事，蝴蝶就成了阳间与阴间的媒介。"九泉"是人死之后去的地方，也叫"黄泉"。

14. Improvised by a Trip to the Suburb
(Song) Cheng Hao

I enjoyed myself thoroughly when walking in the weald of green grass, plant and flower,

Spring has reached the far mountains since it is green all over.

In a high spirit I chased the flying petals and breezed through lanes where willow branches flutter,

Tired I sat on the mossy rock by the river.

One more cup please, and don't decline my toast that is so sincere,

In case everything would be blown away and such is my fear.

So rarely the All Souls' Day is on such a good weather,

Not to forget to return home after you enjoyed enough pleasure.

In Chinese phonetic alphabet and Chinese characters：

jiāo xíng jí shì
郊 行 即 事

（宋）程颢

fāng yuán lù yě zì xíng shí
芳 原 绿 野 恣 行 时 ，

chūn rù yáo shān bì sì wéi
春 入 遥 山 碧 四 围 。

xìng zhú luàn hóng chuān liǔ xiàng
兴 逐 乱 红 穿 柳 巷 ，

kùn lín liú shuǐ zuò tái jī
困 临 流 水 坐 苔 矶 。

mò cí zhǎn jiǔ shí fēn quàn
莫 辞 盏 酒 十 分 劝 ，

zhǐ kǒng fēng huā yí piàn fēi
只 恐 风 花 一 片 飞 。

kuàng shì qīng míng hǎo tiān qì
况 是 清 明 好 天 气 ，

bù fáng yóu yǎn mò wàng guī
不 妨 游 衍 莫 忘 归 。

Notes：The poem can be divided into two parts. The first four lines are devoted to his outing and the last four to his reflections on the outing. While he was sitting on the mossy rock，he saw the fallen flowers being carried away in the river，he might have thought of the precious time，of so many departures from friends and so few gatherings with them，and that things nice would not last long，and he might have concluded that to treasure what is good today is to treasure his entire life.

【说明】此诗可分为两部分。前四句写的是郊游，后四句写的是对郊游的想法。当他坐在长满青苔的岩石上，看落花被河水带走时，他可能会想到时间之宝贵，可能会想到与朋友离多聚少，也会想到好东西往往不长久，他可能会得出这样的结论：珍惜今日所有的美好，就是珍惜了自己的一生。

15. On a Swing

(Song) Shi Huihong

With a decorated stand and colored ropes the swing is swaying up to the air,

A young girl is amusing herself with the swing before the building in spring.

While swaying her scarlet skirt is brushing the ground,

The colored ropes are sending her up and she is scared by the swing.

Her sweat, like dews from apricot flowers, is dropping on the stand,

Among willow branches the colored ropes look like a mist hanging.

When she gets off the swing she stands there composed and calm,

As if she was the Moon Goddess and has just finished landing.

In Chinese phonetic alphabet and Chinese characters:

qiū qiān
秋 千

（宋）释惠洪

huà	jià	shuāng	cái	cuì	luò	piān
画	架	双	裁	翠	络	偏，
jiā	rén	chūn	xì	xiǎo	lóu	qián
佳	人	春	戏	小	楼	前。
piāo	yáng	xuè	sè	qún	tuō	dì
飘	扬	血	色	裙	拖	地，
duàn	sòng	yù	róng	rén	shàng	tiān
断	送	玉	容	人	上	天。
huā	bǎn	rùn	zhān	hóng	xìng	yǔ
花	板	润	沾	红	杏	雨，
cǎi	shéng	xiá	guà	lù	yáng	yān
彩	绳	斜	挂	绿	杨	烟。

xià	lái	xián	chù	cōng	róng	lì
下	来	闲	处	从	容	立 ，

yí	shì	chán	gōng	zhé	jiàng	xiān
疑	是	蟾	宫	谪	降	仙 。

Notes：Huihong（1071-1128）was a famous monk of the Song Dynasty. His parents passed away when he was fourteen years old. He became a monk when he was nineteen. He was a student of Huang Tingjian. He accomplished a lot in studies of the Chan sect of Buddhism，education，history，poetry and literature. The poem depicts the pleasure of playing a swing，the beauty of the player，her dress，the decorated swing and pleasant ambience. It is a bit unusual for a monk to care about such matters in the secular world.

【说明】 惠洪（1071—1128）是宋朝名僧。他 14 岁时父母双亡，19 岁时当了和尚。他是黄庭坚的学生，集禅、教、史、诗、文于一身。这首诗写了荡秋千之快乐，荡秋千的美人裙装掠地，秋千的画饰，以及美妙的氛围。一位僧人会对凡间的这种事物如此关注有些不一般。

16. The Qujiang River（1）
(Tang) Du Fu

The dropping of one petal reduces the fullness of spring，
The blowing down of ten thousand of petals makes me worry.
Before my eyes all of them will be blown away，
I no longer refuse to have more liquor that to me was an injury.
Halcyons have nest built in the small chamber by the river，
The stalwart stone unicorns by the high graves are toppled to the ground in deformity.

I pondered and decide I should loose no time to find more
pleasures to enjoy,

And forget the constraining smugness and vanity.

In Chinese phonetic alphabet and Chinese characters：

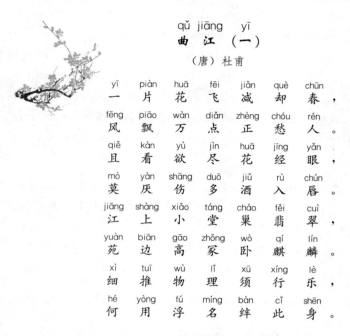

qǔ jiāng　yī
曲　江　（一）

（唐）杜甫

一 片 花 飞 减 却 春，
yī piàn huā fēi jiǎn què chūn

风 飘 万 点 正 愁 人。
fēng piāo wàn diǎn zhèng chóu rén

且 看 欲 尽 花 经 眼，
qiě kàn yù jìn huā jīng yǎn

莫 厌 伤 多 酒 入 唇。
mò yàn shāng duō jiǔ rù chún

江 上 小 堂 巢 翡 翠，
jiāng shàng xiǎo táng cháo fěi cuì

苑 边 高 冢 卧 麒 麟。
yuàn biān gāo zhǒng wò qí lín

细 推 物 理 须 行 乐，
xì tuī wù lǐ xū xíng lè

何 用 浮 名 绊 此 身。
hé yòng fú míng bàn cǐ shēn

Notes：The poet was determined to contribute to the country，
yet he was only a petty official and his recommendations to the state
had been refused. At the sight of the late spring scene at the
Qujiang River，he wrote this poem to release his pent up grief. The
river was a point of interest at the southwest of Xi'an，which is
now dried up. The seemingly broad-mind tones of the poem can not
hide away his profound grief and pain in his heart.

【说明】诗人一心报国，然而官小位卑，他提出的政策建议也
没人采纳。目睹曲江暮春的景色，杜甫写此诗来排遣心中的苦闷。
曲江曾是长安西南的旅游胜地，现在已经干枯了。诗的意境很宏

阔，却也流露出杜甫内心的悲伤与痛苦。

17．The Qujiang River (2)
(Tang) Du Fu

Back from the royal court everyday I had some of my spring clothes pawned，

I went home only when I got drunk by the riverside.

Having wine debt everywhere was my normal deed，

It was rare to become seventy years old.

Butterflies among flowers appeared and disappeared，

Dragonflies moved slowly on the water and sometimes skimmed.

I wish to be with spring time，please pass on this word，

Short our mutual appreciation maybe we should not be parted.

In Chinese phonetic alphabet and Chinese characters：

qǔ jiāng èr
曲 江 （二）
（唐）杜甫

cháo huí rì rì diǎn chūn yī
朝 回 日 日 典 春 衣 ，

měi rì jiāng tóu jìn zuì guī
每 日 江 头 尽 醉 归 。

jiǔ zhài xún cháng xíng chù yǒu
酒 债 寻 常 行 处 有 ，

rén shēng qí shí gǔ lái xī
人 生 七 十 古 来 稀 。

chuān huā jiá dié shēn shēn xiàn
穿 花 蛱 蝶 深 深 见 ，

diǎn shuǐ qīng tíng kuǎn kuǎn fēi
点 水 蜻 蜓 款 款 飞 。

chuán yǔ fēng guāng gòng liú zhuǎn
传 语 风 光 共 流 转 ，

zàn shí xiāng shǎng mò xiāng wéi
暂 时 相 赏 莫 相 违 。

Notes: The poet pawned his spring clothes everyday, so he must have pawned his winter clothes already. Did he need the money for his food or things urgent? No, he used his money to get drunk. When he had pawned all his clothes, he had to buy wine on credit. When he wrote this poem he was forty-six, it was really a rare matter for any person at his time to be seventy. In other words, he thought he would not live that long, so he should get enough to drink at the present since it was not possible to realize his own will. The fifth and sixth lines have been famous in presenting a tranquil, free and beautiful ambience, which would be gone very soon. The poet now wanted to tell the spring that he wished to stay with spring longer for he loved it so much.

【说明】诗人每天都要当掉一件他春天穿的衣服，冬衣已经当完了。他急着用钱买粮食或有什么急用吗？不是的。他用钱买酒为了把自己灌醉。把衣服都当完了，就只好赊账了。他写此诗时 46 岁，那时候的人活到 70 岁是很少见的。换句话说，他觉得自己活不长了，既然无法实现自己的抱负，就喝个够吧。第五、第六句是写静谧、无拘无束的美妙氛围的名句。对诗人来说，这氛围很快就要失去了。诗人要告诉春天，他热爱春天，希望春天能留得久一些。

18. The Tower of Yellow Crane
(Tang) Cui Hao

The immortals left by riding on the yellow crane in the past,
Leaving behind the Tower of Yellow Crane vacant.
Cranes never made a second visit,
For thousand years the tower watched white clouds float.
Over the river trees in Hanyang are so distinct,
Green grass is so vivid on the Land Bar of Parrot.

I don't know where hometown is at this time of sunset,
The mist on the river troubles my heavy heart.

In Chinese phonetic alphabet and Chinese characters:

huáng hè lóu
黄 鹤 楼
（唐）崔颢

xī	rén	yǐ	chéng	huáng	hè	qù	
昔	人	已	乘	黄	鹤	去	，

cǐ	dì	kōng	yú	huáng	hè	lóu	
此	地	空	余	黄	鹤	楼	。

huáng	hè	yí	qù	bú	fù	fǎn	
黄	鹤	一	去	不	复	返	，

bái	yún	qiān	zǎi	kōng	yōu	yōu	
白	云	千	载	空	悠	悠	。

qíng	chuān	lì	lì	hàn	yáng	shù	
晴	川	历	历	汉	阳	树	，

fāng	cǎo	qī	qī	yīng	wǔ	zhōu	
芳	草	萋	萋	鹦	鹉	洲	。

rì	mù	xiāng	guān	hé	chù	shì	
日	暮	乡	关	何	处	是	，

yān	bō	jiāng	shàng	shǐ	rén	chóu	
烟	波	江	上	使	人	愁	。

Notes: Cui Hao （704? – 754） was Head of the Transportation Department and Deputy Head of Land Distribution. Other than that we don't know much about him. Yet, this poem of his has been known to every person in China who attended school. The Tower of Yellow Crane was first built in the period of the Kingdom of Wu （229 AD-280 AD） at the city of Wuchang by the side of the Changjiang River. According to some legends an immortal named Zi'an once stayed in the tower. It was said Fei Yi, an important official of the Kingdom of Shu left the secular world by riding on a crane from this tower and became an immortal. Hanyang is on the other side of the river and in direct opposite of the tower. The Land

Bar of Parrot was to the northeast of the tower, so named because someone contributed parrot to the then Chief Administrator of the region in the Han period when he was throwing out a party on the Land Bar. It was said when Li Bai ascended the tower and saw Cui Hao's poem on the wall, he sighed that he could not write another poem on the tower even though he had much to say, fearing his might not be as good. Some critics say among all seven-characters octaves Cui Hao's ranks number one.

【说明】崔颢（704？—754）曾任太仆寺丞、司勋员外郎。他的其他情况我们所知甚少。但是，这首诗在中国家喻户晓，上过学的都学过这首诗。黄鹤楼始建于三国之吴国时期（229—280），修建在武昌长江岸边。传说仙人子安曾在黄鹤楼休憩。据说蜀国一名重要的官员费祎就是在此楼乘黄鹤离开了尘世成为仙人的。汉阳在江对面正对着黄鹤楼的地方，鹦鹉洲在楼的东北；汉朝太守在此大宴宾客，有人给他献了鹦鹉，此后，这个地方就叫鹦鹉洲了。有人讲李白曾登上此楼，看到崔颢在墙上题的这首诗后，深有感触地说："眼前有景道不得，崔颢题诗在上头。"也有评论家认为，在所有的七律作者中，崔颢排第一。

19. Thoughts on Staying away from Home
(Tang) Cui Tu

Merciless are both the floating water and withering flower,
They see off the east wind to the former Chu area.
I was a butterfly in my dream and back to my hometown ten thousand miles afar,
The cuckoo cries on a tree branch when the moon is sliding at night.
No letters reached me from home through the year,
Spring has turned my temples hair grayer.

I don't choose to return home even though I could do so whenever,

For the mist scene at the Five Lakes I could fine no contender.

In Chinese phonetic alphabet and Chinese characters:

lǚ huái
旅 怀

（唐）崔涂

shuǐ	liú	huā	xiè	liǎng	wú	qíng
水	流	花	谢	两	无	情 ，
sòng	jìn	dōng	fēng	guò	chǔ	chéng
送	尽	东	风	过	楚	城 。
hú	dié	mèng	zhōng	jiā	wàn	lǐ
蝴	蝶	梦	中	家	万	里 ，
dù	juān	zhī	shàng	yuè	sān	gēng
杜	鹃	枝	上	月	三	更 。
gù	yuán	shū	dòng	jīng	nián	jué
故	园	书	动	经	年	绝 ，
huá	fà	chūn	cuī	liǎng	bìn	shēng
华	发	春	催	两	鬓	生 。
zì	shì	bù	guī	guī	biàn	dé
自	是	不	归	归	便	得 ，
wǔ	hú	yān	jǐng	yǒu	shuí	zhēng
五	湖	烟	景	有	谁	争 。

Notes：Cui Tu （? – approx. 887） was born in today's Zhejiang Province，but lived for a long time in Sichuan，Hunan and Hubei. He called himself a "lonely alien". Most of his poems were about his wandering life，and in a depressed and desolate tone. The Chu area in the original is Chu city，both mean areas of the former State of Chu. The Five Lakes in the poem refer to the areas of Lake Taihu. This is a poem about missing home. The whole poem is soaked in the home missing feeling，yet the poet did not use the words "missing home."

【说明】崔涂（? —约887）生在今日浙江，长期生活在四川、

165

湖南和湖北。他称自己为"孤独异乡人"。他的诗大都写他漂泊的生活，情调抑郁苍凉。诗中的楚城指过去楚国的地域。五湖泛指太湖一带。这首诗写的是乡愁。全诗都浸泡在思乡的情感中，然而，诗人并没有使用"思乡"一词。

20. Reply to Li Dan
(Tang) Wei Yingwu

Last year we parted when flowers were in full bloom,

Today flowers flourish again and another year is now a past time.

Things in the world are ambiguous and difficult to predict,

Unable to sleep because of spring melancholy and boredom.

I am disease-ridden and missing home,

I don't found shelters for all the homeless and it's a shame.

I heard you want to come and see me,

I hope you can be here before the moon over the west tower takes its next round form.

In Chinese phonetic alphabet and Chinese characters:

dá lǐ dān
答 李 儋

（唐）韦应物

qù	nián	huā	lǐ	féng	jūn	bié
去	年	花	里	逢	君	别 ，

jīn	rì	huā	kāi	yòu	yì	nián
今	日	花	开	又	一	年 。

shì	shì	máng	máng	nán	zì	liào
世	事	茫	茫	难	自	料 ，

chūn	chóu	àn	àn	dú	chéng	mián
春	愁	黯	黯	独	成	眠 。

shēn	duō	jí	bìng	sī	tián	lǐ
身	多	疾	病	思	田	里，

yì	yǒu	liú	wáng	kuì	fèng	qián
邑	有	流	亡	愧	俸	钱。

wén	dào	yù	lái	xiāng	wèn	xùn
闻	道	欲	来	相	问	讯，

xī	lóu	wàng	yuè	jǐ	huí	yuán
西	楼	望	月	几	回	圆。

Notes: This poem was composed in 784 when the poet was transferred to Chuzhou as the Chief Administrator there. Li Dan was a member of the imperial family and a good friend of the poet. They often exchange poems. The poem was composed when there was a turbulent change in the imperial court. The poem showed his sympathy towards common folks, his loneliness and his longing for the visit of his friends as well.

【说明】这首诗作于 784 年，此时诗人已经到滁州当刺史了。李儋是皇亲，也是诗人的朋友。两人经常交换诗作。作此诗时正逢朝廷有大的变故，此诗表现出他对普通百姓的同情、他的孤寂以及他期盼朋友来访的心情。

21．Village by the River
(Tang) Du Fu

The clear and meandering river encircles the village,
In the long summer days everything seems to have polish.
Swallows come to rest on the beams and leave as they wish,
The amicable white gull couples fully enjoy their marriage.
My wife is drawing a chessboard on paper and would soon finish,
My youngest son is hammering a needle to make a barb to fish.

I am disease-ridden and what I need most is medicine,

Other than that my humble body doesn't need anything.

In Chinese phonetic alphabet and Chinese characters:

jiāng cūn
江 村

（唐）杜甫

qīng	jiāng	yì	qū	bào	cūn	liú
清	江	一	曲	抱	村	流 ，
cháng	xià	jiāng	cūn	shì	shì	yōu
长	夏	江	村	事	事	幽 。
zì	qù	zì	lái	liáng	shàng	yàn
自	去	自	来	梁	上	燕 ，
xiāng	qīn	xiāng	jìn	shuǐ	zhōng	ōu
相	亲	相	近	水	中	鸥 。
lǎo	qī	huà	zhǐ	wéi	qí	jú
老	妻	画	纸	为	棋	局 ，
zhì	zǐ	qiāo	zhēn	zuò	diào	gōu
稚	子	敲	针	作	钓	钩 。
duō	bìng	suǒ	xū	wéi	yào	wù
多	病	所	须	惟	药	物 ，
wēi	qū	cǐ	wài	gèng	hé	qiú
微	躯	此	外	更	何	求 。

Notes：This poem was composed in 760 when the poet finally ended his four-year long turbulent life and settled down in the near suburb of Chengdu, a south-western city, and where his family was able and had time to do things for their pleasure; yet, regrettably, the poet's health was ruined and he didn't want to ask more for life, enough medicine was all he needed.

【说明】此诗作于 760 年，杜甫终于结束了 4 年颠沛流离的生活，在西南方成都市的郊区安顿了下来。他的家人和他都有时间做喜欢的事了。但遗憾的是诗人的身体不好了，他对生活的要求不多，能有足够的药吃就行了。

22. On a Summer Day

(Song) Zhang Lei

The sun is high and breeze goes through the village on a long summer day,

Having become fully fledged, finches on the eaves are so happy.

Butterflies open their wings for the sunlight on the flower spray,

Adding to the web in the bright corner the spider is so busy.

The curtain invited the moonlight to keep its sparse strips company,

With my head on the pillow the rippling stream is heard clearly.

For a long time my hair on the temples has been gray,

In the rest of my life I wish to live as a fisherman or a woodcutter everyday.

In Chinese phonetic alphabet and Chinese characters:

xià rì
夏 日

（宋）张耒

cháng	xià	jiāng	cūn	fēng	rì	qīng
长	夏	江	村	风	日	清 ，

yán	yá	yàn	què	yǐ	shēng	chéng
檐	牙	燕	雀	已	生	成 。

dié	yī	shài	fěn	huā	zhī	wǔ
蝶	衣	晒	粉	花	枝	舞 ，

zhū	wǎng	tiān	sī	wū	jiǎo	qíng
蛛	网	添	丝	屋	角	晴 。

luò	luò	shū	lián	yāo	yuè	yǐng
落	落	疏	帘	邀	月	影 ，

cáo cáo xū zhěn nà xī shēng
嘈 嘈 虚 枕 纳 溪 声 。

jiǔ bān liǎng bìn rú shuāng xuě
久 斑 两 鬓 如 霜 雪 ,

zhí yù qiáo yú guò cǐ shēng
直 欲 樵 渔 过 此 生 。

Notes：Zhang Lei was born in 1054 and passed away in 1114. As far as his official career is concerned，he had a rugged path，yet in the sphere of literature，he was widely known as one of the Four Scholars of the Su Shi School（Qin Guan，Huang Tingjian and Chao Buzhi are the other three），and as he lived longer than the other three，he had more followers and his works were repeatedly printed. One contemporary collection of his works includes over 2,300 poems and more than 300 essays. We can find motion in the quiescence and vise versa in this poem. The movements of finches，butterflies and spiders reflect the tranquility in the poet's village，which is full of life and fun. Through the moonlight，the bamboo curtain，the rippling stream，the poet has made himself one element of the nature；and further，we can see the poet was fond of the country life and understand why he wanted to become a fisherman or a woodcutter.

【说明】张耒（1054—1114）仕途坎坷，然而在文学界素负盛名，是苏门四学士之一（其他三人是秦观、黄庭坚和晁补之），由于他活得比其他三人久，他的门生很多，其作品亦流传很广。有一部文集收入他的诗作 2 300 首，文章 300 多篇。这首诗静中有动，动中有静。在诗人的村子里，燕雀、蝴蝶和蜘蛛营造出静谧的状态，而且充满生机和乐趣。透过月光、竹帘和溪声，诗人也成了大自然的一部分。进一步说，诗人喜爱农村的生活，我们也明白了诗人何以要做渔夫和樵夫了。

23. After a Long Rain at Wangchuan

(Tang) Wang Wei

Kitchen smoke ascends late for the long rain has damped the firewood,

To farmers working east to the village some pot luck was delivered.

A row of egrets dashed up to the sky from the vast paddy field,

Loriots are chirping from the dark shades in the summer forest.

I've been trying to improve my morality by watching quietly the hibiscus day and night,

A vegetarian, under a pine, I snap an okra, still having dew on it, and eat.

Having scrambled for a seat was the rustic old man who just visited,

On what ground the sea gulls are suspecting the intention of the child?

In Chinese phonetic alphabet and Chinese characters:

wǎng chuān jī yǔ
辋 川 积 雨

（唐）王维

jī	yǔ	kōng	lín	yān	huǒ	chí
积	雨	空	林	烟	火	迟 ，

zhēng	lí	chuī	shǔ	xiǎng	dōng	zī
蒸	藜	炊	黍	饷	东	菑 。

mò	mò	shuǐ	tián	fēi	bái	lù
漠	漠	水	田	飞	白	鹭 ，

yīn	yīn	xià	mù	zhuàn	huáng	lí
阴	阴	夏	木	啭	黄	鹂 。

shān	zhōng	xí	jìng	guān	zhāo	jǐn
山	中	习	静	观	朝	槿 ，

sōng	xià	qīng	zhāi	zhé	lù	kuí
松	下	清	斋	折	露	葵 。

yě	lǎo	yú	rén	zhēng	xí	bà
野	老	与	人	争	席	罢 ，

hǎi	ōu	hé	shì	gèng	xiāng	yí
海	鸥	何	事	更	相	疑 。

Notes: This is one of the most famous georgics written by Wang Wei, who has been reputed as a "Buddha Poet". For an ordinary man, watching hibiscus all day long and eat plants as food was almost unbearable. Yet, the poet was so pleased and contented to do so, and actually, such lines reveal his Buddhist mind-set. To the poet, elegant, peaceful and retiring life is a pleasure. I should point out that each of the last two lines contains one classical allusion. Literally the 7th line reads: Having scrambled for a seat was a rustic old man. Such a line is apparently adopted from a Classic—*Zhuangzi*, which collected sayings of Zhuangzi, the most renowned Taoist master only next to Laozi. In the Classic, a scholar went to ask for instruction from Laozi, and when he came to a guest house where Laozi stayed, "the host arranged his seat and the hostess handed him a basin of water, a towel and a comb. The guests gave their seats to him and those who were warming themselves by the stove stepped aside to let him take over the spot. But when he returned from his talk with Laozi, the other visitors scrambled for the best seat with him." That means his talk with Laozi has changed him so much, that others no longer treated him specially. With this story, Wang Wei was saying he had become a rustic villager, just as everybody around him who stayed far from the madding crowd. The last line reads literally: On what ground the sea gulls are suspecting the intention of the child? Again, there is a story behind it. The story, adopted from another Classic—*Liezi*, goes like this: a child used to play by a seaside with a number of sea gulls, who enjoyed his company. But, one day after playing, the child went back home and his father said to him, "please bring one sea gull back tomorrow for me to play with." The next day, when the child came to the seaside, all of the sea gulls were flying high in the sky and none of them had the intention to land at the beach. With this story, Wang Wei was asking on what ground the sea gulls are suspecting the intention of the child. The last two lines may sound somewhat strange to English readers, and I hope the stories could help a bit in their reading.

【说明】这是王维最有名的田园诗之一。王维被誉为"诗佛"。对一个普通人来说，整日观看木槿，采露葵而食，未免过分孤寂寡淡。但是，对于诗人来讲这却是一件令他心满意足的事情。从这几句诗可以看出他信佛的心境。对于他来说雅致、平静的事物和禅寂的生活就是他最大的乐趣。应该指出最后两句里，每句都含有一个典故。第七句："野老与人争席罢"，典出《庄子》。此书收集的是庄子的讲话。庄子是名声仅次于老子的道家大师。《庄子》里说一位学者去向老子请教，他刚到老子所住的店时，店主人给他让座，女主人递给他一盆热水、一条毛巾和一个梳子。其他客人也让出地方来让他烤火。但是，他与老子谈话完毕后，其他客人跟他一起抢夺座位。这就是说，他与老子谈话后变化巨大，其他人不再把他当外人看待了。王维用这个典故是想说，那位学者也变成了粗野的村民，与周围的其他人一样远离喧闹的人群，与世无争了。诗的最后一行说：海鸥何事更相疑。这里面也有从《列子》里引用的一个故事。这个故事说一个小孩在海边与一群海鸥戏耍，这群海鸥跟他玩得也开心。一天，玩过之后，这小孩回到家中，他父亲说，"明天带一只海鸥回来给我玩玩"。第二天，小孩又来到海边，所有的海鸥都在天上飞着，没有一点落下来的意思。王维用这个故事问道：海鸥为什么会怀疑这个孩子呢？最后这两句对英语读者来说可能有些怪异，希望这两个故事能帮助大家理解原文。

24. Fresh Bamboo

(Song) Lu You

I planted a hedge of shrubs to give fresh bamboo a good care,

Rippling in the water is the bamboo verdure.

When a gust swept over you found autumn was here,

The sun is high and you don't realize it is noon time proper.

When the outer skin was peeling off, a rustle sound you may
hear,

When jointing is growing out, their shadows on the ground
scatter.

I make frequent visits for I've retired and live in pleasure,

So, bamboo pillow and mats are with me always and ever.

In Chinese phonetic alphabet and Chinese characters:

xīn zhú
新 竹
（宋）陆游

chā	jí	biān	lí	jǐn	hù	chí
插	棘	编	篱	谨	护	持 ，
yǎng	chéng	hán	bì	yìng	lián	yī
养	成	寒	碧	映	涟	漪 。
qīng	fēng	lüè	dì	qiū	xiān	dào
清	风	掠	地	秋	先	到 ，
chì	rì	xíng	tiān	wǔ	bù	zhī
赤	日	行	天	午	不	知 。
jiě	tuò	shí	wén	shēng	sù	sù
解	箨	时	闻	声	簌	簌 ，
fàng	shāo	chū	jiàn	yǐng	lí	lí
放	梢	初	见	影	离	离 。
guī	xián	wǒ	yù	pín	lái	cǐ
归	闲	我	欲	频	来	此 ，
zhěn	diàn	réng	jiào	dào	chù	suí
枕	簟	仍	教	到	处	随 。

Notes：Lu You （1125－1210）, is known as "Fangweng",

174

who served as an Ombudsman at two places, he stood firmly for recovering the lost land in the north. He is the most proliferous poet of China; he composed over ten thousand poems in his life time. Most of his poems are vehement, stirring, moving and encouraging. One late Qing critic Liang Qichao wrote down such a comment after he read the collection of Lu's poems, "For a thousand years, the atmosphere in the poetry circle has been soft and frail, where the strong and masculine militancy was lost and the soul of our nation was dead. Fang Weng was the only man in so long a period, who was longing for defending the country and elated for having joined the army in ninety percent of his poems." But, this poem is not militant at all, it described how much the poet was fond of the fresh bamboo and whereby his noble and chaste sentiment was reflected.

【说明】陆游（1125—1210），号放翁，在两个地方当过通判。他坚决主张抗金，收复失地。他是中国最高产的诗人，一生作诗超过万首。他的诗大都热情洋溢、激动人心、感人至深、促人上进。清末评论家梁启超读过他的诗集后写道：“诗界千年靡靡风，兵魂销尽国魂空。篇中什九从军乐，亘古男儿一放翁。”但是，我们读的这首诗没有任何战斗性。它描写了诗人喜爱新竹，这种爱好反映了诗人高尚纯真的性情。

25. A Night Reminiscing with My Cousin
(Tang) Dou Shuxiang

At night the courtyard was filled up with the scent of evening primrose,

We sobered up when it drizzled in the small hours.

Precious were our letters, but they never reached our relatives,

We could no longer bear to recall our past miseries.

The children at our departure are now grown-ups,

Half of our relatives and friends have left us.

I shall again depart lonely by a boat tomorrow,

A sight at the wine shop banner by the river would arouse forlornness.

In Chinese phonetic alphabet and Chinese characters:

biǎo xiōng huà jiù
表 兄 话 旧
（唐）窦叔向

yè	hé	huā	kāi	xiāng	mǎn	tíng
夜	合	花	开	香	满	庭 ，

yè	shēn	wēi	yǔ	zuì	chū	xǐng
夜	深	微	雨	醉	初	醒 。

yuǎn	shū	zhēn	zhòng	hé	yóu	dá
远	书	珍	重	何	由	达 ，

jiù	shì	qī	liáng	bù	kě	tīng
旧	事	凄	凉	不	可	听 。

qù	rì	ér	tóng	jiē	zhǎng	dà
去	日	儿	童	皆	长	大 ，

xī	nián	qīn	yǒu	bàn	diāo	líng
昔	年	亲	友	半	凋	零 。

míng	zhāo	yòu	shì	gū	zhōu	bié
明	朝	又	是	孤	舟	别 ，

chóu	jiàn	hé	qiáo	jiǔ	màn	qīng
愁	见	河	桥	酒	幔	青 。

Notes: No dates of birth and death are available for Dou Shuxiang. The highest position he held in the government was the Minister of Works. Only nine of his poems are available. Most critics like this poem, because it describes things very normal, and it says what everybody would say, yet it said the normal words in a provoking way. When the poet said he would depart again tomorrow, it implied that when he comes back again today's children may grow old and half of his relatives and friends would no longer be alive. And such is the saddest thing for a human being.

【说明】窦叔向的生卒年不详。他官至工部尚书。他的诗只有九首存世。很多评论家都喜欢这首诗，因为此诗写人人同有之事、人人欲说之话，不叹他写得出来，却叹他写得出人意料。"明朝又别"四字，隐然言他日再归，今日的孩童已变得年迈，今日的亲友也所剩无几。可不谓之大哀也哉？

26. An Extempore
(Song) Cheng Hao

In my secluded life，things are done with ease，
When I wake up，the red sun often hangs on the eastern window.
I always gain some ideas by watching things that are still，
The zest people have for each of the four seasons is never low.
Basic truth is contained in things both tangible and intangible，
Thoughts would permeate through even when changes are forceful.

If a man keeps his high spirit when he is straitened and humble.

If he refuses luxurious pleasure when he's rich，he then is a true hero.

In Chinese phonetic alphabet and Chinese characters：

ǒu chéng
偶　成
（宋）程颢

xián	lái	wú	shì	bù	cóng	róng
闲	来	无	事	不	从	容 ，
shuì	jiào	dōng	chuāng	rì	yǐ	hóng
睡	觉	东	窗	日	已	红 ；
wàn	wù	jìng	guān	jiē	zì	dé
万	物	静	观	皆	自	得 ，

sì	shí	jiā	xìng	yǔ	rén	tóng
四	时	佳	兴	与	人	同 。

dào	tōng	tiān	dì	yǒu	xíng	wài
道	通	天	地	有	形	外 ，

sī	rù	fēng	yún	biàn	tài	zhōng
思	入	风	云	变	态	中 ；

fù	guì	bù	yín	pín	jiàn	lè
富	贵	不	淫	贫	贱	乐 ，

nán	ér	dào	cǐ	shì	háo	xióng
男	儿	到	此	是	豪	雄 。

Notes：This is the fourth poem composed by Cheng Hao in this collection. The poem reveals the poet's attitude towards life. He no longer cares about personal gains or losses，he feels no pressure whatsoever，he can get sufficient sleep，he finds things interesting by watching still objects，he is able to savor different taste of each season and gains endless pleasure from the nature. He tells us what a true hero is，and he wants to be such a man，who does not bend to desires for extravagant life and he is always in his high spirit no matter being poor or rich，noble or humble.

【说明】这是本集所收程颢的第四首诗。此诗揭示了诗人对待生活的态度。他不再在乎个人得失，在生活中全然没有压力，他能得到足够的睡眠，他观察静物可以发现有趣之事，他能品味四季中不同的美味，从大自然里得到无穷的乐趣。他告诉我们何为真英雄，他想做这样的人，一个不为奢侈的生活而改变初衷的人，一个不论贫富、不论贵贱都始终保持高昂斗志的人。

27. Touring the Moon-Shaped Pond
(Song) Cheng Hao

Around the pond I wander，
To the north there is a hundred-foot high tower.
When autumn wind blows，everywhere is a bleak picture，
Why not dry up a glass before the evening is colder.

The images of clouds look at each other in the water，

In quietness in the forest，the flowing sound of spring we can hear.

Unexpected changes of matter is nothing we should bother，

We should make appointments to meet for festivals in the future.

In Chinese phonetic alphabet and Chinese characters：

yóu yuè bēi
游 月 陂

（宋）程颢

yuè	bēi	dī	shàng	sì	pái	huái
月	陂	堤	上	四	徘	徊

běi	yǒu	zhōng	tiān	bǎi	chǐ	tái
北	有	中	天	百	尺	台

wàn	wù	yǐ	suí	qiū	qì	gǎi
万	物	已	随	秋	气	改

yì	zūn	liáo	wéi	wǎn	liáng	kāi
一	樽	聊	为	晚	凉	开

shuǐ	xīn	yún	yǐng	xián	xiāng	zhào
水	心	云	影	闲	相	照

lín	xià	quán	shēng	jìng	zì	lái
林	下	泉	声	静	自	来

shì	shì	wú	duān	hé	zú	jì
世	事	无	端	何	足	计

dàn	féng	jiā	jié	yuē	chóng	péi
但	逢	佳	节	约	重	陪

Notes：By noting down his travel at the pond，the poet also tells us his attitude towards life. His mind is so peaceful，he sees how the images of clouds looking at each other and he could hear the sound of spring in the forest. He does not wish to be bothered by anything else，parties with relatives and friends are most important.

【说明】通过记录游月陂的情况，诗人吐露了他的生活态度。

179

他心中静谧，看到"水心云影闲相照，林下泉声静自来"；他不想被世间事务所打扰，只要在佳节能约几个亲友相聚就是最重要的事情了。

28. Being Prompted by the Autumn (1)

(Tang) Du Fu

Maple tress are withering, being bitten by autumn dew,

A bleak and cold mist hangs over the Wushan valley and hill.

The river is surging ahead billow after billow,

The blanket of dark clouds is pressing down so low.

I could not hold back my tears seeing daisy has bloomed twice,

The lonely boat can witness how much I miss homeland.

People are organized to rush out cotton-padded clothes,

On top of the city wall cloth are being beaten and washed in exigence.

In Chinese phonetic alphabet and Chinese characters：

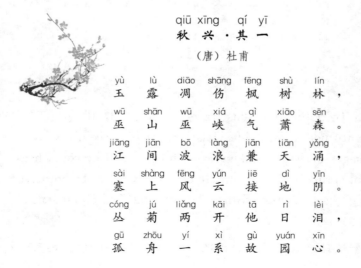

qiū xīng · qí yī
秋 兴 · 其 一

（唐）杜甫

yù	lù	diāo	shāng	fēng	shù	lín
玉	露	凋	伤	枫	树	林 ，
wū	shān	wū	xiá	qì	xiāo	sēn
巫	山	巫	峡	气	萧	森 。
jiāng	jiān	bō	làng	jiān	tiān	yǒng
江	间	波	浪	兼	天	涌 ，
sài	shàng	fēng	yún	jiē	dì	yīn
塞	上	风	云	接	地	阴 。
cóng	jú	liǎng	kāi	tā	rì	lèi
丛	菊	两	开	他	日	泪 ，
gū	zhōu	yí	xì	gù	yuán	xīn
孤	舟	一	系	故	园	心 。

hán	yī	chù	chù	cuī	dāo	chǐ
寒	衣	处	处	催	刀	尺 ，

bái	dì	chéng	gāo	jí	mù	zhēn
白	帝	城	高	急	暮	砧 。

Notes：This poem was composed in 766 when the poet was 55 years old when he was still trying to stay away from wars and living temporarily at Kuizhou，and when autumn wind rose，he felt so chilly and misery and then this poem was conceived，which turned out to be one of the most representative of his poetry. The whole poem，soaked in sorrow，is soul-stirring. Its deliberately arranged meter and cadences project a tragic and profound conception，which is most touching. It should be pointed out that there are altogether eight of them under the same title，and the eight of them constitute a group in its entirety.

【说明】此诗作于766年，诗人当时55岁，仍在躲避战乱，暂时住在夔州。秋风起时，他感到寒冷、凄凉，于是构思了这组诗。此诗也成为他的代表作。全诗浸透在凄清哀怨中，动人心魄。此诗词彩华茂，沉郁顿挫，悲壮凄凉，意境深远，读来令人荡气回肠。这组诗共有八首，是一篇完整的乐章。

29. Being Prompted by the Autumn (3)
(Tang) Du Fu

In the fall，morning sun casts at the hilly city and its inhabitants quietly.

I sit in the tower by the river and face the verdant scene everyday.

The fisherman is still drifting in the river having slept two nights on the boat already.

Swallows seem flying to and fro before me deliberately.

Kuang Heng was promoted after submitting a memorial, but for me it was a different story,

Like Liu Xiang, I also preached classics, yet, he was awarded, but not me.

Most of my teenager classmates went up the social ladder rapidly,

Living in rich quarters and their life is spent in real luxury.

In Chinese phonetic alphabet and Chinese characters:

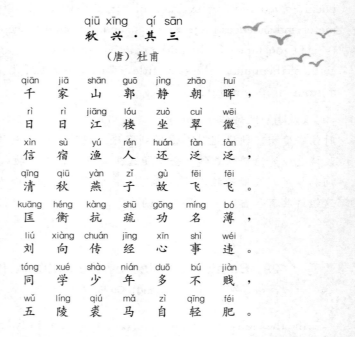

qiū xīng · qí sān
秋 兴 · 其 三

（唐）杜甫

qiān	jiā	shān	guō	jìng	zhāo	huī
千	家	山	郭	静	朝	晖 ，
rì	rì	jiāng	lóu	zuò	cuì	wēi
日	日	江	楼	坐	翠	微 。
xìn	sù	yú	rén	huán	fàn	fàn
信	宿	渔	人	还	泛	泛 ，
qīng	qiū	yàn	zǐ	gù	fēi	fēi
清	秋	燕	子	故	飞	飞 。
kuāng	héng	kàng	shū	gōng	míng	bó
匡	衡	抗	疏	功	名	薄 ，
liú	xiàng	chuán	jīng	xīn	shì	wéi
刘	向	传	经	心	事	违 。
tóng	xué	shào	nián	duō	bú	jiàn
同	学	少	年	多	不	贱 ，
wǔ	líng	qiú	mǎ	zì	qīng	féi
五	陵	裘	马	自	轻	肥 。

Notes: The first four lines portray a scene of the river, the tower, the fisherman and the swallows, something the poet saw every day. In such a dull life, he compared himself to two persons, one is Kuang Heng of the Han Dynasty, who was so lucky after criticized the emperor and got promoted so unexpectedly while the poet was deposed for voicing some different opinions on a fellow official; the other was Liu Xiang, a famous Confucian scholar of the Han Dynasty as well, who lectured on classics and was given more important work to do by the imperial court. The poet was capable to do the same, yet he was never given a chance. The poet then thought of his teenager classmates, and most of them had become high officials and led a luxurious life while he himself was staggering in poor health and misery at a tiny hilly city.

【说明】诗的前四行写江、楼、渔人和燕子这些我们每天都可以看到的事物。在如此乏味的生活中,诗人将自己与两个人物进行了比较。一位是汉朝的匡衡,匡衡上书评议朝政,却出乎意料地得到提拔;而诗人自己因为一同僚说了几句好话却被贬黜。另一个人物是刘向,刘向是汉朝著名的儒家学者,由于他讲经颂道,皇室给了他更重要的事情做。他能做的事情,我们的诗人同样可以做,却从未得到刘向那样的机会。诗人又想到他少时的朋友,他们大都做了高官,过着奢侈的生活,而诗人此时却疾病缠身,步履艰难,在一座小山城里过着凄惨的日子。

30. Being Prompted by the Autumn (5)
(Tang) Du Fu

Facing directly the Southern Mountains in the distance is the Hall of Peng Lai,

The plate containing dew, on top of the copper pillar, sits high in the sky.

The splendid hall is as beautiful as the Jade Pond, where Mother Goddess resided,

The atmosphere is as auspicious as the purple mist at the Hangu Pass from which Laozi disappeared.

An array of pheasant feather fans held by palace maids is moving ahead in the clouds,

The gleaming dragon scales on the banners under the sun that is shining on the emperor's face.

All of a sudden, I woke up on the river, where I've been sick for a year,

Several times I was also in the arrays of officials as I remember.

In Chinese phonetic alphabet and Chinese characters:

qiū xīng   qí wǔ
秋 兴 · 其 五

（唐）杜甫

péng lái gōng què duì nán shān
蓬 菜 宫 阙 对 南 山 ，

chéng lù jīn jīng xiāo hàn jiān
承 露 金 茎 霄 汉 间 。

xī wàng yáo chí jiàng wáng mǔ
西 望 瑶 池 降 王 母 ，

dōng lái zǐ qì mǎn hán guān
东 来 紫 气 满 函 关 。

yún yí zhì wěi kāi gōng shàn
云 移 雉 尾 开 宫 扇 ，

rì rào lóng lín shí shèng yán
日 绕 龙 鳞 识 圣 颜 。

yí wò cāng jiāng jīng suì wǎn
一 卧 沧 江 惊 岁 晚 ，

jǐ huí qīng suǒ diǎn cháo bān
几 回 青 琐 点 朝 班 。

Notes: The poem described a full panoply of the imperial court when it was in session before the social unrest broke out. The Mother Goddess was a figure in a myth who was the head of fairies in the Jade Pond. Laozi was the founder of the Taoist and the author of *The Tao Te Ching*, and according to a legend, a purple gust was blowing after he left behind the book and disappeared from the Hangu Pass. By recalling how splendid the official life was, the poet sighed at how drastically things had changed.

【说明】诗歌描述了安史之乱前皇室气势恢宏的景象。王母娘娘是神话里的人物，是瑶池众仙人的首领。老子开创了道教，是《道德经》的作者，根据传说，老子将《道德经》留下后，一阵紫气吹来，便从函谷关消失了。诗人通过回忆官方生活之辉煌，对事物的巨变发出了感叹。

31. Being Prompted by the Autumn (7)
(Tang) Du Fu

Emperor Wu of Han conducted navel exercise on the Kunming Lake,

War banners are still waving in the wind.

The statue of woman weaver has let down the beautiful night，

Yet，in the fall wind the scales of the stone whale vibrated.

Wild rice stems looked like a tract of dark cloud，

Petals fell from lotus pod and make the water pink.

Only birds could fly over the high pass，

I had to remain a fisherman，being confined by waters.

In Chinese phonetic alphabet and Chinese characters：

qiū xīng   qí qī
秋 兴 · 其 七

(唐) 杜甫

kūn　míng　chí　shuǐ　hàn　shí　gōng
昆　明　池　水　汉　时　功 ，

wǔ　dì　jīng　qí　zài　yǎn　zhōng
武　帝　旌　旗　在　眼　中 。

zhī　nǚ　jī　sī　xū　yè　yuè
织　女　机　丝　虚　夜　月 ，

shí　jīng　lín　jiǎ　dòng　qiū　fēng
石　鲸　鳞　甲　动　秋　风 。

bō　piāo　gū　mǐ　chén　yún　hēi
波　飘　菰　米　沉　云　黑 ，

<table>
<tr><td>lù</td><td>lěng</td><td>lián</td><td>fáng</td><td>zhuì</td><td>fěn</td><td>hóng</td></tr>
<tr><td>露</td><td>冷</td><td>莲</td><td>房</td><td>坠</td><td>粉</td><td>红 。</td></tr>
<tr><td>guān</td><td>sài</td><td>jí</td><td>tiān</td><td>wéi</td><td>niǎo</td><td>dào</td></tr>
<tr><td>关</td><td>塞</td><td>极</td><td>天</td><td>惟</td><td>鸟</td><td>道 ,</td></tr>
<tr><td>jiāng</td><td>hú</td><td>mǎn</td><td>dì</td><td>yì</td><td>yú</td><td>wēng</td></tr>
<tr><td>江</td><td>湖</td><td>满</td><td>地</td><td>一</td><td>渔</td><td>翁 。</td></tr>
</table>

Notes: In the poem our poet recalled how the Kunming Lake was. There was such a lake in the southwest of Chang'an, and Emperor Wu of Han did drill his navy there. When the lake was first dug, statues of both the woman weaver and her cowboy lover were erected. In the lake there was also a stone whale carved. When the poet wrote about the magnificent scene of the lake, he was still preoccupied with the idea of returning to the capital and work there. Yet, the naked fact is that he was straitened at a remote and hilly city, where only birds could fly pass, the only thing he could do was to continue to be a fisherman there.

【说明】作者在诗中回忆了昆明湖过去的模样。长安西南曾有昆明湖，汉武帝曾在那里训练他的水师。最初挖湖时，竖立了织女和她的情郎牛郎的雕像。在湖中还有一条雕塑的鲸鱼。诗人写昆明湖之壮丽，实则对返回都城做官念念不忘。然而，冷酷的事实是，他正被困在遥远的山城，这山城只有飞鸟能飞过来。继续当一个渔翁是他唯一能做的事情。

32. Boating in the Moonlight
(Song) Dai Fugu

My boat, filled to the brim with moonlight, seems wandering in the void,

The air comes out of still water is biting and cold.

I am lost in poetic thoughts, which may be creeping up the mast,

Into the sound of sculls my soul has drifted.

In the deep green water stars sparsely scattered,

Among riverside plants swan geese cried out their lament.

Behind the old berth a few lamp lights shimmered,

From the phoenix tree onto the broken bridge dew dropped.

In Chinese phonetic alphabet and Chinese characters:

yuè yè zhōu zhōng
月 夜 舟 中

（宋）戴复古

mǎn chuán míng yuè jìn xū kōng
满 船 明 月 浸 虚 空，

lù shuǐ wú hén yè qì chōng
绿 水 无 痕 夜 气 冲。

shī sī fú chén qiáng yǐng lǐ
诗 思 浮 沉 樯 影 里，

mèng hún yáo yè lǔ shēng zhōng
梦 魂 摇 曳 橹 声 中。

xīng chén lěng luò bì tán shuǐ
星 辰 冷 落 碧 潭 水，

hóng yàn bēi míng hóng liǎo fēng
鸿 雁 悲 鸣 红 蓼 风。

shù diǎn yú dēng yī gǔ àn
数 点 渔 灯 依 古 岸，

duàn qiáo chuí lù dī wú tóng
断 桥 垂 露 滴 梧 桐。

Notes: By describing what he thought in the boat and what he saw: the bright moon, deep green water, stars, the wailing swan geese, the lamps, the broken bridge, the parasol tree, the poet dramatized loneliness and desolation. Most critics regard this poem as one with high aesthetic value. The poet did name the riverside plants, which in English might be called "Kiss Me Over the Garden Gate."

【说明】通过描写诗人在船上所思、所见：如明月、碧水、星座、大雁的哀鸣、灯火、断桥以及梧桐树等，他对自己的孤寂和凄凉的处境进行了夸张。多数批评家认为此诗具有高度的艺术价值。诗人给出了河边草的汉语名称，其英文或许可以叫"Kiss Me Over the Garden Gate"。

33. An Autumn Scene at Chang'an
(Tang) Zhao Gu

Chilly clouds flew in the dawn,
Palace buildings domineered over the town.

When sparse stars shimmer, swan geese were flying toward the pass at the boundary,

When a flute tune was piped, I, the only person in the tower, leaned on a balcony.

By the fence the quiet chrysanthemum would soon bloom,
Red petals fell from the lotus on the sand bar, a scene so gloom.

It was high time to have perch in my home town, but I could not make the return trip,

I simply can not become the captive who insisted on wearing his homeland cap.

In Chinese phonetic alphabet and Chinese characters:

cháng ān qiū wàng
长 安 秋 望

（唐）赵嘏

yún	wù	qī	liáng	fú	shǔ	liú
云	物	凄	凉	拂	曙	流 ，
hàn	jiā	gōng	què	dòng	gāo	qiū
汉	家	宫	阙	动	高	秋 。
cán	xīng	jǐ	diǎn	yàn	héng	sài
残	星	几	点	雁	横	塞 ，
cháng	dí	yī	shēng	rén	yǐ	lóu
长	笛	一	声	人	倚	楼 。

zǐ	yàn	bàn	kāi	lí	jú	jìng
紫	艳	半	开	篱	菊	静 ，
hóng	yī	luò	jìn	zhǔ	lián	chóu
红	衣	落	尽	渚	莲	愁 。
lú	yú	zhèng	měi	bù	guī	qù
鲈	鱼	正	美	不	归	去 ，
kōng	dài	nán	guān	xué	chǔ	qiú
空	戴	南	冠	学	楚	囚 。

Notes：The poet had to stay in the capital for sometime，even though in his hometown，it was a high time in the autumn to have perch，unlike Zhang Han in the Western Jin period，who missed the fish cuisine of home town so much，he resigned from his official post and went home. The poet had to stay on. The poet said that he could not become a person like Zhong Yi，the captive in the State of Jin from the State of Chu in the Spring and Autumn Period，who not only insisted on wearing his homeland cap，but also successfully restored good relations between the two countries. The poem is remarkable in portraying a home missing mind. In line two，the poet used "palaces of the Han Dynasty"，actually he was referring to the palaces of the Tang.

【说明】诗人还必须在都城待一段时间，尽管此时在他的家乡正是吃鲈鱼的好时候，可是他不能像西晋的张翰那样，想吃家乡的鲈鱼，便辞职回家。他必须待下去。诗人说他也不能像春秋时被晋俘虏的楚人锺仪那样，坚持佩戴楚帽，而且成功地恢复了晋楚的关系。此诗在表现思乡方面非常出色。第二句所谓"汉家"实则说的是"唐家。"

34. Early Autumn
(Tang) Du Fu

Among mountain peaks the burning clouds are still lingering，

I was startled on my pillow seeing a single leaf falling.

In gardens and woods there are sounds of rustling,

Silence is broken by cloth beating and washing.

Cicadas chirp while the moon is lowering,

Up and down in the sky glowworms are flying.

I wish to present again my prosaic verse at the Golden Gate,

While pondering, I scratch my hair into a thatch late at night.

In Chinese phonetic alphabet and Chinese characters：

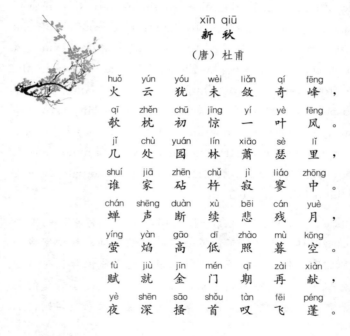

xīn qiū
新 秋

（唐）杜甫

huǒ yún yóu wèi liǎn qí fēng
火 云 犹 未 敛 奇 峰 ，

qī zhěn chū jīng yí yè fēng
欹 枕 初 惊 一 叶 风 。

jǐ chù yuán lín xiāo sè lǐ
几 处 园 林 萧 瑟 里 ，

shuí jiā zhēn chǔ jì liáo zhōng
谁 家 砧 杵 寂 寥 中 。

chán shēng duàn xù bēi cán yuè
蝉 声 断 续 悲 残 月 ，

yíng yàn gāo dī zhào mù kōng
萤 焰 高 低 照 暮 空 。

fù jiù jīn mén qī zài xiàn
赋 就 金 门 期 再 献 ，

yè shēn sāo shǒu tàn fēi péng
夜 深 搔 首 叹 飞 蓬 。

Notes：I have left out something from the original. In the fifth line, the chirping of cicadas was off and on, and in the sixth line the glowworms lightened up the sky are missed out. In the poem, the poet sighed at the fleeting of time and also voiced his emotional distress for having not obtained any success or fame. The Golden Gate is the gate of the Han Imperial Court.

【说明】第五句的蝉鸣之断断续续、第六句的萤焰照空在英文译文中未予体现。在诗中诗人叹息光阴之快，表达了因尚未取得功名而产生的郁闷的心情。金门系汉朝宫殿之门。

35. Mid Autumn

(Song) Li Pu

In the sky the bright moon ascends,

It is soundless in the Fair land above clouds.

The moon is round and full when half of autumn is gone,

The track of the moon among clouds is so long.

When the moon is waning, let the hare shuffle out,

Never let the toad come to the fore-front.

I wish to be on the same raft with the moon,

To travel the space when the Milky Way becomes clear and

clean.

In Chinese phonetic alphabet and Chinese characters:

zhōng qiū
中 秋

（宋）李朴

hào	pò	dāng	kōng	bǎo	jìng	shēng
皓	魄	当	空	宝	镜	升 ，
yún	jiān	xiān	lài	jì	wú	shēng
云	间	仙	籁	寂	无	声 。
píng	fēn	qiū	sè	yì	lún	mǎn
平	分	秋	色	一	轮	满 ，
cháng	bàn	yún	qú	qiān	lǐ	míng
长	伴	云	衢	千	里	明 。
jiǎo	tù	kōng	cóng	xián	wài	luò
狡	兔	空	从	弦	外	落 ，
yāo	má	xiū	xiàng	yǎn	qián	shēng
妖	蟆	休	向	眼	前	生 。

<table>
<tr><td>líng</td><td>chá</td><td>nǐ</td><td>yuē</td><td>tóng</td><td>xié</td><td>shǒu</td></tr>
<tr><td>灵</td><td>槎</td><td>拟</td><td>约</td><td>同</td><td>携</td><td>手，</td></tr>
<tr><td>gèng</td><td>dài</td><td>yín</td><td>hé</td><td>chè</td><td>dǐ</td><td>qīng</td></tr>
<tr><td>更</td><td>待</td><td>银</td><td>河</td><td>彻</td><td>底</td><td>清。</td></tr>
</table>

Notes: Li Pu (1063 - 1127) was a petty official, yet during his lifetime his name was very broadly known. His biography was included in the *History of Song*, which was rare for an official of his rank. His audacity of speaking his mind was most remarkable, in particular when the Queen was ousted, he wrote a memorial to the emperor saying such a profane action was smearing the royal court and the emperor should not listen to the calumny on the queen. His words caused a stir in the royal court and immediately he was removed from his office since nobody has ever had the guts to blame the emperor. Facing all the charges, Li Pu was not at all scared. Fortunately sometime later the emperor regretted on what he did to the Queen and Li Pu was given another job. Another thing that was really rare is that starting from his uncle; the Li family produced seven candidates to the final imperial examinations in 33 years.

In one of Chinese myths, the moon is also called Chang E, a lady who took some medicine and ascended to the moon, and some said that in the moon she transformed into a toad; others said that there was also a hare, whose main job was to smash herbal medicine for the lady. The poet compared traitorous officials to these two animals.

【说明】李朴（1063—1127）官职很小，在当时却极负盛名。《宋史》专门为他立传，为他这么小的官立传很罕见。他忠勇敢言，特别是在皇后被废黜时，他写了一道奏折，指出此事是宵小之辈败坏朝纲、亵渎圣听的把戏。李朴的奏折在朝廷引起轩然大波，他立即遭到贬黜，因为从未有人敢于指责皇上。面对所有的指控，李朴毫无惧色。好在，皇上后来对他废黜皇后深感后悔，李朴重新被启用。还有一件事情是绝无仅有的，那就是从李朴的叔叔开始，他家在 33 年的时间里出了 7 位进士。

在中国的神话里月亮也被称为嫦娥，嫦娥因误食草药升到天上；有人说在月亮里她变成了蟾蜍；也有人说月亮里有一只兔子，其主要工作是为嫦娥研药。诗中将朝廷里的宵小之辈比喻成这两种动物。

36. In Cui Village at Lantian on the Ninth Day
(Tang) Du Fu

For an overage in this dreary fall the best thing to try is to cheer up,

While in high spirit on the Double Ninth day we should all whoop up.

It would be embarrassing if my cap is blown away to expose my sparse hair,

So I asked someone with a smile to set my cap right and proper.

Having funneled from many brooks far away the river is with us here,

Two peaks of Yushan Mountains, so aloft and cold, stand alongside each other.

Who would be at this party with a good health next year?

In drunkenness I look at the cornel in my hand with care.

In Chinese phonetic alphabet and Chinese characters:

jiǔ rì lán tián cuī shì zhuāng
九 日 蓝 田 崔 氏 庄

（唐）杜甫

lǎo qù bēi qiū qiáng zì kuān
老 去 悲 秋 强 自 宽,

xìng	lái	jīn	rì	jìn	jūn	huān
兴	来	今	日	尽	君	欢 。

xiū	jiāng	duǎn	fà	hái	chuī	mào
羞	将	短	发	还	吹	帽 ，

xiào	qiàn	páng	rén	wèi	zhèng	guān
笑	倩	旁	人	为	正	冠 。

lán	shuǐ	yuǎn	cóng	qiān	jiàn	luò
蓝	水	远	从	千	涧	落 ，

yù	shān	gāo	bìng	liǎng	fēng	hán
玉	山	高	并	两	峰	寒 。

míng	nián	cǐ	huì	zhī	shuí	jiàn
明	年	此	会	知	谁	健 ，

zuì	bǎ	zhū	yú	zǐ	xì	kàn
醉	把	茱	萸	仔	细	看 。

Notes: This poem has been considered the best of Du Fu's octaves. In China, there is a day for the old aged—the ninth day of the ninth month, which is referred to as the Double Ninth Day. On this day the poet joined a party in the Cui village. In the Chinese original each character in the first line has a parallel in the second, to be specific, "getting old" versus "high spirit", "sad autumn" versus "this day", "trying" versus "going out", "myself" versus "gentlemen", and "cheer up" versus "bacchanal pleasure." Usually, there must be such parallels in the third and fourth lines and in the fifth and sixth lines of Chinese octaves poems. In the third line, the poet was referring to an anecdote of the Eastern Jin period. At a party given by a general, the hat of a staff officer was blown away, and then the general asked another staff to write a poem to make fun of the officer. Apparently, the party the poet joined was also held in the open, in order to avoid possible embarrassment the officer encountered, the poet asked someone to set his cap right. Why the poet was looking at cornel in his hands at the party? Because on the Double Ninth Day, the aged is supposed to climb high and have cornel planted in the earth. Some critics say that each of the eight lines is extraordinary and each character in each line is extraordinary. When it came to the sixth line with the two peaks, the poet aroused vigor of his readers. The last line with the cornel provides much food for afterthought.

【说明】此为杜甫七律中的代表作。中国有一个老年人的节日，即重阳节。重阳日杜甫参加了崔庄的一个聚会。第一句的中文原文的每个词在第二句里都能找到对偶词。如"老去"对"兴来"、"悲秋"对"今日"、"自宽"对"君欢"。通常，第三句和第四句，以及第五句和第六句是需要对仗的。第三句提到东晋时期的一个典故。这个典故说一位参军的帽子被风吹掉，然后主人就让人写诗取笑这位参军。很显然，杜甫参加的聚会也是在室外进行的，为了避免那位参军的尴尬，诗人就找人将他的帽子正了一下。诗人为何要看手中的茱萸呢？因为在重阳日，老人们要登高，然后将茱萸插在高处。有评论家说此诗"字字亮，笔笔高"。第六句的两峰，以壮语唤起了一股精神。最后一句，诗人盯住手中茱萸细看，不置一言，却胜过万语千言。

37. Autumn Thoughts
(Song) Lu You

Driven by cupidity is like ten thousand bulls dashing madly with their tails on fire,

It's better to be a sand bird to roam and rove freely any where.

When one gets nothing to do a day for him is like a year,

When one had a drop too much things as huge as a hill he would not care.

Amid the sound of cloth beating and washing the moon in the long lane is lowering in the west,

Leaves falling from the parasols tells me autumn is in sight.

I wish to look far with my old eyes, yet there is no where I can scale a height,

Unlike Yuan Long who, on top of a high tower, slept.

In Chinese phonetic alphabet and Chinese characters:

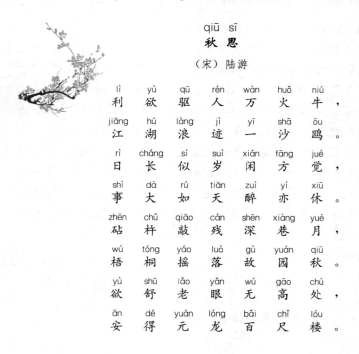

qiū sī
秋 思

（宋）陆游

lì　yù　qū　rén　wàn　huǒ　niú
利　欲　驱　人　万　火　牛，

jiāng　hú　làng　jì　yī　shā　ōu
江　湖　浪　迹　一　沙　鸥。

rì　cháng　sì　suì　xián　fāng　jué
日　长　似　岁　闲　方　觉，

shì　dà　rú　tiān　zuì　yì　xiū
事　大　如　天　醉　亦　休。

zhēn　chǔ　qiāo　cán　shēn　xiàng　yuè
砧　杵　敲　残　深　巷　月，

wú　tóng　yáo　luò　gù　yuán　qiū
梧　桐　摇　落　故　园　秋。

yù　shū　lǎo　yǎn　wú　gāo　chù
欲　舒　老　眼　无　高　处，

ān　dé　yuán　lóng　bǎi　chǐ　lóu
安　得　元　龙　百　尺　楼。

Notes: Ten thousand bulls dashing madly with their tails on fire were a tactic used by the State of Qi and defeated invading armies of the State of Yan in the Warring States period. Yuan Long mentioned in the last line was a devoted Chief of a prefecture. When some one was commenting on him before the ruler of the Shu Kingdom and resented that Yuan used a big bed in a high place and left his guest at lower places, the ruler then said that was because the one who was resenting was preoccupied with family matter while Yuan was doing things good for the public, and if I were him, I would have slept in a tower of a hundred foot high and leaving the resenting person at the same place as he did. The poem

196

showed that the poet despised those who were driven by cupidity,
and he was not satisfied with himself for being so idle. We can
detect from the poem his pains for not being able to serve the
motherland.

【说明】尾巴被点着后，一万头牛往前冲是战国时期齐国打败
燕国的一种战术。最后一句提到的元龙是一位尽忠职守的地方官。
有人向蜀主抱怨说元龙自顾自地上大床高卧，而让客人们坐在下
床；蜀主说你们一心只考虑自己的田地房舍，而元龙在为国家效
力，要是我也肯定会上百尺高楼去高卧，而让你们睡在地下。我们
从此诗可以看到诗人讨厌贪心之人，对自己无所事事也不满意，他
因不能为国家效力而心痛。

38. My Southern Neighbor Zhu
(Tang) Du Fu

My neighbor always wears a black kerchief and lives at a place
called Jinli,

He grows taros and chestnuts, not in abject poverty.

His children greets guests with juvenile and convivial smile,

Birds frequently visit and peck at millets on the steps, never
frightened by people.

In autumn the river is only four or five foot deep,

The ferry can carry two or three in a single trip.

In dusk the beach sand is still white and the bamboo forest
green,

Standing by the wood door, the host is seeing off visitors
under the new moon.

In Chinese phonetic alphabet and Chinese characters:

yǔ zhū shān rén
与 朱 山 人
（唐）杜甫

jǐn 锦	lǐ 里	xiān 先	shēng 生	wū 乌	jiǎo 角	jīn 巾 ，
yuán 园	shōu 收	yù 芋	lì 栗	wèi 未	quán 全	pín 贫 。
guàn 惯	kàn 看	bīn 宾	kè 客	ér 儿	tóng 童	xǐ 喜 ，
dé 得	shí 食	jiē 阶	chú 除	niǎo 鸟	què 雀	xùn 驯 。
qiū 秋	shuǐ 水	cái 才	shēn 深	sì 四	wǔ 五	chǐ 尺 ，
yě 野	háng 航	qià 恰	shòu 受	liǎng 两	sān 三	rén 人 。
bái 白	shā 沙	cuì 翠	zhú 竹	jiāng 江	cūn 村	mù 暮 ，
xiāng 相	sòng 送	chái 柴	mén 门	yuè 月	sè 色	xīn 新 。

Notes：The poem has two titles，one is "To the Recluse Zhu"，and the other is "My Southern Neighbor Zhu". The poem portrays a special figure—a recluse，who is so sociable even birds treat his family as their friends. The scenes the poem draws of a life in seclusion are so natural and simple.

【说明】此诗有两个标题："南邻"和"与朱山人"。此诗写一类特殊的人——隐居的人。隐居者很好交，连鸟儿都把他和家人看成自己人。诗人笔下的隐居生活非常自然与简朴。

39. Listening to a Flute
(Tang) Zhao Gu

Someone is piping a flute in the beautiful building，
The flute is on when the wind is strong and off when the wind is declining.

The sound of the flute is halting clouds from floating,

Cold moonlight that casting on windows is softly touching.

It reminds me of Huanzi who once played three tunes with his flute for a stranger,

And of Ma Rong whose "Poetic Prose on Flute" I still remember.

The flute has stopped, nobody knows if the player is still there,

Yet, the clear sound continues to linger in the air.

In Chinese phonetic alphabet and Chinese characters:

wén dí
闻 笛

（唐）赵嘏

shuí	jiā	chuī	dí	huà	lóu	zhōng
谁	家	吹	笛	画	楼	中，

duàn	xù	shēng	suí	duàn	xù	fēng
断	续	声	随	断	续	风。

xiǎng	è	xíng	yún	héng	bì	luò
响	遏	行	云	横	碧	落，

qīng	hé	lěng	yuè	dào	lián	lóng
清	和	冷	月	到	帘	栊。

xìng	lái	sān	nòng	yǒu	huán	zǐ
兴	来	三	弄	有	桓	子，

fù	jiù	yī	piān	huái	mǎ	róng
赋	就	一	篇	怀	马	融。

qǔ	bà	bù	zhī	rén	zài	fǒu
曲	罢	不	知	人	在	否，

yú	yīn	liáo	liàng	shàng	piāo	kōng
余	音	嘹	亮	尚	飘	空。

Notes: Some scholars challenge if this poem was written by Zhao Gu. The poem is not included in the *Complete Collection of Tang Poems*, neither in Zhao's individual collections. The reason for its inclusion, I guess, is because it provides an excellent example of how to appreciate flute music. Huanzi was an established flute musician in the Eastern Jin period, one day the son of a most famous calligrapher run into the musician and asked, out of admiration, if he could pipe the flute for him. The musician immediately piped three tunes for the stranger and then left without saying a word and without getting a "thank you" from the stranger. Ma Rong was a famous musician in the Eastern Han period.

【说明】有学者认为此诗不是赵嘏所作。《全唐诗》未收此诗；赵嘏个人的集子里也没有这首诗。它之所以被收进《千家诗》，我个人认为它提供了一个很好的关于如何欣赏笛子的案例。桓子是东晋著名的笛子演奏家，一天一位著名书法家的儿子与他相遇，出于对桓子的仰慕之心，年轻人问桓子可否为他吹支曲子。桓子立即为这位陌生人吹了三支曲子，然后，没等对方说声谢谢，就一声不吭地走掉了。马融是东汉著名的音乐家。

40. A Winter Scene
(Song) Liu Kezhuang

I like to rise up early to look out of the window, for the rays of morning sun is my love,
Late autumn is assuming great airs in the bamboo grove.
I asked a servant to get my new room heated and ready,
Then had my paddy clothes ironed by the boy.
Tender tea leaves floating in the cup while wine is being warmed,
Fat crabs are inviting, yellow oranges have been cut.
The garden is so rapturous with flowers and plants,
From now on I shall never miss such sheer delights.

In Chinese phonetic alphabet and Chinese characters:

dōng jǐng
冬 景

（宋）刘克庄

qíng	chuāng	zǎo	jué	ài	zhāo	xī
晴	窗	早	觉	爱	朝	曦

竹 外 秋 声 渐 作 威 。
zhú wài qiū shēng jiàn zuò wēi

命 仆 安 排 新 暖 阁 ，
mìng pú ān pái xīn nuǎn gé

呼 童 熨 贴 旧 寒 衣 。
hū tóng yùn tiē jiù hán yī

叶 浮 嫩 绿 酒 初 熟 ，
yè fú nèn lǜ jiǔ chū shú

橙 切 香 黄 蟹 正 肥 。
chéng qiē xiāng huáng xiè zhèng féi

蓉 菊 满 园 皆 可 羡 ，
róng jú mǎn yuán jiē kě xiàn

赏 心 从 此 莫 相 违 。
shǎng xīn cóng cǐ mò xiāng wéi

Notes：The poet didn't say much about the winter scene，instead，he described much trifling matters of daily life，and what he did was to get himself ready for winter，thus he told us how much he enjoyed his life with a blithe heart.

【说明】关于冬景，诗人并未用多少笔墨；相反，他描写了很多日常的琐事，他做的事就是为过冬做好准备。这样，他告诉我们他在如何无忧无虑地享受生活。

41. The Winter Solstice

(Tang) Du Fu

Seasons，weather and human affairs change every day，

When Winter Solstice comes days are longer and the spring is not far away.

The embroider girls would use a few more threads for longer

working hours,

The burnt ashes of reed membrane would fly out of the six bamboo tubes.

The river bank is urging the twelfth month to pass by so that new shoots could grow on the willows,

Longing for the bloom of plum the hills are trying to break through the coldness.

Many things here and home can match-up,

I just take over a cup from my son and have a bottom-up.

In Chinese phonetic alphabet and Chinese characters:

dōng zhì

冬 至

（唐）杜甫

tiān	shí	rén	shì	rì	xiāng	cuī
天	时	人	事	日	相	催 ，
dōng	zhì	yáng	shēng	chūn	yòu	lái
冬	至	阳	生	春	又	来 。
cì	xiù	wǔ	wén	tiān	ruò	xiàn
刺	绣	五	纹	添	弱	线 ，
chuī	jiā	liù	guǎn	dòng	fēi	huī
吹	葭	六	管	动	飞	灰 。
àn	róng	dài	là	jiāng	shū	liǔ
岸	容	待	腊	将	舒	柳 ，
shān	yì	chōng	hán	yù	fàng	méi
山	意	冲	寒	欲	放	梅 。
yún	wù	bù	shū	xiāng	guó	yì
云	物	不	殊	乡	国	异 ，
jiāo	ér	qiě	fù	zhǎng	zhōng	bēi
教	儿	且	覆	掌	中	杯 。

Notes: Winter Solstice is one of the 24 weather markers of China, and it used to be an important festival in China. It was the New Years Day in the Zhou Dynasty. On this day the emperors of both the Tang and Song dynasties would hold grand ceremonies to

202

offer sacrifices to the Heaven in the suburbs. In China, northerners would eat Jiaozi—dumplings and southerners would eat Tangyuan—sweet dumplings on this day. Since Du Fu wrote this poem in 766, it has been cited on this day every year in China. In ancient times, people used bamboo pipes to determine weather periods, for instance, they used to stuff the pipe with burnt bamboo membrane and when Winter Solstice came, the ashes would be blown out automatically of the pipes. The poem reveals the joy of the poet with the weather change and his longing for a more stable life.

【说明】冬至是中国二十四节气之一，在过去冬至是个隆重的节日。周朝时以冬至为新年。唐宋时皇帝会在郊区举行盛大的祭天活动。到那天，北方人会吃饺子，南方人会吃汤圆。自杜甫766年写了这首关于冬至的诗后，每年冬至人们都会念这首诗。古时候，人们用竹管来确定节气，譬如，人们把竹膜烧成灰放到竹管里，冬至这一天到来时，灰粉就会自动地从竹管里被吹出来。此诗表现了天气变化给诗人带来的快乐，以及他对安稳生活的向往。

42. Plum

(Song) Lin Bu

You are embroidering your beauty when all other flowers have withered,

In the whole garden your charm is so prominent.

Your sparse shadows slanting down on the shallow water,

Floating in the twilight air is your feint aroma.

While landing, the white crane is peeking at you first,

White butterflies would be scared if they saw your graceful look.

Fortunately I could approach nigh you by my new verse in a whisper,

Rather than toasting to you with a golden cup while beating

wood clappers, which is a bit vulgar.

In Chinese phonetic alphabet and Chinese characters:

méi huā
梅 花

（宋）林逋

zhòng	fāng	yáo	luò	dú	xuān	yán
众	芳	摇	落	独	暄	妍 ，

zhàn	jìn	fēng	qíng	xiàng	xiǎo	yuán
占	尽	风	情	向	小	园 。

shū	yǐng	héng	xié	shuǐ	qīng	qiǎn
疏	影	横	斜	水	清	浅 ，

àn	xiāng	fú	dòng	yuè	huáng	hūn
暗	香	浮	动	月	黄	昏 。

shuāng	qín	yù	xià	xiān	tōu	yǎn
霜	禽	欲	下	先	偷	眼 ，

fěn	dié	rú	zhī	hé	duàn	hún
粉	蝶	如	知	合	断	魂 。

xìng	yǒu	wēi	yín	kě	xiāng	xiá
幸	有	微	吟	可	相	狎 ，

bù	xū	tán	bǎn	gòng	jīn	zūn
不	须	檀	板	共	金	尊 。

Notes: Lin Bu （967 - 1028） was born into a family of Confucian scholars in Hangzhou, Zhejiang Province. In his early years, he travelled quite extensively and when he was over forty years old, he became a recluse in the Gushan Mountains near Hangzhou, and since then he had never stepped out of his solitude, where he planted plum and raised cranes and people used to say plum was his wife （he never got married） and cranes were his children. It must be pointed out that in China's history of poetry and since this poem came into being, many important poets began to write about plum. Su Shi, for instance, used this poem to teach his sons.

【说明】林逋（967—1028）出生在浙江杭州一个儒家学者家

204

庭。年轻时漫游甚广，40 岁后隐居杭州附近的孤山，并在孤山终老。他一生不仕不娶，唯喜植梅养鹤，自谓"以梅为妻，以鹤为子"，人称"梅妻鹤子"。必须指出的是，自他这首写梅的诗问世后，很多大诗人都开始写梅了。譬如苏轼就用这首诗教他的儿子们。

43. Words to my Nephew at the Languan Pass
(Tang) Han Yu

In the morning I submitted a note of remonstrance to the emperor,

In the evening I was demoted to Chaoyang, which is eight thousand miles far.

I intended to rid the dynasty of misrule,

I was fully committed without sparing any efforts.

Clouds now hang horizontally at the Qin Ridges leaving my home far behind,

Snow has almost buried the Languan Pass and horses refused to go ahead.

I know why you came here to see me at this juncture,

You can thus collect my bones by the side of Zhangjiang River.

In Chinese phonetic alphabet and Chinese characters:

zuǒ qiān zhì lán guān shì zhí sūn xiāng
左　迁　至　蓝　关　示　侄　孙　湘

（唐）韩愈

yì　　fēng　zhāo　zòu　　jiǔ　chóng　tiān
一　封　朝　奏　九　重　天　，

xī　　biǎn　cháo　yáng　lù　　bā　　qiān
夕　贬　潮　阳　路　八　千　。

běn　　wéi　shèng　míng　chú　　bì　　zhèng
本　为　圣　明　除　弊　政　，

gǎn	jiāng	shuāi	xiǔ	xī	cán	nián
敢	将	衰	朽	惜	残	年 。

yún	héng	qín	lǐng	jiā	hé	zài
云	横	秦	岭	家	何	在 ，

xuě	yōng	lán	guān	mǎ	bù	qián
雪	拥	蓝	关	马	不	前 。

zhī	rǔ	yuǎn	lái	yīng	yǒu	yì
知	汝	远	来	应	有	意 ，

hǎo	shōu	wú	gǔ	zhàng	jiāng	biān
好	收	吾	骨	瘴	江	边 。

Notes：The poet was an unflinching Confucian scholar who opposed firmly against Buddhism. When the emperor decided to bring into the imperial court one finger bone of an important and deceased Buddhist figure to display and worship，the poet immediate wrote a note to the emperor saying how bad the idea was. Yet，on the evening of the day the letter was sent in he was deposed and sent to a remote place in today's Guangdong Province. As the poem told us the way to the new post was hard，the snow storm he encountered was so sever even his horse refused to move ahead. Fortunately，his nephew joined him on the way. Not knowing what he was going to face，he found a little solace in his nephew，for in case he ended his life，his nephew would be able to collect his bones and send them home. The poem revealed his bitterness and wrath at the fact that he was so quickly and so severely handled for a note he wrote，which was intended for the good of the emperor and the dynasty. He may feel much better if he could know that the note of remonstrance has become one of the master pieces in the history of Chinese literature.

【说明】诗人是一位无畏的儒家学者，坚决地反对佛教。当他听说朝廷要将释迦文佛的一节指骨迎入宫廷供奉，便写了一篇奏折（《论佛骨表》），反对这一做法，并劝谏阻止唐宪宗。然而，他早上上书给皇上，当天晚上，就被贬到如今广东一个遥远的地方。正如诗里所讲，前去赴任的道路很艰难，他遇到的暴风雪都使马匹却步。幸好，他的侄子半道来送他。如若遇到不幸，他侄子尚可将他的尸骨送回家乡。此诗道出了他心中的委曲、愤慨和悲伤，被如此之快、如此严厉地惩罚是他始料未及的，他本是为了皇帝和朝廷呀。他若地下有知，这篇劝谏书已成为中国文学史上的一篇力作，或许会感觉好一些。

44. War Is the Bane of My Life
(Song) Wang Zhong

I don't know what to do with the war that has been raging for so long,

My temple hair is grey, but nothing has been achieved and so much time has by-gone.

My drifting life and that of Wang Can at late Han is almost the same,

Like Du Fu of Tang, my mind was often filled with grief and gloom.

When brothers are thousand miles apart, they don't hear from each other,

Under the moon on a branch the magpie is resting in her cold bower.

If I could find the thing that makes one drunk for a thousand days and drink the liquor,

Let me sober up only when it is peace all over.

In Chinese phonetic alphabet and Chinese characters:

gān gē
干 戈
（宋）王中

gān　gē　wèi　dìng　yù　hé　zhī
干　戈　未　定　欲　何　之　,

yī	shì	wú	chéng	liǎng	bìn	sī
一	事	无	成	两	鬓	丝 。
zōng	jì	dà	gāng	wáng	càn	zhuàn
踪	迹	大	纲	王	粲	传 ,
qíng	huái	xiǎo	yàng	dù	líng	shī
情	怀	小	样	杜	陵	诗 。
jí	líng	yīn	duàn	rén	qiān	lǐ
鹡	鸰	音	断	人	千	里 ,
wū	què	cháo	hán	yuè	yì	zhī
乌	鹊	巢	寒	月	一	枝 。
ān	dé	zhōng	shān	qiān	rì	jiǔ
安	得	中	山	千	日	酒 ,
mǐng	rán	zhí	dào	tài	píng	shí
酩	然	直	到	太	平	时 。

Notes: We don't know much about the poet, except that he was a poet of the Southern Song period and that his adult name is Jiweng. However, from the poem we know he had a very bumpy life and had been drifting around because of war. In the fifth line, he used "wagtails" to compare to brothers, and this usage was adopted from *The Book of Songs*, in which there is a line saying wagtails (brothers) help each other in emergence out of fraternity. The liquor that can make a person drunk for a thousand days in the seventh line is adopted from a legend, which says a man by the name of Di Xi was able to brew this kind of liquor.

【说明】我们对诗人知之甚少，只知道他生于南宋，字积翁。但是，从诗中我们了解到他生活坎坷，四处躲避战乱。第五句，他用鹡鸰比喻兄弟，此用法源自《诗经》，《诗经》中有这样的句子："脊令在原，兄弟急难。"后世便使用"脊令"比喻兄弟。第七句所说使人醉一千天的酒取自一个传说，说一个叫狄希的可以酿造这样的酒。

45. My Solitude

(Song) Chen Tuan

In the past ten years I have travelled the secular world,

Thinking back only green mountains appear in my dream so frequent.

Splendid a purple ribbon may be, it is not good as a sound sleep,

Eminent a red gate may look like, it lacks a merrily mood that only a poor life can provide.

What faces new rulers after numerous battles is anxiety,

What can be morose is to listen to pipes that urge you to sleep your life away.

Thus, I prefer to stay in solitude and keep reading my old books,

And enjoy spring among chirping birds and wild flowers.

In Chinese phonetic alphabet and Chinese characters：

guī yǐn

归 隐

（宋）陈抟

shí	nián	zōng	jì	zǒu	hóng	chén
十	年	踪	迹	走	红	尘 ，
huí	shǒu	qīng	shān	rù	mèng	pín
回	首	青	山	入	梦	频 。
zǐ	shòu	zòng	róng	zhēng	jí	shuì
紫	绶	纵	荣	争	及	睡 ，
zhū	mén	suī	fù	bù	rú	pín
朱	门	虽	富	不	如	贫 。
chóu	wén	jiàn	jǐ	fú	wēi	zhǔ
愁	闻	剑	戟	扶	危	主 ，
mēn	tīng	shēng	gē	guō	zuì	rén
闷	听	笙	歌	聒	醉	人 。
xié	qǔ	jiù	shū	guī	jiù	yǐn
携	取	旧	书	归	旧	隐 ，

Notes: Chen Tuan (871 - 989) was a most famous hermit, Taoist scholar and poet in the late Tang, Five Dynasties and the early Song periods. He was well known for his ability of sleeping for a long time, sometimes for a hundred days, he argued that keeping oneself busy for success and fame is not as good as a nice sleep. After failure at the national examinations, he decided to seek a different life that is to become a hermit deep in the mountains. This poem was composed when the poet was sixty years old. The solitary life made it possible for him to concentrate on the writing of a few important Taoist books, which were most influential at his time and in later developments of Chinese philosophy. He was called upon by two emperors to work for the imperial court, he declined them and returned to his peaceful life, which lasted for 118 years.

【说明】陈抟（871—989）是晚唐五代、宋初著名隐士、著名道教学者、著名诗人。相传陈抟嗜睡，常百余日不起。他认为与其为功名利禄忙忙碌碌，不如关门大睡。因屡试不第，遂不求入仕，以山水为乐，在深山里当起了隐士。写此诗时，他已经60岁了。隐居的生活，使他能集中精力完成几部重要的道教著作。这些著作无论当时还是现在都对中国哲学的发展产生了重要的影响。两位皇上曾请他到朝廷为官，他都予以谢绝。他更愿回到他平静的生活里，并在这样的生活里活了118年。

46. The Widow in the Mountains
(Tang) Du Xunhe

She was left stranded in the thatched room after her husband died in war,

Her hair at the temples had turned grey and ramie cloth was something she wore.

Silk tax had to be paid while mulberry and cudrania trees were not attended at all,

Green shoots charges were not exempted though the fields lay in waste and not producing any more.

She had to live on wild herbs she could found and eat even their roots,

To warm up her room she burnt woods and their leaves.

No matter how sequestered one's home was deep and deep in the mountains,

One could never escape from the corvee or paying taxes.

In Chinese phonetic alphabet and Chinese characters:

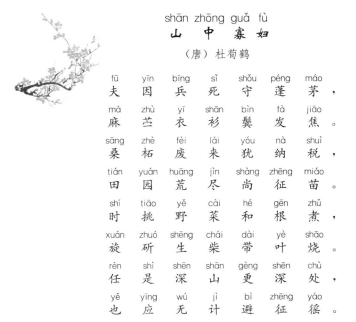

shān zhōng guǎ fù
山 中 寡 妇

（唐）杜荀鹤

fū yīn bīng sǐ shǒu péng máo
夫 因 兵 死 守 蓬 茅，

má zhù yī shān bìn fà jiāo
麻 苎 衣 衫 鬓 发 焦。

sāng zhè fèi lái yóu nà shuì
桑 柘 废 来 犹 纳 税，

tián yuán huāng jìn shàng zhēng miáo
田 园 荒 尽 尚 征 苗。

shí tiāo yě cài hé gēn zhǔ
时 挑 野 菜 和 根 煮，

xuán zhuó shēng chái dài yè shāo
旋 斫 生 柴 带 叶 烧。

rèn shì shēn shān gèng shēn chù
任 是 深 山 更 深 处，

yě yīng wú jì bì zhēng yáo
也 应 无 计 避 征 徭。

Notes: Du Xunhe (846 – 904) was a child born out of

211

wedlock，his father was said to be the famous poet Du Mu. He grew up in poor conditions with his mother. He took poetry writing as his career. Over 300 of his poems are still in existence today.

【说明】杜荀鹤（846—904）是个私生子，相传他的父亲是杜牧。他跟着母亲长大，生活很贫困。他将作诗视为自己的事业。现有他的 300 多首诗存世。

47. Seeing Off the Heavenly Master
(Ming) Zhu Quan

The city was covered with frost and the shadows of willow are sparse，

By the lakeside I saw off genially the guest of importance.

The seal he used to produce thunder is in the gold case，

The chart that can drive sun and moon is encapsulated in a red damas.

He used to fly on a crane in the morning，

And sometimes landed down from wild ducks for purpose of sleeping.

In a big hurry he went back to his immortal courtyard，

To check if the fairy land peaches are already ripened.

In Chinese phonetic alphabet and Chinese characters：

sòng tiān shī
送　天　师

（明）朱权

shuāng luò zhī chéng liǔ yǐng shū
霜　落　芝　城　柳　影　疏　，

yīn qín sòng kè chū pó hú
殷　勤　送　客　出　鄱　湖　。

huáng	jīn	jiǎ	suǒ	léi	tíng	yìn	
黄	金	甲	锁	雷	霆	印	，

hóng	jǐn	tāo	chán	rì	yuè	fú	
红	锦	韬	缠	日	月	符	。

tiān	shàng	xiǎo	xíng	qí	zhī	hè	
天	上	晓	行	骑	只	鹤	，

rén	jiān	yè	sù	jiě	shuāng	fú	
人	间	夜	宿	解	双	凫	。

cōng	cōng	guī	dào	shén	xiān	fǔ	
匆	匆	归	到	神	仙	府	，

wèi	wèn	pán	táo	shú	yě	wú	
为	问	蟠	桃	熟	也	无	。

Notes：Zhu Quan （1378 - 1448） was the 17th son of the first emperor of Ming—Zhu Yuanzhang. He was persecuted by his uncle，who usurped the imperial power. Instead of trying to get back the political power，he devoted all his efforts in the study of Taoism，drama and literature. He was not happy in the most of his life and eventually died at the age of 71. He was the playwright of twelve poetic operas. "The Heavenly Master" referred to a Taoist priest，who was believed to have super-natural powers.

【说明】 朱权 （1378—1448） 是明太祖朱元璋第 17 子。他被夺取了皇权的叔父迫害，但并未为了夺回政权而战，而是投身于对道教、戏剧和文学的研究。他一生大部分时间都郁郁寡欢，71 岁离世。作有杂剧 12 种。"天师"是对道士的尊称，据说"天师"会法术。

48. Seeing Off Mao Bowen
(Ming) Zhu Houcong

General，you're leading the expedition to the south with gallant spirit，

The broad sword in the shape of a goose feather at your waist shone so brilliant.

Land and hills shudder when drums sound like gale blowing,

The sun and moon are high while banners flutter like lightening.

The people you're defending are posterities of unicorn,

The ones you're fighting are trashes like ants that can not escape and live on.

When you return after peace is restored in the southern land,

I shall untie your war robe with my hand.

In Chinese phonetic alphabet and Chinese characters:

sòng máo bó wēn
送 毛 伯 温
（明）朱厚熜

dà	jiàng	nán	zhēng	dǎn	qì	háo
大	将	南	征	胆	气	豪 ，
yāo	héng	qiū	shuǐ	yàn	líng	dāo
腰	横	秋	水	雁	翎	刀 。
fēng	chuī	tuó	gǔ	shān	hé	dòng
风	吹	鼍	鼓	山	河	动 ，
diàn	shǎn	jīng	qí	rì	yuè	gāo
电	闪	旌	旗	日	月	高 。
tiān	shàng	qí	lín	yuán	yǒu	zhǒng
天	上	麒	麟	原	有	种 ，
xué	zhōng	lóu	yǐ	qǐ	néng	táo
穴	中	蝼	蚁	岂	能	逃 。
tài	píng	dài	zhào	guī	lái	rì
太	平	待	诏	归	来	日 ，
zhèn	yǔ	xiān	shēng	jiě	zhàn	páo
朕	与	先	生	解	战	袍 。

Notes: Zhu Houcong (1507 – 1566) is the 11th emperor of the Ming Dynasty. In the first part of his forty-five years reign, he tried to accomplish something for the country. This poem was composed in that period for purpose of boosting up the morale of his army led by General Mao Bowen in an expedition to the south to wipe out rebels there. He used the word "unicorn" —an auspicious legendary animal in China to say the posterities of that land are of noble origin. In the remaining years of his rule, he indulged in his fetish for Taoism and failed to attend to imperial affairs for almost 20 years, and thus he was regarded as one of most disputed emperors in China. Mao Bowen (1487 - 1544) was the Minister of Defense at the time.

【说明】朱厚熜 (1507—1566) 是明朝第 11 位皇帝。在他当政 45 年的前期尚有所作为。此诗就是在他当政前期所写。写诗的目的是为毛伯温所率南征平乱的部队鼓舞士气。他所用"麒麟"一词是古代的一种瑞兽，此处是说他们要收复的国土的后代出身高贵。在他当政的后期，痴迷道教，有 20 余年不理朝政，成为历史上最有争议的皇帝。毛伯温 (1487—1544) 是当时的兵部尚书。

Part III "Five-Characters a Line" Quatrains

卷三　五绝

In a "five-characters a line" quatrain, there are only four lines, each line has five characters, so there are all together twenty characters in one quatrain of this type. It can rhyme at the end of each line; it can also rhyme at the end of every second line. It rhymes with flat tones. Tonal patterns must be strictly followed. As far as antithesis is concerned the requirement is not as strict as in regulated (octave) poems. The third part of this primer is devoted to the "five-characters a line" quatrains. There are thirty-nine poems in it. Now, let's look at each of them.

五言绝句只有四句，每句五个字，共二十个字。可以每行押韵，也可以隔行押韵。韵押平声。五绝也讲究平仄。对仗则不像律诗那样严格。这一部分专讲五绝，共三十九首。现在，让我们一首一首地读一下。

1. Day Break in Spring

(Tang) Meng Haoran

Day always breaks without me knowing it while I'm in a sound sleep in spring,

I wake up to find everywhere birds are chirping.

I seem remember last night wind was whistling and rain pattering,

Many flowers might have fallen and are still falling.

In Chinese phonetic alphabet and Chinese characters:

chūn xiǎo

春 晓

（唐）孟浩然

chūn	mián	bù	jué	xiǎo
春	眠	不	觉	晓 ，

chù	chù	wén	tí	niǎo
处	处	闻	啼	鸟 。

yè	lái	fēng	yǔ	shēng
夜	来	风	雨	声 ，

huā	luò	zhī	duō	shǎo
花	落	知	多	少 。

Notes: Meng Haoran (689 - 740) looked after his parents at home in the first half of his life. He had never been an official, but he was the pioneer of eclogue of the Tang Dynasty. This poem has been one of the most popular poems in China, almost every child starts his learning of Tang poetry from this poem. The words in it are simple, plain and natural, yet the feeling it contains is condensed and true.

【说明】孟浩然（689—740）的前半生专事父母，一生不仕，是唐朝田园诗的先锋。这首诗在中国家喻户晓，几乎每个学习唐诗的孩子都从这首开始。此诗语言简单、朴素、自然，却饱含真情实感。

2. An Unsuccessful Visit

(Tang) Meng Haoran

I came to see the gifted scholar at his home,

Yet he was sent to the far away ridges and to suffer from ostracism.

Even though plum blooms earlier over there,

The spring here is still more superior.

In Chinese phonetic alphabet and Chinese characters:

fǎng yuán shí yí bú yù
访　袁　拾　遗　不　遇

（唐）孟浩然

luò yáng fǎng cái zǐ
洛　阳　访　才　子，

jiāng lǐng zuò liú rén
江　岭　作　流　人。

wén shuō méi huā zǎo
闻　说　梅　花　早，

hé rú cǐ dì chūn
何　如　此　地　春。

Notes: In the Chinese title, the poet told us whom he was trying to call on, it was Mr. Yuan, an official in charge of ritual affair and his good friend. However, the friend was not home, and was sent into exile at a remote mountain area. The poet came to the capital to see if he could be recruited as an official and as soon as he got in he called on this friend of his. That shows how profound their relation was. Reading the comparison between the spring in the capital and the early plum in the remote mountain ridges, we can feel how much the poet was missing his friend.

【说明】我们从诗的题目得知，诗人去造访他的朋友——袁拾遗。但是，朋友不在，已然被流放到遥远的山区了。诗人自己来京

220

城，是看看在官场有无机会，一到京城就去看他的朋友，可见他们的关系不一般。诗人说南方山区的梅花虽然早开，仍无法与都城的春天相比，表现了他对朋友深深的怀念。

3. Seeing Off Mr. Guo
(Tang) Wang Changling

Under the moon the green color of the Huai River is reflected on the gate，

I wish you will not leave me and your mind can stay with me，and also your horse and cart.

I hope moonlight can always accompany you，my good official，

When you hear surging spring tide at night it would be me pining for you.

In Chinese phonetic alphabet and Chinese characters：

sòng guō sī cāng
送 郭 司 仓

（唐）王昌龄

yìng mén huái shuǐ lù
映 门 淮 水 绿 ，

liú qí zhǔ rén xīn
留 骑 主 人 心 。

míng yuè suí liáng yuàn
明 月 随 良 掾 ，

chūn cháo yè yè shēn
春 潮 夜 夜 深 。

Notes：Wang Changling（694？－765？）was an important frontier poet of the Tang. He enjoyed friendship with famous poets such as Li Bai，Gao Shi，Wang Wei，Wang Zhihuan，Cen Shen and so on. His "seven-characters a line" quatrains are the best among all his poems. The person the poet was seeing off was a granary keeper，a petty official of the lowest rank.

【说明】王昌龄（694？—765？）是唐朝重要的边塞诗人。他与很多诗人过从甚密，如李白、高适、王维、王之涣和岑参等。在他所有的诗歌中，其"七绝"最出色。诗人送行的是一位官阶最低的仓库管理员。

4．The Luoyang Avenue
(Tang) Chu Guangxi

On the broad and straight Luoyang Avenue，

The spring sun is radiant and the landscape is a pleasant view.

Dapper kids from prestigious neighborhoods are galloping on horse back，

Their jade ornaments on horses give out a colliding sound.

In Chinese phonetic alphabet and Chinese characters：

luò yáng dào
洛 阳 道
（唐）储光羲

dà dào zhí rú fà
大 道 直 如 发 ，

chūn rì jiā qì duō
春 日 佳 气 多 。

wǔ líng guì gōng zǐ
五 陵 贵 公 子 ，

shuāng shuāng míng yù kē
双 双 鸣 玉 珂 。

Notes：Chu Guangxi（706 - 763）was one of the most famous eclogue poets of Tang. He once served as a discipline inspector in the central government. Unfortunately，he was forced to work for rebels for a while, and for that he was degraded. In the first line the poet was saying the road was as straight as a hair, which is a rare metaphor even in Chinese. The understatement of this poem is his contempt for the sons of rich families, but he expressed it in a moderated way.

【说明】储光羲（706—763）是唐朝最有名的田野诗人。官至监察御史。不幸的是他曾被迫受伪职，平乱后被降职。诗的第一句说"大道直如发，"此种比喻在中文里也很少见。此诗以很缓和的口吻对富家子弟表示了蔑视。

5. Sitting Alone in the Jingting Mountains

(Tang) Li Bai

All birds have vanished in the high sky,
A single piece of cloud has leisurely gone by.
My tryst is with the Jingting Mountains here,
We never had enough of looking at each other.

In Chinese phonetic alphabet and Chinese characters:

dú zuò jìng tíng shān
独 坐 敬 亭 山

（唐）李白

zhòng niǎo gāo fēi jìn
众 鸟 高 飞 尽 ，

gū yún dú qù xián
孤 云 独 去 闲 。

xiāng kàn liǎng bú yàn
相 看 两 不 厌 ，

zhī yǒu jìng tíng shān
只 有 敬 亭 山 。

Notes: This poem was composed in 753 when the poet left the capital out of his disappointment with the politics there and went to Xuancheng city for a second time and climbed the nearby Jingting Mountains, where a southern dynasty poet Xie Tiao used to elocute his poems. Unlike the last time, in which his friends were with him drinking, composing and chanting in the mountains. However, now he was alone, not even the birds and clouds were with him. Lonely as he was, this poem has become a masterpiece that has been reciting for ages.

【说明】此诗作于 753 年，这时他由于对长安的政治很失望，已离开都城，第二次来到宣城，并登上这附近的敬亭山，这是南朝诗人谢朓经常诵读诗歌的地方。第一次来宣城时很多朋友一起在山上饮酒、赋诗唱和；这次完全不同，只有他一人，甚至连飞鸟、乌云都没有。尽管他独自一人，却吟下了这千古绝唱。

6. On the Stork Tower

(Tang) Wang Zhihuan

The sun disappeared into the back of the mountain,
To the sea the Yellow River flows with emotion.
If you wish to look much farther,
Then ascend one more stair.

In Chinese phonetic alphabet and Chinese characters：

dēng guàn què lóu
登 鹤 雀 楼

（唐）王之涣

bái rì yī shān jìn
白 日 依 山 尽，

huáng	hé	rù	hǎi	liú	
黄	河	入	海	流	。

yù	qióng	qiān	lǐ	mù	
欲	穷	千	里	目	，

gèng	shàng	yī	céng	lóu	
更	上	一	层	楼	。

Notes: Wang Zhihuan (688 – 742) is one of the famous Tang poets. During his life time, most of his poems were rendered into music. He was known of dancing with a sword while chanting poetry. Only six of his poems are available today, but each is of high artistic value. The Stork Tower is in today's Shanxi Province, it is a three-storied building. The poem not only portrays the majestic land in the north, but also reveals the poet's grandeur of soul and his positive mind.

【说明】王之涣（688—742）是唐朝著名诗人。他在世时许多他写的诗已被谱曲传唱。他以边吟诗边舞剑出名。目前只有他的 6 首诗存世。但是，每一首都有极高的艺术价值。鹳雀楼在当今的山西省，是一座三层建筑。诗歌不但表现了北方宽广的大地，也显示了诗人高尚的灵魂和积极的精神。

7. The Princess Being Married to a Neighboring State
(Tang) Sun Ti

There are no orioles or flowers at the frontier,
No spring scene is in sight in the New Year.
From the Heaven the fairy lady is descending,
Immediately the frontier pass is in spring.

In Chinese phonetic alphabet and Chinese characters:

guān yǒng lè gōng zhǔ rù fān
观 永 乐 公 主 入 蕃
（唐）孙逖

biān dì yīng huā shǎo
边 地 莺 花 少 ，

nián lái wèi jué xīn
年 来 未 觉 新 。

měi rén tiān shàng luò
美 人 天 上 落 ，

lóng sài shǐ yìng chūn
龙 塞 始 应 春 。

Notes：Sun Ti（696？－761）once served as an assistance Minister of Justice. He was chosen as the tutor of the crown prince. The princess was Princess Yongle，and she was married to the King of Khitan. The poet was saying as soon as the Princess came to the border area with Khitan，spring came and replaced the desolate scene before her arrival.

【说明】孙逖（696？—761）曾任刑部侍郎、太子詹事。诗中的"美人"指永乐公主，她被嫁给契丹王。诗人说随着公主驾临契丹边境，春色立即跟了过来，代替了荒凉的景致。

8. Her Grievance in Spring
(Tang) Jin Changxu

I brushed away the yellow oriole，

It's chirping is so annoying on the branches of willow.

It awoke me with a start，

Otherwise，I would have been to the border to see my husband.

In Chinese phonetic alphabet and Chinese characters：

chūn yuàn
春 怨

（唐）金昌绪

dǎ	qǐ	huáng	yīng	ér
打	起	黄	莺	儿 ，

mò	jiào	zhī	shàng	tí
莫	教	枝	上	啼 。

tí	shí	jīng	qiè	mèng
啼	时	惊	妾	梦 ，

bù	dé	dào	liáo	xī
不	得	到	辽	西 。

Notes：We don't know much about this poet. This is his only poem in the *Complete Collection of Tang Poetry*. The words used in the poem are easy and simple. Each line does not make much sense by itself，yet it means a lot in the entire poem. It expressed the complaints of a young wife，whose husband was serving in the frontier army. She was meeting her husband in her dream，yet，before the meeting she was wakened up by the chirping of an oriole. The last line mentions a specific place where her husband was.

【说明】我们对诗人知之甚少。此诗是《全唐诗》中唯一一首由他创作的诗篇。此诗用词简易，每一句单独看没什么意义，但是全诗通篇却意义非凡。此诗写一位年轻妻子的哀怨，她丈夫在边塞服役，她在梦里将与丈夫相见，在马上见面之际，她被黄莺的叫声吵醒了。诗的最后一句点出了她丈夫服役之处的地名。

9. Pear Flowers in the Courtyard of the Left Office
(Tang) Qiu Wei

Your white seems colder and more elegant than snow,
Your aroma can get into my body and soul.

Spring wind, please don't stop blowing up the fallen petals,
May they fall on the jade steps and sit there still.

In Chinese phonetic alphabet and Chinese characters:

zuǒ yè lí huā
左 掖 梨 花
（唐）丘为

lěng	yàn	quán	qī	xuě
冷	艳	全	欺	雪 ，

yú	xiāng	zhà	rù	yī
余	香	乍	入	衣 。

chūn	fēng	qiě	mò	dìng
春	风	且	莫	定 ，

chuī	xiàng	yù	jiē	fēi
吹	向	玉	阶	飞 。

Notes: Qiu Wei (694? – 784?) is another eclogue poet of
Tang. The left office was the Office of Imperial Affairs, because it
was on the left side of the Imperial Court. Jade steps indicate the
Imperial Court.

【说明】丘为（694？—784？）是唐朝又一位田园诗人。左掖即
门下省，因位处皇室左边，故名。玉阶指皇宫。

10. Longing for the Intimacy with His Majesty
(Tang) Linghu Chu

Oriole's singing in the imperial garden has ceased,
Butterflies are dancing before the palace gate.
Spring season would soon be gone again,
Yet His Majesty's verdant cart hasn't come in.

In Chinese phonetic alphabet and Chinese characters:

sī jūn ēn
思 君 恩
（唐）令狐楚

xiǎo yuàn yīng gē xiē
小 苑 莺 歌 歇，
cháng mén dié wǔ duō
长 门 蝶 舞 多。
yǎn kàn chūn yòu qù
眼 看 春 又 去，
cuì niǎn bù céng guò
翠 辇 不 曾 过。

Notes：Linghu Chu（766 - 837）was once a military governor. Aside from his poetry，he was also well known for his writing of rhythmical prose. The poem describes a young lady who was selected into the imperial palace as one of the concubines of the emperor. These concubines stayed deep in the palace，not allowed to have contacts with the outside world. One would be lucky if she could have had copulation with the emperor once in her life time，most of them were forgotten，yet each of them longed for the intimacy with the emperor. This poem tells us how anxious one of them was longing for the coming of the emperor.

【说明】令狐楚（766—837）曾任节度使。除赋诗外，还善于写骈文。此诗写一年轻女子被选进皇室做皇帝的嫔妃。一旦迈入皇宫，这些嫔妃便终身幽居深宫，不准和宫外有任何联系。这些女子平生若能得到一次皇帝的宠幸，就是很走运了。她们中的大多数都会被遗忘，但是每个人都巴望能与皇帝亲近。此诗写了其中一位嫔妃盼望皇帝临幸的焦急心情。

11. The Villa of the Yuan Family
(Tang) He Zhizhang

I don't know the owner of the villa,

In this fortuitous trip，I wish to see his forest and spring here.
I told the owner buying wine is nothing he should worry about，
For I have money in my own pocket.

In Chinese phonetic alphabet and Chinese characters：

tí yuán shì bié yè
题　袁　氏　别　业

（唐）贺知章

zhǔ　rén　bù　xiāng　shí
主　人　不　相　识　，

ǒu　zuò　wéi　lín　quán
偶　坐　为　林　泉　。

mò　màn　chóu　gū　jiǔ
莫　谩　愁　沽　酒　，

náng　zhōng　zì　yǒu　qián
囊　中　自　有　钱　。

Notes：He Zhizhang（659？－744？）was once Assistant Minister of Rites．He was reputed as one of the Eight Wine Immortals with Li Bai and six others．He was widely admired for his broad mind and jovial mood．His cursive and clerical scripts of writing was often applauded．Apparently the owner of the villa in the poem was a Mr．Yuan，someone the poet didn't know．When he was passing by this villa，he found the forest and spring there attractive，so he came in and told the owner not to worry about how to receive him，and if he wanted to drink wine，he could buy it himself.

【说明】贺知章（659？—744？）曾任礼部侍郎。他与李白等人被誉为酒中八仙。他宽阔的心胸和欢快的性情被人们广为赞誉。他的草书和隶书也常被人称赞。很明显，这园林的主人姓袁，诗人并不认识他。当诗人路过此园林时，为其森林和泉水所吸引，便走了进来，告诉主人不用招呼他，他会自便，如果需要酒喝，他自己会买的。

12. Seeing off Zhao Zong at Night

(Tang) Yang Jiong

The Zhao State gem stone was worth of fifteen cities,
It had been highly regarded since ancient times.
Tonight I see you off for you're returning to your home state,
All your way ahead is under moonlight.

In Chinese phonetic alphabet and Chinese characters：

yè sòng zhào zòng
夜 送 赵 纵

（唐）杨炯

zhào shì lián chéng bì
赵 氏 连 城 璧 ，

yóu lái tiān xià chuán
由 来 天 下 传 。

sòng jūn huán jiù fǔ
送 君 还 旧 府 ，

míng yuè mǎn qián chuān
明 月 满 前 川 。

Notes：Yang Jiong （650 - 692） was reputed as a child prodigy when he was a teenager. He was known for his cruel manner in office. The Zhao State gem stone was rare and precious, the State of Qin coveted it and asked to exchange it with fifteen cities. We don't know what kind of a person Zhao Zong was, but the poet compared him to the precious gem stone, and the poem was brimmed with profound feelings toward his friend.

【说明】杨炯 （650—692） 十几岁时被誉为 "神童"。其吏治以严酷著称。赵国的和氏璧价值连城，秦国对此璧垂涎三尺，想用15座城池来换。我们对赵纵所知甚少，但是，诗人将他比喻为和氏璧，用此诗表达了对他的仰慕之情。

13. My Bamboo Forest Retreat

(Tang) Wang Wei

I sit alone deep in the bamboo forest,
I also whooped while plugging my lute.
Nobody cares my whereabouts,
Only the moon regards me as her sublunar friend.

In Chinese phonetic alphabet and Chinese characters:

zhú lǐ guǎn
竹 里 馆

（唐）王维

dú zuò yōu huáng lǐ
独 坐 幽 篁 里，

tán qín fù cháng xiào
弹 琴 复 长 啸。

shēn lín rén bù zhī
深 林 人 不 知，

míng yuè lái xiāng zhào
明 月 来 相 照。

Notes: This is Wang Wei's best "five-characters a line" quatrain. Words in each line are so plain and simple, there is no aphorism, nothing is touching or stimulating, yet it is full of artistic charm. In the poem the moon and the poet is at one.

【说明】这是王维最好的"五绝"。每行的字句都很朴实，没有什么警句，没有动人的话语，没有振奋人心的句子，却充满艺术魅力。在诗中，月亮和诗人已融为一体。

14. Seeing off Zhu Da

(Tang) Meng Haoran

You're going to the capital to seek a better fate,

My sword is worth of a thousand ounces and a gold object.

I now untie it from my waist and give it to you,

It carries my heart sincere and real.

In Chinese phonetic alphabet and Chinese characters：

sòng zhū dà rù qín
送 朱 大 入 秦
（唐）孟浩然

yóu	rén	wǔ	líng	qù
游	人	五	陵	去 ，

bǎo	jiàn	zhí	qiān	jīn
宝	剑	值	千	金 。

fēn	shǒu	tuō	xiāng	zèng
分	手	脱	相	赠 ，

píng	shēng	yī	piàn	xīn
平	生	一	片	心 。

Notes：We don't know who Zhu Da was. The title in Chinese says Zhu Da was going to Qin，because Changan，the capital was where the State of Qin used to be. The first line says Zhu Da was going to the Five Tombs area，which was tombs of five emperors situated in the capital，and the area became one of high end properties. The poet was encouraging his friend by giving his own sword to him.

【说明】我们不知道朱大是谁。诗的中文题目说朱大要入秦。因为长安所在地过去属于秦国，故有此说。诗的第一句说朱大要到五陵去，五陵曾安葬过五位皇帝，当时豪侠多在此居住。为了鼓励朋友，诗人将自己的佩剑赠送给他。

15. A Chang Gan Tune
(Tang) Cui Hao

Gentleman，may I ask where you are from?

Hengtang is my humble self's home.

I wish to stop the boat and get an answer,

For he might be my fellow villager.

In Chinese phonetic alphabet and Chinese characters:

cháng gān xíng
长 干 行
（唐）崔颢

jūn jiā hé chù zhù
君 家 何 处 住 ，

qiè zhù zài héng táng
妾 住 在 横 塘 。

tíng chuán zàn jiè wèn
停 船 暂 借 问 ，

huò kǒng shì tóng xiāng
或 恐 是 同 乡 。

Notes: The collection of folk songs and ballads in the Han Dynasty was called "The Official Conservatory". In it there was one category— "Assorted Songs. " "Chang Gan Tune" was a part of this category，which depicted women living in the area of Chang Gan by the riverside in today's Nanjing. The forlorn lady in the poem lived in a boat，which she used to carry people over the river. She was lonely，had no one to talk to. Therefore，when she overheard her hometown accent from a man，she was so delighted and wanted to speak to him and find out if he was a fellow villager.

【说明】汉朝所采集的民歌称为"乐府"。其中有"长干曲"，属于"杂曲歌词"一类。此类曲目专门描写生活在今日南京河边长干地区的妇女。此诗写一位生活在船上的孤寂女人，她用船摆渡人过河。她很孤独，没有人与她交谈。当她听到一个男人操家乡口音的时候，她非常兴奋，想找到这个人，看看他是不是老乡。

16. An Interlude in History

(Tang) Gao Shi

He gave Fan a robe made of thick coarse silk fabric,
Out of his pity for Fan's straitened state.
Not knowing Fan had become a state affair administer,
So still he took Fan as a commoner.

In Chinese phonetic alphabet and Chinese characters:

yǒng shǐ

咏 史

（唐）高适

shàng	yǒu	tí	páo	zèng
尚	有	绨	袍	赠，

yīng	lián	fàn	shū	hán
应	怜	范	叔	寒。

bù	zhī	tiān	xià	shì
不	知	天	下	士，

yóu	zuò	bù	yī	kàn
犹	作	布	衣	看。

Notes: Gao Shi（701? −762）was an assistant minister of justice, and a close friend of both Li Bai and Du Fu. The poem presents us an interlude in the Warring States period. Fan Ju was a hanger-on at the residence of Xu Jia, a minister in the State of Wei. Xu, however, charged Fan with false information before the King of the State of Wei, and then Fan was beaten, wrapped up with a mat and thrown into a dirty lavatory. Fan was rescued by someone, and he managed to escape to the State of Qin in another name and later became Qin's Prime Minister. When Qin was going to wage a war against Wei, Xu Jia was sent to Qin for a peace talk. Putting on wore clothes, Fan Ju went to see Xu Jia. Seeing Fan was still his scrubby little self, Xu gave him a robe made of coarse material. Later, when Xu found out Fan was the Prime Minister of Qin, he immediately went to Fan to apologize for what he did before. Considering Xu had given him that robe, Fan didn't revenge and set him free.

【说明】高适（701？—762）官至刑部侍郎，是李白和杜甫的好友。此诗所说是战国时期的一段往事。范雎曾是魏国中大夫须贾的门客，须贾在魏王面前诋毁他，然后鞭打范雎，范挨打后被卷入竹席，扔进厕所。幸而被人救出，用假名逃亡秦国，不久为相。秦欲伐魏，须贾奉命使秦止兵。范雎破衣求见。须贾见他如此贫寒，就送他一件绨袍。当他发现范雎就是秦相时，立即前往谢罪。范雎因为有绨袍之事，便没对他进行报复，还放走了他。

17. After My Resignation
(Tang) Li Shizhi

I've just resigned from the post of the Prime Minister,
As a wine saint I quaffed the liquor.
Then I asked: among past visitors,
Today how many of them are here?

In Chinese phonetic alphabet and Chinese characters:

bà xiàng zuò
罢 相 作

（唐）李适之

| bì | xián | chū | bà | xiàng |
| 避 | 贤 | 初 | 罢 | 相 ， |

| lè | shèng | qiě | xián | bēi |
| 乐 | 圣 | 且 | 衔 | 杯 。 |

| wèi | wèn | mén | qián | kè |
| 为 | 问 | 门 | 前 | 客 ， |

jīn   zhāo   jǐ   gè   lái
今　　朝　　几　　个　　来 。

Notes: Li Shizhi（? - 747）was a member of the imperial family and served once as the Minister of Justice. When this poem was composed he had just resigned from the post of the Left Prime Minister, because the Right Prime Minister was treacherous and tried every means to elbow him out of the post. The poet was a capacity drinker of liquor and one of the eight drinking "immortals", so he was much relieved after the resignation and he knew only a few of those frequent visitors in the past would still come, yet he still asked how many were there on the day to show his despite of timeservers.

【说明】李适之（? —747）是皇室后裔，曾任刑部尚书、左相。他作此诗时刚刚辞去左相的职务，因右相是一位奸臣，千方百计地要将他排挤出内阁。诗人酒量大，是酒中八仙之一。辞职后如释重负。辞职后，他知道只会有少数人来看他，而过去则门庭若市。明知如此，他还是问了一下，现在会有几人来看他呢？此一问，表达出他对趋炎附势者的蔑视。

18. The Knight I Met
(Tang) Qian Qi

People remember bold knights from Yan and Zhao in their mournful songs,

The hometown of Ju Meng happened to be our meeting place.

I still have much in my mind to tell you,

Yet the sun is setting and you got to go.

In Chinese phonetic alphabet and Chinese characters:

féng xiá zhě
逢 侠 者
（唐）钱起

yān zhào bēi gē shì
燕 赵 悲 歌 士 ，

xiāng féng jù mèng jiā
相 逢 剧 孟 家 。

cùn xīn yán bú jìn
寸 心 言 不 尽 ，

qián lù rì jiāng xiá
前 路 日 将 斜 。

Notes： Ju Meng was a hero and a swordsman，his hometown was Luoyang，where the poet met him. This poem was devoted to this knight out of his admiration of gallantry and valor.

【说明】诗人遇到一位侠客，出于对他的侠义和勇猛的敬佩写此诗送给他。他们相遇之处正好是剧孟的家乡洛阳，而剧孟也是西汉时期的一位侠者。

19. Looking at the Lushan Mountains from My Boat
(Tang) Qian Qi

I am discouraged by the rain storm，
The mount is before me，but I can not climb.
I figure the peaks are encapsulated by clouds and fog，
It seems the one from former dynasties is still the eminent monk.

In Chinese phonetic alphabet and Chinese characters：

jiāng xíng wàng kuāng lú
江 行 望 匡 庐
（唐）钱起

zhǐ chǐ chóu fēng yǔ
咫 尺 愁 风 雨 ，

kuāng	lú	bù	kě	dēng	
匡	庐	不	可	登	。

zhǐ	yí	yún	wù	kū	
只	疑	云	雾	窟	，

yóu	yǒu	liù	cháo	sēng	
犹	有	六	朝	僧	。

Notes: Some people believe that this poem was not composed by Qian Qi and it was the product of his great grandson Qian Xu. The Lushan Mountains was an important place for Buddhism. When the poet was not able to climb the mountain, he figured the monks from the Six Dynasties (222 – 589), that is say at least monks who came some 150 years ago might still be in the mountains, which were enclosed at the time of his visit by heavy clouds and fog. The Chinese original does mention specifically monks of the Six Dynasties while the translation only uses a singular for the monk and a general term for the dynasties for rhyming purpose.

【说明】有人认为此诗并非钱起所作，而是其曾孙钱翊所作。庐山是佛教重地。当诗人无法登山时，他设想六朝（222—589）的僧人还在山上，也就是说150年前，甚至更早的时候来的僧人仍然健在。诗人到庐山时，浓云密布，雾气腾腾。为了押韵起见，译文只说前朝僧人，且用的是单数，没有像原文那样说六朝僧。

20. Reply to Li Huan
(Tang) Wei Yingwu

After I finished reading "The Book of Changes" in the forest,
I watched idly by the brook how gulls frolicked.
The Chu region used to beget more poets,
With whom do you have frequent contacts?

In Chinese phonetic alphabet and Chinese characters:

dá lǐ huàn
答李浣
（唐）韦应物

lín zhōng guān yì bà
林　中　观　易　罢　，
xī shàng duì ōu xián
溪　上　对　鸥　闲　。
chǔ sú ráo cí kè
楚　俗　饶　词　客　，
hé rén zuì wǎng huán
何　人　最　往　还　。

Notes：We don't know who Li Huan was，except that he was a friend of Wei Yingwu．The poet projected affability with a few easy touches on trifles in a family manner．

【说明】李浣是韦应物的朋友，除此之外我们对他一无所知。诗人所说是生活中的琐事，但淡淡几笔，却写出了朋友之间的亲切感情。

21．Prelude to the Autumn Wind
（Tang）Liu Yuxi

From where comes the autumn wind？
In swish rows of wild geese fly overhead．
In the morning when the wind gets onto the trees in the yard，
The traveler in solitude is the first to detect．

In Chinese phonetic alphabet and Chinese characters：

qiū fēng yǐn
秋风引
（唐）刘禹锡

hé chù qiū fēng zhì
何　处　秋　风　至　，
xiāo xiāo sòng yàn qún
萧　萧　送　雁　群　。

<table>
<tr><td>zhāo</td><td>lái</td><td>rù</td><td>tíng</td><td>shù</td></tr>
<tr><td>朝</td><td>来</td><td>入</td><td>庭</td><td>树，</td></tr>
<tr><td>gū</td><td>kè</td><td>zuì</td><td>xiān</td><td>wén</td></tr>
<tr><td>孤</td><td>客</td><td>最</td><td>先</td><td>闻。</td></tr>
</table>

Notes: The poet, by writing about the autumn wind, is telling us how he felt when stayed far away from home and how much he longed for an earlier return.

【说明】诗人通过写秋风，表达了其远离故乡的感受，以及他想尽早还乡的心情。

22. To Landlord Qiu
(Tang) Wei Yingwu

It is in the late autumn night that I am missing you,
I whine about the cold frost in my stroll.
Pine nuts are falling in this hollow hill,
You in the hermitage must be sitting up late still.

In Chinese phonetic alphabet and Chinese characters:

qiū yè jì qiū yuán wài
秋 夜 寄 丘 员 外

（唐）韦应物

<table>
<tr><td>huái</td><td>jūn</td><td>shǔ</td><td>qiū</td><td>yè</td></tr>
<tr><td>怀</td><td>君</td><td>属</td><td>秋</td><td>夜，</td></tr>
<tr><td>sàn</td><td>bù</td><td>yǒng</td><td>liáng</td><td>tiān</td></tr>
<tr><td>散</td><td>步</td><td>咏</td><td>凉</td><td>天。</td></tr>
<tr><td>shān</td><td>kōng</td><td>sōng</td><td>zǐ</td><td>luò</td></tr>
<tr><td>山</td><td>空</td><td>松</td><td>子</td><td>落，</td></tr>
<tr><td>yōu</td><td>rén</td><td>yīng</td><td>wèi</td><td>mián</td></tr>
<tr><td>幽</td><td>人</td><td>应</td><td>未</td><td>眠。</td></tr>
</table>

Notes: This landlord Qiu was a hermit and a younger brother of Poet Qiu Wei. The hermit often exchanged poems with the poet, and this one was composed as an answer to the hermit. We can certainly feel the strong and profound thoughts contain in the plain words of the poem.

【说明】此员外是一位隐者，是丘为的弟弟。隐者经常与韦应物交换诗作。此诗就是为答隐者所作。此诗语淡而情浓，言短而意深。

23. A Day in Autumn
(Tang) Geng Wei

The rays of setting sun slant in the deep lane，
I can not find any one who could listen to my groan.
On this old road there is no pedestrian，
With the rustling of crops in the wind I'm sorrow-stricken.

In Chinese phonetic alphabet and Chinese characters：

qiū rì
秋 日

（唐）耿沛

fǎn	zhào	rù	lú	xiàng
返	照	入	闾	巷 ，
yōu	lái	shuí	gòng	yǔ
忧	来	谁	共	语 。
gǔ	dào	shǎo	rén	xíng
古	道	少	人	行 ，
qiū	fēng	dòng	hé	shǔ
秋	风	动	禾	黍 。

Notes：We don't know much about this poet，except that he was one of the "Ten Da Li Calibers" we mentioned in the foregoing. This poem depicts an autumn scene in the capital after a rebellion broke out. The poet was frustrated and saddened by the demolished buildings and deserted roads.

【说明】我们对这位诗人所知甚少，只知他是前面提到的"大历十才子"之一。此诗描写了安史之乱后京城破败的景象，表现了诗人面对山河寥落、城乡破败时心中的凄凉和无助。

24. On the Lake in Autumn
(Tang) Xue Ying

I'm having a boat tour on Lake Tai in the sunset,
The entire water is under a haze blanket.
So many vicissitudes in the long past the water has witnessed,
Nobody cares to ask who have been washed away east-ward.

In Chinese phonetic alphabet and Chinese characters:

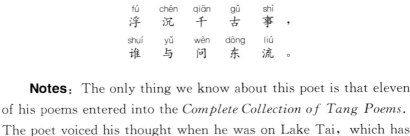

qiū rì hú shàng
秋 日 湖 上
（唐）薛莹

luò rì wǔ hú yóu
落 日 五 湖 游 ，

yān bō chù chù chóu
烟 波 处 处 愁 。

fú chén qiān gǔ shì
浮 沉 千 古 事 ，

shuí yǔ wèn dōng liú
谁 与 问 东 流 。

Notes: The only thing we know about this poet is that eleven of his poems entered into the *Complete Collection of Tang Poems*. The poet voiced his thought when he was on Lake Tai, which has been a strategically important location and was subjected to contending by various powers. In the Chinese original it refers the area of Lake Tai as the Five Lakes. Even though many who rose and fell，nobody cares to know or remember who，like the water，was being washed away toward the east.

【说明】诗人有 11 首诗被收入《全唐诗》，除此而外，我们对诗人一无所知。此诗写诗人游太湖时的感受。太湖是战略要地，是兵家必争之地。诗中将太湖一带称为五湖。历史上的兴衰，无人记得，千百年不断发生的事件像太湖上的水面浮浮沉沉，随着湖水向东流去。

25. The Imperial Court
(Tang) Li Ang

The special road for the imperial carriage is overgrown，
Flowers are in full bloom in the garden.
I don't have to ask my courtiers if I wish to scale higher，
It is now not necessary to inform my retinue any of my idea.

In Chinese phonetic alphabet and Chinese characters：

gōng zhōng tí
宫　中　题

（唐）李昂

niǎn lù shēng qiū cǎo
辇　路　生　秋　草　，
shàng lín huā mǎn zhī
上　林　花　满　枝　。
píng gāo hé xiàn yì
凭　高　何　限　意　，
wú fù shì chén zhī
无　复　侍　臣　知　。

Notes：Li Ang（809 – 840）was the second son of Emperor Mu of Tang. At the age of nineteen，he became the Emperor owing to the plot and support of a group of eunuchs. He was on the throne for fourteen years, during his reign he sent over 3,000 palace maids out of the court and fired over 1,200 officials. He failed to destroy the rule by eunuchs and as a result, he was put under house arrest and was finally killed by the eunuchs at the age of 32. Seven of his poems are still available today. This poem aims to cry out his melancholy and feelings of impotence.

【说明】李昂（809—840）是唐穆宗第二子。19 岁时由于一批太监的谋划和支持而登上皇位，在位 14 年。他当政期间将 3 000 多名宫女送出皇宫，罢黜了 1 200 多位官员。但是，他未能打破宦官的统治，结果自己却被软禁，在 32 岁时丧命于太监之手。现存他所作诗歌 7 篇。此诗道出了他的苦闷和无奈。

26. The Hermit Was Not In
(Tang) Jia Dao

Under a pine tree I asked a boy servant where the master was,
The boy replied: he left to gather medical herbs.
But he is just in this mount,
The clouds are so thick I don't know his exact where-about.

In Chinese phonetic alphabet and Chinese characters:

xún yǐn zhě bú yù
寻 隐 者 不 遇

（唐）贾岛

sōng xià wèn tóng zǐ
松 下 问 童 子 ，
yán shī cǎi yào qù
言 师 采 药 去 。
zhǐ zài cǐ shān zhōng
只 在 此 山 中 ，
yún shēn bù zhī chù
云 深 不 知 处 。

Notes：The poet intended to call on a hermit，but he was not successful. The last three lines are answers from a boy servant at the hermitage. The simple words in the question and answers reveal to us the admiration of the poet towards the hermit.

【说明】诗人拜访一位隐者，隐者却不在住处。诗的后三句是隐者的书童的答话。问答之中简朴的话语显示出诗人对隐者的敬重之情。

27. Being Startled by Autumn on the Fen River
(Tang) Su Ting

The north wind is blowing the white clouds away，
After crossing the river I have to cover a long way for a remote county.

The withering plants are being blown into my melancholy，
I can no longer bear the autumn sound that is sheer droudgery.

In Chinese phonetic alphabet and Chinese characters：

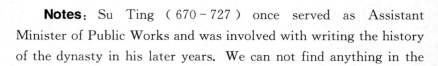

fén shàng jīng qiū
汾　上　惊　秋

（唐）苏颋

běi　fēng　chuī　bái　yún
北　风　吹　白　云　，

wàn　lǐ　dù　hé　fén
万　里　渡　河　汾　。

xīn　xù　féng　yáo　luò
心　绪　逢　摇　落　，

qiū　shēng　bù　kě　wén
秋　声　不　可　闻　。

Notes：Su Ting（670－727）once served as Assistant Minister of Public Works and was involved with writing the history of the dynasty in his later years. We can not find anything in the

246

first three lines saying how startled the poet was，yet，the white clouds，to which he compared himself，are being blown away，the long distance he has to cover is scaring and the sight of falling leaves from withering plants shocked him. So he is really startled by the autumn scene and therefore he can no longer bear the sound of autumn.

【说明】苏颋（670—727）曾任工部侍郎，晚年时参与编修国史。从诗的前三句我们看不出诗人是如何吃惊的。他将自己比作白云，然而，白云飘走了；去路遥远，景象可畏；树木枯萎，落叶飘零，他感到吃惊。秋天的景色确实吓着他了，于是他也不忍去听那秋声。

28. Behind Schedule
(Tang) Zhang Yue

I was away on business and started to count down time and day，

I have prepared an itinerary.

But the autumn was in a hurry，

It got to Luoyang ahead of me.

In Chinese phonetic alphabet and Chinese characters：

shǔ dào hòu qī
蜀 道 后 期

（唐）张说

kè xīn zhēng rì yuè
客 心 争 日 月 ，

lái wǎng yù qī chéng
来 往 预 期 程 。

qiū fēng bù xiāng dài
秋 风 不 相 待 ，

xiān zhì luò yáng chéng
先 至 洛 阳 城 。

Notes：Zhang Yue（667 – 730）served as Minister of Defense and Prime Minister of the Tang. As the title in Chinese suggests his business trip was to Sichuan. The first line says that his mind was competing with time. Unfortunately，he could not return home to Luoyang before autumn as planned，so he blamed the autumn wind for getting home earlier than him.

【说明】张说（667—730）曾任兵部尚书、宰相。正如中文标题所示，作诗时，他正在四川出差。诗的第一句说诗人正与时间赛跑。遗憾的是，他不能像事先计划的那样在秋天之前回到洛阳的家中，他便指责秋风抢在了他的前头。

29. Thoughts in the Still Night
(Tang) Li Bai

The ground is covered by moonlight before my bed，
I wonder if it was frost.
Looking up the moon is so bright，
Looking down I miss my homeland.

In Chinese phonetic alphabet and Chinese characters：

jìng yè sī
静 夜 思
（唐）李白

chuáng	qián	míng	yuè	guāng
床	前	明	月	光 ，
yí	shì	dì	shàng	shuāng
疑	是	地	上	霜 。
jǔ	tóu	wàng	míng	yuè
举	头	望	明	月 ，
dī	tóu	sī	gù	xiāng
低	头	思	故	乡 。

Notes：This poem was composed in 726 when the poet was twenty-six years old and was staying in Yangzhou, far from home. There is no novel imagination, no flowery vocabulary in the poem, it simply narrates a traveler's homesickness, and it meant much to readers ever since it came into being. The actions of the poet, the wondering, looking up and down betrays his thought. The poem turned out to be so nice and neat out of the expectation of the poet himself.

【说明】此诗写于 726 年，诗人 26 岁时，他正在远离家乡的扬州。诗中没有新奇的想象，没有华丽的辞藻，只是简单地道出了旅者的乡情。此诗问世后，对读者产生了巨大的吸引力。诗人的举动，亦即他抬头所见，低头所思，流露出诗人的思想。此诗不但美妙，而且工整。

30. The Song of Qiupu

(Tang) Li Bai

My white hair is three thousand meters long,
The causation is the anxiety that has been dragging on.
Looking at my image in the mirror,
I don't know where I got the grey hair.

In Chinese phonetic alphabet and Chinese characters：

qiū pǔ gē
秋 浦 歌

（唐）李白

bái　fà　sān　qiān　zhàng
白　发　三　千　丈，

yuán　chóu　sì　gè　cháng
缘　愁　似　个　长。

bù　zhī　míng　jìng　lǐ
不　知　明　镜　里，

hé   chù   dé   qiū shuāng

何　处　得　秋　霜　。

Notes：*The Song of Qiupu* contains seventeen poems，and this is the fifteenth. They were composed approximately in 754，when he was at Qiupu for the second time. It was ten years since he was ostracized from the capital. Seeing the country was damaged by the rebels，he was very depressed at this period. The length unit used in the Chinese original is "zhang"，which is ten Chinese foot that equals to a bit over three meters. The first line is shocking，it sounds like a volcanic eruption. How can one's hair be so long？ Nobody challenges this exaggeration. This was his way of depicting anxiety and worries. Why did he have so many worries？ Well，he was repeatedly squeezed out of the imperial court，he was ostracized more than once；he could never realize his dreams. His lonely whining has been heard in each and every generation of the Chinese，who can fully understand his grief and indignation.

【说明】《秋浦歌》共 17 首，此为第 15 首。大约在 754 年诗人第二次到秋浦时，创作了此诗。那时距他被逐出长安已经 10 年了。看到大唐被叛军搞得支离破碎，这段时间他感到很压抑。"丈"是中国的长度计量单位，等于市尺 10 尺，合 3 米多一些。第一句就令人惊愕，听起来像火山爆发一样。一个人的头发怎么会这么长？然而，从来没有人对这种夸张提出怀疑。这是诗人表达忧愁和思虑的方式。他怎么有这么多忧愁？他多次被排挤出皇室，不止一次被罢黜；他无法实现自己的理想。读者都听到了他的心声，都能理解他悲伤和愤怒的情感。

31. To Examiner Qiao
(Tang) Chen Ziang

The Han court tended to honor those good at wheeling and

dealing,

Its memorial hall ignored heroes in the border fighting.

The generals at border areas would have my sympathy,

Nobody has ever appreciated their gallantry till their hair turned grey.

In Chinese phonetic alphabet and Chinese characters:

zèng qiáo shì yù
赠 乔 侍 御

（唐）陈子昂

hàn tíng róng qiǎo huàn
汉 廷 荣 巧 宦 ，

yún gé báo biān gōng
云 阁 薄 边 功 。

kě lián cōng mǎ shǐ
可 怜 骢 马 使 ，

bái shǒu wéi shuí xióng
白 首 为 谁 雄 。

Notes: Chen Ziang （661－702） was born into a rich family in Sichuan. Being a chivalrous and straight forward young man, his talents of writing was not known. Therefore, one day he bought, in front of a big crowd, a lute with two thousand ounces of gold and told everybody present he would give a performance with the lute the next day. The next day more people came to listen to him, yet he smashed the lute and told the audience that his purpose was to show them his writings because wherever he went with his poetry and essays, he was cold-shouldered, now he wished to let all of crowd to have a look of his writings. He handed out his writings and almost every body applauded for his literary talent. And since that day he became well known. The poem criticized the Tang court instead of Han. There was a particular hall to display the portraits of meritorious officials and generals. There was a general in the Han, who was famous for riding a horse of greenish white color and who contributed much in safeguarding the frontier, yet was neglected by the Han court and his portrait was not displayed in the memorial hall. The third line mentions this general. Actually the poet meant to resent with this poem for the examiner who had been neglected.

【说明】陈子昂（661—702）出生在四川一个富足的家庭。他是一个侠义豪爽的年轻人，但是他的写作才能未被人看中。一天，在一个集市上，他当着一大堆人的面，用两千两黄金买下一把琴，而且告诉大家次日他将为大家抚琴演奏。第二天，来了很多人，他却当着大家的面把琴摔碎了，他说他让大家来，是想展示一下他的文笔，因为不管他将作品送往何处，总是受到冷落；他想让在场的人看看他的文笔到底怎样。于是，他将作品分发给大家看，结果，在场的几乎每个人都为他的写作叫好。从那一天起，他的名声就传了开来。此诗批评的虽是汉朝，实则说的是唐朝。为了表彰有功的文武官员，专门开设了一个肖像厅。汉朝有一位将军总骑一匹青白色的马，在边塞立了大功，其肖像却没有被展示在纪念厅里。诗的第三句提到这位将军。此诗实则是为乔侍郎鸣不平。

32. Reply to the Wuling Viceroy
(Tang) Wang Changling

Before I embark on a long journey with sword in my hand,
May I take the liberty to humbly say the following word?
The one who was a brain man at Daliang,
Never let Lord Xinling down.

In Chinese phonetic alphabet and Chinese characters:

dá wǔ líng tài shǒu
答 武 陵 太 守
（唐）王昌龄

zhàng jiàn xíng qiān lǐ
仗 剑 行 千 里 ，

wēi qū gǎn yī yán
微 躯 敢 一 言 。

céng wéi dà liáng kè
曾 为 大 梁 客 ，

bù fù xìn líng ēn
不 负 信 陵 恩 。

Notes：The poet himself was a brain man at the place of the Wuling viceroy. Before his departing, the viceroy gave a farewell dinner. The host must have toasted a farewell, and this poem was a return toast of the poet. The brain man at Da Liang refers to a chivalrous man, who had enjoyed much bounty from Lord Xinling, and at a critical juncture the brain man's idea saved the lord from much trouble. The poet minced his words here to say that he was like this brain man, and would live up to the hopes of the viceroy.

【说明】诗人曾是武陵太守的门客。诗人离开武陵前，太守设宴送别。主人敬酒后，此诗是答词。大梁客是一位侠义之人，曾受到信陵君不少恩惠。在关键时刻，此门客的一个主意让信陵君免去很多麻烦。诗人借用典故来说明他今后不会让太守失望。

33. Missing the Home Garden in Chang'an on the Double-Ninth Day while on a March
(Tang) Cen Shen

I forced myself to climb to a height,
Yet there is no wine that is a must on this date.

I am so regretful for the chrysanthemum flowers way back at home,

It is a battle field by their side when they blossom.

In Chinese phonetic alphabet and Chinese characters:

xíng jūn jiǔ rì sī cháng ān gù yuán
行 军 九 日 思 长 安 故 园

（唐）岑参

qiáng yù dēng gāo qù
强 欲 登 高 去 ，

wú rén sòng jiǔ lái
无 人 送 酒 来 。

yáo lián gù yuán jú
遥 怜 故 园 菊 ，

yīng bàng zhàn chǎng kāi
应 傍 战 场 开 。

Notes: We talked about the Double-Ninth Day in the foregoing. On this day people would climb to higher places and drink chrysanthemum wine. The hometown of the poet was Chang'an, the capital, which was occupied when the poet was composing this poem by rebels. The poem spelt out the poet's worry about the nation's fate and miseries people were suffering.

【说明】我们前面谈到过重阳节。重阳日人们会登高、喝菊花酒。诗人的家乡是京城长安，作此诗时，长安正被叛军占领。诗人为民族的前途和百姓遭受的苦难而深深地忧虑着。

34. The Concubine's Grievance
(Tang) Huangfu Ran

A bevy of maids have left their palace to wait on the emperor,
My heart ached when flurries of piping are blown over.

May I ask those who are now in favor,

How long your eye-brows are?

In Chinese phonetic alphabet and Chinese characters:

jié yú yuàn
婕 妤 怨

（唐）皇甫冉

huā zhī chū jiàn zhāng
花 枝 出 建 章 ，

fèng guǎn fā zhāo yáng
凤 管 发 昭 阳 。

jiè wèn chéng ēn zhě
借 问 承 恩 者 ，

shuāng é jǐ xǔ cháng
双 蛾 几 许 长 。

Notes：Huangfu Ran （718? - 767） was one of the "Ten Da Li Calibers". His regulated poems were well known. The title, which bears a name of a particular concubine, used to be a rubric of the Han Official Conservatory. This concubine was the aunt of the famous historian Ban Gu. The poem described her mind when she lost the favor of the emperor. The pipe music from the emperor's hall was disturbing, the last line actually asks: how long could the new favor be. The poet used the concubine's mouth to resent about his own frustration of not being recognized by the imperial court.

【说明】皇甫冉 （718? —767） 是 "大历十才子" 之一，以写律诗著称。诗的题目里有一位嫔妃的名字，这样的题目经常出现在汉乐府诗里。这位嫔妃是汉朝历史学家班固的姑姑。此诗道出了她失宠后的想法。皇室里传出来的笛声很恼人；最后一句问得很直接：新人受宠又能长几时？诗人借嫔妃之口，道出了自己因朝廷不看重他而生的怨愤。

35. For the Bamboo Forest Temple

(Tang) Zhu Fang

Years and months in the human world are so short,

Mist and clouds at this place are more frequent.

To this temple I am very much attached,

In the rest of my life how many more times can I come and visit?

In Chinese phonetic alphabet and Chinese characters:

tí zhú lín sì
题 竹 林 寺

（唐）朱放

suì	yuè	rén	jiān	cù
岁	月	人	间	促 ，

yān	xiá	cǐ	dì	duō
烟	霞	此	地	多 。

yīn	qín	zhú	lín	sì
殷	勤	竹	林	寺 ，

gèng	dé	jǐ	huí	guò
更	得	几	回	过 。

Notes: Zhu Fang (? – 788?) was a very popular figure at his time, many poets were his close friends. He declined offers to work in the government. There is one volume devoted to his poetry in the *Complete Collection of Tang Poetry*. This bamboo forest temple was where the famous "Seven Bamboo Forest Scholars" used to gather. They were representatives of meta-physics thought and active in the late "Three-Kingdom" period. The poet expressed in the poem how much he adored the scholars and his wish to live in solitude like them.

【说明】朱放（? —788?）在世时就享有名声，很多诗人都是他的好友。他曾谢绝出仕的邀请。《全唐诗》专有一卷收他的诗作。

此竹林寺是有名的"竹林七贤"聚会的地方。这七个人是玄学的代表，在三国后期非常活跃。此诗表达了作者对七贤的仰慕，以及他要像他们那样过隐居生活的愿望。

36. The Qu Yuan Temple

(Tang) Dai Shulun

Rivers Yuan and Xiang run for ever,
Grievance of Qu Yuan we can still hear.
Autumn wind rises at dusk,
And swishes are sounding through the maple forest.

In Chinese phonetic alphabet and Chinese characters:

sān lú miào
三 闾 庙

（唐）戴叔伦

yuán xiāng liú bù jìn
沅 湘 流 不 尽 ，

qū zǐ yuàn hé shēn
屈 子 怨 何 深 。

rì mù qiū fēng qǐ
日 暮 秋 风 起 ，

xiāo xiāo fēng shù lín
萧 萧 枫 树 林 。

Notes: Dai Shulun （732－789） was a famous poet of mid-Tang period. Unlike his father and grandfather, who were hermits, he worked as head in several local governments. Qu Yuan is one of the greatest poets of China, whose *Grievance* is China's first long lyric. When his home state—Chu was over taken by others, he saw no hope of realizing his political aspirations, he drowned himself in a river, and when people heard about this, they tried

257

to chase him in their boats, and such became the "Dragon Boat Festival" in China. The title in Chinese says "The Qu Yuan Temple", because Qu was the Minister of Patriarchal Affairs. The Temple is still there today. River Yuan and River Xiang are all in the State of Chu. The maple forest was just at the side of the temple. The second line in the original says that the grievance of Qu was very deep. Critics say that the last two lines only touch on the scenery without any comments, yet such a method has been regarded as a much better way to cry out the sorrows for the great poet.

【说明】戴叔伦（732—789）是唐中期著名诗人。与其父和祖父不同，他没有做隐士，而是在地方政府担任刺史等官职。屈原是中国最伟大的诗人之一，其《离骚》是中国第一首抒情长诗。当他的故乡——楚国被别人侵占后，他失去了实现自己政治抱负的希望，便投江自尽了。人们听到这个消息后，就划船追赶他，这个行动后来演变为中国的"龙舟节"。中文的题目提到"三闾庙"，因为屈原曾任三闾大夫。此庙今日仍在。沅江和湘江都在楚国，枫树林就在庙的外面。诗的第二句道出了屈原深深的哀怨。有评论说诗的最后两句只写景，没有一字进行评论，却是喊出伟大诗人心中悲痛的最好方法。

37. Farewell by the Yishui River
(Tang) Luo Binwang

He said farewell to the Prince of Yan by the riverside,
Out of rage his hair erected and propped up his hat.
It has been long since the hero deceased,
The water in the river is just as cold.

In Chinese phonetic alphabet and Chinese characters:

yì shuǐ sòng bié
易 水 送 别
（唐）骆宾王

cǐ	dì	bié	yān	dān
此	地	别	燕	丹 ，

zhuàng	shì	fà	chōng	guān
壮	士	发	冲	冠 。

xī	shí	rén	yǐ	mò
昔	时	人	已	没 ，

jīn	rì	shuǐ	yóu	hán
今	日	水	犹	寒 。

Notes：Luo Binwang （638？ - 685？） was one of the four most outstanding scholars in early Tang. This poem depicts the hero who was sent by the Prince of the State of Yan to assassinate The First Emperor of Qin. The prince saw off the hero at the side of Yishui River. There was a musician to play his lute to boost up the spirit of the hero，who also sang out：wind whistles and the water of the Yishui River is cold，I shall take my leave and not possible for me to come back. The hero failed and was killed. The poem above echoed to the hero's own words by saying the water was just as cold as it was when he left.

【说明】骆宾王 （638？ —685？） 是初唐四位最杰出的学者之一。此诗写的是被燕国太子派去刺杀秦王的英雄。太子在易水河岸为英雄送行。一位音乐家当场击筑为英雄鼓舞士气。英雄唱道：风萧萧兮易水寒，壮士一去兮不复还。英雄刺杀未成，牺牲了。此诗对英雄的吟唱做出了回应：易水仍然像他离开时一样寒冷。

38. Departing Mr. Lu
(Tang) Sikong Shu

Though the date has been set for our next appointment，

Tonight it is still difficult to part.

To let you stay on, this wine toasted by friend,

Can be more effective than the strong head wind.

In Chinese phonetic alphabet and Chinese characters：

bié lú qín qīng
别 卢 秦 卿

（唐）司空曙

zhī	yǒu	qián	qī	zài
知	有	前	期	在 ，

nán	fēn	cǐ	yè	zhōng
难	分	此	夜	中 。

wú	jiāng	gù	rén	jiǔ
无	将	故	人	酒 ，

bù	jí	shí	yóu	fēng
不	及	石	尤	风 。

Notes：Sikong Shu (720? – 790?) was one of the "Ten Da Li Calibers", the highest official post he held was a director of urban affairs. He was well known for describing feelings of staying at alien places and feelings for living in a straitened condition. We don't know who Mr. Lu was. In the Chinese original the head wind is named "Shi You", which are family names of a couple, the husband was doing business away from home, the wife died of missing her husband, and before her death, she wished head wind could stop all men from leaving their wives. Since then head wind was named by "Shi You".

【说明】司空曙（720？—790？）是"大历十才子"之一，官至虞部郎中。其诗以表现异乡流落之感知名。我们不知道卢秦卿是谁。中文原文将逆风称为"石尤"风，而石与尤是一对夫妻的姓，丈夫离开家乡到远处做生意，妻子因思念丈夫而亡。她故去之前，希望逆风可以阻挡丈夫们离别他们的妻子。自此，逆风被称为"石尤"风。

39. An Answer
The High Hermit

Occasionally I come to the pine,

Rest my head on the stone I sleep sound and fine.

In the mountains there is no calendar,

When the cold days are gong I don't know I am in which year.

In Chinese phonetic alphabet and Chinese characters:

dá rén
答 人
太上隐者

ǒu	lái	sōng	shù	xià
偶	来	松	树	下 ，

gāo	zhěn	shí	tóu	mián
高	枕	石	头	眠 。

shān	zhōng	wú	lì	rì
山	中	无	历	日 ，

hán	jìn	bù	zhī	nián
寒	尽	不	知	年 。

Notes: The poet, or the hermit was anonymous, so people asked him who he was, then he composed this poem as an answer. The poem says how the hermit enjoyed his blithe life away from the outside noisy world.

【说明】诗人，或者说这位太上隐者是位匿名之人。当人们问他是何人时，他作此诗来回答。诗人讲他远离尘世，非常享受静谧的生活。

A **P**rimer of **A**ncient **P**oetry 千家诗

Part IV "Five-Characters a Line" Octaves

卷四　五律

For a "five-characters a line" octave, there must be eight lines in it. There must be antitheses between the third and the fourth lines, and between the fifth and the sixth lines. Tonal patterns must be strictly followed. Usually it rhymes at the end of each even number line at a flat tone. There are forty-five poems in this part. Now, let's look at each of them.

五言律诗必须有八句。第三句和第四句，第五句和第六句必须对仗。平仄要求严格。一般来讲，在偶数行押韵。此卷收诗四十五首。现在，让我们一首一首地读一下。

1. Going through Jianmen Pass from Sichuan
(Tang) Li Longji

The Jianmen Mountains piercing through clouds,

Having finished inspections I now return with my retinues.

Verdant are the screen like high peaks,

Red are the stone walls built by the Five Giants.

Now and then banners seem to be entangled with shrubs,

Clouds are coming to brush the horses.

To get along with our times morality is important,

I applaud what has been achieved by my officials.

In Chinese phonetic alphabet and Chinese characters:

xìng shǔ huí zhì jiàn mén
幸 蜀 回 至 剑 门

（唐）李隆基

jiàn gé héng yún jùn
剑 阁 横 云 峻 ，

luán yú chū shòu huí
銮 舆 出 狩 回 。

cuì píng qiān rèn hé
翠 屏 千 仞 合 ，

dān zhàng wǔ dīng kāi
丹 嶂 五 丁 开 。

guàn mù yíng qí zhuǎn
灌 木 萦 旗 转 ，

xiān yún fú mǎ lái
仙 云 拂 马 来 。

chéng shí fāng zài dé
乘 时 方 在 德 ，

jiē ěr lè míng cái
嗟 尔 勒 铭 才 。

Notes: Li Longji （685 – 762）, one of the emperors of the Tang, whose reign was the longest among all Tang emperors. During 713 – 741, the society was most developed. In 755 a rebellion broke out, Li Longji had to go to Sichuan when the rebels took the capital, This poem was composed in 757 when order was restored and when he had crossed the Jianmen Pass on his way back to the capital, He said he had finished inspections rather than running away from rebels. "The Five Giants" are adopted from a legend, which says that when King Hui of Qin was waging a war against the State of Shu, he didn't know how to get to Shu. He built five stone cows and under the tail of each cow, he put some gold there and said that those cows could shit out gold. Hearing this the King of Shu sent five giants to pull back the stone cows. And thus marked out the way for the Qin troops. Going ahead in his political life, he realized morality would be important. In the poem he praised his officials who helped restore the social order.

【说明】李隆基（685—762）是唐朝的皇帝之一，当政时间最长。713—741 年，唐朝社会很发达。755 年爆发安史之乱，在叛军攻占京城后，李隆基不得不逃往四川。此诗作于 757 年，当时已恢复社会秩序，他已经过了剑门关，在回长安的路上，他说自己是巡视回朝，而不是逃亡后返京。"五丁之说"引自一个传说，说秦惠王伐蜀不识道路，于是造五只石牛，置金牛尾下，扬言牛能屙金。蜀王负力信以为真，派五壮士拉牛回国，为秦开出通蜀的道路。李隆基意识到，他的国家往下走，道德非常重要。诗中赞扬了为恢复社会秩序而努力的官员。

2. Reply to Prime Minister Lu
(Tang) Du Shenyan

Only those officials who work far away from hometown,
Are often startled by the new climate change phenomenon.
Rosy clouds are splendid when the sun is rising behind the sea,

Spring has just crossed the river when in the south trees blossom happily.

Prompted by warm spring air orioles sing with joy,

Under the bright sun the green of duckweed becomes heavy.

When I suddenly hear the antiquated song you're singing,

I begin to miss home and my clothes get wet from weeping.

In Chinese phonetic alphabet and Chinese characters:

hé jìn líng lù chéng zǎo chūn yóu wàng
和 晋 陵 陆 丞 早 春 游 望

（唐）杜审言

dú yǒu huàn yóu rén
独 有 宦 游 人 ，

piān jīng wù hòu xīn
偏 惊 物 候 新 。

yún xiá chū hǎi shǔ
云 霞 出 海 曙 ，

méi liǔ dù jiāng chūn
梅 柳 渡 江 春 。

shū qì cuī huáng niǎo
淑 气 催 黄 鸟 ，

qíng guāng zhuǎn lù pín
晴 光 转 绿 蘋 。

hū wén gē gǔ diào
忽 闻 歌 古 调 ，

guī sī yù zhān jīn
归 思 欲 沾 巾 。

Notes: Du Shenyan （648? – 708） once served as Rector of the Imperial College. He contributed much to the development of regulated poems. The poem was a reply to Prime Minister Lu, who was from Jinling. Line four mentions two trees—plum and willow, which were in blossom in south of China. While giving an affirmative view on the poem by the Prime Minister, the poem also expresses the poet's serious home-sickness.

【说明】杜审言（648？—708）曾任国子监主簿，对律诗的发展做出过很大的贡献。诗的中文题目反映出晋陵是陆丞相的家乡。第四句提到梅、柳两种树木，暗指南方已经春意盎然。诗人对陆丞的诗予以肯定，同时也抒发了思乡之情。

3. In Praise of Zhongnan Mountains
(Tang) Du Shenyan

The Big Dipper hangs over the city edge,
To the mountains the three halls are leverage.
Magnificent halls are so high that clouds often emerge,
Exquisite chambers and lofts seem to be pendants on tree branch.
Half way on the mountain refreshing aura hangs,
Auspicious clouds encircle mountain peaks.
I, a humble official, wish to toast the Emperor longevity,
May our country live in eternal peace and prosperity.

In Chinese phonetic alphabet and Chinese characters:

péng lái sān diàn shì yàn fèng chì yǒng zhōng nán shān
蓬 莱 三 殿 侍 宴 奉 敕 咏 终 南 山

（唐）杜审言

běi dǒu guà chéng biān
北 斗 挂 城 边 ，

nán shān yǐ diàn qián
南 山 倚 殿 前 。

yún biāo jīn què jiǒng
云 标 金 阙 迥 ，

shù miǎo yù táng xuán
树 杪 玉 堂 悬 。

bàn lǐng tōng jiā qì
半 岭 通 佳 气 ，

zhōng	fēng	rào	ruì	yān
中	峰	绕	瑞	烟 。

xiǎo	chén	chí	xiàn	shòu
小	臣	持	献	寿 ，

cháng	cǐ	dài	yáo	tiān
长	此	戴	尧	天 。

Notes： The poet was asked to come to the birthday banquet of the Emperor，during the banquet the Emperor asked him to compose a poem on the Zhongnan Mountains. So，the poem was an impromptu on the spot. There were three big halls named "Peng Lai" in the imperial court of the Tang，which were filled with guests at the Emperor's birthday party. The original Chinese of the last line says：may the days like those during the reign of Yao last for ever. Yao was the earliest ruler in China，who was nice and brought peace and prosperity to the nation.

【说明】诗人应邀出席皇帝的寿宴，并受命写一首以终南山为题的诗。因此，此诗是当场即兴之作。在唐朝皇宫里有三座名为"蓬莱"的宫殿，寿宴时，这一天会坐满群臣。原文最后一句说：长此戴尧天。尧是上古时期领袖，他为民族带来了和平与繁荣。

4. Saying Goodbye to a Friend in a Spring Night
(Tang) Chen Ziang

White candles emit wisps of dark smoke，
I raise a golden cup at this grand banquet.
The departing hall is filled with cordial disposition，
Regardless of the ensuing journey through the mountain.
The moon has retreated to the back of tall trees，
Into the light of early dawn the Milky Way disappears.

The trip to Luoyang is a long distance ahead,

We don't know when is our next meeting date.

In Chinese phonetic alphabet and Chinese characters:

chūn yè bié yǒu rén
春 夜 别 友 人

（唐）陈子昂

yín zhú tǔ qīng yān
银 烛 吐 清 烟 ，

jīn zūn duì qǐ yán
金 尊 对 绮 筵 。

lí táng sī qín sè
离 堂 思 琴 瑟 ，

bié lù rào shān chuān
别 路 绕 山 川 。

míng yuè yǐn gāo shù
明 月 隐 高 树 ，

cháng hé méi xiǎo tiān
长 河 没 晓 天 。

yōu yōu luò yáng qù
悠 悠 洛 阳 去 ，

cǐ huì zài hé nián
此 会 在 何 年 。

Notes: The first four lines depict things indoor and how the poet felt. The second four lines move to the outdoor when the moon is setting and the first ray of dawn is coming. The poet has to depart without any idea of when they can meet again in the future.

【说明】诗的前四句写室内的景物及诗人的感受，后四句移到室外，写月落和第一线曙光。诗人不得不离别友人，而且不知道他们何时才能再聚首。

5. Banquet at the Palace of the Princess
(Tang) Li Qiao

The palace is in the suburb near the dark green fields,

While the bells ring the Imperial cart descends.

Like the landing rows of bird officials have flanked the long tables,

The phoenix tune was played by flute and other instruments.

Tall trees stand next to the Nanshan Mountains,

The mist also extends to the river in the distance.

All had a drop too much thanks to the majestic favor,

Being carried by the bacchanalian atmosphere there is no sign of his departure.

In Chinese phonetic alphabet and Chinese characters:

cháng níng gōng zhǔ dōng zhuāng shì yàn
长　宁　公　主　东　庄　侍　宴
（唐）李峤

bié　yè　lín　qīng　diàn
别　业　临　青　甸　,

míng　luán　jiàng　zǐ　xiāo
鸣　銮　降　紫　霄　。

cháng　yán　yuān　lù　jí
长　筵　鹓　鹭　集　,

xiān　guǎn　fèng　huáng　diào
仙　管　凤　凰　调　。

shù　jiē　nán　shān　jìn
树　接　南　山　近　,

yān　hán　běi　zhǔ　yáo
烟　含　北　渚　遥　。

chéng　ēn　xián　yǐ　zuì
承　恩　咸　已　醉　,

liàn　shǎng　wèi　huán　biāo
恋　赏　未　还　镳　。

Notes: Li Qiao（644 - 713）served four emperors in his

political career as Minister of Personnel and Chief of the Secretariat. On April 1, 710, the Emperor went to the residence of his daughter—Princess Changning and had a dinner there. The poet was asked to accompany the Emperor and during dinner he was ordered to compose a poem. The first three lines tell us how the villa of the princess was. The rest depict the grand style of the royal family.

【说明】李峤（644—713）服务过四任皇帝，官至吏部尚书、中书令。710 年 4 月 1 日，皇帝去他女儿长宁公主处赴宴。诗人被命令作为随从同往，宴会期间被命赋诗。前三句写公主居所的状况，其余写皇家的宏大与豪华。

6. A Poem Rhyming with the Sound of "Lin"
(Tang) Zhang Yue

An academy is set up in the Imperial Library,

It's the venue for us scholars to come for our assembly.

Having read "The Book of Songs" we will conduct state administration,

Having expounded "The Book of Changes" we would know the intention of the Heaven.

My duty is prodigious as a Prime Minister,

By the grace of the Emperor I drank too much and almost fall into a slumber.

I'm so delirious that I sing and extol spring,

To show my gratitude to the Emperor for his trust and understanding.

In Chinese phonetic alphabet and Chinese characters:

ēn cì lì zhèng diàn shū yuàn cì yàn yīng zhì dé lín zì
恩 赐 丽 正 殿 书 院 赐 宴 应 制 得 林 字

（唐）张说

dōng bì tú shū fǔ
东 壁 图 书 府，

xī yuán hàn mò lín
西 园 翰 墨 林。

sòng shī wén guó zhèng
诵 诗 闻 国 政，

jiǎng yì jiàn tiān xīn
讲 易 见 天 心。

wèi qiè hé gēng chóng
位 窃 和 羹 重，

ēn tāo zuì jiǔ shēn
恩 叨 醉 酒 深。

zài gē chūn xìng qǔ
载 歌 春 兴 曲，

qíng jié wéi zhī yīn
情 竭 为 知 音。

Notes: An academy was established in 725, the poet was appointed the rector to over look the studies of classics by officials. For the inauguration the Emperor gave a banquet, and at the banquet the Emperor asked the poet to compose a poem. The Emperor also gave a sound for the rhyming. The hall that housed the academy was called "the eastern wall", which, in Chinese astronomy, means two constellations that were in charge of books and education, therefore, the Imperial Library was also in the same building. The original of the second line mentions "a western garden", which used to be a place for the scholars in the period of the Three-Kingdoms to gather. In the poem the academy was compared as a western garden. The Emperor asked the poem must rhyme with the sound of "lin". As it turned out the poem rhymes at the end of every other line with the sound of "lin", "xin", "shen" and "yin", which all ends with "n".

【说明】725 年丽正殿设立了书院，诗人被任命为书院使。在正式启用书院的宴会上，皇帝命诗人赋诗，而且要押"林"字韵。书院设在东壁，按中国天文学的说法，东壁指两个星座、两个掌管天上文章和图书的秘府。因此，皇家书院也在东壁。诗的第二句提到的"西园"是三国时期学者们聚会的地方。在诗里，书院被比喻为"西园"。诗人隔行所押"林"字韵的用字为"林"、"心"、"深"和"音"，这几个字的尾音都是"n"。

7. Seeing off a Friend

(Tang) Li Bai

Outside the northern outer wall the green hill lies,
Around the eastern city the clear river circles.
At this place I would wish you a safe and sound journey,
Like drifting dried grass you would be blown far away.
Being floated like clouds is a wanderer,
The sun is setting down much slower.
We wave at each other at your departure,
With a long trip ahead your horse neighs much louder.

In Chinese phonetic alphabet and Chinese characters:

sòng yǒu rén
送 友 人

（唐）李白

qīng shān héng běi guō
青 山 横 北 郭 ，

bái shuǐ rào dōng chéng
白 水 绕 东 城 。

cǐ dì yì wéi bié
此 地 一 为 别 ，

gū péng wàn lǐ zhēng
孤 蓬 万 里 征 。

fú	yún	yóu	zǐ	yì
浮	云	游	子	意 ，
luò	rì	gù	rén	qíng
落	日	故	人	情 。
huī	shǒu	zì	zī	qù
挥	手	自	兹	去 ，
xiāo	xiāo	bān	mǎ	míng
萧	萧	班	马	鸣 。

Notes：The poem was composed in 754，when the poet said farewell to a friend at Xuancheng city. The poet used a handful of dried grass and floating clouds to describe the wanderer，who was lonely and had to travel from place to place. He used the setting sun to describe his reluctance in parting with his friend. A neighing horse added sorrow to the departure.

【说明】此诗作于 754 年，当时诗人在宣城正与一位友人告别。诗中把友人的漂泊比喻为蓬草和浮云，别后的旅途将会寂寞，漂泊不定。他用落日比喻自己不舍的心情。马的嘶鸣又添几分悲伤。

8. Seeing off a Friend to Sichuan
(Tang) Li Bai

People say this is the road to （Sichuan） the State of Shu，
Not easy to travel for it is rugged and tough.
Cliffs always plunge at your side，
Clouds swirl and billow in front of horse head.
Trees and branches on the cliff provide shade to the plank road，
Cities surrounded by spring river are in sight.
Your fate in official career has been ordained，
There is no use to ask a diviner to predict.

In Chinese phonetic alphabet and Chinese characters：

sòng yǒu rén rù shǔ
送 友 人 入 蜀
（唐）李白

jiàn shuō cán cóng lù
见 说 蚕 丛 路，
qí qū bú yì xíng
崎 岖 不 易 行。
shān cóng rén miàn qǐ
山 从 人 面 起，
yún bàng mǎ tóu shēng
云 傍 马 头 生。
fāng shù lǒng qín zhàn
芳 树 笼 秦 栈，
chūn liú rào shǔ chéng
春 流 绕 蜀 城。
shēng chén yīng yǐ dìng
升 沉 应 已 定，
bú bì wèn jūn píng
不 必 问 君 平。

Notes：This poem was composed in 743. By saying how difficult to travel back to Sichuan, the poet showed his concern of the friend. He was persuading his friend not to care too much about his official position and privilege. The last line in the original gives a name of a diviner in the Han Dynasty, to refer to diviners in the Han Dynasty; apparently, his friend was going to see a diviner to find out how his fate in the officialdom would be.

【说明】此诗作于743年。诗人说回川之路困难，表达了对朋友的关心。他试图说服友人不要太在意官场的地位和得失。诗的最后一句给出了汉朝一位占卜者的名字，在此代指任何一位占卜者。他的友人将拜访某位占卜者，去看看他的官运如何。

9. At the Foot of Beigu Mountains
(Tang) Wang Wan

Travelers are passing through the green mountain foot,

The verdant water is carrying their boat forward.

Water is surging up and the river is being widened,

The sail is full with a tail wind.

In the residuals of night from the sea the sun is an earlier riser,

Spring seems entering into the remaining of the year on the river.

When can my letter be delivered home I wonder,

The returning wild geese may get there sooner.

In Chinese phonetic alphabet and Chinese characters:

cì běi gù shān xià
次 北 固 山 下

（唐）王湾

kè lù qīng shān wài
客 路 青 山 外 ，

xíng zhōu lù shuǐ qián
行 舟 绿 水 前 。

cháo píng liǎng àn kuò
潮 平 两 岸 阔 ，

fēng zhèng yì fān xuán
风 正 一 帆 悬 。

hǎi rì shēng cán yè
海 日 生 残 夜 ，

jiāng chūn rù jiù nián
江 春 入 旧 年 。

xiāng shū hé chù dá
乡 书 何 处 达 ，

guī yàn luò yáng biān
归 雁 洛 阳 边 。

Notes：Wang Wan（693 – 751）was born in Luoyang. He was once a local city register, a proof-reader at the Imperial Academy. Not many of his poems survived, but the few that are still available are well known. The poem is famous for its description of the scene along the lower ridges of the Changjiang River and his homesickness by way of writing about the wild geese that were returning to the north.

【说明】王湾（693—751）生在洛阳。曾任地方主簿，曾编校丽正书院藏书。他的诗存世很少，仅存的几首均非常有名。此诗以描写长江下游的景色以及见雁思亲而著称。

10. The Villa of the Su Family
(Tang) Zu Yong

Villa can serve as a retreat,
It's where you can live as a hermit.
The distant Southern Mountains is my window view,
Into the river the garden casts its shadow.
What remains on the bamboo branches are the winter snow,
The courtyard is already dim before the sun is low.
It's so quiet and still as not in a mundane world,
I sit and listen leisurely to the spring bird.

In Chinese phonetic alphabet and Chinese characters:

sū shì bié yè
苏 氏 别 业
（唐）祖咏

bié yè jū yōu chù
别 业 居 幽 处 ，

dào lái shēng yǐn xīn
到 来 生 隐 心 。

nán shān dāng hù yǒu
南 山 当 户 牖 ，

lǐ shuǐ yìng yuán lín
澧 水 映 园 林 。

zhú fù jīng dōng xuě
竹 覆 经 冬 雪 ，

tíng hūn wèi xī yīn
庭 昏 未 夕 阴 。

liáo liáo rén jìng wài
寥　寥　人　境　外　,
xián zuò tīng chūn qín
闲　坐　听　春　禽　。

Notes：Zu Yong（699 – 746?）was constantly ostracized in his political career，and then decided to become a hermit and lived on fishery and woodcutting. He was a famous pastoral poet of the Tang Dynasty.

【说明】祖咏（699—746?）在政治生涯中多次遭贬，于是做起了隐者，以打鱼打柴为生。他是唐朝著名的田园诗人。

11. On Duty in a Spring Night
(Tang) Du Fu

Flowers hide behind the low wall of the hall on the left，
Chattering birds are flying past to their nest for the night.
When stars appear lamp lights in a thousand rooms shimmer，
The imperial hall receives more moon light because they're much higher.
I sit up late and heard the opening of the gate lock，
I think of the horse bells as I hear the rustling night wind.
Tomorrow morning we have to deal with many issues，
I asked what hour it was several times.

In Chinese phonetic alphabet and Chinese characters：

chūn xiǔ zuǒ shěng
春　宿　左　省
（唐）杜甫

huā yǐn yè yuán mù
花　隐　掖　垣　暮　,
jiū jiū qī niǎo guò
啾　啾　栖　鸟　过　。

xīng	lín	wàn	hù	dòng
星	临	万	户	动 ，
yuè	bàng	jiǔ	xiāo	duō
月	傍	九	霄	多 。
bù	qǐn	tīng	jīn	yào
不	寝	听	金	钥 ，
yīn	fēng	xiǎng	yù	kē
因	风	想	玉	珂 。
míng	cháo	yǒu	fēng	shì
明	朝	有	封	事 ，
shuò	wèn	yè	rú	hé
数	问	夜	如	何 。

Notes: This poem was probably composed in 758 when the poet was the Left Adminisher in the General Office of the Imperial Affairs, which was on the left side of the Imperial Hall. The poem described what he saw from the dusk to the early morning when he was on duty and it shows to us how prudent and cautious he was.

【说明】此诗可能作于 758 年，当时杜甫任门下省左拾遗。门下省在皇宫的左侧。该诗详细描述了门下省自黄昏到第二日拂晓的情况，表现出诗人谨慎敬业的态度。

12. Inscription for the Mural in the Monk's Room
(Tang) Du Fu

Nobody knows in which year the Tiger Head Gu drew the mural on this wall,

The coves and seas in it are so vivid and real.

The sun can not deprive the forest and peaks of their verdure quality,

Under the azure sky the river surges towards the sea.

The monastery is just on the opposite of the White Crane Temple on the other side,

In between the veteran monk crosses the river by riding a wooden cup.

I suddenly felt I'm familiar with the roads here,

An impelling force in my carnal body asks me to follow the great monk afar.

In Chinese phonetic alphabet and Chinese characters：

tí xuán wǔ chán shī wū bì
题 玄 武 禅 师 屋 壁

（唐）杜甫

hé nián gù hǔ tóu
何 年 顾 虎 头 ，

mǎn bì huà cāng zhōu
满 壁 画 沧 洲 。

chì rì shí lín qì
赤 日 石 林 气 ，

qīng tiān jiāng hǎi liú
青 天 江 海 流 。

xī fēi cháng jìn hè
锡 飞 常 近 鹤 ，

bēi dù bù jīng ōu
杯 渡 不 惊 鸥 。

sì dé lú shān lù
似 得 庐 山 路 ，

zhēn suí huì yuǎn yóu
真 随 惠 远 游 。

Notes：Tiger Head Gu is the nick name of Gu Kaizhi (344 – 405)，one of the most important artists in China. The mural was on the wall of a room of one monk at the Xuanwu Temple. The fifth line contains a story in the Southern Dynasties，a Buddhist monk and a Taoist priest chose the same place for their venue，the emperor at their time asked each to contest in their supernatural skills. The Taoist set free his white crane and the Buddhist throw his walking stick into the sky. Just before the crane touched down， the stick already got there and stood upright on the ground. So the chosen spot was given to the monk and the Taoist built his temple at where the crane landed. The sixth line tells a legend about a monk，who used to shuttle between the monastery and the temple on water by riding a wooden cup. What is missing in the translation is that when the monk is crossing the river on a wooden cup no gulls were startled. The last line in the original does mention the name of the great monk—Hui Yuan，who was a close friend of the famous poet in the Jin Dynasty—Tao Yuanming（352－427）. Hui Yuan used to live in the Lushan Mountains，the seventh line actually says the poet felt the roads at Xuanwu Mountains as familiar as those in the Lushan Mountains. In the last line，the poet compared himself to Tao Yuanming.

【说明】顾虎头是顾恺之（344—405）的外号，他是中国最重要的画家，壁画画在玄武寺一僧人房间的墙上。第五句说了一个南朝的故事：一个僧人和一位道士都选中了同一个地方修建他们的修行之地。当时的皇帝，让他们比法术来决定谁建。于是，道士放飞了他的仙鹤，僧人则将拐杖扔到天空。就在仙鹤快要落地的时候，拐杖已直直地戳在了地上。这样，他们看中的地方就给了僧人，道士则在仙鹤落脚的地方修了道观。第六句也讲了一个传说，说一位僧人在水面上往来于道观和寺庙之间，其往来就靠站在一只木杯上。译文未能表示出如下的意思：僧人站在木杯上过江，江里的鸥鸟丝毫未被惊吓。诗的最后一句提到的惠远和尚是晋朝诗人陶渊明（352—427）的好朋友，惠远生活在庐山。诗的第七句说诗人觉得玄武山有些像庐山。在最后一句，诗人将自己比喻为陶渊明。

13. The Zhongshan Mountains
（Tang）Wang Wei

The Taiyi Peak soars nigh on the Heavenly Capital，

The mountains extend to the sea through ridges and hill.

Looking back the parted white clouds are merging into one again,

When I entered into the pale grey mist, the mist is nowhere to be seen.

A separator is what the central peak tries to play,

Some coves are sunny and some dales are cloudy.

Someone wants to find a place to lodge in the mountains,

He asked a woodman across the river for directions.

In Chinese phonetic alphabet and Chinese characters：

zhōng nán shān

终　南　山

（唐）王维

tài yǐ jìn tiān dū
太 乙 近 天 都，

lián shān dào hǎi yú
连 山 到 海 隅。

bái yún huí wàng hé
白 云 回 望 合，

qīng ǎi rù kàn wú
青 霭 入 看 无。

fēn yě zhōng fēng biàn
分 野 中 峰 变，

yīn qíng zhòng hè shū
阴 晴 众 壑 殊。

yù tóu rén chù sù
欲 投 人 处 宿，

gé shuǐ wèn qiáo fū
隔 水 问 樵 夫。

Notes：Taiyi is the highest peak in the Zhongnan Mountains. The poet had a villa in the mountains. He loved the scenery there and wrote many poems about the mountain. There are over 1,800 poems describing this mountain in the *Complete Collection of Tang*

Poetry, yet, this is the only one that is entitled with the name of the mountain. The poem started from looking at the mountain from a distance, the high peaks piercing into the clouds and extends to the sea; and when the poet is half way on the mountain, he saw parting and converging clouds and mist; when he got to the top he had a bird-eye view of the coves underneath. A dialogue about finding a place to lodge, between a traveler and a woodman was also echoing in the valleys.

【说明】太乙山是终南山的最高峰。诗人在山里有一所房子。他喜爱那里的景色，写过多首关于终南山的诗。《全唐诗》里共有1 800多首诗是写终南山的。但是，题目就叫终南山的只有这一首。诗以远看山脉开始，最高峰直插云霄，山连着山一直蜿蜒到海边；当诗人走到半山腰时，白云不见了，青霭又合拢过来；诗人登顶时可以俯瞰山谷的全景。此时，听到一位旅客与樵夫关于找地方投宿的对话在山里回响。

14. To Inspector Du
(Tang) Cen Shen

We used to ascend together in quickened gaits the red steps,
I work in the Privy Council and you at another office.
Every morning we follow the guards of honor to start working hours,
Every evening we left office with our outfit smell imperial incense.
As my hair has turned grey I bewail at the sight of falling flowers,
Looking at the infinite azure sky I admire the high flyers.
There seems to be no wrongs to be corrected in the court,
My memorials to the Emperor for admonition have decreased.

In Chinese phonetic alphabet and Chinese characters:

jì zuǒ shěng dù shí yí
寄左省杜拾遗
（唐）岑参

lián bù qū dān bì
联 步 趋 丹 陛 ，

fēn cáo xiàn zǐ wēi
分 曹 限 紫 微 。

xiǎo suí tiān zhàng rù
晓 随 天 仗 入 ，

mù rě yù xiāng guī
暮 惹 御 香 归 。

bái fà bēi huā luò
白 发 悲 花 落 ，

qīng yún xiàn niǎo fēi
青 云 羡 鸟 飞 。

shèng cháo wú quē shì
圣 朝 无 阙 事 ，

zì jué jiàn shū xī
自 觉 谏 书 稀 。

Notes：The poet used to go to his office，which was on the right side of the imperial court，with Du Fu whose office was on the left side. The job of both were to find faults and offer ways of remedies. Yet，the poet was disappointed and unsatisfied，not because there were no faults，but because officials were not encouraged to criticize. So，under the garish cloak of working in the central government，the poet was not happy.

【说明】诗人的办公室在皇宫的右侧，他经常与杜甫一起上朝，杜甫的办公室在左侧。两人的工作都是查找政府工作中的问题，并提出改进的方案。由于诗人对君王文过饰非的失望与不满便戏说圣朝没有过失，也就写不出谏书来了。所以，在天子脚下做事听起来冠冕堂皇，可是诗人根本高兴不起来。

15. The Temple of Absolute Control

(Tang) Cen Shen

Almost reaching the residence of deities, the lofts are so high,

When I scalded and find the sun is just nearby.

In a clear day distinctive are the houses, wells and trees,

The mist in the area of Five Tombs is just like morose persons.

Off the balustrade the Qinling Ridges are much lower,

Outside the window the Weishui River is a miniature.

If I learned the doctrines of purity earlier,

I would have rendered my service to the image of Buddha.

In Chinese phonetic alphabet and Chinese characters:

dēng zǒng chí gé
登　总　持　阁

（唐）岑参

gāo	gé	bī	zhū	tiān
高	阁	逼	诸	天 ，
dēng	lín	jìn	rì	biān
登	临	近	日	边 。
qíng	kāi	wàn	jǐng	shù
晴	开	万	井	树 ，
chóu	kàn	wǔ	líng	yān
愁	看	五	陵	烟 。
jiàn	wài	dī	qín	lǐng
槛	外	低	秦	岭 ，
chuāng	zhōng	xiǎo	wèi	chuān
窗	中	小	渭	川 。
zǎo	zhī	qīng	jìng	lǐ
早	知	清	净	理 ，
cháng	yuàn	fèng	jīn	xiān
常	愿	奉	金	仙 。

Notes: The temple was on the Zhongnan Mountains. By describing the height and size of the temple, the poet felt somewhat detached from the noisy world. The Qinling Ridges winds from the

286

west to the east for 1,500 kilometers.

【说明】总持阁在终南山上。诗人描写此阁之高之大，自己似乎也远离了尘世。秦岭自西往东绵延 1 500 公里。

16. Ascending the Yanzhou City Tower
(Tang) Du Fu

I was in Yanzhou to visit my father，

It was my first time to look far from the southern tower.

The floating clouds blend the Eastern Sea and the Tai Mountains，

The flat fields stretch to the Qing and Xu prefectures.

Lonely as Mount Tai the Qin Emperor's stone tablet was still there standing upright，

Deserted as the county the Hall of Lu still remains as a point of interest.

I Having been passionately nostalgic，

I pace on the tower alone and lost in a pensive thought.

In Chinese phonetic alphabet and Chinese characters：

dēng yǎn zhōu chéng lóu
登 兖 州 城 楼

（唐）杜甫

dōng　jùn　qū　tíng　rì
东　郡　趋　庭　日　，

nán　lóu　zòng　mù　chū
南　楼　纵　目　初　。

fú　yún　lián　hǎi　dài
浮　云　连　海　岱　，

píng　yě　rù　qīng　xú
平　野　入　青　徐　。

gū　zhàng　qín　bēi　zài
孤　嶂　秦　碑　在　，

荒　城　鲁　殿　余　。

huāng chéng lǔ diàn yú

cóng lái duō gǔ yì
从　来　多　古　意　，

lín tiào dú chóu chú
临　眺　独　踌　躇　。

Notes：Du Fu's father was a local officer at Yanzhou, which was called Dongjun County before Tang. The poet was young at the time, yet the image he created in the poem is grandiose and vast. The Hall of Lu was built in the Han Dynasty.

【说明】杜甫的父亲在兖州做地方官，此地唐以前称为东郡。那时诗人尚年轻，然而，他在诗中描述的景观却很宏大壮观。鲁殿系汉朝所建。

17. Before Du Takes His Office in Shu
(Tang) Wang Bo

Three areas are guarding the capital in the front,
The view of the five ferries is blurred in the mist.
Both of us are plaintive at the parting moment,
We are all officials far away from homeland.
Vast as the four seas there must be one who knows me best,
Even he is at a remotest place I still feel he's in my neighborhood.
Let's say farewell at this fork road,
Not letting tears wet our clothes as what the lads did.

In Chinese phonetic alphabet and Chinese characters：

sòng dù shǎo fǔ zhī rèn shǔ zhōu
送　杜　少　府　之　任　蜀　州

（唐）王勃

chéng què fǔ sān qín
城　阙　辅　三　秦　，

fēng	yān	wàng	wǔ	jīn
风	烟	望	五	津 。

yǔ	jūn	lí	bié	yì
与	君	离	别	意 ，

tóng	shì	huàn	yóu	rén
同	是	宦	游	人 。

hǎi	nèi	cún	zhī	jǐ
海	内	存	知	己 ，

tiān	yá	ruò	bǐ	lín
天	涯	若	比	邻 。

wú	wéi	zài	qí	lù
无	为	在	歧	路 ，

ér	nǚ	gòng	zhān	jīn
儿	女	共	沾	巾 。

Notes：Wang Bo（650 - 676）was an outstanding poet in the early Tang period. He was drowned on his way visiting his relatives. Du was a local security officer，who was assigned to a new post in Shu—Sichuan. There are over eighty of his poems available today. The three areas that are mentioned all belonged to the former Qin. The fifth and sixth lines in this poem have been on the lips of Chinese to describe friendship.

【说明】王勃（650—676）是初唐杰出的诗人。他在探望亲友的途中被淹死。杜少府是一县尉，被派往四川担任新职。王勃的诗仍有 80 多首存世。诗中所说"三秦"过去均属秦朝。诗的第五、六句是中国非常流行的形容友谊的名句。

18. Seeing off Cui Rong
(Tang) Du Shenyan

The emperor is appointing a general for the expedition，
It's the post of a staff in the army you've taken.
The tents for the farewell party run from palace to the riverside，

In the city interest in the army's dignity has been aroused.

Banners flutter in the cold air,

At night frontier pipes are played at the border.

You would sit in the camp scheming attacking plans,

When autumn wind rises there will come news of your victories.

In Chinese phonetic alphabet and Chinese characters:

sòng cuī róng

送 崔 融

（唐）杜审言

jūn	wáng	xíng	chū	jiàng
君	王	行	出	将 ，

shū	jì	yuǎn	cóng	zhēng
书	记	远	从	征 。

zǔ	zhàng	lián	hé	què
祖	帐	连	河	阙 ，

jūn	huī	dòng	luò	chéng
军	麾	动	洛	城 。

jīng	qí	zhāo	shuò	qì
旌	旗	朝	朔	气 ，

jiā	chuī	yè	biān	shēng
笳	吹	夜	边	声 。

zuò	jué	yān	chén	sǎo
坐	觉	烟	尘	扫 ，

qiū	fēng	gǔ	běi	píng
秋	风	古	北	平 。

Notes：Cui Rong was a friend of the poet and joined the army as a staff member to quell the rebels in the border area. Not knowing what awaits his friend, the poet didn't say a sad word, by writing about the size of the army and their dignified bearing, the poet successfully hid his reluctance in saying farewell to his friend.

【说明】崔融是诗人的朋友，在军中担任参谋，被派往边塞平叛。诗人不知崔融此战前景如何，在诗中没有用任何不吉祥的字词。他通过描写军队规模之庞大、军人仪表之威武，成功地掩饰了自己对朋友的依依不舍之情。

19. On Her Majesty's Sacrificial Offer

(Tang) Song Zhiwen

On top of the mountain tents gathered into a cluster，

The scene of Her Majesty's tour is spectacular.

While streamers are blown up dawn clouds are rolling away，

Lamp lights intrude into the star-lit sky.

Thousand banners appear from the dim dales，

Her Majesty's cart has come and the mountain hails and cheers.

Such a tour is worth praising with a verse.

After all I don't have extraordinary writing abilities.

In Chinese phonetic alphabet and Chinese characters：

hù cóng dēng fēng tú zhōng zuò
扈从登封途中作

（唐）宋之问

zhàng diàn yù cuī wéi
帐　殿　郁　崔　嵬　，

xiān yóu shí zhuàng zāi
仙　游　实　壮　哉　。

xiǎo yún lián mù juǎn
晓　云　连　幕　卷　，

yè huǒ zá xīng huí
夜　火　杂　星　回　。

gǔ àn qiān qí chū
谷　暗　千　旗　出　，

shān míng wàn shèng lái
山　鸣　万　乘　来　。

hù　cóng　liáng　kě　fù
扈　从　良　可　赋　，
zhōng　fá　shàn　tiān　cái
终　乏　挨　天　才　。

Notes：Song Zhiwen（656？ - 712）was once a supervising officer of appliances for the Imperial Court. He was considered to have laid a foundation for the development of regulated poetry，in particular the "seven-characters a line" poetry. There was a lady emperor in the Tang Dynasty. The poet was in the retinue in one of her trips to offer sacrifices to mountains. This poem was composed on the way.

【说明】宋之问（656？ —712）曾任尚方监丞。他对近体诗的定型起过重要的作用，尤其是"七言"诗。唐朝有一位女皇帝，她去祭山时，诗人就在她随从的队伍里。此诗是在祭山的途中所写。

20. An Inscription for the Room of the Respected Monk
(Tang) Meng Haoran

To practice ways to reach sustained concentration in the mind，

The respected monk had his house built by the side of the forest.

Outside the gate the beautiful peak is so steep，

Before the steps the dales are so deep.

After the rain the setting sun has appeared，

Verdant woods cast their shadows in the courtyard.

Learning from lotus flowers that are so pure and sacred，

Would make one's heart untarnished.

In Chinese phonetic alphabet and Chinese characters：

tí yì gōng chán fáng
题 义 公 禅 房

（唐）孟浩然

yì gōng xí chán jì
义 公 习 禅 寂 ，

jié yǔ yī kōng lín
结 宇 依 空 林 。

hù wài yī fēng xiù
户 外 一 峰 秀 ，

jiē qián zhòng hè shēn
阶 前 众 壑 深 。

xī yáng lián yǔ zú
夕 阳 连 雨 足 ，

kōng cuì luò tíng yīn
空 翠 落 庭 阴 。

kàn qǔ lián huā jìng
看 取 莲 花 净 ，

fāng zhī bù rǎn xīn
方 知 不 染 心 。

Notes：The inscription was for the monk，rather than the room. The monk was practicing Dhyana，the surroundings of the room，the quiet forest，beautiful peak，the deep dales，the setting sun after rain，the shady courtyard，all smelt Zen. We don't hear about or see the monk in the poem，but we can feel about him. Lotus is a sacred token of Buddhism. By trying to be pure and clean as lotus flowers，one can reach the state of mind of sustained concentration.

【说明】诗人是位禅师，该诗是为禅师题词，而不是给房屋题词。此僧人正在修炼禅宗。房屋的周围、寂静的山林、美丽的山峰、幽深的山谷、雨后的落日、郁郁葱葱的庭院都洋溢着禅的味道。在诗中，我们没有听到僧人讲话，也没有看到他。但是，我们可以感觉到他的存在。莲花是佛教神圣的象征。如若像莲花一样纯洁和清净，一个人就可以长时间地入定。

21. To Zhang Jiuxu When I Got Drunk

(Tang) Gao Shi

People make friends with almost anybody,

But with this old man it's a different story.

When he is in the right mood he writes the best calligraphy,

When he had a drop too much he was crazy and spoke madly.

When his hair turned grey he was care-free,

At present he was put on top of the rank luckily.

With a pot of liquor at his bedside,

How many times could he fall into sleep at night?

In Chinese phonetic alphabet and Chinese characters:

zuì hòu zèng zhāng jiǔ xù
醉　后　赠　张　九　旭

（唐）高适

shì　shàng　màn　xiāng　shí
世　上　谩　相　识　，

cǐ　wēng　shū　bù　rán
此　翁　殊　不　然　。

xìng　lái　shū　zì　shèng
兴　来　书　自　圣　，

zuì　hòu　yǔ　yóu　diān
醉　后　语　尤　颠　。

bái　fà　lǎo　xián　shì
白　发　老　闲　事　，

qīng　yún　zài　mù　qián
青　云　在　目　前　。

chuáng　tóu　yì　hú　jiǔ
床　头　一　壶　酒　，

néng　gēng　jǐ　huí　mián
能　更　几　回　眠　。

Notes: Zhang Jiuxu, also known as Zhang Xu, is one of the most important calligraphers in China; he has been reputed as a saint of cursive script. He was one of the eight "drinking immortals" headed by

294

Li Bai. This poem was composed in 736. When the poet said Zhang Xu didn't easily make friends, that he was a saint of the cursive script and that he often got drunk, because of these traits, the poet was worrying about Zhang's future even though zhang was given an important job by the emperor when this poem was written.

【说明】张九旭，也叫张旭，是中国最重要的书法家之一，他被称为"草圣"，也是以李白为首的酒中八仙之一。此诗作于736年。当诗人说张旭不轻易交友、说他是"草圣"、说他常常喝醉时，他是由于张旭的这些特性，而为他的前途担心，尽管写此诗时，皇帝给了张旭一份很重要的工作。

22. The Yutai Temple

(Tang) Du Fu

It was the King of Teng who built this Taoist temple,
Visiting it is just like touring an ancient chancel.

The immortal standing in the colored clouds is playing a flute in the fresco,

The King's inscriptions still enlightens as a classic article.
Its halls can connect with heavenly emperors,
All ten prefectures constitute the world of the immortal.
People say when pipes sound and the crane calls,
It is Prince Qiao who is flying over the hill.

In Chinese phonetic alphabet and Chinese characters:

yù tái guàn
玉 台 观

（唐）杜甫

hào   jié   yīn   wáng   zào
浩　劫　因　王　造，

píng tái fǎng gǔ yóu
平 台 访 古 游 。

cǎi yún xiāo shǐ zhù
彩 云 萧 史 驻 ,

wén zì lǔ gōng liú
文 字 鲁 恭 留 。

gōng què tōng qún dì
宫 阙 通 群 帝 ,

qián kūn dào shí zhōu
乾 坤 到 十 洲 。

rén chuán yǒu shēng hè
人 传 有 笙 鹤 ,

shí guò běi shān tóu
时 过 北 山 头 。

Notes: The Yutai Temple was built by the King of Teng in the Tang Dynasty. The poet used some legends and myth to describe the temple. Line three mentions a legendary figure—Xiao Shi, who used to play a flute and one day ascended to the sky. Line four mentions about King Gong of Lu who found from between walls some Confucian classics. By citing this story the poet is saying that the inscription by the King of Teng in the temple is as enlightening as classical canons. Line five shows that Taoists believe there are emperors in five directions in the heaven. The ten prefectures in line six resemble the entire country. Taoist believers could communicate with their emperors from this temple. The last two lines refer to Prince Qiao, son of King Ling of the Zhou, who used to play a pipe instrument and finally ascended to the sky on the back of a crane.

【说明】玉台观是唐朝腾王所建。诗人用了一些传说和神话来写此观。第三句提到关于萧史的传说,萧史善吹笛,已然升天做了神仙。第四句提到鲁恭王,他在墙的夹缝里发现了儒家的经典,诗人用此典故,是想说腾王的题词就像经典一样可以启迪人生。第五句是说道观可以直通五方天帝诸神。第六句所说十洲是指全国。最后两句说到周灵王的儿子乔太子,他好吹笙,曾驾鹤而去,离开了人世。

23. Viewing a Landscape Painting
(Tang) Du Fu

The Fangzhang Mountains and the sea are blended,

The Tiantai Mountains are blanketed by a mist.

I can only see such a scene in paintings,

Regretfully for my old age I never saw such a real landscape with my eyes.

Fan Li's boat is too small to let me on,

Prince Qiao's crane has long been gone.

It seems I could only be drifted along to follow the tides,

Not knowing how to get out of the secular ambience.

In Chinese phonetic alphabet and Chinese characters:

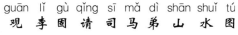

guān lǐ gù qǐng sī mǎ dì shān shuǐ tú
观 李 囧 请 司 马 弟 山 水 图

（唐）杜甫

fāng zhàng hún lián shuǐ
方 丈 浑 连 水 ，

tiān tái zǒng yìng yún
天 台 总 映 云 。

rén jiān cháng xiàn huà
人 间 长 见 画 ，

lǎo qù hèn kōng wén
老 去 恨 空 闻 。

fàn lǐ zhōu piān xiǎo
范 蠡 舟 偏 小 ，

wáng qiáo hè bù qún
王 乔 鹤 不 群 。

cǐ shēng suí wàn wù
此 生 随 万 物 ，

hé chù chū chén fēn
何 处 出 尘 氛 。

Notes: Fangzhang Mountains only exist in myths while Tiantai Mountains do stand on shore. Fan Li was a high ranking official of the State of Yue in the Spring and Autumn period, who, after helping the state defeating its enemies, disappeared on a small boat. We mentioned about Prince Qiao in the last poem. But the original in line six says the prince had only one crane and there wasn't one to spare to the poet.

【说明】方丈山只在神话里才有，而天台山则是矗立在海边的。范蠡是春秋时越国的一位高官，他在击败敌国后，乘小舟消失了。上首诗里我们曾提到过乔太子。原文第六句说乔太子只有一只仙鹤，无法与诗人共享。

24. My Mind during a Nocturnal Trip
(Tang) Du Fu

Breeze winnows tender grass on the bank,
The lonely boat with a spar is berthed at night.
Stars hang in the sky over the vast plain,
Rapid currents push out the moon.
Why should my writings made me famous?
I resigned on the pretext of a poor health.
What do I look like, a person being drifted around?
In between the sky and earth I am merely a sand bird.

In Chinese phonetic alphabet and Chinese characters：

lǚ yè shū huái
旅 夜 书 怀
（唐）杜甫

xì   cǎo   wēi   fēng   àn
细   草   微   风   岸，
wēi   qiáng dú   yè   zhōu
危   樯   独   夜   舟。

xīng	chuí	píng	yě	kuò
星	垂	平	野	阔 ，

yuè	yǒng	dà	jiāng	liú
月	涌	大	江	流 。

míng	qǐ	wén	zhāng	zhù
名	岂	文	章	著 ，

guān	yīn	lǎo	bìng	xiū
官	因	老	病	休 。

piāo	piāo	hé	suǒ	sì
飘	飘	何	所	似 ，

tiān	dì	yī	shā	ōu
天	地	一	沙	鸥 。

Notes：This poem was composed in 765 when he had to leave his thatched house in Chengdu and resigned from his official post. He thought he was more capable in administering government organs than writing, yet what made him famous were his writings. The reason for his resignation was not really because of his health; the real reason was that some of his colleague had been trying to crowd him out. The poem, which spelt out very well the pathos of his loneliness, has been widely commended.

【说明】此诗作于 765 年，诗人当时不得不离开在成都的茅草房，而且辞去了他的官职。他认为自己管理政事的能力要比写诗强，但是，他却因写诗出名。他辞去官职并不是因为身体不好，而是因为他的同僚处处排挤他。这首道出他内心孤寂和凄楚的诗被人们广为传颂。

25. Ascending the Yueyang Tower

(Tang) Du Fu

I heard about Lake Dongting before,
Today I ascend the Yueyang Tower.
The lake separates States Wu and Chu southeastern ward,

The sun, moon and stars float on the lake surface day and night.
Haven't heard from relatives and friends, not even a word,
I am old and sick on this lonely boat.
Hearing a war broke out again in the northern frontier,
Leaning on the window I could not hold back my tear.

In Chinese phonetic alphabet and Chinese characters:

dēng yuè yáng lóu
登 岳 阳 楼

（唐）杜甫

xī	wén	dòng	tíng	shuǐ	
昔	闻	洞	庭	水	，
jīn	shàng	yuè	yáng	lóu	
今	上	岳	阳	楼	。
wú	chǔ	dōng	nán	chè	
吴	楚	东	南	坼	，
qián	kūn	rì	yè	fú	
乾	坤	日	夜	浮	。
qīn	péng	wú	yí	zì	
亲	朋	无	一	字	，
lǎo	bìng	yǒu	gū	zhōu	
老	病	有	孤	舟	。
róng	mǎ	guān	shān	běi	
戎	马	关	山	北	，
píng	xuān	tì	sì	liú	
凭	轩	涕	泗	流	。

Notes: The Yueyang Tower is on the bank of Lake Dongting. In the Spring and Autumn period, State Wu was on the southeastern side of the lake and State Chu was on its northwestern side. This poem has been regarded as the best "five-characters a line" octave of the Tang Dynasty Poetry.

【说明】岳阳楼就在洞庭湖边上。春秋时吴国在湖的东南方，楚国在湖的西北方。此诗被视为唐诗中最好的五言律诗。

26. My Travel in the South
(Tang) Zu Yong

The ridges in the Chu area are rolling on without end,

The homebound road is undulate and desolate.

Sunrise and colored clouds herald rain,

When waves roar the tide would come soon.

I was stranded in the region under the Sagittarius,

My letters are like the wild geese that could only fly south when north wind blows.

I wish to send home some tangerines that are fully grown,

The pity is that nobody could deliver them to Luoyang.

In Chinese phonetic alphabet and Chinese characters:

jiāng nán lǚ qíng
江 南 旅 情
（唐） 祖咏

chǔ	shān	bù	kě	jí
楚	山	不	可	极 ，
guī	lù	dàn	xiāo	tiáo
归	路	但	萧	条 。
hǎi	sè	qíng	kàn	yǔ
海	色	晴	看	雨 ，
jiāng	shēng	yè	tīng	cháo
江	声	夜	听	潮 。
jiàn	liú	nán	dǒu	jìn
剑	留	南	斗	近 ，
shū	jì	běi	fēng	yáo
书	寄	北	风	遥 。
wèi	bào	kōng	tán	jú
为	报	空	潭	橘 ，
wú	méi	jì	luò	qiáo
无	媒	寄	洛	桥 。

Notes: The poet was on his way home and was passing through an area that belonged to the former State of Chu. The fifth line in the original says the poet was stranded at a place under the Sagittarius, which was presumably where the former State of Wu was. The original also says he was keeping his sword at this place, which means he was staying there. In ancient times, when a learned person was away from home to pursue his career, he would bring his sword along with his books. The last line mentions a bridge on the Luoshui River, because it was a symbol of the city of Luoyang.

【说明】诗人正在回家的途中，路过以前属于楚国的地区。诗的第五句说他被羁绊在南斗星下，而此处正是过去吴国的地界。原文说他把佩剑留在那里，是说他停留在那里了。古时候，当一个书生离家去闯荡时，会带上他的佩剑和书籍。最后一句提到的洛水桥是洛阳的标志性建筑。

27. Spending a Night at the Longxing Temple
(Tang) Qiwu Qian

Visiting the temple I forget to go home at night,
Behind the pine trees the doors of halls hide.
The head monk's room is brightly lit,
On his robe a string of rosary is attached.
On the day he preaches with his integrity,
The green lotus is an analogy of sutra's subtlety.
Flowers keep falling from the sky,
Yet birds are removing all of them away quietly.

In Chinese phonetic alphabet and Chinese characters:

sù lóng xīng sì
宿 龙 兴 寺

（唐）綦毋潜

xiāng chà yè wàng guī
香 刹 夜 忘 归，

sōng qīng gǔ diàn fēi
松　清　古　殿　扉　。

dēng míng fāng zhàng shì
灯　明　方　丈　室　，

zhū jì bǐ qiū yī
珠　系　比　丘　衣　。

bái rì chuán xīn jìng
白　日　传　心　净　，

qīng lián yù fǎ wēi
青　莲　喻　法　微　。

tiān huā luò bú jìn
天　花　落　不　尽　，

chù chù niǎo xián fēi
处　处　鸟　衔　飞　。

Notes：Qiwu Qian（692 - 749?）was once an official responsible for recording history. He later became a hermit，he was one of the representatives of eclogue poets.

【说明】綦毋潜（692—749?）曾任左拾遗和著作郎。后来做了隐士，是田园派诗人的代表人物。

28. An Inscription for the Monk's Room
(Tang) Chang Jian

I came into the archaic temple in the morning for a visit，
When the forest is bathed in the early sunlight.
The serpentine path leads me to where it is deep and quiet，
Around the monk's room flowers and woods are exuberant.
In the enchanting mountain the birds are delightful and pleasant，
Any mundane thoughts are cleared when looking into the pond.
Everything is so quiet and quiescent at this moment，
Bell and chime stone are the only things can be heard.

In Chinese phonetic alphabet and Chinese characters:

tí pò shān sì hòu chán yuàn
题 破 山 寺 后 禅 院
（唐）常建

| qīng | chén | rù | gǔ | sì |
| 清 | 晨 | 入 | 古 | 寺 ， |

| chū | rì | zhào | gāo | lín |
| 初 | 日 | 照 | 高 | 林 。 |

| qū | jìng | tōng | yōu | chù |
| 曲 | 径 | 通 | 幽 | 处 ， |

| chán | fáng | huā | mù | shēn |
| 禅 | 房 | 花 | 木 | 深 。 |

| shān | guāng | yuè | niǎo | xìng |
| 山 | 光 | 悦 | 鸟 | 性 ， |

| tán | yǐng | kōng | rén | xīn |
| 潭 | 影 | 空 | 人 | 心 。 |

| wàn | lài | cǐ | jù | jì |
| 万 | 籁 | 此 | 俱 | 寂 ， |

| wéi | wén | zhōng | qìng | yīn |
| 惟 | 闻 | 钟 | 磬 | 音 。 |

Notes: We don't have the dates of birth and death of this poet. We only know he was once a local military officer and an important member of the eclogue group of the poets. The title in Chinese gives the name of the temple. The poem reveals to us the longing of the poet to live as a monk.

【说明】无诗人的生卒年记载。我们只知道他曾任地方校尉，是田园派的重要人物。诗的中文题目有寺院的名称，此诗表达了诗人想过出家人生活的愿望。

29. An Inscription at the Songting Courier Station
(Tang) Zhang Hu

Endless ridges join the sky in the distance,

The mist over the water countryside in the east is boundless.

If the surface of the lake is bright, the sun would soon rise,

If the rapids of water are white, you would hear the sound of wind from a distance.

The road, so narrow that only birds can fly over, leads to the plateau,

The cursive path would bring a village to you.

My dear hermit friend, I have scouted,

The entire Five Lakes and still can't find your where about.

In Chinese phonetic alphabet and Chinese characters:

tí sōng tīng yì
题 松 汀 驿

（唐）张祜

shān sè yuǎn hán kōng
山　色　远　含　空　，

cāng máng zé guó dōng
苍　茫　泽　国　东　。

hǎi míng xiān jiàn rì
海　明　先　见　日　，

jiāng bái jiǒng wén fēng
江　白　迥　闻　风　。

niǎo dào gāo yuán qù
鸟　道　高　原　去　，

rén yān xiǎo jìng tōng
人　烟　小　径　通　。

nà zhī jiù yí yì
那　知　旧　遗　逸　，

bú zài wǔ hú zhōng
不　在　五　湖　中　。

Notes: Zhang Hu (782 – 852) never worked in the government, but was known not only for his poetry, but also his gallantry and masculinity. He was one of the most important poets in the late Tang period. The Five Lakes refer to the area of Lake Tai.

【说明】张祜（782—852）一生未仕，但是，其名声不只源自他的诗作，还来自他的侠义和英勇。他是晚唐的重要诗人之一。五湖即太湖一带。

30. The Shengguo Temple

(Tang) Monk Chumo

The road on the middle peak can take us to the temple,
On the serpentine road wisteria droop and vines coil.
Reaching the river you realize the land of the Wu ends here,
The undulating hills of Yue are on the other side of the river.
The verdant and old woods are cloaked in mist,
Into the white waters the horizon has been soaked.
The temple provides a panorama of the city,
Into the fluting and sing the bell and chime stone are melted
away.

In Chinese phonetic alphabet and Chinese characters:

shèng guǒ sì
圣　果　寺
（唐）释处默

lù　zì　zhōng　fēng　shàng
路　自　中　峰　上　，

pán　huí　chū　bì　luó
盘　回　出　薜　萝　。

dào　jiāng　wú　dì　jìn
到　江　吴　地　尽　，

gé　àn　yuè　shān　duō
隔　岸　越　山　多　。

gǔ　mù　cóng　qīng　ǎi
古　木　丛　青　霭　，

yáo　tiān　jìn　bái　bō
遥　天　浸　白　波　。

xià	fāng	chéng	guō	jìn	
下	方	城	郭	近	，

zhōng	qìng	zá	shēng	gē	
钟	磬	杂	笙	歌	。

Notes：The temple was on the Phoenix Mountains to the South of the Hangzhou city. We don't know much about this monk poet. Wu and Yue were all states in the Spring and Autumn period. The river is the Qiantang River，which divided the two states in the north-south direction.

【说明】此寺位于杭州市城南的凤凰山上。我们对此僧家诗人所知甚少。吴、越是春秋时期的诸侯国。钱塘江将两国从南北方向上分割开来。

31．A View of the Fields
（Tang）Wang Ji

I look into the distance from Donggao at dusk，
Not knowing what to rely on I'm so hesitate.
The dull autumn color is on every tree，
With each hill sun setting is the same scenery.
Driving their calves back the cowboys are happy，
On their horses the hunters are coming home with their prey.
Among so many returnees there is no body I know，
I sing an old song to remember the solider hero.

In Chinese phonetic alphabet and Chinese characters：

yě wàng
野 望

（唐）王绩

dōng	gāo	bó	mù	wàng	
东	皋	薄	暮	望	，

xǐ	yǐ	yù	hé	yī
徙	倚	欲	何	依 。

shù	shù	jiē	qiū	sè
树	树	皆	秋	色 ，

shān	shān	wéi	luò	huī
山	山	惟	落	晖 。

mù	rén	qū	dú	fǎn
牧	人	驱	犊	返 ，

liè	mǎ	dài	qín	guī
猎	马	带	禽	归 。

xiāng	gù	wú	xiāng	shí
相	顾	无	相	识 ，

cháng	gē	huái	cǎi	wēi
长	歌	怀	采	薇 。

Notes: Wang Ji (586 – 644) was the younger brother of the famous Confucian scholar Wang Tong and was once responsible for emendating classic works. He wrote a book on the history and brewing skills of liquor. His contribution to the development of Tang poetry has been commended. Donggao was where his hermitage was. The last line mentions the name of the song the poet was singing— "Gathering Pea Seedlings", which was in *the Book of Songs*, depicts the mind of a soldier who was returning home from a long station at the frontier.

【说明】王绩（586—644）是著名儒家学者王通的弟弟，曾负责对经典著作的校勘。他写过一本关于白酒历史和酿造技术的书。他对唐诗发展所做的贡献被普遍认可。东皋是他隐居的地方。最后一行提到诗人所唱歌曲的名称——采薇歌，此歌出自《诗经》，这是一首形容一位战士长期驻守边防后返回家乡的歌曲。

32. Before Cui Joins the Battle in the East
(Tang) Chen Ziang

In the golden season of autumn cold wind rustles，

On white dew days the expedition starts.

The royal armed forces do not love wars,

In maneuvering troops you got to be cautious.

Your battle would sweep the south like a sea current,

Your army would wipe the invaders out of the north and be triumphant.

With victory I hope you'll not boast and become arrogant,

Don't wish to enter the Memorial Hall and be on the list of merit.

In Chinese phonetic alphabet and Chinese characters:

sòng bié cuī zhù zuò dōng zhēng
送 别 崔 著 作 东 征

（唐）陈子昂

jīn tiān fāng sù shā
金 天 方 肃 杀 ，

bái lù shǐ zhuān zhēng
白 露 始 专 征 。

wáng shī fēi lè zhàn
王 师 非 乐 战 ，

zhī zǐ shèn jiā bīng
之 子 慎 佳 兵 。

hǎi qì qīn nán bù
海 气 侵 南 部 ，

biān fēng sǎo běi píng
边 风 扫 北 平 。

mò mài lú lóng sài
莫 卖 卢 龙 塞 ，

guī yāo lín gé míng
归 邀 麟 阁 名 。

Notes: Cui is the same as the one in poem 18 of this section. Cui was responsible for recording history in the army. The expedition was targeted on the Khitan invaders. The poet was sure of the victory, but he admonished Cui not to be arrogant when the war was won. The original of line seven sited one incident in 207 A. D. when a member of staff offered the idea of luring the enemy to Lulong Pass and then won the battle. The superior of the staff wanted to grant a title to him for the sound plan, but the staff refused saying that he didn't have a heart to receive such a title, which was given at the expense of a strategic pass. The last line mentions about the Hall of Unicorn, which housed the portraits of most important officials and generals of the Tang Dynasty.

【说明】这位崔某与本卷第 18 首所说的是同一位崔先生。此时崔某人负责记录军中的历史。队伍要征讨的是契丹侵略者。诗人对获胜很有把握，但是他还是劝告崔得胜后，不能忘乎所以。第七句引用了 207 年发生的一件事，即一位参谋出了一个用卢龙塞诱敌深入的计策，并取得了胜利。当部队首领要给此参谋授予称号时，这个参谋拒绝了，说用牺牲一个战略要地的代价换来的称号他无心领取。诗的最后一句提到的麒麟阁，是唐朝悬挂有功的文武官员肖像的地方。

33. Encountering Rain at Night when Enjoying the Cool Accompanied by Singing Girls (1)
(Tang) Du Fu

It is the best time to enjoy the cool on a boat when the sun has set,

Breeze rises and the lake ripples are so quiet.

Deep in the bamboo forest is an opportune place to entertain our guest,

The green lotus leaves and the air are so temperate.

While sons of the nobles are mixing cold drinks,

The singing girls are shredding lotus roots.

The overhead clouds become black all of a sudden,

It must be the rain that is urging poetry composition.

In Chinese phonetic alphabet and Chinese characters:

xié jì nà liáng wǎn jì yù yǔ · qí yī
携 妓 纳 凉 晚 际 遇 雨 · 其 一

（唐）杜甫

luò rì fàng chuán hǎo
落 日 放 船 好 ，

qīng fēng shēng làng chí
轻 风 生 浪 迟 。

zhú shēn liú kè chù
竹 深 留 客 处 ，

hé jìng nà liáng shí
荷 净 纳 凉 时 。

gōng zǐ diào bīng shuǐ
公 子 调 冰 水 ，

jiā rén xuě ǒu sī
佳 人 雪 藕 丝 。

piàn yún tóu shàng hēi
片 云 头 上 黑 ，

yīng shì yǔ cuī shī
应 是 雨 催 诗 。

Notes：The poet was with sons of rich families were sons of rich families and who were seeking pleasure after sun set on a boat accompanied by some singing girls. Rain came when the boys were preparing cold drinks and girls were shredding lotus roots. The poet was not annoyed by the rain; instead, he thought the rain was urging people to write poems.

【说明】诗人与一群富家子弟在太阳落山后乘船去纳凉，并有歌妓陪同。子弟们准备冷饮、歌女们准备切藕片时却下雨了。雨水并没有惹恼诗人，相反，诗人觉得雨水让他突生作诗的兴致。

34. Encountering Rain at Night when Enjoying the Cool Accompanied by Singing Girls (2)

(Tang) Du Fu

The rain has wetted our seats so through,

The gale slashed on the prow.

The red skirts of southern girls are drenched,

The foreheads of northern girls furrowed.

We hurriedly tied the rope onto the willow tree,

The veiling on the boat is fluttering madly.

The wind is soughing on the way home,

The May weather is just like cold autumn.

In Chinese phonetic alphabet and Chinese characters：

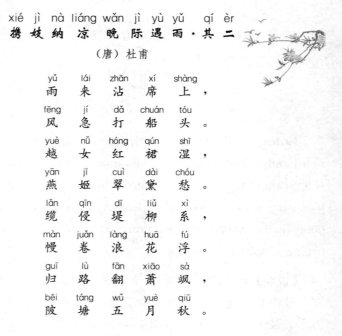

xié jì nà liáng wǎn jì yù yǔ　qí èr
携 妓 纳 凉 晚 际 遇 雨 · 其 二

（唐）杜甫

yǔ　lái　zhān　xí　shàng
雨 来 沾 席 上 ，

fēng　jí　dǎ　chuán　tóu
风 急 打 船 头 。

yuè　nǚ　hóng　qún　shī
越 女 红 裙 湿 ，

yān　jī　cuì　dài　chóu
燕 姬 翠 黛 愁 。

lǎn　qīn　dī　liǔ　xì
缆 侵 堤 柳 系 ，

màn　juǎn　làng　huā　fú
幔 卷 浪 花 浮 。

guī　lù　fān　xiāo　sà
归 路 翻 萧 飒 ，

bēi　táng　wǔ　yuè　qiū
陂 塘 五 月 秋 。

Notes：Closely following the poem above，the poet describes the embarrassment of the group in the rain and their discomposure on their way back. You may wish to know that the third line mentions about girls from the Yue State, which was situated in the south and the fourth line mentions girls from the Yan State, which was situated in the north.

【说明】紧接上诗，诗人描写了他们一群人在雨中的尴尬，以及回程途中的慌乱之状。第三句所说的越女来自南方，第四句所提燕姬来自北方。

35. Spending a Night at the Garret of the Yunmen Temple
(Tang) Sun Ti

The scented temple sits at the foot of the Eastern Mountain,
The quietness of blooming flowers does not seem to be mundane.
The pendent lamps are lit while at dusk peaks stand straight,
When draperies are blown up the autumn crispy air of the lake is felt.
Only a few wild geese remain on the archaic fresco,
Stars of the Altair intersperse outside the screen window.
I figure the temple is staying nigh in the sky,
And in my dream, together with white clouds, I joyfully fly.

In Chinese phonetic alphabet and Chinese characters:

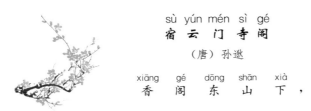

sù yún mén sì gé
宿 云 门 寺 阁

（唐）孙逖

xiāng gé dōng shān xià
香 阁 东 山 下，

yān	huā	xiàng	wài	yōu
烟	花	象	外	幽 。

xuán	dēng	qiān	zhàng	xī
悬	灯	千	嶂	夕 ，

juǎn	màn	wǔ	hú	qiū
卷	幔	五	湖	秋 。

huà	bì	yú	hóng	yàn
画	壁	余	鸿	雁 ，

shā	chuāng	sù	dòu	niú
纱	窗	宿	斗	牛 。

gèng	yí	tiān	lù	jìn
更	疑	天	路	近 ，

mèng	yǔ	bái	yún	yóu
梦	与	白	云	游 。

Notes：Sun Ti（696？－761）was a memorial drafter and well known scholar. This poem contains queer imaginations and reveals the poet's intention to live as a monk.

【说明】孙逖（696？—761）是有名的学者，曾任中书舍人。诗中想象奇特，道出了诗人想出家为僧的想法。

36．Ascending the North Xie Tiao Tower
(Tang) Li Bai

Beautiful as a painting is the riverside city,

At dusk I climbed up the tower to look at the clear sky.

Between two rivers the lake seems like a mirror,

The two bridges seem like two rainbows of a simple color.

Looming behind chilling kitchen smoke are trees of orange and pomelo,

Aged in the autumn grey are trees of parasol.

Except me，who else would care to climb up the tower?

To remember Xie while the autumn wind roars to flicker.

In Chinese phonetic alphabet and Chinese characters:

qiū dēng xuān chéng xiè tiǎo běi lóu
秋　登　宣　城　谢　朓　北　楼
（唐）李白

jiāng chéng rú huà lǐ
江　城　如　画　里　，

shān wǎn wàng qíng kōng
山　晚　望　晴　空　。

liǎng shuǐ jiá míng jìng
两　水　夹　明　镜　，

shuāng qiáo luò cǎi hóng
双　桥　落　彩　虹　。

rén yān hán jú yòu
人　烟　寒　橘　柚　，

qiū sè lǎo wú tóng
秋　色　老　梧　桐　。

shuí niàn běi lóu shàng
谁　念　北　楼　上　，

lín fēng huái xiè gōng
临　风　怀　谢　公　。

Notes: During his second trip to Xuancheng city, Li Bai wrote this poem to express his memory of Xie Tiao. The tower was built when Xie was the Chief Administrator of the city.

【说明】李白第二次到宣城，并作此诗怀念谢朓。此楼是谢朓在宣城当太守时所建。

37. By the Side of Dongting Lake
(Tang) Meng Haoran

In August the water in the lake is vast and plane,
In mist the water and sky come into a twain.
White steam is rising on the lake steadily,
Turbulent waves are trying to rock the Yueyang city.

I wish to cross the lake, but there is no oar or boat,

I feel regret for seeking leisure at times of sacred and clean government.

I can only look at other people, who are fishing by the lakeside,

There is nothing I can do except admiring their fishing harvest.

In Chinese phonetic alphabet and Chinese characters:

wàng dòng tíng hú zèng zhāng chéng xiàng
望　洞　庭　湖　赠　张　丞　相

（唐）孟浩然

bā　yuè　hú　shuǐ　píng
八　月　湖　水　平　，

hán　xū　hùn　tài　qīng
涵　虚　混　太　清　。

qì　zhēng　yún　mèng　zé
气　蒸　云　梦　泽　，

bō　hàn　yuè　yáng　chéng
波　撼　岳　阳　城　。

yù　jì　wú　zhōu　jí
欲　济　无　舟　楫　，

duān　jū　chǐ　shèng　míng
端　居　耻　圣　明　。

zuò　guān　chuí　diào　zhě
坐　观　垂　钓　者　，

tú　yǒu　xiàn　yú　qíng
徒　有　羡　鱼　情　。

Notes: This poem was written for the then Prime Minister Zhang Jiuling, and the purpose was to groom himself for an official career. The poet compared crossing the lake to working in the government. The fishermen are those already working in the government. The poet said that if there wasn't anyone to help him, he could only be an onlooker.

【说明】此诗是写给时任宰相张九龄的，其目的是推荐自己。诗人将在朝做官比作渡过洞庭湖，将渔家比作已经在朝做官的官员。诗人说，如果没有人帮他出仕，他只能做一个旁观者。

38. Visiting the Xiangji Temple
(Tang) Wang Wei

I didn't know where the temple was，
It was several miles above the clouds.
Everywhere seemed untrodden in the old woods，
The bell was echoing deep in the mountains.
It sounded like sobbing when spring water flew by the precipitous rocks，
It was gloomy and cold under the sun and thick pines.
At early dusk by the empty pond some music was played，
When get deep in meditation improper desires would be removed.

In Chinese phonetic alphabet and Chinese characters：

guò xiāng jī sì
过 香 积 寺

（唐）王维

bù zhī xiāng jī sì
不 知 香 积 寺 ，
shù lǐ rù yún fēng
数 里 入 云 峰 。
gǔ mù wú rén jìng
古 木 无 人 径 ，
shēn shān hé chù zhōng
深 山 何 处 钟 。
quán shēng yàn wēi shí
泉 声 咽 危 石 ，
rì sè lěng qīng sōng
日 色 冷 青 松 。
bó mù kōng tán qǔ
薄 暮 空 潭 曲 ，

安　禅　制　毒　龙　。

Notes：This is a representative work of Wang Wei. The poem was intended to write about the temple，but it only touched on its surroundings. The last line mentioned about "poisonous dragon"，which in the Buddhist sutra means one's improper desires. The poet meant to say only when evil thoughts are overcome，can one really grasp the essence of Buddhism. The fifth and sixth lines have been regarded as a fine example of diction in China.

【说明】此为王维的代表作。诗写的是寺，然而只着墨于寺的四周。原文最后一句所说"毒龙"，是指人心中的杂念。诗人是说只有克服了头脑中坏的想法，才能掌握佛教的真谛。第五、六句在中国被视为字句锤炼的典范。

39. Before Zheng Was Ostracized to Fujian
(Tang) Gao Shi

I wish you will not bear any grudges for being ostracized，

I was in Fujian in the past.

People seldom see any wild geese there，

At night ape-cry is what you would hear.

On your way to the east there are endless mountains and clouds，

It's humid in the south，but the miasma and plague are not so rampant.

I'm sure bounties will be bestowed on you soon，

In the journey you got to watch the ambiance and stay in good condition.

In Chinese phonetic alphabet and Chinese characters：

sòng zhèng shì yù zhé mǐn zhōng
送　郑　侍　御　谪　闽　中

（唐）高适

zhé　qù　jūn　wú　hèn
谪　去　君　无　恨 ，

mǐn　zhōng　wǒ　jiù　guò
闽　中　我　旧　过 。

dà　dōu　qiū　yàn　shǎo
大　都　秋　雁　少 ，

zhǐ　shì　yè　yuán　duō
只　是　夜　猿　多 。

dōng　lù　yún　shān　hé
东　路　云　山　合 ，

nán　tiān　zhàng　lì　hé
南　天　瘴　疠　和 。

zì　dāng　féng　yǔ　lù
自　当　逢　雨　露 ，

xíng　yǐ　shèn　fēng　bō
行　矣　慎　风　波 。

Notes：In the poem the poet tried to console his friend Mr. Zheng，who was a courtier and was ostracized to a remote place. The poet also gave him some advice，encouragement，and cautioned him that he should be careful on the way and when he gets to Fujian，he should stay away from trouble，because someday the emperor would call him back to the imperial court.

【说明】诗人写诗安抚他的朋友郑先生。郑某是一位侍臣，被贬到一个遥远的地方。诗人安慰他，给他鼓励，并告诉他此去福建，途中要多加小心，尽量躲避麻烦，保重自己，说他早晚会得到皇室的恩泽。

40．Assorted Poems at Qinzhou

(Tang) Du Fu

The war is still going on at Fenglin，

The way to Yuhai is difficult and trouble-ridden.

Beacon fires are on all the high peaks,

The forces went alone into the enemy found no water in the wells.

The west-most frontier is being shaken by the strong wind,

At the northern pass the moonlight is extremely cold.

The veterans are missing the Flying General,

When could we discuss the new appointment proposal?

In Chinese phonetic alphabet and Chinese characters:

qín zhōu zá shī
秦 州 杂 诗
（唐）杜甫

fèng	lín	gē	wèi	xī
凤	林	戈	未	息 ，
yú	hǎi	lù	cháng	nán
鱼	海	路	常	难 。
hòu	huǒ	yún	fēng	jùn
候	火	云	峰	峻 ，
xuán	jūn	mù	jǐng	gān
悬	军	幕	井	干 。
fēng	lián	xī	jí	dòng
风	连	西	极	动 ，
yuè	guò	běi	tíng	hán
月	过	北	庭	寒 。
gù	lǎo	sī	fēi	jiàng
故	老	思	飞	将 ，
hé	shí	yì	zhù	tán
何	时	议	筑	坛 。

Notes: The poet wrote twenty *Assorted Poems at Qinzhou* and this is the nineteenth. The poet offended the emperor when he was trying to defend another official, and he was relegated. There was a famine going on in central Shanxi area, he had to move all his family to Qinzhou, which is where today's Tianshui is. While there for three months in 759 the poet wrote over one hundred poems including the twenty. Both Fenglin and Yuhai are place names. The northern pass refers to a place in today's Xinjiang region. The "Flying General" refers to General Li Guang of the Han Dynasty who successfully defended frontier areas. The original of the last line asks when the discussion, on building an altar to officially name a general, could be conducted.

【说明】杜甫写了《秦州杂诗二十首》，这是第 19 首。杜甫在为一个朋友进行辩护时，得罪了皇帝，因此被降职。当时，陕西正闹饥荒，他不得不搬到秦州去住，秦州即今日之天水。他 759 年在那里待了 3 个月，写了 100 多首诗，其中包括《秦州杂诗二十首》。凤林和鱼海都是地名。北庭在今天的新疆地区。"飞将军"指汉朝李广将军，李广是保卫边塞的有功之将。原文的最后一句问道：什么时候才能建好坛台讨论任命将军的事呢？

41. The Da Yu Temple
(Tang) Du Fu

The Da Yu Temple sits lonely in the dale,

The setting sun slants in while the autumn wind is blowing like hell.

In the deserted yard tangerine and pomelo are pendent on the trees,

On old room fresco there are some blurring images of dragons and snakes.

Clouds drift around the stone wall chiseled long ago,

The pace of the river going along the white sand is not slow.

We knew Da Yu drove four kinds of vehicles in fighting flood,

By chiseling and dredging the floods in the Sichuan area were tamed.

In Chinese phonetic alphabet and Chinese characters：

yǔ miào
禹 庙
（唐）杜甫

yǔ	miào	kōng	shān	lǐ
禹	庙	空	山	里 ，
qiū	fēng	luò	rì	xiá
秋	风	落	日	斜 。
huāng	tíng	chuí	jú	yòu
荒	庭	垂	橘	柚 ，
gǔ	wū	huà	lóng	shé
古	屋	画	龙	蛇 。
yún	qì	shēng	xū	bì
云	气	生	虚	壁 ，
jiāng	shēn	zǒu	bái	shā
江	深	走	白	沙 。
zǎo	zhī	chéng	sì	zǎi
早	知	乘	四	载 ，
shū	záo	kòng	sān	bā
疏	凿	控	三	巴 。

Notes：The poet made a special visit to the Da Yu Temple after he left Sichuan. The temple was built by the river on the mountain. At the time of his visit, the temple was deserted and looked bleak. By praising Da Yu for his heroic deeds of controlling flood the poet also satirized implicitly the destitution of the time.

【说明】杜甫离开四川后，专门拜访了禹庙。禹庙建在河边的山上。他到访时，禹庙已经荒芜。他歌颂了大禹治水的英雄事迹，同时含蓄地讽刺了当时社会凋敝不堪的现实。

42. The Area North of the Qinling Mountains
(Tang) Li Qi

I've left the area far behind when looking back at it in the

morning,

From behind the eastern peak the sun is slowly rising.

Hills and rivers in the distance are so clear,

The capital profile is so curvaceous, tall buildings stand layer after layer.

When autumn wind blows bamboo forests in every household rustle,

Pine trees in the Five-Tomb area seem so chill.

The thick fog and cold dew make me feel so gloom,

I sigh this is not a place for me and I'd better go home.

In Chinese phonetic alphabet and Chinese characters:

wàng qín chuān
望 秦 川
（唐）李颀

qín	chuān	zhāo	wàng	jiǒng
秦	川	朝	望	迥 ，
rì	chū	zhèng	dōng	fēng
日	出	正	东	峰 。
yuǎn	jìn	shān	hé	jìng
远	近	山	河	净 ，
wēi	yī	chéng	què	zhòng
逶	迤	城	阙	重 。
qiū	shēng	wàn	hù	zhú
秋	声	万	户	竹 ，
hán	sè	wǔ	líng	sōng
寒	色	五	陵	松 。
kè	yǒu	guī	yú	tàn
客	有	归	欤	叹 ，
qī	qí	shuāng	lù	nóng
凄	其	霜	露	浓 。

Notes： Li Qi (690? — 751?) was a petty military officer at a county when he was forty-five, and was not promoted ever since. He resigned and lived as a hermit until his death. He was on good terms with some famous poets such as Wang Wei, Gao Shi, Wang Changling and etc. This poem was composed after he had resigned from office in 741 and when he had left the capital and on his way home. The Five-Tomb area was a place where noble families gathered.

【说明】李颀（690？—751？）45 岁时才在县里当了一个小官，而且从未得到提拔。他后来做了隐士，直到故去。他与很多诗人如王维、高适、王昌龄等过从甚密。此诗是他 741 年辞职后所写，当时他离开京城，正在回家的路上。五陵地区是贵族家庭聚集的地方。

43. Sharing My Thoughts with Wang at Lake Dongting
(Tang) Zhang Wei

It's a sheer view of autumn at Lake Dongting in August,
Toward north Rivers Xiao and Xiang drift.
I returned home in my dream from ten thousand miles away,
In an alien place and small hours homesickness becomes heavy.
I don't have the heart to open books and read,
The best thing to do is to go to a tavern and drink to my heart's content.

In Chang'an and Luoyang there are numerous relatives and friends of mine,

When can I travel around with them again?

In Chinese phonetic alphabet and Chinese characters:

tóng wáng zhēng jūn dòng tíng yǒu huái
同　王　征　君　洞　庭　有　怀

（唐）张谓

bā　yuè　dòng　tíng　qiū
八　月　洞　庭　秋，

xiāo	xiāng	shuǐ	běi	liú
潇	湘	水	北	流 。
huán	jiā	wàn	lǐ	mèng
还	家	万	里	梦 ,
wéi	kè	wǔ	gēng	chóu
为	客	五	更	愁 。
bú	yòng	kāi	shū	zhì
不	用	开	书	帙 ,
piān	yí	shàng	jiǔ	lóu
偏	宜	上	酒	楼 。
gù	rén	jīng	luò	mǎn
故	人	京	洛	满 ,
hé	rì	fù	tóng	yóu
何	日	复	同	游 。

Notes: We don't have the dates of the poet's birth and death. We know the highest position he held in the government was a deputy minister of the Ministry of Protocol. He was most at home with regulated poems. In the *Complete Collection of Tang Poetry*, there is one volume of his poems. The Mr. Wang to whom this poem was dedicated to was a hermit. The two rivers mentioned in the poem all flow north into the lake.

【说明】我们没有诗人生卒年的资料。他官至礼部侍郎，精通律诗。他的诗在《全唐诗》中专有一卷。此诗是写给王隐士的。诗中所提的两条河都向北流到湖里。

44. Crossing the Yangzi River
(Tang) Ding Xianzhi

When our boat got to the center of the river I looked around，
In the river the scenery along the banks were clearly reflected.
The Yangzi Courier Station was built in the open space of the forest，
On the other side and among hills the prefecture city stood out.

At the far end of waters it was sable and quiet,
When north wind was blowing the river was chill and cold.
The falling of maple leaves could be heard,
The pattering rain delivered an autumn sound.

In Chinese phonetic alphabet and Chinese characters:

dù yáng zǐ jiāng
渡 扬 子 江

（唐）丁仙芝

guì jí zhōng liú wàng
桂 楫 中 流 望 ，

kōng bō liǎng pàn míng
空 波 两 畔 明 。

lín kāi yáng zǐ yì
林 开 扬 子 驿 ，

shān chū rùn zhōu chéng
山 出 润 州 城 。

hǎi jìn biān yīn jìng
海 尽 边 阴 静 ，

jiāng hán shuò chuī shēng
江 寒 朔 吹 生 。

gèng wén fēng yè xià
更 闻 枫 叶 下 ，

xī lì duó qiū shēng
淅 沥 度 秋 声 。

Notes：We don't have the poet's dates of birth and death. We know he was once a petty official at a county. There are fourteen of his poems still available today. The Yangzi River refers to the lower ranges of the Changjiang River. Line four mentions the name of the prefecture city in Chinese. The poem depicted an autumn scene from what the poet saw and heard from a boat, which is very different from other poems on autumn.

【说明】我们没有诗人生卒年的记载。我们只知道他在县里当过小官。现仍有他 14 首诗存世。扬子江指长江的下游。诗的第四句提到了州府名称。此诗描写了诗人在船中的所见所闻，不同于其他写秋天的诗歌。

45. Nightingale at the You Prefecture

(Tang) Zhang Yue

Cold wind is winnowing the night rain,
The chilly forest is panting and shaken.
At the party in the grand army hall,
I can not get rid of my old age mentality at all.
With the military band one should dance with his sword,
At the frontier piping music has been more stressed.
If I hadn't been a general at the frontier,
How could I keenly feel His Majesty's favor?

In Chinese phonetic alphabet and Chinese characters:

yōu zhōu yè yín
幽 州 夜 吟

（唐）张说

liáng fēng chuī yè yǔ
凉 风 吹 夜 雨 ，

xiāo sè dòng hán lín
萧 瑟 动 寒 林 。

zhèng yǒu gāo táng yàn
正 有 高 堂 宴 ，

néng wàng chí mù xīn
能 忘 迟 暮 心 。

jūn zhōng yí jiàn wǔ
军 中 宜 剑 舞 ，

sài shàng zhòng jiā yīn
塞 上 重 笳 音 。

bú zuò biān chéng jiàng
不 作 边 城 将 ，

<pre>
shuí zhī ēn yù shēn
谁   知   恩   遇   深 。
</pre>

Notes：This poem was composed in 718 when the poet was ostracized from the position of the Prime Minister to a frontier military governor. The last two lines do not show any of his resentment，actually this was his way of voice his bitterness and anger. The poem has been regarded as a fine example of diction，especially such words as winnowing，panting and stressing.

【说明】此诗作于 718 年，诗人那时已被罢相，到幽州做了都督。诗的最后两句尽管没发牢骚，实际上却道出了他的苦闷与愤懑。此诗被视为字句推敲的范例，尤其是"吹""动""重"这样的字眼很见功底。